The Last Page

BOOKS BY ANTHONY HUSO

The Last Page
*Black Bottle**

* Forthcoming

The Last Page

ANTHONY HUSO

TOR®

A TOM DOHERTY ASSOCIATES BOOK ◆ NEW YORK

This is a work of fiction. All of the characters, organizations, and events portrayed in this novel are either products of the author's imagination or are used fictitiously.

THE LAST PAGE

Maps by Jon Lansberg

A Tor Book
Published by Tom Doherty Associates, LLC
175 Fifth Avenue
New York, NY 10010

www.tor-forge.com

Tor® is a registered trademark of Tom Doherty Associates, LLC.

ISBN 978-0-7653-2516-7

First Edition: August 2010

Printed in the United States of America

0 9 8 7 6 5 4 3 2 1

FOR

SLEN

ACKNOWLEDGMENTS

I OWE a debt of gratitude to Marc Laidlaw for peddling my jank, Paula Guran for believing in it and Paul Stevens and the people at Tor for taking a chance.

I also want to thank Chris Duden and Gary Webb for their steadfast support and encouragement and James Papworth for being my first real mentor in writing.

Additionally, nothing in this book would be what it is without the infinite lost hours of Poy (Phanty), Chappy (Vlon), Tone (Rill) and Mike (Karakael) or "Jason: the Hermit" (and his assorted bloody sacrifices).

Thanks also to Barno, Bob, Suzy, Ted, Jen, Twi and of course Nikki.

I wrote this story because it Rained.

Bode Royal suggests the thing was commissioned by an Ublisi, authored at Sǫth and bound in cŭrlshydra hide.

Page 349: the Ublisi is actually quoted, "Write[1] the math of Ahvêllę. Write everything your eyes foresee. We must find our way back . . . use a rune of ŭlian ink on the cover . . . it must be slippery . . . this codex must stay hidden in order to survive."

Page 351: it is a red book containing, "Secret patterns on sheets of skin . . . a byname . . . no proper title . . . referred to sometimes as the *Cįsrym Tạ*."

—PERSONAL NOTES OF MORGAN GULLOWS

---

[1] A homographic ambiguity in Dark Tongue: "Write or right/correct the math . . . write or right/correct everything your eyes foresee." I.e. possibly, "Fix/change our fate."

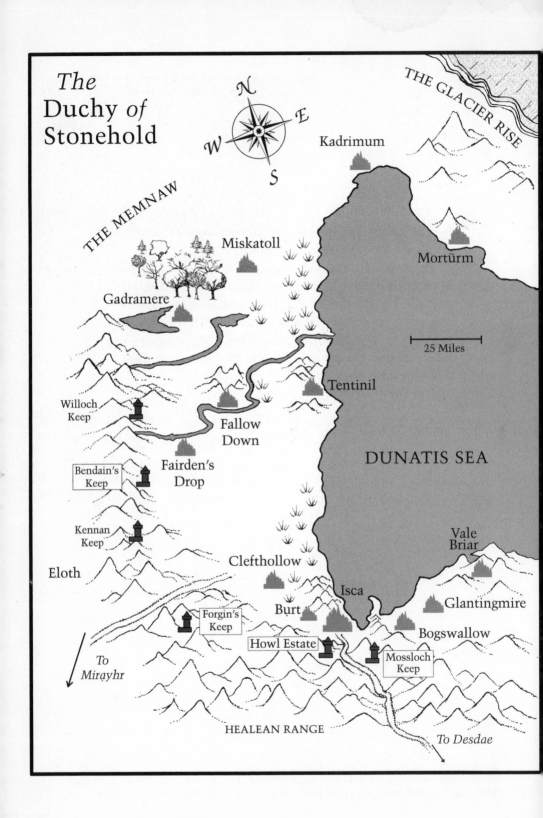

Isca Castle

Temple
Hill

The Hold

Ironside

Barrow Hill

Blekton

Bilgeburg

North Fell

South Fell

Thief
Town

Tin Crow

Growl
Mort

Murkbell

Nevergreen

Grue Hill

Maruchine

Brindle Fen

Ghoul Court

Three
Cats

Daoud's
Bend

Lampfire
Hills

Os Sacrum

West Fen

Candleshine

Monk Worm

Isca
City

Gas End

Winter Fen

The Last Page

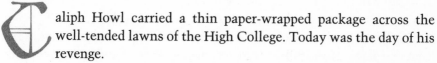

CHAPTER

I

Caliph Howl carried a thin paper-wrapped package across the well-tended lawns of the High College. Today was the day of his revenge.

Tattered shadows slid back and forth under a canopy of danson trees. The old stone buildings of Desdae warmed themselves in the sun like ancient mythic things, encrusted with gargoyles and piled with crippling tons of angled slate. Thirty of the buildings belonged to the township. The other eighteen belonged to the college. Two camps with an uneasy truce watched each other across the lake that separated them; collectively known by one name, Desdae: the gray hamlet of higher learning that crouched at the foothills of the mighty Healean Range.

Behind the campus' thick walls, Caliph knew theory-haunted professors wasted away, frisking books for answers, winnowing grains of truth, pulling secrets like teeth from deep esoteric sockets. This was a quiet war zone where holomorphs and panomancers cast desperately for new ideas, compiling research with frenetic precision.

Desdae might be far away from the mechanized grit of cities like Isca, it might be quiet and sullen, but it wasn't simple. It had small-town villains and small-town gossip and, he thought, small-town skullduggery as well.

Caliph tugged the library's massive door and cracked the seal on the tomblike aromas: dust, buttery wood polish and ancient books.

He scanned for the librarian and slunk smoothly into the aisles.

The system that organized the library was like most other products of northern bureaucracy: a premeditated torture inflicted by the personal preferences of the man in charge. The system required students to memorize the stone busts of dead scholars, thereby reinforcing the school motto, "Truth, Light, Chastity and [especially] Hard Work." The busts marked ogive-shaped burrows into labyrinthine stacks where freshmen soon learned to associate topic and location with the scholar representing a given area of study. Those who didn't, doomed themselves to hours of wandering.

Caliph knew almost all two hundred sixty-three stone heads' names and birth dates as if they had been kin.

Freshmen who became hopelessly lost had two choices: browse endlessly or pay the *expedition fee* senior students demanded in exchange for a *path to wisdom.*

Senior students typically charged one bek for two books. Caliph had quickly become one of the profiteers.

Four more years and he would graduate. Halfway to the embossed vellum that would list the three foci of his degree: economics, diplomacy and holomorphy. He turned down an aisle marked with the bust of Timmon Barbas, born Century of Wind, Year of the Wolverine. Timmon Barbas had been one of the most brilliant military strategists to see siege engines roar.

Caliph gently ran his finger across the leather spines as he walked. Anticipation swelled his stomach and a faint smile marked his still boyish lips.

Roric Feldman would come to the library after lunch today, looking for Timmon Barbas' book, *The Fall of Bendain.* Though only forty-seven pages in length, Caliph knew every word of it from beginning to end. He knew every stitch in the binding, every scuff in the cover, every worn and dog-eared page.

He had written it himself.

Not a bad bit of forgery. Every page had been individually aged and penned in the old tactician's handwriting. The cover and binding Caliph felt particularly proud of, embossed and tooled and edged with metal just like the real thing. Even the rust was authentic.

The Fall of Bendain had not yet been reprinted. Though the new press from Pandragor, dripping with grease and possibilities, would eventually churn out copies, other textbooks had taken priority: *Ǫlisgīrl's Physics Compendium* for instance, and *Blood: A Holomorph's Guide,* which for any student of the discipline was an absolute must.

In another year or two or five, Caliph's careful forgery might not have been feasible. Today, however, the window of opportunity swung wide open.

Morgan Gullows, Caliph's tutor in the Unknown Tongue, had almost caught him aging treated paper over a gas flue. With first draft in hand, Caliph's plan had nearly been discovered. Thankfully, Gullows was a recluse and rarely looked at anyone directly. He had muttered something unintelligible and shambled off, leaving Caliph to watch his paper catch fire.

The whole test had gone up in a mushroom of smoke and shriveled ash.

From then on, Caliph had exercised every precaution he could think of, stowing his drafts and materials behind the massive radiator in Nasril

Hall. He wheedled his way into a job organizing the whirring ticking office of Silas Culden where he graded midterms.

Silas loathed every minute taken up by class-related chores. Twice a week he dumped a slippery pile of paperwork into Caliph's lap and headed back to his research—the only thing that would secure his tenure; therefore the only thing that mattered.

He paid Caliph, of course, and thanked him for assigning an illicit but reasonable ratio of passing grades by way of a weekly pair of tickets to the Minstrel's Stage.

Alone in Silas' office, Caliph had pawed methodically through the wooden cabinets until he found the senior exam Roric would be taking, the one that meant the difference between an eight-year degree and a shameful return to his father's house in the Duchy of Stonehold.

With test in hand, Caliph had begun plotting his revenge, justice for what had happened three and a half years ago on a chilly cloudless night.

He could still remember the articulation of Roric's lips and the perverse smile that framed his abrupt violation of social grace:

"You a virgin?" Roric's eyes gleam through the dormitory shadows.

Caliph's pretense, studying the dead language propped against his thighs, doesn't seem to convince Roric.

"We've got some sugar doughnuts coming up from the village tonight, Caph. Haven't we, Brody?"

Brody is stout but muscular and grows hair on his face faster than a Pplarian Yak. He nods silently and flips a gold gryph across his knuckles.

Caliph smirks. "I'll believe that when I see—"

"You're such a fuck, Caph. You probably say the motto in your sleep. Dean's list . . . oh shit! My grades slipped a tenth of a point. Eaton's assworm. That has a ring to it."

"Fuck off."

"Maybe you'd like old Luney's flock better than our thoroughbreds." Roric picks up a pillow from the stiff dormitory bed and humps it with both hands.

Caliph simpers, "Where are they going to be then?"

"Why would I tell you? You wouldn't know where to stick it in anyway."

Caliph's gaze falls out the window where rain-distorted shapes are making the dash between buildings.

"Suppose they was on Ilnfarne-lascue?"

"How would they get out there?"

"Just suppose they was? Would you chip in? It cost us a bit more than

three weeks' tutoring to get them up here, right Brody? We could use an-other man to bring the cost down for all of us."

Brody's lower lip projects like a ledge as he watches his coin dance.

"How many are there?"

"Three—but plenty to go around, eh?"

"I might chip in," Caliph says slowly, "just to talk." He feels embar-rassed thinking about the possibilities.

Roric and Brody snicker. "Sure, just talk, Caph—whatever you say."

That night, Caliph and Roric swim the cold dark water of the college lake. The tiny island barely conceals the ruined steeple of a shrine the stu-dent body refers to as Ilnfarne-lascue, a Hinter phrase meaning the place of the act.

Rumors of expulsion and unsubstantiated trysts wrap the island in a localized fog of notoriety, but this is the first time Caliph believes such a scenario might actually unfold. Picking their way over the graffiti-covered rocks of the shore, the two of them crouch at the edge of the trees and listen.

"Vanon and the others must already be here," says Roric. Voices and firelight vacillate through the limbs. "I'll meet you at the shrine. Better make sure no one followed us."

Caliph shakes with excitement. The cold, cloying lake smell, wet and fungal; the cry of a night bird; they crystallize suddenly and unexpect-edly, associated from that moment on with young lust.

As he makes his way, he catches sight of the shrine and a notion that he has been overcharged passes through him. He counts not five freshmen but seven. They are wet and shivering around a fire, whispering emphat-ically.

Caliph stops. Where is Brody? He waits in the darkness, suspicions growing.

Roric has not come back from the shore. Where are the women?

Caliph turns and looks out across the lake. On the lawns, the green flicker of a chemiostatic lantern bobs. Several figures are putting a boat in. Not the women. They would have oared from the village.

Caliph scrambles back to the water. He eases himself in, fearful of splashing, and begins pulling slowly and quietly for shore. When he is within range of the lantern, he slips beneath the water's skin and kicks out, submarining until his lungs burn.

On the far side, he finds his clothing gone. His key to the dormitory is gone. Fooled after all!

He darts up the hill toward the unsympathetic edifice of Nasril Hall,

*looking for available windows. Halfway up one of the metholinate pipes
that siphons gas into the boy's dormitory, the pallid cast of a lantern
strikes his nakedness and a commanding voice bellows for him to get
down.*

*In the morning, Caliph is locked in the pillory with the other seven,
each of them bearing bright red welts that run horizontally across their
backsides. Expulsion could have been the penalty, but seeing as how no
felonies had been committed, the chancellor's cane and a dose of public
humiliation have sufficed.*

*Roric Feldman, master of the deception, gathers with the rest of the
student body in front of the Woodmarsh Building to stand and sit and
watch and laugh.*

*Of course, the chancellor knows there has been treachery. Nothing of
consequence that transpires on Desdae's lawns escapes Darsey Eaton.*

*He hears the boys' complaints individually in his office. But the initi-
ation serves his purpose—so he allows it to pass. These freshmen have
learned a code behind the code: violators will be caught and they will be
punished.*

CALIPH'S painful memory of the event was offset by knowledge that
Roric's exam was comprised entirely of essay. Caliph had taken it upon
himself to rewrite all the tactics and all of the figures and many of the
names and dates in *The Fall of Bendain*. It remained a very readable book,
he mused smugly. Very official sounding.

Quietly, he unwrapped the package he had carried into the library and
looked briefly at his handiwork. So much effort had gone into it that it
pained him to leave it here. The exchange took place quickly. A book sliding off a shelf, a book sliding onto a shelf—a completely normal occurrence
that would destroy Roric Feldman.

When the book came back, as they all must the night before final exams, the exchange would take place again and there would be no trace
and no proof to support Roric's distressed complaint.

Caliph stiffened suddenly and turned around. Someone had been watching.

She had just started up the spiral staircase that rose to the balconies.
Caliph had only a vague notion of how her body moved as she went up
the steps one at a time, carrying a small leather pack over her shoulder.
Her jawline bowed, smooth and proud, tracing from gem-studded lobes;
her curls were short for the helmets she wore in fencing class. She passed
through a stray lance of window light and her eyes flared molten blue.

She looked directly at him, lips flickering with a wry vanishing smile, face perfectly illuminated. Then she was gone, radiant head disappearing above the second story floor, soft booted feet lifting her out of sight.

The crocus-blue glare had etched itself into Caliph's mind. For a moment he felt like he had stared straight into the sun. Then he cursed. He knew her. She was in her sixth year but shared some of his classes, probably as audits.

"Byŭrn, byŭrn, byŭrn," he whispered the Old Speech vulgarity for excrement.

Carefully, he wrapped *The Fall of Bendain* in the paper his forgery had been in and slid it into his pack.

Odds were she had not understood what he was doing. Still, Desdae was a tiny campus; if Roric complained loudly enough, she might remember seeing him here and put the two together. He walked quickly to the wrought-iron stairs and spun up them, looking both ways down the third story balcony.

Dark curls and skin that stayed tan regardless of weather, Caliph felt confident despite his size. His torso had hardened from swordplay and his face was already chiseled with the pessimism of higher learning. He might be quiet but he wasn't shy. A subtle nuance that had often worked in his favor.

He saw her down the right, hand on the balcony railing, headed for the holomorph shelves. He caught up with her and followed her into an ogive marked with the bust of Tanara Mae.

When he cleared his throat, her eyes turned toward him more than her body.

"Hello." He kept it simple and upbeat.

"Yes?"

"Are you seeing anyone?"

"Quite direct, are you?" She sauntered down the aisle, slender as an aerialist, fingertips running over unread names. "Yes, I am . . . he doesn't go to school at Desdae though."

Her smell amid the dust was warm and creamy like some whipped confection, sweet as Tebeshian coffee. In the ascetic setting of the library it made him stumble.

"So if we went to Grume's . . . or a play?"

"I like plays." Her eyes seized him. Bright. Not friendly. Caliph had to remind himself that he had no personal interest in her. "There's a new play in town," she was saying. "Some urban gauche piece out of Bablemum. Probably atrocious."

Caliph tapped his lower lip. "I heard about it. What's the writer's name?"

"I don't know. It's called *Rape the Heart.*" She drifted farther down the aisle.

"Tragedy?" Caliph pressed after, trying to corner her in a casuistic way.

She slipped between the shelves like liquid. "Depends on your point of view I suppose."

"And you'd like to see it?"

"I'm seeing a boy," she murmured, twisting the knife.

"But he doesn't go to school here . . ." Caliph whispered.

"No. He doesn't."

"And I don't mind." His voice couched what he hoped was a satisfactory blend of confidence and innuendo.

"Final exams?" She seemed to maintain a constant distance as though the air were slippery between them. "Aren't you busy or worried—or both?"

Caliph shrugged. "I don't study much." It was a blatant lie.

She frowned. "And you have money for a play?"

"I don't pay anyone for notes. Actually I charge—expedition fees—you know?" His slender fingers gestured to the books all around. "I come into a good deal of money this time of year, but I usually get my tickets for free."

"*Rape the Heart* then?" She didn't ask how he managed free tickets. "Tomorrow. I'll meet you here before evening bells."

Caliph tossed her a wan smile. This was not a date of passion. "I'll be here. What's your name?"

She shook her head derisively. "It matters to you?"

"I'm not like other men."

"Boys," she suggested. "If I were you and didn't want to sound pretentious, I'd say, I'm not like other boys."

"Right." Caliph's eyes narrowed, then he feigned a sudden recollection. "It's Sena, isn't it?"

Her lips curled at one corner.

He tipped his head. "Tomorrow evening . . ."

She stopped him just as he turned to go. "I'll see you then . . . Caliph Howl."

Caliph smirked and disappeared.

SENA stood in the dark alcove looking where he had vanished into the white glare of the balcony.

"Caliph Howl," she mused with mild asperity. "Why now? Why here, after four years, do you suddenly decide to give me the time of day?"

Tynan Brakest was the *other* boy. He was sweet. He had been the one to pay her way at college. His father's money ensured their relationship slipped easily from one moment to the next. The coins had purchased Tynan hours, weeks and months until the accumulated stockpile of familiarity had evolved into a kind of watered down love.

But Caliph Howl? Her stomach warmed. *This could be exactly what I am looking for.*

CHAPTER

2

A storm was coming. Caliph lay in wait at the top of the library, surveying the campus through a great circular pane of glass. The black plash of leaves perpetuated through the trees to the west where Naobi drizzled syrupy light on lilacs bobbing near the lake.

The universe snapped ineffectually at the dark silhouettes of students and teachers, human forms distorted by the warm gush of light spilling from the chapel across the lawn. Caliph felt superior to the herd migrating slowly toward Day of Sands vespers.

It was difficult for him to imagine being king. The fact that he was an heir did not present itself at Desdae. Here he found himself treated like any other student, disciplined and cowed under the stern rules of the chancellor. But his father assured him it was for the best.

It's a time of unrest in the Duchy, read one of Jacob's few letters. *Men aspire to the High King's throne. You're safer at Desdae.*

In the belfry, like lonesome beasts, the bells began to toll.

Caliph turned from the window and gazed on the dusty abyss of the library's interior. Eight centuries' worth of interred paper bodies infused the air with spoor. The pages were holomorphically preserved, mummified within this vast sepulcher. It was a temple to the dead, to thought, to maxims and poetry, to plays and battles and vagaries gouged out of antiquity. But it wasn't Caliph's temple.

The bells ceased and a pleasant loneliness poured in with the moonlight, varnishing the railings, tranquilizing every board.

He mouthed the words he planned to use tonight if Sena actually showed up. They were old words, bleak as the air that sighed around Desdae's gables.

Forbidden by most governments, silenced through flames that had once danced on great piles of holomorphic lore, slowly, very slowly, holomorphy was being practiced again. Opportunists seeking an edge in business, politics—they had begun drawing blood.

At Desdae, the focus stayed safely on lethargy crucibles, thaumaturgic reactors that ran off planetary rotation and cow blood, that sort of thing.

The professors never openly admitted that other types of holomorphy were also catalogued in obscure sections of the library. But in the teeth of their frantic scramble to gain tenure, the faculty often followed a much older motto than Truth, Light, Chastity and Hard Work. Theirs was: Don't Ask Don't Tell.

Caliph used a tiny knife to prick his finger. As any holomorph, he needed something to start with, an essential ingredient to begin the chain reaction where matter, memories, reality could be extruded and controlled.

Caliph could still remember the banal demonstration Morgan Gullows had put on for his freshman class: the way he had dropped that book. It had hit the ancient desk with a dusty thud and at that moment he had revealed a simple yet extraordinary idea to his young students: the book must travel half the distance to the desk and then half of that distance and so on, somehow going through an infinite number of divisive repetitions in a finite period of time. Although he had solved this mystery for them with simple mathematics, holomorphy, the Unknown Tongue, was the key to understanding the endless repetition of the spiral, the key to the ancient problem of the circle, the key to unlocking the universe.

Numbers became symbols. Symbols compiled words. "Language shapes reality," said the philosophers and linguists. So the maths of the Unknown Tongue deconstruct reality; form new realities—whatever realities the mathematician desires. "In reality," claimed the holomorphs of Desdae, "there is none."

But Caliph knew that underneath their departmental propaganda, not everything was possible. And despite his natural aptitude for the discipline he distrusted it on a visceral level. To him, the Unknown Tongue was a struggling science propped on the intellectual framework of backward-gazing scholars.

Metholinate burners, chemiostatic cells, ydellium tubing that polarized itself against the weather and somehow generated power out of nothing—practically. Those were the only things that made holomorphy worth studying. Those and the kinds of mischievous legerdemains he had selected for this meeting tonight.

He had learned about holomorphy from his uncle before coming to Desdae: lessons he did not like to think about here, alone in the library. Instead, he examined his oozing fingertip, making the tiny cut open and close like a little red mouth.

"Early, aren't you?"

Caliph spun to see a shape step out from the staircase. He had been expecting a knock. A clumsy tug at the bolted portals. Instead there had been a vacuum of sound, not even the scratch of picks in the lock, something that would have amplified across the library's taut funerary silence.

"You like surprising people." He said it like a palmist giving a reading, trying to sound cool even though his heart was racing.

"Practicing Introductory Psych?" she asked. "Let me try. You're agnostic. Wait, that was too easy . . ."

Caliph grinned. "I'm not agnostic. I just don't like Prefect Eaton. Something about him being chancellor-slash-resident priest causes me cognitive dissonance."

Sena laughed softly. "So you used the handbook's loophole clause? You actually filed a form?"

Caliph shrugged. "Got me out of vespers." He took out his pocket watch. "I'm not sure we can make it into town before the play starts."

"Sooo . . . you have other plans for us?" She walked toward him like a gunslinger.

"Not really. I don't like people who show up late."

She stopped, visibly stunned. "I'm not late."

Caliph took advantage of the moment.

His voice yanked at the air. His wounded hand cut a black shape against the huge moon-drenched pane of glass. The spread of his fingers drew darkness over her eyes and oxygen off her brain.

It was too late for her to whisper a counter.

He was on her, protracting, suboccipital subtraction, siphoning a strand of memory. The suction was mechanical and precise. If he succeeded it would be gone.

Sena cursed and tackled him. They grappled. Caliph's arm caught for the railing. Over thirty feet of empty air separated them from the tiles of the first floor; Caliph felt the antique balustrade give slightly under the pressure of their combined weight.

Sena punched him hard and the formula died in his mouth. Breathless vulgarities struggled from both their lips. A loud crack sounded in one of the worm-eaten balusters. Just as the whole thing seemed ready to break apart, Caliph managed to gain leverage and push her back.

Apparently she either didn't care or didn't comprehend their peril. Her hands clenched in his shirt, pulling him along in a clumsy stumbling dance toward the bookcases.

Their scuffle rocked something near the shelves: the sound of a wooden pedestal base rolling slowly in a teetering circle followed by a splintering smash.

Caliph toppled to the floor and wrestled with the girl who now pressed him from above. Somehow, through a quirk of balance and leverage she had managed to stay on top. He was astonished at her subtle strength.

"Don't-move-I'll-kill-you."

Her lips ran all the words together. He could feel her breath and the icy edge of a small knife touch him on the throat. It was the same kind of knife he had used on his hand, the same kind every student of holomorphy was allowed to carry with them. Meant only for pricking fingers, it was still capable of opening his throat.

Beside him, the fallen bust of Tanara Mae lay facedown in the darkness, nose shattered in pale shards that spun slowly, dissected by moonlight.

"I thought you were simple," she gasped in disgust. "What were you looking for?" She wiped a droplet of blood from her cheek, making a dark line, like a trail of mascara below her eye.

"I think you're bleeding," Caliph said. One of his hands rested on the slender muscles of her waist.

"Actually, that's you bleeding on me." They were entangled, warmth passing through their clothes, a comfortable but awkward closeness.

"Well . . . you have a cut." His finger brushed her cheek.

"Don't tell me you're getting romantic." She tried to push herself off but her leg was pinned.

"Broke Tanara's face too."

Caliph began to laugh, too loud. It echoed off the coffered ceiling.

"It's your fault! If anyone gets expelled for this it will be you." She let up slightly on the blade. "I can't afford another session with the chancellor."

"You must be the one they're gossiping about—"

"Let me up! This is your fault!" She struggled furiously against his weight.

"Miss Iilool . . . what were you doing alone in the library after bells with a boy?" He impersonated the slow deep voice remarkably considering the pressure on his throat. Sena's smile at the mimicry was brief and unpleasant.

"What were you looking for?" she asked.

"If I tell you, it will sort of defeat the purpose—"

"You were doing something in the library yesterday." She scowled thoughtfully and kept the blade on him. "Pranking someone, were you? Stealing a book before finals?"

Caliph looked into her face with an expression of profound malice. For an instant she drew back.

"You think I'd tell?" She extricated her leg and pulled herself up.

Caliph picked up a piece of Tanara's nose. He flipped it, then used it to point at her.

"If you cross me—"

"I won't!" She sounded deeply insulted, almost hurt by the insinuation. "I promise."

"You don't strike me as particularly trustworthy."

She snorted. "Probably the same as you."

"What can you possibly know about me?"

"Everyone knows Caliph Howl, carnally or otherwise."

"Of course. So stupid. I'm one of the Naked Eight." There was an element of shame, a hint of vulnerability in his voice that he recognized and quickly hardened. "You were in the courtyard with everyone else that day—"

"That's who it is then. You're sabotaging Roric Feldman's senior exam. For that wretched joke he played on you when you were a freshman."

When he didn't answer she went on. "You must've been planning this . . . for a long time."

"I don't care if you think . . ."

"Relax. Why should I care?" She stood up and took a step backward. "I don't just know you from the pillory, you know?"

She leaned back against the railing, her posture seemed to communicate a series of wordless invitations.

"Oh? Where else have I been locked under your view?" He glanced up furtively. The memory of her body pressed against him made it difficult to think. She had been warm and light, yet surprisingly strong. His voice leveled, turned cautious. He wasn't about to take her bait. Though he had pretended not to know her, everyone knew Sena Iilool.

"You were ranked second best swordsman last year," she was saying.

Caliph couldn't tell if she was being serious.

"You're not even supposed to know that legerdemain. That's way beyond sixth year holo . . ."

"Thanks," Caliph interrupted, "for the documentary. But I'm not your fool."

"I didn't say you were . . . yet."

"Go piss up a rope."

"I'd get wet. And besides, holomorphy is my first discipline. I think we should study together."

Caliph snorted.

"You think I need you? Just because every boy here follows you around like a trained sledge newt . . . I'm well ahead in my studies. I don't need a . . ." He didn't know what to classify her as and classifying her as

a distraction would betray the what? Infatuation? Lust? . . . that was rapidly thickening inside him.

"Co-conspirator?" Her suggestion startled him. "Look," she said, "I
know you don't want to wind up teaching here like everybody else. I know
who you are." She floated from the railing and sank down in front of him.

"I'm Caliph Howl," he said directly into her face as though it were the
most ordinary name in the world.

She grinned.

"I've got myself a king."

Her face was uncomfortably close, her breath sweet and startling as
black licorice. Caliph could barely keep from kissing her lips despite the
arrogance that snarled behind them.

"I thought you were seeing a lad," he mumbled.

"I was," Sena deadpanned. "Did you get the tickets?"

Caliph made the southern hand sign for yes.

"Then come on, we're going to be late for the play."

CHAPTER
3

I t hits Sena on her second visit that Morgan Gullows' office is not on the brink of relocating to one of Githum Hall's sunny upstairs chambers. The pile of laundry, the lopsided stacks of cardboard boxes, the books, the coffee mugs: none of it has moved.

The mushy darkness is riddled with pipes and objects shrouded in deeper gloom. Sena is familiar with the smell, a previously unidentifiable mustiness she recognizes from all face-to-face encounters with her employer.

Teacher's aide. Hmphf. Teacher's maid is what he needs!

Sena wrinkles her nose. There is a leather chair behind the desk, crippled from years of supporting the professor's enormous carcass. It leans heavily to one side, seams burst, stuffing quite literally pressed out of it.

Sena gets straight to her task, following the bizarre instructions Morgan has given her for locating Bruntis' **A Dictum of Calculating Light** in the office-shaped waste bin.

She hoists a pair of soiled trousers and discovers a crumb-covered saucer and a foil wrapper whose yellow oil has drained down half a sheaf of midterms. These, she pushes aside. Below, are a stack of books whose weight has caved in the top of a cardboard box. Under the box is Bruntis' work, which she jerks free. Coming with it into her hand is a careless half-sheet, brown with dry spillage. It is written in Morgan's handwriting and she can't help glancing it over.

Cisrym Ta?

The little sheet contains two references to Bode Royal wherein a codex is described, bound in cīrlshydra hide. The references sound amusingly theosophic but after delivering Bruntis' work to the professor, Sena goes to the library on a whim and fills out a form that grants her twenty minutes with Bode Royal.

The references are real.

She gets a twinge in her stomach and decides to start chipping at the legend of the Cisrym Ta. The more she chips the harder it becomes to dig out new leads. After several semesters, the amount of information she's

gleaned fills only two and a half pages. The legend jumps between books,
like a bird darting through trees, tracing its history across millennia, in
and out of obscurity. She chases it relentlessly. One of the most out-
landish rumors linked to it concerns the lock and a corresponding recipe
supposedly needed to open it. No key. Just a list of ingredients. The for-
mula makes her stomach turn.

She spends two weeks cross-checking the recipe's veracity on the top
floor of the library, coming to the conclusion that it has been translated
exactly in four different languages when, out of a glaring white ogive,
Caliph Howl invites her to a play.

WHEN she learned about Caliph's plot against Roric Feldman, she took a
hiatus from her pet project in order to analyze the heir.

But getting inside his head, she realized, would require a seduction. She
baited him, employed several previously infallible methods to which he
maddeningly did not succumb. She could tell that he viewed the school
code as a narrow ledge and her as a liability. Getting him to crack became
a game . . . there was a certain purity to him that poured warmth into her
stomach. But his crush on her was growing.

It happened later in the Woodmarsh Building, against a backdrop of
gray paint and bloodless creatures floating in jars. They had been alone,
doing labs, looking through the monocular at slides and taking notes.

She was intentionally unbuttoned, just enough to reveal the ruffle of lace
cupping her breasts. She had worn the lotion that smelled like Tebeshian
coffee. On his second turn at the slide, when he had reached for the monocular, she had pivoted instead of stepping aside. His hand had gone through
the loop of her arm, brushing past her body. They were the same height.
She had stared him down, bitten her lower lip and refused to move.

Finally . . . finally, he had pushed her up against the counter. She remembered him fumbling with her skirt, lifting it up around her waist. She
had pulled his belt away like a snake, gripping it by the head before letting
it clatter dramatically to the floor. The cool laboratory air had shocked
them both, forced them together for warmth, a catalyst, carrying them
into the next stage of their relationship.

IT took a month, but Sena realized slowly that Caliph was becoming part
of the recipe. She found his affections refreshingly devoid of the bravado
and lachrymose fawning she thought of as the two schoolboy extremes.
His attention to her was crystalline, immediately clear yet full of cunning. She saw it in the way he ignored her during class, focusing intently
on the lecture. Then a note would suddenly arrive in her hand, written in

acrostic code. She would read it with amazement and look at him but he would never look back.

As the weeks passed, she returned to her project: something she concealed carefully from Caliph for several reasons . . . collecting every reference she could until suddenly the *Cisrym Tq* vanished, seemingly for good.

The last trace was a holomorph, almost two decades ago in the Duchy of Stonehold. She read that his rise to power had gone sideways. Body surfaced at the base of the sea wall in Isca in the fall of '45. Only his mansion, auctioned and hollow, was left crumbling in the foothills of the Healean Range.

The *Cisrym Tq* must have been auctioned with the rest of the estate amid vast lots of books. It frightened her to think that she had reached the end of what she could read. Her graduation was approaching. If this was what she wanted, she knew she had to shift from thinking to doing. It made her nervous, but Caliph had taught her, in the way he had orchestrated their relationship, how to execute on a plan.

He hadn't wanted the situation they began in: risking expulsion every night, sneaking behind Brie House. But once he had chosen it, he showed no regret. When it came to the code and motto, he had adjusted smoothly from rigid obedience to deft evasion.

During the day, they went to class in Githum Hall and the Woodmarsh Building, vaguely listening to lectures while composing notes that promised, in code, what they would do to each other later that night. Caliph devised ways to meet in the machine shed, the stable, the shadows of the mill. They risked disaster by sneaking into Desdae Hall and altering chore assignments on the chancellor's ledger, ensuring they shared custodial duties in same buildings at like times.

One afternoon, while Professor Blynsk was droning at the blackboard and Sena was watching leaves tantalize window glass, a note poked into her palm written in the usual code. It said simply:

If the haberdasher alters seven threads, only evens need dye.

Her fingers went numb and her stomach turned. Something had gone wrong. The translation was brutally succinct: *It has to end.*

It has to end? Why was he saying this? She looked across the room. For the first time, he looked back. He smiled faintly from his desk near the door, winked at her; then got up and left the room.

Forty minutes later it had spread across campus that Caliph Howl was in the chancellor's office for stealing.

The theft was remarkable. He had taken the clurichaun from Desdae Hall and it was still missing.

"Night watch for sure if he doesn't get expelled . . ."

"He'll get expelled."

"No he won't. He's fucking heir-apparent to the Iscan High Throne. He'll get night watch."

"Why do you think he took it?"

"Attention."

Sena listened to gossip flickering over the lawn. One of her dorm sisters passed her with a sadistic smile. "Looks like no more fun for you . . ."

Sena went to lunch. She went to class. When evening settled, the lights in the Administration Building still burnt. Caliph had not come out.

It had leaked that a sentence was coming down and it would not be expulsion. Bets on the lawn now began circulating as to the duration of Caliph's punishment.

"Nine months. Night watch."

"A year."

"If the clurichaun stays missing, he'll be watchman 'til he graduates . . ."

Students speculated and smoked and drank coffee outside Desdae Hall. Sena loitered, mingling with them, repeatedly denying any knowledge of why her "friend" had stolen the intricate southern mechanism.

Night watch required the student so sentenced to sleep not in the comfort of the dorms, but to stalk the drafty expanse of the library until eighteen o'clock. At midnight, the student could bed down on the floor near one of the radiators. No cots were allowed. A campus watchman checked in on the prisoner once at fifteen and again at two in the morning. If, during his shift, anything was damaged or stolen, the student was expelled without further delay.

At seven, from the Administration Building, the sound of a caning began, which meant—according to popular opinion—that Caliph had yet to divulge the location of the missing clurichaun.

Silence settled over the lawn, partially out of awe for Caliph's cries, which floated through an open window, and partially so the number of strokes could be counted.

Sena winced, marveling at his stupidity.

At seven-o-five the caning was complete. Twenty strokes had been administered, just shy of the maximum.

The Administration Building's doors finally opened at twenty past and a lone figure appeared, a shade in the darkness that dragged over the threshold, stooped and stiff like an old man. It plodded down the steps and across the lawn. Going to him now would lacquer another layer onto the already lustrous veneer of rumors that surrounded the two of them; so Sena stayed with the others, watching as he crossed the empty campus alone, headed directly for the library, a ring of keys in his hand. At the doors, he jingled softly without looking back and disappeared inside.

The knot of students broke up. Sena went home and slept fitfully.

The entire next day, she anticipated her own meeting with the chancellor. It was common talk that she and Caliph were possibly more than friends. It made sense that the chancellor would question her. But surprisingly, no summons ever came. Caliph met her between classes near Nasril Hall, under the shade of an enormous tree. He was disheveled and grim, hollow-eyed and somewhat pale. She had watched him stand rather than sit during class and he was still walking with a limp.

"Everything's set," he said simply. "You can come to the library any night you want."

Sena's jaw dropped. *This had been his plan?*

"Are you crazy?"

"I've minimized our risk. No more stables or closets."

"You didn't do this for me."

"Ever since you crept up on me in the library, I figured you're a damn good sneak. All you have to do is make it to the cellar doors without being seen. Think about it, we're inside a locked building, alone."

"You are crazy." Sena pointed at the brick-gabled windows of the chancellor's house. They faced the library directly.

Caliph responded without agitation. "Do you really think he will be watching? He knows I'm too smart to risk getting caught. Besides," he jingled the ring of keys, "we can go anywhere in the library! Think of the private book collections!"

Sena looked at them. Each had been wired with stiff white paper and labeled with the names of various rooms.

"I know you've had a brush with the chancellor and can't afford another office visit. But I can. He's never going to expel me." Caliph looked at her directly. "He can't afford to expel me."

"Yella byūrn,[2] Caliph! Are you telling me you made a deal with him?"

For a moment his dark eyes burrowed into her face. Finally he said, "No one's going to bother us."

Her stomach soured. She felt queasy-sick inside, but he had not done this extraordinary thing to generate pity. He had done it with the single goal of moving their relationship beyond the reach of the school motto, facilitating something stable and private. She decided not to dwell on the horror of the caning. Instead, she gave him what he wanted, a smile.

"Can I at least get in by myself?"

---

[2] O.S.: Expletive: "Mother's shit!"

"This isn't about picking locks. This is about keeping quiet. Staying hidden."

She played along. "Ooh—an esoteric society. Just the two of us?" Her knuckles rapped an imaginary door. "Will there be secret knocks?"

Caliph grinned despite his obvious pain.

HE had taught her how to execute on a plan regardless of personal cost.

Since then, there had been wine, books and plenty of sex. The library had remained bearable even as Kam faded into Thay, Shem and Oak, reducing the wooded campus to lifeless brown and frosty white.

Sometimes they used the fireplaces. Sometimes they just listened to the coal boiler in the basement, indigestion flushing through its pipes. The night watchman scheduled to check up on Caliph twice a night never came.

Her stomach warmed. Maybe it was love.

But it wasn't Caliph that elicited her strongest emotions. That still came from the scrap of paper she had found in Githum Hall, burning like a cruestone in her brain. Its black sparkle steered her toward a course of actions on which she was now utterly resolved.

Caliph wouldn't understand even if she had been able to tell him. He had steeped himself in the modern cauldron of business and government. For him, holomorphy was quaint. And besides, the recipe was clear. She couldn't tell him.

He'll be fine, she thought. *I need this. He has a whole country waiting for him. I just need him to open the book . . .*

BREATH sweetened through a filter of wanton bouquets, Sena tossed her flower-flavored chewing gum like the pin from a grenade. It landed in the dark, forgotten behind spider-infested bundles of spare pipe while the chemical reaction it had induced continued to swell.

Sena let it go. Her mouth opened; her pelvis flexed forward.

Even in the beginning, despite no history of his own, Caliph had been better than Tynan, better than several sophomoric fumblings she had endured for the sake of release. Tonight, they drew it out, seeming to understand the potential finality of this encounter.

Caliph's breathing changed and Sena shifted her rhythm, calculating their trajectory, applying tension to the spring.

It was her private metaphor: the catapult. The sudden pitch in her stomach that signaled her body going numb. Like being launched into the air at the circus and floating . . . floating . . .

After that came the zoetrope. Warmth washing through her like sheet lightning. She had discovered it with Caliph. The pleasant spinning, her senses so overstimulated that her body stuttered like pictures in a little moving wheel, arching backward in a series of staccato animations.

Catapult then zoetrope. Only with Caliph.

"So soon—?" She uncoiled the playful whisper directly into his ear. "A little unexpected, huh?" She breathed hard, watched Caliph close his eyes and nod.

Her voice took on a whispered ecstasy.

"Wow—I'm kind of proud of myself." And she was. She was happy.

Caliph pinched her earlobe with his lips and rested his forehead on her shoulder. She adjusted her body.

Blue light from the clurichaun bubbled across them. It stood politely all of six inches tall with its back to them. The glass bulb full of solvitriol fluid illuminated tiny sprockets and whirring, jewel-crusted gears that comprised its internal organs.

Caliph had hidden the object of inestimable worth in the library. Several professors of engineering had been able to replicate it (except for its esoteric power source) with variable results.

It had been two years since the play, two years since they had broken Tanara's nose; two years since Roric Feldman had failed at school and gone home in shame.

After-sex hunger was making Sena's stomach growl. Caliph put his ear to the hollow of her navel and listened.

"It's talking," he grinned, raising a finger. "Wait, wait . . ." He paused intently. "It says . . . we should eat!"

The muscles of her abdomen tightened under the tickle of his chin. "Mm—I want ice cream. I want to get fat as an airship." She looked at him expectantly; blue clurichaun fire ghosting her eyes.

"I wouldn't mind."

His candor frightened her as she realized he meant a pregnancy. She turned it quickly into a joke. "Oh? You like 'em big? Huh?" She cupped her breasts and shook them at him. "Aren't I broad enough for you to ride?" She laughed at her own pun. "Fat as a zeppelin, I swear!"

He tugged her toward him, kissed her skin. "Have you ever been on a zeppelin?"

"My mother didn't have the money. We took a coal ship from Greenwick to the Coasts of Gath."

"What were you on Greenwick for?"

"I was born there."

"You told me you were from Miṛayhr."

"I am. But I was born on Greenwick—I belong to the isles."

She regretted that Mirąyhr had entered the conversation. She could see him thinking about it. He had pestered her only occasionally over the past two years for information about the Witchocracy.

"You know the cane-eyen legend?" he asked suddenly. "The one where all the Mirąyhric farmers wake up to find a third eye grown in the top of their dogs' heads? Is that true? Did the Shrądnæ Sisterhood really do that?"

Sena scowled but didn't scold him for asking. It was only natural for him to be interested.

Widespread rumors trickled through the north, endorsed and disseminated by several watchful governments. They gave an accounting of what were said to be Shrądnæ witches captured in Isca. Their beauty had been erased. They had no eyes, no legs and half a tongue; they pulled themselves through the slums of Ghoul Court in wheeled boxes inches off the ground. The High King put them there: broken, blind, stitched-up pets that wandered the streets until winter came and froze them in their wheeled crates.

By the end of Tes, their bodies became small humps of gray statuary that huddled under fire escapes. Eventually the street sweepers pulled them out into wintry light. They had to pry the bodies out with crowbars. Urine had frozen, grafted them to wood. They fell like bags of cement into Bragget Canal where virulent waters opened black steaming holes in the ice. Then the street sweepers watched without malice, smoking and talking as the legless forms went down, sinking in an undertow drawn by turbines in lower Murkbell, far beyond the opera house.

It was dramatic. Possibly embellished. But it was also at least partly true and the reason Sena kept her secret. Caliph could not know she was a witch.

CALIPH'S eyes followed her lips as she answered the question. She remembered that he had once told her they were overly sensual, as if her lips could run away and fornicate with him behind her back. He had told her once that they were cheating lips.

Sena watched the clurichaun as it took two clicking steps and dispatched a black crawling shape with its tiny metal claw.

"I've got two more years," Caliph mentioned. "I suppose you're going to start forgetting me tomorrow."

"Are you telling me what you want me to do?" She kept her smile lighthearted.

"Maybe. Maybe I don't want to think about you after you're gone."

She laughed and looked into the rafters. She knew what he really meant—that the loneliness would be painful for him despite his best effort to keep these intimacies cordoned off.

The attic was so old it could not keep all the wind out and low oscillating moans gave voice to drafts with origins impossible to trace.

The clurichaun was stomping around, as much as a one-pound mechanism could stomp, casting weird blue halos from its power source. The light disturbed other creatures and somewhere below the rafters came the soft rustle of leathery shapes and the faint chitter of obscure winged things that posed no threat to humans or machines.

"I don't think you'll be able to help it," Sena said.

"Sometimes . . ." Caliph paused. "I think you love me."

"It's only two years." She curled into him, pressing for warmth as the air chilled her back. "I'll visit you, or you can visit me after you get your degree."

"Sounds too . . ."

"Trust me," she whispered. "You make truth, and I'm making it so."

Caliph sighed. "Eight years. Nothing seems simple anymore—"

A spring moon glowed in the transom they had cleaned. Sky the color of exotic olives moiled Naobi's halo while fragile whiplike branches scraped the glass. Wind coming under the shingles made the attic sound too familiar. The smell, the darkness, the soft sounds; these secret nights in the guano-besmirched loft had become part of them. Tomorrow everything would change.

"Listen, Caliph. I'm going south. I'm headed for trouble." She grinned and slid her finger over his mouth. "I'm looking for something special. Something Professor Gullows managed to leave out of his lessons."

Caliph turned his head. "What is it?"

"It's a book," she whispered. "Every holomorph in the Hinterlands would die to get their hands on it . . . if they knew about it."

"Sounds like something made up."

"It's real. I'm going to find it."

Caliph sat up. "Then it's a sure candidate for the printing press—"

"Listen, you fool. Stop joking. I need you. You have to find me after you graduate. It's important. I love you Caliph."

His eyes narrowed. She had never said it before.

"You love me?"

She smiled and leaned in to kiss him.

Caliph stopped her.

"There's something you're not telling me."

"So single-minded—" She tousled his hair. "I love that about you."

She bent forward, plucked at his mouth with her lips; moved her leg slowly over his waist and brushed her warmth against him.

"What aren't you telling me?" He pushed her gently away.

"Nothing," she whispered. "But I'll tell you this . . . I know a secret about you . . . something nobody else at Desdae knows." She made the southern hand sign for yes. "You're Hjolk-trull. Like me."

Caliph frowned. "What? What does that matter? How . . ." He raised his hand.

"I've fallen in love with you," she whispered. "You know I mean it. I wouldn't have dragged you up here so often if it weren't true. Think, Caliph. You and I—we don't even belong to a country. We belong to the stars. We can make things right . . ."

"Right? The only thing wrong is you just brought up—" He stopped, sighed. "I don't belong to the stars."

Sena tried to regroup. "Caliph, I didn't mean . . . look-abrupt, tomorrow I'm gone . . . don't . . . you love me?"

It was a mistake. She saw it in his eyes, black mirrors that reflected her lie. *He knows. He knows I wouldn't have asked if it were true. Stupid. Stupid. But it is true! It is! I need this. For the recipe, I need this to be true.*

Now what? Would he remember her like this? Framed in the groundwork of an agenda he couldn't begin to understand? She could feel it, silly and stupid, how her few sentences had excavated a chasm between them. But she was smart enough to know that it was time to shut her mouth. Leave. Act hurt. Give him time to think and hope that the sex had been good enough to compensate for her last impression.

She stood up and pushed the toggles through the eyelets on her cloak.

The clurichaun, sensing that its duties were over, whirred off on a brave expedition through the clutter.

Yella byūrn, she thought and then out loud, "In two years, we'll see. Hynnsạ ŭllạ,[3] Caliph."

The Old Speech formality left Caliph in the dark, listening to the sound of wind under the shingles and goatsuckers in the trees.

IN the morning, Caliph watched from an obscure rain-flecked dormer as Sena went through the ritual in her scholar's robe. He felt sour. He wanted her to come looking for him. The ceremony made his stomach hurt.

He hadn't noticed her talking with anyone beforehand but immediately after the ceremony, a group of women in somber cloaks met her on

---

[3] O.S.: "Shade and sweet water."

the lawn. Their cowls covered their heads and faces against the rain. He wished he could hear what they were saying.

Sena glanced over her shoulder as though trapped, looking for help. Maybe she could feel his eyes. Caliph jerked his face back from the glass. She did not look happy to see the women and Caliph wondered who they were. Sena didn't talk about her family. It was a preclusion they shared.

For several minutes he deliberated. Finally he dashed, nearly falling down four flights of stairs. He struggled with the heavy door and burst out onto the lawn.

A light mist greeted him on the face, but Sena and the women were gone.

CHAPTER

4

wo years later Caliph dreamt the dream.

It had been with him since memory, coming and going on sub-liminal cycles. In the dream, man-shaped shadows beaded and ran like black oil across machines and towers made semi-acrylic with soot. Police sabers glittered amid a chaos of searchlights and shouts.

As always, the dream man plucked him from the confusion and carried him away.

It was not a dream that needed interpretation, not a misty plunge into oneiromancy or egocentrism. The tatters of his childhood parted slowly, dragging like strips of heavy cloth off Caliph's brain, releasing him to the waking world.

Spring filmed the dormitory air with an almost imperceptible fetor, a warm moist stink that evanesced from the wood around his windowpane. The High College graduated on the tenth but Caliph had opted to stay for spring semester. It was a decision he couldn't explain adequately even to himself. He had amassed enough credit hours to graduate early, yet he remained.

The Council wouldn't allow it to happen again. In Pash they would come for him.

Caliph looked out the window at the newest crop of not-quite-alumni. No more classes. No more tests. They had nothing left but to break the code in as many ways as eight pent-up, frustrated years could help devise. They would smash it. They would trample it; crush it completely. By week's end they would leave its smoking wreckage in their past and move on to new lives and new locations. The chancellor appeared unannounced at the frat house once or twice but everyone knew that, for the seniors, his rule had ended.

Spring was an exodus. Caliph washed, got dressed and went outside.

A venerable building crouched at the edge of the lake, poised in the shade like a giant toad, ready to either jump into the water or fall apart at any moment. Caliph went inside, unlocked the musty box with his number and found two letters, one from his father, the other in a familiar boy-

ish cursive that made his stomach feel like it was falling. He opened the
first.

Tarsh 4, Day of the Sowing

Caliph,

*I got word of your success at school today but the Council says
you plan to stay another semester. Don't do it. Come home. There's
turmoil near Clefthollow. Unfortunately I have men there to lead
and will not likely be able to attend your graduation. Such are the
responsibilities of serving the Council. I smile when I think that I
may soon be serving you.*

—Jacob

Caliph's hand crumpled it and released it somewhere near the trash. It
was forgotten even before he turned the second letter over for further inspection. He could feel something heavy inside. It wouldn't be drivel. This
letter would require something of him. His stomach fell again. Unable to
do anything else, he tore off the corner with a flourish and shook its contents into his palm. A date nearly a month old crabbed the top of the page.

Mrẹsh 8, Y.o.T. Falcon

Caliph,

Congratulations! I don't have to tell you that you're brilliant.

*I have my own place now, not far from Sandren, in the Highlands
of Tue. You could be here in a week if you take the steam rail. I enclosed a map. The fact that you did most of my cartography for me is
my only excuse.*

*I have something to show you. Something that might put our last
conversation in a better light. And no, that's not the only reason I
want you to come.*

*It gets lonely out here. I bought some things I know you like. I
can probably find a use for them if you don't show up but . . .*

*Don't worry. If you decide against coming—for any reason—I'll
understand and wish you good luck. Hynnsạ ŭllạ.*

—Sena

There was a key, their key, tucked inside a wrecked attempt at a map. To
his surprise, the key affected him profoundly like a talisman. He thought
of throwing it in the pond.

At noon he met the rest of the Naked Eight at Grume's for a drink. Since Roric's expulsion, Caliph had become their genearch; the one they toasted while skirting the humiliating topic that had forged their fraternity.

With graduation bearing down, they promised to stay in touch, look each other up; look Caliph up in particular since he would be king. They joked about taking advantage of his featherbeds and the fictitious chambermaids that gave sponge baths.

Caliph forced a laugh but he had to wonder whether it might be true that they clung to him primarily because of the power he would soon command. He wanted to believe that regardless of his distinction, there was some invisible unbreakable bond between them. They were the Naked Eight. Unfortunately it sounded cheap and mawkish, sincerity that with time would turn into the oldest kind of lie.

Caliph left Grume's feeling depressed.

By Day of Dusk, his isolation was complete.

He went to the chapel where a heavy brocade of dove-colored stone seemed to shout. Choking-sweet clouds of incense smudged the tierceron vault under which twenty-nine graduates milled as though eight years of school had left them confused.

Caliph walked in, spotted with jewel-colored light and found Belman Gorn's eyes watching him.

"Here for a gown?"

Caliph felt sheepish. "I opted out of that pomp. I'm staying one more semester. There's a class on lethargy crucibles: slow power. I couldn't pass it up."

"Engineering?"

"No. It's an overview of how they run, but mostly economics. Impact, cost, infrastructure . . . that kind of thing."

Belman chuckled. "Let no one say Caliph Howl doesn't love school. You probably won't miss much at commencement tonight."

Caliph smiled but knew Belman was wrong. Suddenly he understood that this should have been his night. Belman wasn't giving him advice. Belman wasn't talking to him like a student anymore. Some miraculous transformation had almost taken place. Caliph imagined all the doors and windows in Desdae being suddenly flung open, releasing him—every part of him—like a startled flock of birds.

But that didn't happen.

Instead, he watched his friends accept their degrees on the lawn. It was different than Sena's graduation, an evening ceremony with an audience that included no one he knew and the occasional lacewing that fluttered like white fire through the last rays of evening translucence.

Caliph met the chancellor in the Administration Building on the eleventh. Enthroned behind his desk in a riveted oxblood chair, Darsey looked up from his work through a set of thick, half-moon spectacles to see the clurichaun standing on his desk. He stared at it for several moments; then his eyes flicked to Caliph. He wore a sad expression that Caliph didn't want defined. "A deal is a deal, is that it?" the chancellor asked.

He pushed himself back, turned precisely ninety degrees in his chair and drew a roll of vellum from the great brooding bookshelf behind him.

Caliph didn't answer. The chancellor opened the document, examined it briefly, re-rolled it and held it out. "I think you'll find everything in order . . . your majesty."

The words struck Caliph in the chest, solidly. He looked at Darsey for a moment, then reached out and took his diploma. "Be careful, Mr. Howl. I doubt the Duchy of Stonehold will be as quiet as the library."

Caliph nodded faintly and left the room without a word. After that, he knew he was dead. He could feel it when he went to class. The hollowness. The emptiness of the campus. He had done spring and summer semester every year, but this year was different. This year he had fallen like too-ripe fruit.

Tarsh to Maom to Myhr to Paṣh. It was really only two and a half months. The class on lethargy crucibles made three hours of every day tolerable. The rest of the time he found himself coping with ghosts. Everywhere he turned he saw places where someone he used to know had done or said something. Usually that someone was Sena. He carried the key in his pocket like a weight.

On the fourth of Paṣh Caliph sat up in bed.

The cracked sink grimaced at him like a chrome-eyed creature backed against the wall. The place where the plaster had given out; the small pencil marks near his bed where he had written Sena's name seemed sullen at being left behind.

A pillar of antiseptic sunlight fell through the window, whitewashing his sheets.

This morning, the Council was coming.

Outside, silken banners curled softly in the early summer air, barely moving in a shady breeze from the west.

Caliph had no energy. The final class had sucked him dry. His husk fell back into bed. Rather than face another day, another hour, he chose the oblivion of sleep.

TWIGHLIGHT arrived. Still no Council. Word came by pigeon that there had been a storm, heavy snow and wind that prevented any navigation of the narrow crack through the Healean Range.

Caliph couldn't breathe. He paced, watched the sun choke on sky as thick and bright as peach jelly. He walked to Karthŭrl Hall and found Nihc Pag smoking in the shadows of the pitted front steps.

Nihc was a Pandragon but had lost most of his accent during eight years of school. He had gone through graduation and stayed for spring. Unlike Caliph, he had good reason. A two-focus degree in bioscience and exotic ecologies demanded additional time in the labs of the Woodmarsh Building. Soon, he too would vanish.

"Hey, Caph."

Caliph sat down. Nihc stubbed his smoke against the wall and joined him. The sun was totally gone. Naobi had crawled out of the glutinous shadows like a white beetle that had been feeding on the day. She was in her waning half-phase: slender, livid and cadaverous. From the steps they could see the lake. Blue fireflies flickered sporadically, casting double images in the water, occasionally vanishing forever in the mouth of a leaping fish.

They said nothing for a long time. The splishing fish and the leaves that pitched and moaned around Desdae's blackened gables were enough to keep the silence comfortable.

Finally Nihc made the first real effort at conversation. "Thought you were leaving today."

Caliph envisioned the Council, the uniforms, the offices waiting for him in Stonehold. "Yeah. I am."

Nihc plucked a killimore weed from beside the step and chewed it. "Not much of today left."

"There's enough. What about you?"

Nihc spat. "Headed out next week. Down south. Something lined up for me in the Empire, Pandragonian, of course. I wouldn't serve Iycestoke if it killed me."

"Really? What'll you be doing?"

"There's hunters in Pandragor that go out and trap all kinds of things so they can entertain the Emperor—or so they've got something to feed criminals to."

Caliph mused sardonically, "Must cut long-term prison costs."

Nihc shrugged. "I'm not a politician. I'm just going to advise the hunters on care and feeding. Think of it! Catch me a Khlohtian ground sloth or a sintrosa—one of them ax-beaks, you know? Or—biggest damn thing to walk on four legs—a norkocis!"

"Sounds dangerous."

Caliph glanced beyond the library at the dark shadows of the north woods. "I got a letter from Sena back in Tarsh. I think I'm going to see her."

Nihc stood up, indicating that good-byes would soon be in order. "Must be excited. Over half the campus was in love with her."

Caliph yawned and rubbed his eyes.

"She's different." He doubted *love* was the word Nihc should have used.

"Nobody could understand how you two never got caught . . . you know . . . together."

Caliph pulled the key from his pocket and clenched it until its teeth bit into his palm.

"Anyway," said Nihc. "If I was you, I'd be glad. A girl like that you hold on to."

THE Council arrived at the High College the following morning. Two official representatives touched down in a zeppelin bristling with armed men and women. Caliph imagined them scouring the town, the buildings and the forest to the north, thinking immediately of abduction, ransom, assassination. It would never occur to any of them that the rational, notoriously reclusive heir might simply walk away.

He had left shortly after wishing Nihc Pag good luck, used a black cotton shirt to cover his escape and crawled through the attic of Nasril Hall. From there, he'd gotten onto the roof and into the branches of a danson whose limbs tore savagely at the shingles every time there was a storm.

Down the trunk and through the shadow-painted lawn, behind the lilacs and south along the pond.

He'd gone between the chapel and the mill, feeling giddy, and crossed the stream connecting the tiny lake and Ilnfarne-lascue to the cattail marshes southeast of the village.

At the fork a quarter mile down Grey Road he had headed through the village, passing Mim's Grocer, the Whippoorwill and Grume's Café.

By morning, Caliph had left the High College of Desdae far behind. He was free.

A tractor headed for South Oast passed him, flappered stack retching a mixture of blackness and motes of colored light. It lurched over the hill like a sick tippler and disappeared.

Caliph glanced at his compass and kept on. He traveled marshland to canebrake, canebrake to holt; over smooth drumlins left from Kjnardag's glacial reign. He saw the world as a series of textbook illustrations.

He crossed geography he had learned in class, the Grey River by thirteen o'clock on his second day while dusk piled clouds like blue ashes on a white marble floor.

An old stone barn with an empty loft served as a hostel for the night. In the morning he ate some of his provisions and headed west.

The third day put him through a wide forest of danson trees and planted him on the steam rail platform at Maiden Heart. He had enough money for a ticket to Crow's Eye, which he bought at a window fitted with brown iron bars and a bizarre perforated funnel on a flexile pipe for speaking to the hidden seller inside.

The platform was ugly and myriad. Horses in strange barding lashed the air with their complex tails. Chickens hacked into millet bags with sawtooth beaks and forked tongues. Their bloodred eyes glared ferociously at children who stepped too close. Hairless purple dogs pulled two amputees in a pair of rolling midget thrones. Flowered hats, pipe smoke, stale booze and shit of all kinds stunk together on the platform. Bodies pressed into queues like hülilyddite waiting to explode. There were scuffles. Eventually men in uniform started getting the animals sorted.

Steam and sound shrieked from whistles and pistons as Caliph handed a thin man his ticket and climbed aboard. Inside, the air was so close it felt infected. One couple kissed obliviously despite their proximity to a woman shaped like piled trash and a reading man who snorted every thirty seconds.

The Vaubacour Line ran west to Woonsocket and from there to Mirạyhr or south a thousand miles into the Theocracy of the Stargazers.

Sena's map would be of no use until he reached the Highlands of Tue. It showed only a small section of country and did even that poorly.

Caliph found room as the engines screamed. He sank into a red leather seat whose springs and stuffing erupted like fungi. *Maybe I want to get lost,* he thought. *Maybe I want to get lost and I'm never coming back.*

ynan doesn't come to her graduation. He has never seen her time at Desdae as important.

Commencement goes off, bitter, solitary and anticlimactic, concluding with rain.

It doesn't matter, *she tells herself. I did this for me. But she feels desolate.* Fuck Tynan Brakest. Fuck Caliph Howl too for not showing up.

Then they *arrive.*

Women in rain-dark storm cloaks looking bizarre, so pragmatically dressed amid the throng of suit coats and corsets. As parasols pop open and people bustle into Desdae Hall, the three women move against the current, directly toward her.

Sena's heart stammers as though she is losing her balance on a ledge. She considers running but then, paradoxically heroic and at the same time alarming, Darsey Eaton swoops in.

The undisputed master of his domain, Chancellor Eaton faces the three women uncowed and unaware of his peril. Sena finds a touch of comedy in watching him bring them up short. He towers, pear-shaped, leaning forward, hands behind his back, the welcoming smile on his face in perfect counterpoint to the deep-set eyes that wield disdain like a pair of clubs. Sena sees it in third person: the whole uncomfortable little crowd grazing the lip of satire, smiling thinly over introductions and regarding one another with cordial skepticism.

Shucking fear, Sena makes her way to Darsey's side and joins the conversation. She can tell that the chancellor doesn't believe any of it: neither that Megan is her grandmother nor that the other two are her cousins. He offers to escort all of them to Desdae Hall where refreshments are already being served.

Megan returns his invitation with procuress-arrogance. "Thank you but we'll be along. No need to wait."

Sena watches the cords in Darsey's neck stretch; he smiles and glances sideways into her face. It happens so quickly that Sena barely has time to understand he is checking with her, making certain everything is fine. It shocks her to realize that, in a cool and businesslike way, he is genuinely concerned.

When Sena nods faintly he immediately looks elsewhere, scanning the lawn, overseeing the mass of people. Then the chancellor bows, rainwater dribbling from his hat, turns squarely and abandons her, striding purposefully toward the bright open doors of the cultural hall.

"So good to see you, Sienæ," Megan chirps after he is gone. Sena listens for irony but detects none. She still wonders if she is in trouble. The Shrạdnæ Mother never ventures outside of Mirạyhr and her presence at Desdae is bizarre. The ancillas seem tense. They stare at Sena, all business. Maybe they know about Caliph . . . or Tynan. But Darsey is gone. There is no one on the lawn anymore and they would have taken her by now, in the Shrạdnæ grip, hauling her off to a fiery end.

Sena watches Megan dig inside a gloomy paisley corduroy bag for her hand mirror. "The only femininity I have left is melting." She powders her cheeks and pulls her cowl forward. "Let's get out of the rain."

"My things . . ."

"Pshh—" Megan's finger taps her temple. "Anything you need should already be up here. We don't have time to dawdle."

Sena subdues her glare. "Yes, Mother."

"Don't be crabby with me. It's bad enough you wasted eight years of your own life in this trash heap of positivist thinkers. You won't be wasting what little time I have left. We'll get you all new things in Skellum. Come along."

SENA is whisked away clutching only her gown and her diploma. She goes back to the familiar shadowed buildings that released her nine years ago as an adolescent spy, to the socket vaults of old parliament made strange by Shrạdnæ Witchocracy.

As Megan's shịe-sịn,[4] Sena retains access to Deep Cloister and the archives. But the privilege costs her. She must work for the Sisterhood.

SUMMER begins with warm arguments between Sena and Megan. As usual, Sena gets her way. She is assigned to Sandren and leaves parliament behind, supported by authentic government papers identifying her with a list of verfiable lies. In an attaché, she carries an array of padparadschas rationed from the Sisterhood's vaults. When she reaches the city state, she liquidates them at the most affluent jewelry shop she can find. It is enough to live well for a year and it gets her a footing in local

---

[4] D.W.: Witch's pupil.

circles without turning her into a celebrity. She begins donating to Emolus, the most popular church in town, and thereby makes Bishop Wilhelm's acquaintance. He is a man on everyone's guest list and seizes each opportunity to take her to parties where he introduces her to Sandren's powerful elite.

At Megan's request, Sena sleeps with three of them, diplomats out of Iycestoke and Pandragor. It is easy work. They are reasonably attractive, clean shaven and rich enough to make it seem more like a first date than what it really is.

The information she collects goes to a half-sister named Clea who runs a potion shop near Litten Street.

It is tiring. Compartmentalizing Clea from Tynan, Tynan from Wilhelm from the diplomats she has fucked. There is an embarrassing moment at a fund-raiser when Tynan's father sees her. She knows instantly that despite her best efforts, rumors have reached him. Sandren's influential circles are small and Tynan's father is in all of them. He crosses the room calmly and whispers three sentences into her ear. "You look lovely tonight. Amazing what jewelry can do. Stay away from my son."

TYNAN never mentions the incident. He remains loyal, funding her cottage off the books.

A graduation present.

As the cottage begins to form, blueprints to foundation to framework, Sena realizes it is more than a building. Not only is it a delightful way to exact her pound of flesh from Tynan's father, but it is also her first real stab at independence—sort of. It is definitely her first act of outright defiance against the Sisterhood.

She is supposed to stay in Sandren, seduce men and gather information. That's what the Sisterhood is paying her for. But she builds her cottage in the countryside, well away from the city state.

A gleaming padparadscha comes in a nondescript envelope every month to her box on Goorin Street. The stipend allows for plenty of luxuries when combined with Tynan's allowance. She meets him on weekends, risking death out of spite.

For those that marry in the name of the Witchocracy, Sena suspects the lines sometimes blur, but for field agents such as her, pårın[5]—the duty—is rigorously enforced.

---

[5] Pårın and fårǫn are respectively "The Duty" and "The Betrayal". Pårın specifically is sex work to advance the Sisterhood's political agenda. Fårǫn is sex for personal reasons and seen as jeopardizing the Sisterhood's veil of secrecy.

When Tynan and she stay at Sandren's posh hotels she tries to revel in
it, but anger leaves her empty. For a while, at college, sex had very nearly
slipped from being a political tool to a pastime. Now, with Megan's influence enveloping her again, all of that is gone.

She is back. Deeper than ever. An Ascendant of the Seventh House.
Apart from that there is the undeniable sense of family she attaches to the
organization. She buries it. She ridicules it internally as an affectation but
the feelings persist, a vague sense of belonging. Unable to verbalize such a
grotesquery, Sena sums it as crassly as she can in her journal, "They still
have a use."

She moves out of Sandren even before her cottage is complete and begins skipping social functions, fading from Sandrenese galas, shrugging
her duties to focus on her project. Megan's letters become persistent. The
cottage secret slips.

"The Highlands of Tue? Within eyeshot of the Porch of Soth? Are you
mad?"

Sena doesn't argue. Megan is right.

She still remembers her first journey below the Walls of Tue, looking
up at the grim dark circle perched on the brink of cliff and sky; she had
seen something in the air, transparent ommatophorous images, like light
trapped in ancient glass.

Sena won't admit that the monument frightens her. In the end, it
doesn't matter. Her goal, her search, wins out. The Stones are linked to
something abstruse and awful, something that can protect her if she actually finds the Cisrym Ta.

Much different than the modernists in Sandren, Sena sees herself as a
believer in sweet black secrets, rich as chocolate cake, visceral and
bloody with cosmic truths learned and lost on the tides of other civilizations. In the cities, in the gleaming dirty bustle and rush, Sena thinks, we
are on the edge of something . . . not the future. Something so old it only
feels new . . .

Sena keeps working for the Sisterhood even after her cottage is finished. She fudges on her hours. And then, after nearly two years, everything pays off.

"New electroplate angel on my altarpiece," Bishop Wilhelm murmurs.
Sena says nothing as they pass a pharmacopolist. "God-jarring marvel
pales in comparison to you."

The bishop is smoldering. He swings himself around her like a censer.
Cologne and wealth pour off him like smoke.

Lines of sight intersticed by momentary objects and rushing people *allow others to glimpse their eastward passage along the Avenue of Lights. They catch snippets of Sena. The fleeting blond tantrum in the wind. The gem-blue eyes italicized in mascara. The movement of her hips caroms sunlight, sets the black jewel fastened in her navel flashing. It is a chronotropic spell. Some of her gawkers collide with city things, remembering their places in the street on impact.*

Sena slices east between the buildings with purpose.

At the outlet to Rum Street she and the bishop say good-bye. His questionable eloquence fades into city sound as she pays for teagle fare and enters one of the gondolas blackened by a century of weather. In her hand is a colorful shopping bag, stretched by something heavy . . .

It hadn't been found in some forsaken temple or ruined attic. Rather it was to be had off March Street for five gold scythes.

"I WANT this one," she had said, holding up the book.

The proprietor had smiled with lips like wood shavings—pale, smooth and tight.

"That's from Stonehold . . . very old. Can't open it though. Latch's rusted shut, see?"

"How much do you want?" Sena had given him a coy look, then turned away, pretending to consider while his thin fingers had kept caressing the leather.

"The binding suggests it might have come from the islands before I found it."

"I'll give you three gold scythes."

A simper.

"Five?"

THE machine lurches down a wind-scraped cliff, carrying Sena with it, scudding through iron rib cages draped in grease. She watches the operator throw his switches and apply the brakes whenever they descend too fast. His eyes are furtive and lochetic. As soon as the great old lift clanks against its coupling in the ghettos of Seatk'r, Sena leaves.

Her animal is stabled nearby. It takes her out of the reeking enclave, pounding east and home along the lip of the plateau.

Delusions of robbery and loss stem her excitement. It is the fastest, most panicked ride she has ever made from Sandren.

When she finally arrives, she crosses the threshold of her cottage and locks the door, touching a chemiostatic lamp and flooding the kitchen with shadows more than light. When she slides her new possession out onto the table, the room sways around it. Reality seems to buckle. Her fingers twist her hair into ringlets while the object groans. There is no actual sound. But she can hear it, feel it, blasting her tabletop with psychomantic darkness.

She moves to wind a thermal crank in the corner. Yellow dials wobble to life as the metal snaps, expands and infuses the room with warmth incapable of dispelling the chill she feels pouring from the book.

For a while she frets, examines the metal ferrules riveted at the corners, beaten to resemble coiled Neķrytian serpents whose bodies have worn smooth under centuries of handling. There are greenish pits where air works the metal. Like bariothermic coils, strange power sources in the south, the cover shocks her fingertips with cool. It does not have a title but a faint rune on the front reassures her that this is the object, the unbelievable end of her search.

Its ornate lock peers at her from where the tumblers nest like the rusted legs of a metal spider, crawled inside and curled up to sleep. Her rakes and picks are useless. Cutting the spine, sawing bits off, all would be equally futile and dangerous.

Her eyes trace its shape in the middle of the table. Awful, like a murdered child. She can only stare and think about the recipe.

On the twenty-third of Myhr her letter to Caliph remained unanswered. Light dribbled through the trees, pattered around the leaves from last fall. Sena sat at her kitchen table looking out the window. Her head was killing her. She got up, uncorked a honey-colored bottle and tapped the glass against her palm. Four aspirin rolled out. She drank them with milk, flipped out her pocket watch.

Eight sixty-four. Sixteen minutes 'til noon. A soft tapping echoed through the house.

Tynan? Three more taps.

She noticed a shadow fall across the curtains near the front door. Even through the gently tossing lace, the sound of mercurial breathing prickled over her skin like vinegar. Not breathing. It was mechanical, ill-regulated, gasping, then whispering, then whining like the draft beneath a door.

She moved around the back of the table carefully.

The shadow was massive and bent, like a huge cowl vent on a ship's deck. The thing's breathing fluttered strangely, disloyal to its origins. The sound bounced off glass, floor, coming from behind her, wet and unpredictable, like wind through a storm drain.

Sena jumped catlike to the top of her table with only a whisper of sound. She could look out at a better angle from here, bracing one hand against the ceiling, leaning out into the room, craning to see around the edge of the window.

The filthy shape of the visitor eluded her, wavering in and out of view. A mountain of rags. When it swung left she could see the tatters hanging from its bulk, heavy, barely swinging in the breeze, like dripping bandages. No visible feet. Its carcass was wrapped every inch in the sopping swaddling. *How can it move?* The rags poured down and pooled where torso met ground in an oozing pile the same consistency as wet cigar ash. The upper yards of fabric stretched taut across the creature's hump, a great pile of muscle it seemed, where the body made its ninety degree turn like an elbow joint, undiminished in size or thickness, defying its own center of gravity.

Finally an appendage, impossibly thin, like pencils taped together end to end, articulated from a small lump of gray meat. It swung from a powerful rack of bone that must have connected somewhere beneath the rags to that enormous hump. Sena watched as the limb uncurled. There were nails, almost talons, eight inches long, uncurling like digits. One of them extended, the middle one, a stiletto poised. It drew back with dramatic acuity then struck forward against the door, tapping again with soft, almost human decorum.

She could see the shadow of the fingernail on her curtain. It was banded as though parts of it were translucent and parts of it were opaque, like a tropical fish spine, she thought, painted in bands of white and brown. Its staccato movement against her door stopped. The limb withdrew under the haystack of rags.

Sena had seen enough. She walked down her table like she would have walked down a staircase, stepping from table to chair seat, chair seat to floor. She was headed for the back door when Niṣ brayed like a snake. The cat was off the wall, through the back door and gone in a flash.

Sena gasped as the coldness passed through her. It did not hurt immediately but when she looked down she saw the slash on her bare waist. Like a slice through her finger in the kitchen; she didn't want to look.

Instinctively she mashed her hand over her side. A warm tingling wash of red was gushing down her thigh.

Time slowed.

She noticed the long fingernail hovering above her wound, the rags swinging behind her like drapery. The huge presence was with her in the kitchen but the front door had not opened.

Where was the sound?

A fecal smell like tooth decay filled the room. She felt herself topple, fall toward the back doorway, clutch at the stones. She could see points of light now, oozing out of darkness. Sidreal. Slippery. Galaxies dripping dizzy. The bent torso of the rag-thing above her was fuzzy. Everything was fuzzy. A hand like a branch drooled cosmic cold.

She tried to talk but either she couldn't hear or her lungs weren't moving air. Tingling numbness was coursing through her sex, down into her legs, spreading from the wound. She couldn't feel her ass. Her arms refused to work properly. She flailed.

Her numb body was sliding across flagstones now, out of the house. One of her fingernails caught on something and tore, a fibrous shredding that ripped it to the quick. But there was no pain. Her body was moving backward now. Back into the house. She was being fought over. Her torso hit the door frame with a limp solid sound.

Sena felt broken inside, like ceramic dishes dashed against the floor. She tried to steady herself and realized she could move her arm. Her finger slipped into the cut on her waist, brushed the hot slick pulse of her own entrails. She heard herself cry. Sound was coming back but there was nothing she could do. It no longer mattered where the rag-thing was or what it did. She was powerless to stop it.

Golden light fluttered down through the ghostwoods by the well. Shadows kissed back and forth across her face. She wanted the light to dissolve her, absorb her, reflect her off the stones, into the sky.

The bent, maggot form of the rag-thing covered the sun, haloed in streaming white light. It was trying to pull her out of the house. But for some reason it wasn't succeeding. It looked at her not from a face but from a hole, a burrow in that dark cylinder of wrappings. It seemed to regard her as though suddenly surprised and then . . . the cottage took it.

Sena heard the creature bellow as it tumbled through the air into the room. It sounded like someone blowing across wide hollow pipes to make sound, bass and strange and much softer and more resonant than it was loud.

The Porch of Soth, connecting to her home like a tension snare, had finally sprung. An invisible force grappled the rag-thing with a vengeance, flinging the enormous grub body with careless childlike violence, repeatedly against the floor.

Sena held her wound together and fumbled for a hidden latch beneath the stairs.

From the front of the house something large struck the door. Boards splintered. The sound of talons sunk into wood with a squeak. Then, just as quickly, everything went quiet.

Sena felt nauseous. She drew up on her knees and looked around the shaken room. Her connection to the Porch was broken. But she could feel again. She pulled the hidden door to her study open and went wobbly and clumsy down a set of uneven steps. The room below reeked of mice.

It was getting hard to think.

Sena groaned. Five staggering steps. She touched the lanthorn above her worktable and flooded the cellar with light. There was a medical kit. She cracked it, rifled through and doused herself in antiseptic, yelping at the pain. She irrigated with a bottle of saline solution and realized she needed sutures. Hand quivering, she took the needle driver from the box and did the best she could, pulling her flesh together, forcing the bleeding to stop.

It was makeshift and ugly. She knew she needed help. She wrapped a bandage around her waist and jammed the *Cisrym Ta* and a few other objects into her pack.

She hesitated a moment, weighing the odds, wondering if it was worth the energy. Then, finally committing to the task, she reached for her bookcase and pulled a thin book from the shelves. She set it in the middle of her worktable like a centerpiece, then turned and left the room.

In her kitchen, she took a moment to scrawl a note and tack it to her corkboard. Then she set out on the two-minute walk that took her to the Stones.

The Porch of Soth gathered starlines from all across the world, angles, lines through the Nocripa. The Shradnæ Sisterhood used them for navigation and connecting space. Megan claimed no one outside the Sisterhood knew how to use them, that they were forgotten like the very monuments that marked them.

But the Porch of Soth was different. Its numerology was skewed. Routes taken to the Stones from other places did not always have reciprocal lines. And lines taken away from Tue were often difficult to retrace.

But there was one place she could go and return from and she had planned it from the beginning.

At the Stones, Sena's body shimmered and unwound, a two-dimensional cicatrix, a spool of black ribbon thrown from the mile-high cliff by holomorphy, fading north into nothingness.

Where she went, she hoped, would be impossible for anyone except Caliph Howl to deduce.

he train crawled between the Spine Mountains and howled over the Medysan Bog. Caliph got off at Crow's Eye. Even stopped, the great hideous thing flickered with people: bodies adjusting behind three stories of slotted white windows. The obscene black cars repeated like segments of a myriapede, fading back along the Vaubacour Line.

Caliph dispersed with the rest of the passengers, fading from the platform like engine steam.

In the east, the sun had left ruins in the clouds. He found the toilets locked and crouched behind the station. Far away, the horizon crumpled with distant humidity. A glimmer that might have been an airship floated south. Caliph finished up. There was no shortage of waste paper. He wrinkled his nose and made due.

Just then, a man's cough startled him. A slender silhouette emerged from the deserted platform, utterly featureless in the dark. Caliph buckled his belt. He watched the man, who didn't seem to notice him, take a set of cement stairs down behind a fence that was alive with spectral bits of paper.

Caliph took one step and his foot hit a can. It sang mournfully off the gravel. The man stopped and turned in Caliph's direction. He stood there, too long, staring directly into the blackness. Maybe he was frightened. Maybe he was a thug.

"It's just me," Caliph finally said, feeling stupid. "The toilets were locked."

The man said nothing. He continued to stare.

Caliph stepped out into a gray tangent of streetlight. When he did, he thought he heard the other man gasp.

Caliph tried again. "I didn't mean to startle you . . . nowhere else for me go—"

"You rode from Greymoor?" The other man's voice was older, slightly stretched and tinged with emotion: anxiety or perhaps disbelief. Caliph felt trapped, uncertain how to answer. Certainly people were looking for him, probably a great many people by now. Maybe this man worked for the Stonehavian government.

"I'm a butcher," said the man. There was no further explanation but his accent indicated a degree of education. His vowels sounded vaguely like he usually spoke Gnah Lug Lam or maybe High Malk. "Name's Alani."

Do I dare use my name? "I'm Caliph."

"There's a pushing school on the south side of town," said Alani. "But you're not going there, are you?"

Caliph wished he could see the man's face.

"I don't know . . . I . . ."

"No. You're headed for that little skirt's place on the lip of the plateau."

"Who are you?"

Alani stepped back; lamplight caked his face suddenly like butter. Caliph recognized him. He couldn't find the circumstance but he had definitely seen him before, wearing different clothes . . . a uniform.

"Turn around. Go to Stonehold." Then the man shifted position and abruptly walked away.

Caliph let him go. He was too frightened to run after him. He was still trying to find a setting to pair with the bald head, pocked cheeks and well-kept goatee.

A thin man in his fifties.

It had to have been at college. Mentally, Caliph dressed him in baggy pants and a shirt. No. He imagined Alani in Desdae Hall selling books. A professor? A cook? Maybe in town at the theater or Grume's . . . No. He tried a different angle: *who could have known he was going to see Sena? Who would have had access to the letter? Who could have seen the map?*

Caliph searched his mind, trying to remember the faces at the campus post office. All he found were the pouts and freckles of two or three sullen women.

It seemed useless. Whoever Alani was, he obviously knew both where Caliph Howl was supposed to be and where he was going. *Maybe I should turn around . . .*

Caliph stood in the dark for a long time, wondering, doubting.

Finally he decided. On his first step he rebuked the can that had given him away, kicking it fiercely. It seemed to float rather than fly, barely scraping the bricks before vanishing into the dark. On his second step he set his feet toward the cement steps that led down into Crow's Eye. He was not going back.

At a point just north of the barren arches of Tibiŭrn, Caliph could see the Walls of Tue, black and misty through miles of humid sky. It was the eleventh of Pash and he had reached the crossroads.

Sena would have no way of knowing he had stayed another semester. Maybe her invitation had expired. She might even be with someone else by now. The thought thickened the back of his throat.

Caliph wished he had brought a friend, someone to make it less obvious that he had traveled all this way just to see her. The thought of knocking on her door alone terrified him.

There was a crumbling thread of trail that climbed from the cross-roads up into Tue. When Caliph topped the final switchback, he was gasping. Five thousand feet below, the landscape swept away, creating an indigo vista of lakes and trees. Caliph dug Sena's map out of his pack and looked at it with some dismay. A nostalgic smile haunted his lips.

"Can't draw so well," he whispered to himself.

A damp breeze swelled and flapped out of the lowlands.

Caliph looked up from the crackling paper and studied his surroundings. The sweat from his climb had chilled, inducing vast tracts of horripilated flesh across his arms and back. At least he told himself it was the temperature. A freakish mood had settled, oozing from the angular, purpurean shadows around the Stones. Caliph walked toward them, pulled by an itching in his brain. He touched one like a child on a dare. It felt slick and cool, the crowded patterns stained by an unidentifiable pers residue. There was nothing recognizable in the carvings. As if the very subject matter were distortion. Flux.

The air felt sticky, smelled sweet.

Caliph shuddered.

Maybe he had heard it: that insane high-pitched gibbering he didn't want to acknowledge. Whether it really existed or not was a matter he might debate later over pints when the horrible subtlety of the sound had dissolved into memory. For now, Caliph preferred to label it a trick or figment of the wind.

He left the monument and trudged uphill. A meadow above the Stones tossed mournfully, tumbled down from a small wood that Caliph recognized from Sena's map. He scanned the trunks, looking for a trail and found one.

He checked his compass and gripped the paper, wading through the whipping weeds and into the wood. Giant drops were splattering everywhere, on boulders, bark and patches of stony dirt. The warm musty rain assaulted him like soft slimy food hurled in a theater.

Just ahead, a small cottage came into view and Caliph made a dash for it. Crimson flowers in a barrel drooped darkly by the door. A window had been left open and lace curtains slapped about like desperate fingers.

Caliph thumped hard only to have the door swing open under his blows.

He fumbled into a broad kitchen, pungent with spice and tried to shut the door but the latch seemed broken. He set his pack on the table and slammed the sash on the moaning window.

Caliph wiped water from his face and began winding the thermal crank. After the dials started glowing, he clicked a chemiostatic lantern and held it up to examine the room.

Delicate chairs and copper kettles poised like swans. A pair of tall soft boots sat crumpled by the door. The cottage smelled of her, but in a dusty faint way. Panning the lantern, he could see that the floor by the window had been ruined by weather.

"Sena?"

His voice, coinciding with a blast of wind, seemed to rattle the leaded glass. The cottage was tiny. A brown tailless cat blinked at him from the stairs, but there was something else, something dark and somber on the floor.

Grume streaked the floorboards, rusty and dry. Caliph found more at the threshold. He backed into the kitchen, feeling the warmth drain from his face.

Caliph reexamined the front door. The lock had been broken, but the bolt had splintered the frame as though hit from the inside.

Caliph shook off his queasiness. There was no body. He poked his face above the second floor and peered at Sena's bedroom, noting the carved headboards. Maybe she'd made it to a hospital in Sandren. Maybe the blood wasn't hers.

A deafening crack of thunder split the air just the other side of the roof. Caliph's body hair prickled.

The sound of torrential rain on the vague and somehow unsettling geometry of the windows lessened.

He panned the lantern, scanning the room. His name leapt out from a corkboard in the kitchen. Plucking the pushpin, he quickly read the note:

Caliph:

Currently, hospitals employ cytoclastic kymographs. Unless new doctors emerge, redundant therapy heightens egregious symptoms, taking all intrinsic remedies south . . .

The old game. *C*-urrently, *h*-ospitals *e*-mploy *c*-ytoclastic *k*-ymographs . . . *check under the stairs*. He spun immediately, took two steps forward and knelt down.

A small latch had been cleverly hidden at the corner of the first step. Caliph unhooked it and a crack appeared along the baseboard. He raised his eyebrows, gripped the lip of the bottom step and stood up. The entire staircase rose smoothly into the air like the lid of a counter-weighted trunk. Underneath, a second set of steps descended into a narrow pit lined with mortared stones. He felt immediately apprehensive about what he might find.

The chemiostatic light spilled like old wash water down the secret steps; it picked out the silver glints of bottles and flasks from the cellar gloom. Caliph swung the hood around and the light lapped over a book-case filled with volumes, a table cluttered with powders, charcoal drawing sticks and dried roots.

"Witch."

The word came softly to his lips.

Upstairs, the hinges on the kitchen door creaked in the wind. Caliph paused, listening, but nothing stirred. When he turned his attention back to the table of powdered roots, he noticed *The Fall of Bendain* sitting in the middle of the workspace with a fingerprint inked in blood in the center of its cover.

It wasn't the real thing. She had asked for his forgery of *The Fall of Bendain* after Roric had left school.

He picked it up. The blood stopped here. There was a bookmark. He opened to it and discovered that it was actually a note addressed to him.

He scowled. It was dated nearly a year ago and everything about it was wrong.

Tes 13, Year of the Search

Caliph,

I'm not paranoid, really. This is just in case something goes wrong, which of course it won't because if it does I'll probably wind up dead . . . so this is really pointless anyway.

Sick, I know. Still, there's a bit of time to kill out here on the edge of the world especially when it's been snowing for four days.

Long waits can kill you.

I wish it was just the two of us again, battling the brigade of books, picking up the splinters of broken stone noses. For a kiss I'd give my soul.

Anyway, I'll probably show this to you and we'll both laugh. I just thought I should let you know how much I loved you—since I never told you.

Things slip by unsaid and you regret it later. "Opportunities are the blossoms of seconds," Belman used to say and "Eternal love orders the heart." I say: love is the origin of theft.

—Hynnsą Ŭllą

SENA had never been sloppy in love. *For a kiss I'd give my soul!*

Caliph wrinkled his nose.

And the Old Speech farewell had been misspelled. Ŭllą should have been left uncapitalized to infer you as the person addressed.

She was fluent in Old Speech and couldn't have made the mistake unintentionally. She also knew that he had memorized every word in *The Fall of Bendain* and in the original there had been a paragraph about snow.

The author, Timmon Barbas had been a general and he had written that long waits will kill a city cut off from its supplies. It was snowing. For four weeks Bendain remained without its provisions. Not four days but four weeks.

Caliph did not have to second-guess whether she was being clever. This was code specifically for his eyes and it seemed her reason for writing it had been justified. If she had the foresight to write it nearly a year ago she must have foreseen her danger; their last conversation in the attic came back to him.

What had she been after? A book? The lines in the note were taking form now.

Just the two of us, battling the brigade of books, picking up . . .

In the original copy Caliph had quoted Timmon Barbas.

I WISH it was I alone, entrenched in this sorrow, battling the brigade of foes, but alas I cannot do it alone. I am left picking up the splinters of broken bodies and shattered plans of war. For a hiding place I'd give my soul.

CALIPH found the passage on page thirty-one. The words *"you clever boy"* had been written in the margin and they bracketed a paragraph that Caliph had composed himself.

IN desperate times you must flee and we fled and hid ourselves where none would think—amid the buried dead in the hills. And we ate among

*the graves and slept amid the sepulchers, regaining what strength we
could. And I had but two thousand men left in my army. Two thousand
that lived in the hills like dead men. And we were four weeks from home.*

THERE was the time frame of four weeks again. Caliph riffled through
the shelves and pulled down a thin atlas of sorts with crude maps of the
Hinterlands.

Four weeks from home, hiding with the dead . . .

His eyes ran over the map. There had to be hundreds of cemeteries
within four weeks' travel from here.

Wait!

Eternal love orders the heart?

Belman had said nothing of the sort. His eyes went from the words to
the map and back again.

Eternal love orders the heart . . .

E-l-o-t-h.

The Valley of Eloth, otherwise known as the Lost Dale.

The ruins of Esma lay at the far northern end of the valley. A mortuary
temple resting above a small lake in the middle of thickly wooded mountains.

Hynnsạ Ŭllạ: shade and sweet water. Not a farewell addressed to anyone, left capitalized it formed a description of a literal place: the lake in
the woods below Esma. She was alive. That much seemed obvious.

Caliph felt pleased with himself, pleased with Sena for being so clever
and with himself for being equally clever. He had his heading. In the
morning, he would set out for Eloth.

He went back upstairs, pushed the table against the front door and
took off his clothes. He hung them over the thermal crank where they
dribbled and hissed.

The dark house, strange as it was, did not threaten him. It was Sena's
house, with Sena's things, infused with a faint but familiar blend of in-
toxicating smells.

SLEEPING in her bed, the man's face mocked him. The one from the train
platform; it was supported by the official vest of a courier, the scarlet coat
of a doctor. The man wore priest's clothing, a gardener's smock. He held
a paintbrush, knives, files full of paper. Nothing fit.

Slowly, Caliph's dreams shifted, moving from the man on the platform to the soot-covered walls, the brown fans and the running shadows.
Once again, the police sabers glittered and the dream man plucked him
from the chaos. Then, in dreamlike fashion, Caliph found himself run-

ning through the halls of his uncle's mansion where blood had been so common.

He woke late, twisted in her sheets, cock stiff, smelling her smell in the linens. He had chased vague dreams of her toward morning.

Caliph left the loft and found a bite to eat. There was a tin of biscuits in the pantry with a label showing a clown holding a magic wand. A Sandrenese brand he didn't recognize. More searching produced fruit preserves sealed in wax. He dug into them while songbirds rummaged outside, making music discordant with his thoughts. The cat slept in a patch of sunlight on the floor, its snubbed nose and batlike ears twitched with dreams.

When he finished, he cleaned up and looked at the map he had torn from one of Sena's atlases. Eloth was four weeks away if he walked, but he had found some money in her desk to help with train fare and there was a horse stabled out back that he could ride to Crow's Eye.

What am I doing? I should go to Stonehold . . .

Outside, the late morning sun steamed dew into a sultry fog around the house. Insects were crooning but the songbirds had vanished. Caliph picked up Sena's cat and stepped through the back door, not looking at the gruesome stains on the threshold.

"You're thin as a stick," Caliph whispered to the animal. "I can't very well leave you here to starve." The garden behind the house had grown into a jungle. Enormous pink and orange speckled blooms hung in the tangled foliage, humming with blue bees. Caliph fought his way to the fence line where a solitary horse grazed near a steaming pond. There was a shed nearby with tack and harness. He set the cat down on the split-rail fence and opened the door.

"Horse thief."

Caliph stumbled backward. Crouched on her haunches atop the shed's small peak was a woman in dark clothing.

The soft impact of another woman embraced him from behind. Her body was close, her arms cradled him strangely. There was a knife, curved perfectly against his throat, a razor choker that warned him not to move.

From the flowers another woman appeared. She too had dark clothes and like the one on the roof, there was something strange about her eyes. They glittered profoundly, as if faceted by a jeweler's chisel, liquid flickers of light scintillating while they watched him.

For a moment, only the insects trilled across the breezy green shapes of the forest. Caliph blew a mosquito from his lips but couldn't speak. The knife around his neck was too tight.

"He doesn't look like he belongs out here," said the second woman.

Then a voice behind his head said, "I'll bet he knows her." She was talking into his ear now. "You came out here for some fun, didn't you?"

Caliph still couldn't answer. He held these women up to the memory of those he had seen at Sena's graduation.

"What are you doing here?" asked the one on the roof. Then she spoke in a language Caliph couldn't understand. Instantly the pressure on his throat lessened.

"That's the important question." Her voice was calm and pleasant as it shifted back to Trade. "What *are* you doing here?"

Shrạdnæ Witches . . . do they know I'm the future king of Stonehold? If they do I'm dead . . . And then another realization.

Sena is one of them . . .

It kept going through his head, combined with all the occasions he had pressed Sena for information about the Shrạdnæ Witches based solely on the fact that she had grown up in the Country of Mirạyhr, when in fact she had been one.

"I'm not going to ask again," said the woman on the shed. She was beautiful. The sunlight trickling across her nose; her smile, a pleasant disguise for the threat she represented.

Caliph knew he had to answer and that the more truth he injected into the conversation, the less likely he was to wind up dead.

"I came to see Sena."

"Boyfriend?"

Caliph had been briefed at school. As the future ruler of Stonehold, he had been given access to certain antiseptic details about who the Shrạdnæ Witches were and how they worked. Shrạdnæ field agents were forbidden from any kind of relationship that could compromise them: pregnancy in the all-female organization was strictly regulated. For Shrạdnæ operatives, sex was part of their training. It was an art form they perfected just like assassination and like their trademark knife sheaths, their legs didn't open unless it was part of the job.

She knew I was going to be king . . . was she using me the whole time? Caliph's brain froze around a new thought. *Her letter! Just to lure me out where they could kill me? Ransom?* He couldn't help himself. He pitched forward on his hands and knees, retching; everything he'd just eaten turned out in the grass.

For a while he stared at the weeds, watching the slick amber liquid attract bugs. His torso convulsed again; he didn't care what the women were doing.

"Sena's always taken her men watered down."

"Not her boyfriend," Caliph managed to croak. He wiped his mouth on the back of his hand. He felt dizzy from the heat, like he might pass out.

"You must know her well enough to walk through her house and take her horse."

"I wish I *was* her boyfriend. I went to school with her." He picked one of the Naked Eight at random. "Name's David."

"Get up, David . . ."

aliph stood up. As he did, the woman on the roof pitched forward like a gargoyle breaking loose from a building. She plummeted into the weeds at Caliph's feet, landing with a simultaneous crunch-thud; she did not move again.

He turned around. The woman behind him was standing perfectly still with a shaft of gleaming metal sticking out of her cheek. She fell forward into the flowers, brushing Caliph's shoulder on her way down.

Caliph ran.

He vaulted the split-rail fence and landed in the pasture, heading for the horse. He saw its tentacle tails flipping gently like a fistful of snakes, its slab teeth shearing contentedly through grass. It looked up, watched him for a moment, then roared. Its claws ripped massive clods of sod from the ground as it bolted away, racing for the far end of the pasture.

Caliph slipped and skidded in a patch of mud; the momentum flipped him onto his back like a turtle, speeding him over moss and horse shit down a gentle slope and finally depositing him near the edge of the pond.

When Caliph opened his eyes, the sun had gone behind a cloud and everything looked gray. There were men with duralumin wings and chemiostatic cells on their backs, landing in the pasture. They cradled gas-powered bows and huge compression guns in their arms. Their goggles were chrome blue. Their flight suits black.

Caliph heard heavy propellers and looked up. Not a cloud. A vast porcine airship blotted out the sun.

There were men surrounding him. They wore rapiers and made signals with their hands, telling each other what to do. So fast. Caliph couldn't tell where they had come from but he assumed they too had dropped from the zeppelin.

"Caliph Howl?"

A man was shouting from slightly uphill. He reached down and pulled Caliph from the mud. "Caliph Howl?"

Dazed beyond speaking, Caliph could only nod.

"I'm Master Sergeant Timms." He shook Caliph's hand, seemingly unfazed by the thick muck covering almost every inch of Caliph's body. "Trying to give us the slip there again, literally . . ." He smiled. His teeth were slightly crooked but very white.

Caliph looked around. It seemed obvious that Stonehold had found him. Snipers had killed the Shrạdnæ Witches and this man was now taking him north. Far north. Over the Country of Mirạyhr, east of Eloth, past Sena—wherever she was—beyond the Greencap Mountains and down into the Duchy of Stonehold.

Caliph knew he didn't have a choice in this. He didn't have a choice that the women were dead, or that he didn't want to be king. He knew that now, suddenly. He didn't want to be king. But he wasn't sure he wanted to find Sena either. Everything between them must have been a lie. *Or was it?*

His mind was already toying with ways to suspend judgment. Maybe there had been a mistake.

He was walking, letting Master Sergeant Timms steer him like a cow toward a harness that hung from a cable like a tail trailing into the sky.

"Don't worry, your majesty. You're safe now. Everything's going to be fine."

Caliph felt the buckles snap around his chest, his groin, his legs. He looked across the pasture to where more men were corralling the horse, maneuvering it toward a horse-sized sling. *Why would they do that? It's not even my horse . . .*

Master Sergeant Timms was grinning in Caliph's face, white teeth and blue goggles reflecting Caliph's sordid condition like a mirror. He jerked the cable several times and Caliph felt himself float up into cool air, away from the squalid heat of the pasture, reeled in like a fish by the hand of providence.

He moved from thoughts of Sena to thoughts of Stonehold. *What will happen when I get there? Wretchedly submit to the tenure of public service?* And then there was the other logical notion that being High King might not be so bad a thing.

Caliph vomited again from a hundred feet above the ground, hoping he missed Sergeant Timms. Landing on the deck was a blur. The winch stopped. There was a smell of hot machine grease. Then Caliph was in a small metal shower stall cleaning off, getting dressed, crawling into a bunk that smelled of bleach. He shivered from the trauma, the violence . . . but was soon asleep.

A change in engine pitch woke him. It was dark. He rubbed his eyes, trying to remember where he was. He pulled a robe from the back of the tiny room's door, tied it on and stepped out into a gray corridor.

There was a man stationed outside his room who said nothing. Caliph looked both ways and arbitrarily chose right. The passage led him outside onto a deck that stared into the night. Flashing lights reflected on the railing from the overhead zeppelin skin.

Below, in the black abyss, green-lensed gas lamps erupted from turrets, hooded and massive like grotesque helmets. Their ornate leaded glass launched groaning beacons into the dark, lighting an aerial highway not just for this ship, but for pilots ferrying metholinate to the Independent Alliance of Wardale and the Free Mercantilism of Yorba.

Beyond the beacons, twinkling in the distance, a massive sprawl of lights smoldered beneath a pancake of brown clouds. Naobi burned, staring out from just beneath the cloud cover, turning the Dunatis Sea into a hypnotist's cauldron flecked with light.

Master Sergeant Timms appeared at Caliph's side, summoned suddenly by the look of it. His short ash-brown hair was slightly crimped and his eyes looked bleary. "Did you sleep, your majesty?"

Caliph made the hand sign for yes. "I guess so."

"Not very luxurious," Timms said, "but it's the best we could do for you on this ship." He looked out at the approaching landscape of lights. "They know we're coming. Tomorrow's going to be a busy day. Can I get you anything to eat?"

Three hours later, Caliph Howl landed in Isca.

MAPS lay scattered across the old tactical table of the High King's tower, rustling in a breeze from the window where Caliph stood staring out at the city.

He tried to follow the arcaded gutters that sluiced rain and night soil and anything else that oozed or floated but tracking them was impossible. His eyes drifted through the blackened spires of Temple Hill, down into Ironside where the Iscan navy bristled and the Dunatis shone like a colony of golden beetles.

Almost mythic, Caliph thought.

The Duchy of Stonehold had not been a true duchy since Donovan Blek liberated it from the Kingdom of Greymoor six hundred sixty-eight years ago and shortly thereafter choked on his own tongue.

As the years passed, a queer mongrelization of southern technology and northern hocus-pocus settled across the land.

Much of the original tribal ferocity persisted in aristocratic form, as barristers with familiar chieftain surnames like Cumall and Hynsyil flung opinions like spears around the courtrooms of the north. Others became constables and burgomasters and sometimes even kings.

Backward by most accounts, the Duchy of Stonehold was a pseudo-feudal monarchy buttressed by a complex aristocracy composed of wealthy merchants, factory owners, artisans and businessmen. It was a cobbled mess of governmental offices and overstated positions. It was five duchies, five kingdoms really. Four lesser kings unified by the High King in Isca, all of which echoed obsolete tribalism: tribalism that stoked the main fires of Stonehold's nameless hybrid political engine.

Miles away, the industrial yards of Growl Mort and East Murkbell spewed smoke as cohesive as black ink. From the weltering ooze, little golden lights winked and twinkled—all that remained of holomorphic energies poured into furnaces at Vog Foundry and the shipbuilding yards of Bilgeburg.

Caliph turned his back on the phantasmagoric vista and focused once again on the gruff interplay of voices barking all around him.

King Lewis had just said something outlandish and there were whispers from the crowd.

Lewis laid claim to a well-thinned head of hair the color of used engine grease that he combed straight back and a body like a glutted wineskin that slumped in his chair, leaning forward into a dramatic pitch of evening light.

"Mayor Ashlen knows more about war campaigns . . ."

Ashlen Kneads, whose last name had become a pun, sat quietly in the corner ferrying occlusions from his nose to some hidden sticking point beneath his chair.

Another voice, one that Caliph was only recently acquainted with, came from Yrisl Dale, the Blue General and Caliph's chief military advisor. He too was whispering angrily.

"He is the High King. Show him some respect!"

"Respect? He's staring off into space . . ." Without looking, Lewis tossed a hand in Caliph's direction. "The least he could do is pretend we are here!"

Snickers twittered in the assembly, subdued because everyone could see that Caliph was now paying attention.

One of the power players, Prince Mortiman of Tentinil, sat laconically, one foot resting on the seat of a nearby chair, listening to Lewis vent. He wore a cold smile that matched his platinum jewelry.

Lewis continued. "I've put off meeting with Pplarian ambassadors for two days because of this."

"Don't treat it like it's nonsense," the prince chirped. His dark eyes flashed across the room and bored into Caliph's face with a strange mixture of warmth and aggression. "Why do you think my mother is still in

Tentinil? Saergaeth will turn the zeppelins coming from the Memnaw into war engines! He can turn off our supply of gas like that!" He snapped his fingers. "We've seen fires in Bellgrass. There are troops maneuvering and engines massing in the hills north of Newt Lake." His lips moved like sculpted rubber, perfect and pale.

Lewis snorted. "Saergaeth could be on maneuvers . . . or logging trees for all we know."

The whole room suddenly exploded. Everyone had an opinion and all of them started coming out at the same time. Cries about proving whether there was a valid threat from Saergaeth clashed with statements that questioned old alliances, loyalty, greed and cowardice.

Through the jungle of bodies, Mortiman continued to stare. Caliph looked away.

One of the burgomasters was saying, "I doubt it, but the Council wants to appear vigilant. Saergaeth is angry the High King's throne is going to be filled by a boy just out of Desdae. I think he thought he still had a chance of seducing the Council until this week."

Another burgomaster seated nearby responded and his words echoed in Caliph's ears. "Well it's got to be clear to Saergaeth now that he's not going to be High King. Saergaeth's diplomacy is at an end."

Caliph realized now that most of the burgomasters were here, curious to know firsthand how a civil war might affect the economy of their respective boroughs.

Mortiman spoke up. "Does his majesty have a voice?"

The room stilled. Roughly two dozen heads turned expectantly toward Caliph.

"He's speechless," said Lewis, starting to look away.

"Maybe," agreed the prince. "Maybe he's worrying about his father in Fallow Down, ordered to garrison there with the rest of the fodder."

What the fuck are you on about? thought Caliph.

Lewis chuckled. "Forgive him, everyone. He's still mourning the loss of those witches—"

Despite the Council's strict mandate that the events in the Highlands remain undisclosed, too many people knew about Caliph's rescue. And since the Council's ability to enforce its own will had dissolved along with it, details had invariably leaked.

Caliph knew his moment had come. If he waited a second longer his persona would slip from silent, past mute to join Ashlen Kneads in the rank and file of the dumb. He had to take control of the room. He had to make them understand that he knew he was the king.

But the men around him wore business suits and jewels while Caliph had come to the meeting in prosaic black. He wore a sweater for the chilly evening air, riding pants and dusty black boots.

"All right," said Caliph. Lewis stopped, midsentence. The soft, distinct syllables of Caliph's voice seemed to have more impact than if he had shouted.

The prince was smiling.

"This isn't a parliament," said Caliph. "And I don't know why all of you are talking."

"Maybe if you—"

Caliph shot a look at the prince who stopped speaking but kept smiling, a sort of silent laughter.

"Saergaeth Brindlestrom is a hero," said Caliph. "He's served this country for almost thirty years. I believe he still wants what . . . he thinks . . . is best for the Duchy . . . and I plan to establish some dialogue with him about that. In the meantime, we are not at war."

"We are at war," said the prince, "or might as well be. Saergaeth isn't going to stop until he's sitting on your throne. I really thought you'd be clever enough to grasp that."

Caliph looked directly at the prince. "Would you like to apologize now or later?"

The room collectively caught its breath.

Mortiman simpered, "Your majesty . . . this really isn't the place . . ." His smile was insincere and his tone glib. "Besides, without me . . . Saergaeth will lay siege to Isca by autumn."

The crowd waited, watching as Caliph found his words.

"Assuming that were true, you'd be dead or conquered by then. It's not really in your interest to advise me on what follows, is it?"

The crowd gasped.

Everyone knew what Caliph meant. The notion that Mortiman was more of a queen than a prince was old news. Likewise, the fact that Saergaeth held the prince in contempt on account of his preferences had been widely recognized for years. But that Caliph was brash enough to expose Mortiman's posturing with artillery based on such sensitive trivia actually seemed to impress many of the more reptilian burgomasters.

Mortiman had no real choice in his allies. If he wanted to stay Prince of Tentinil he had to side with Caliph Howl.

Caliph hardened his gaze but tempered his voice with genuine sincerity. "I don't want to alienate you. I respect your doubts . . . in me. If you didn't have doubts, it would mean somehow that you didn't care about Stonehold. But don't ever speak to me like that again."

"Majesty—" Yrisl whispered.

"You advise me," Caliph raised his palm, "never interrupt me." He let the same hand he had raised fall slowly to rest on the pommel of his sword—it was the only weapon allowed in the chamber and a solid reminder of his unquestionable power in this place.

The Blue General of Isca raised his eyebrows and fell silent.

Caliph stood up and faced the assemblage. "I'm well aware I'm not the king many of you wish I was. I've had no opportunity to stand in the shadow of a real king and watch him work. But I have spent the past eight years learning about Stonehold. Learning about you.

"I have a sound grasp of this city's laws and I know there are a host of outdated, still-viable punishments able to be handed down for insulting a High King."

He smiled softly as the audience went pale. They were gauging now, how they could explain away the hasty remarks, cast their unforgivable sauciness in a better light by adding meaning and rationale after the fact.

"I'm insulted.

"But I'm also patient." He looked at the prince. "If any of you doubt me, I respect that. I will earn your trust. I will secure Stonehold's future. And I will do that, hopefully, by not choosing war. I will not *choose* war. If war comes, that will be Saergaeth's choice."

After the silence ebbed in, Lewis was the first to speak. "Forgive me, your majesty." He bowed slightly and began to clap.

Whether they felt he deserved it or not, everyone else followed suit.

After that, the meeting broke up. Whispers slithered between the burgomasters but by and large Caliph had come out on top. At a different time or place his words might have turned the same audience against him.

But this had been a critical moment. Caliph knew that Stonehold needed a decisive leader. With less unified military power than most northern countries, the High King of Stonehold had to exude power from his pores. He could not flinch in the face of overwhelming or unknowable odds.

He heard the whispers but in their own draconian way he sensed that the burgomasters were pleased. Yrisl had warned him beforehand that many of them were dreading this audience, distressed by the possibility of a meeting with an academic milquetoast fresh from Desdae's idealistic lecture halls.

Everyone was crowding toward the door, drawn down a series of staircases and passageways by an alluring smell that propagated from the kitchen. The Blue General met them at the exit and fed them the usual lies for good measure.

"Everything will be answered in due time. We'll call you back once this [completely absurd, fatuous] meeting has been assessed and compared with intelligence reports from the field."

Caliph listened to them go. When the room was nearly empty, Yrisl approached him.

"I'm not sure about how you handled that. We needed to cement Lewis and Vale Briar as an ally. This is a war, your majesty . . . no amount of diplomacy is going to save us and calling Saergaeth a hero . . ."

"He is a hero," said Caliph. "His popularity north of Tentinil approaches legend. He's protected the people near the Glacier Rise better than any High King."

Yrisl sighed. "Well, two percent of the region where your hero lives is comprised of military. That means eight thousand airborne, engineers and regular army. If he musters from Gadramere and Mortûrrm he'll have a legion over that. Vale Briar has to be solid with us!"

Caliph nodded. "I'm sorry for jumping on both of you," he looked at the prince who had stayed behind and was listening intently, "in front of everyone."

Yrisl's eyebrows levitated.

Mortiman looked hungry. "Nonsense. You did exactly what you should have. I was just glad you had it in you."

"Oh? And what did I have *in* me?"

"You showed those fickle bastards that you don't give a shit about etiquette when you are forced into a fight. You fought dirty. More importantly, you won. I like that and so do they."

Caliph looked at the floor. "Thank you . . . but . . . none of this is the issue. I'm the issue. If it wasn't for me, there wouldn't be a threat. I wonder if we held some kind of election, found another way to turn the crown over to Saergaeth."

He looked up to see both Yrisl's and Mortiman's jaws go slack.

"I mean it," said Caliph. "I'm sure Saergaeth knows how to manage Stonehold better than I do. Why not let him? If war comes, think of all the blood that will be spilled. Think of our countrymen fighting each other. All because of me? It doesn't make sense."

"No," said Yrisl. "If this is a test of our loyalties, so be it. Nevertheless I'll respond as if your concerns are genuine. If the High King's throne were turned over to the first challenger, where would that leave the sovereignty of the Duchy? I'll tell you where. *In question.* This government isn't up for auction. Nor is it subject to contestation—by anyone. You, your majesty, are not the issue. The issue is, pardon my saying so, much bigger than yourself. The issue is the security of the Duchy—which no one except you is authorized to ensure."

The prince nodded.

Caliph sighed through his nose. He walked to the window and looked out on the distant turmoil of Temple Hill.

"All right, tell me about Saergaeth." He sounded apathetic.

Yrisl glanced at the prince.

"His only challenge, your majesty, will be feeding all his troops. Without Lewis, we die."

The maps rustled in a breeze that pulled into the high tower and Caliph began to feel the discomfort of the stomach that he suspected was common to all the High Kings of history.

The prince, seeming to sense that there was nothing else to say, extended his hand and offered a solicitous smile.

Caliph grinned and shook. "I won't hang you out to dry."

"I appreciate that. I leave for Tentinil in the morning. Good luck managing Isca. I'll send word the minute anything changes."

The Blue General paused, waiting for a formal dismissal before following the prince out.

"Go ahead, Yrisl. Get something to eat." Caliph remained at the window.

"I could have something sent up," Yrisl offered.

Caliph shook his head and waved the departing tactician away.

Alone, he pondered the past two days.

The zeppelin had dumped him off directly at the castle. The next morning, at his coronation, the Council had been disbanded and a great crowd of people had cheered. Or, thought Caliph, maybe they had only shouted.

For several days he had been free. An anonymous . . . mostly anonymous . . . wanderer in the north, chasing what he thought was love or adventure. Maybe it was just stupidity. But now his fate had finally caught up.

He wished his father could be High King but Jacob wasn't a Howl. In fact, Jacob, according to the one instance of him saying so, was a half-blooded Hjolk-trull that had come from the Gwymrin Sward, a place he had never described or explained.

The family history was murky and embarrassing. "Unfortunately, when you were two," Jacob had once told him, "your mother . . . got sick . . . with the rest of her family. Since you were a Howl and therefore related to the High King, he sent his physicians out to the estate. They decided it was likely bad food, something you had avoided eating due to your tender age. Your Uncle Nathaniel came from Greymoor soon after, inheriting the house and you with it."

Caliph could remember living with his uncle in the vast dark house. The dream man had come to live with them in the fall.

Suddenly, Caliph wondered about the dream man as a real person instead of a dream person. Cameron was the man in the dream, the real man that had carried him down that rope so long ago. It had been at least sixteen years but if Cameron was still alive, he might be able to help run the kingdom. He had been a soldier, a tactician maybe. Words spoken so long ago echoed indistinctly out of the past.

Jacob would know. After his uncle's death, Jacob had been the only reliable figure in his life. He had taken Caliph to Isca's south side, to Candleshine.

It wasn't until Caliph's eighteenth birthday, for reasons unknown, that the Iscan Council had decided Caliph's mother's blood was good enough to call him a Howl. They removed him from school and gave him the entrance examination to the High College of Desdae.

Apparently he had passed.

Now he was in Isca again, the past leaking into the present, alone in the tallest tower in the Duchy of Stonehold.

Caliph thought again of Cameron, the dream man. He recognized it as wishful thinking, smoke puffs in the sudden wind of responsibility facing him, but it was still worth a try. If nothing else it would provide some closure: finally tying off the loose end that had generated so many dreams.

He left the tower, locked it and descended a set of corkscrewing stairs.

He went directly along one of the few hallways he knew—to his bedroom, festooned with wood and marble and occupied by several newly carved wardrobes.

Caliph sat down at a desk and took a sheet of parchment that seemed to be waiting at attention. He pulled a gold-nibbed quill from an elaborate inkwell and looked down at the empty page.

Jake,

I've been curious about your old friend, Cameron. If you know where to find him, please tell him I'd like to see him as soon as possible.

—Caliph

Caliph smiled, somewhat amused with himself.

He blew the ink dry and pulled one of the ropes that, through pulleys and bells, summoned one of the servants.

"Have this delivered to my father in Fallow Down at once."

The servant took the note and ran.

"At once," Caliph whispered to himself.

He pushed himself away from the desk and opened the bedroom windows. Outside, the sky sagged under a host of stars. They were framed perfectly by the sharp geometry of the battlements. A hundred thousand points of light trapped between the crenels seemed to represent all the people of Stonehold.

Maybe he was being maudlin. Maybe he was just beginning to understand what the burgomasters already knew: that lifestyles were at stake. Futures were at stake. People's lives and homes hung in the balance.

He had studied war. Sena had handpicked the best books on tactics to augment his required reading. She had said, "You can't ignore it, Caliph. War defines the king."

CHAPTER
8

Voices come and go.

They speak in Withil.

A cold front pulls down into the Country of Mirąyhr. Gold, generator-powered lights caramelize the intricate sockets of brown medical equipment. Sena can hear the slow regular tick of a thermal crank but she is freezing.

"Nie slipsou,"[6] says Megan. She is not talking to Sena. She is talking to a harridan at the edge of the room, a decayed crone like a strange animal folded in half. Giganalee's voice makes Sena whimper like a dreaming dog. "What news from our half-sisters in Sandren?"

Megan tightens. "There are signs the Wįllin Droul has returned."

Wįllin Droul? Sena listens from the heavy drapery of half-sleep. She understands from inside the framework of argot, an Ilek phrase unchanged by Withil: Wįllin Droul means Cabal of Wights.

The voices move like clouds, in and out of existence. Sena catches only bits when Giganalee speaks. "They can no longer . . . Chamber . . . Last Page."

"Let us hope . . . Clea will send us word . . ."

The rain increases for a few moments, falling hard against the glass.

SENA woke with a start. Something stirred in the darkened room. She relaxed.

"You came quietly," said Sena.

The candle's halo obscured Megan. "But you have not come quietly, Sienæ."

Sena ignored her birth name.

Megan sat in an armchair near the bed. "What have you been doing in the Highlands of Tue?"

"What day is it?" Sena tried to divert the conversation to anything else.

"Black Moon, the fourteenth of Pạsh. You've been sleeping for sixteen

---

[6] W.: "Sena sleeps."

days. You were lucky to catch us in Eloth. We were planning to leave the next day because of weather."

"I didn't want to disturb you . . ." Sena's voice trailed off.

Megan leaned forward, face melting from the gloom. Her night-blue robe was trimmed with black. Setting her apart however was the slender coronet of tunsia that marked her as Coven Mother.

"What is it, Sienæ?"

Sena could feel her own clouded emotions passing through the muscles of her face. Megan was reading them. For a moment they might have been real mother and daughter.

Sena fought it. She unclenched her jaw, tried to relax, forced a faint smile. "Thank you for taking care of me, Mother."

Megan's stern expression splintered. *Into what? Compassion? The smudge of insoluble guilt?* The Coven Mother reached out, tentatively, visibly aching in her core. Sena felt a surge of nausea. She envisioned Megan's heart as a zombie lab of barely lurching emotions; the final resting place of matriarchal instinct strangled so long ago.

Sena didn't pull away. She closed her eyes and submitted to Megan's caress.

It didn't last. Sena heard her sigh after only a few moments and opened her eyes to see Megan scowling at the wound. The old woman touched it lightly. It was swollen, blackish-purple, crusted and awful in the light.

Megan drew a bowl of steaming antiseptic from the top of the thermal crank. "There's been an incident," she said. "Three Sisters murdered in the Highlands of Tue. Shot by Stonehavian troops."

Sena's mind reeled. "Three? Why three?"

"Shh. It wasn't a qloin.[7] I sent them to fetch some of your things. But tell me, what was the future King of Stonehold doing at your cottage?"

"What? Why? What happened?"

"You don't know? It's right here." Megan nudged a neatly folded newspaper on the nightstand like bait.

Grabbing for it would be a mistake. Sena forced herself to reply coolly, "I knew him at school."

"And you didn't tell me? *Sienæ* . . ."

Sena closed her eyes.

"We only made one attempt at school," Megan said softly. "It was too difficult. He was surrounded by secret police. Almost every cook and gardener at Desdae was a bodyguard. We didn't assign you to him because of your inexperience. And now I find out he went looking for you?"

---

[7] D.W.: A hit squad of witches composed of three Ascendant Sisters.

"It was his idea."

"There's no mention of you in the papers. No one knows why he was in Tue. Only that he was found, quote, in the company of witches." Megan put the antiseptic back on the thermal crank. "Difficult headlines for a new king I'm sure . . . but if it's still possible . . . I want you in his bed, Sienæ. I want you in Stonehold right away."

Sena wanted to ask *why* but could only nod her head softly. Her cheeks felt hot and seemed to throb. Great droplets of sweat welled up between her breasts and across her face. She felt sick. Truly, suddenly sick. "Mother . . . ?"

The room whirled around her, spinning out like a vomit-inducing centrifuge of purest black.

THE morning after his Council meeting, the High Seneschal brought Caliph breakfast and his itinerary for the day.

Caliph sat up in bed and looked at the concise schedule, bemused.

> Pash 16th, 561
> 4:40   Breakfast
> 5:00   Zane Vhortghast (tour of the city)

That was it.

Gadriel seemed to sense Caliph's puzzlement.

"From my experience, your majesty, you will be spending several long days in Mr. Vhortghast's company, touring different locations. Although I have never been, it is my understanding that the High King's tour is extensive and . . . unusual."

Caliph laid the sheet of paper aside, greatly interested and eager for five o'clock to arrive. "Who is this Mr. Vhortghast?"

"The spymaster of Isca," Gadriel said somberly. He glanced at Caliph above his glasses as he poured tea.

The High Seneschal was an immaculate man, poised and fastidious to a fault.

"I heard nothing of him in Desdae."

Gadriel clucked. "Of course not. He used to be a knight. Now he ensures that the business of the burgomasters falls in line with your wishes. There is little that Zane Vhortghast does not know."

"My wishes? How does he know what my wishes are?"

"I'm sure he knows quite a bit already," said Gadriel. "Saergaeth made several attempts on your life while you were at college."

Caliph scowled. "How could I not have known—"

Gadriel smiled reassuringly. "Discretion of that caliber is his job and the reason I'm afraid his salary is considerably higher than mine."

Caliph thought about the implications. It felt strange knowing that he was about to meet someone who had supposedly saved his life. "How did the Council hire him?"

Gadriel shrugged. "I wish I could tell you."

The forty-minute half-hour between four-forty and five o'clock passed torturously slow. Caliph read part of the *Iscan Herald*. It had been toasted in the oven. It was crisp and still slightly warm. One of the front-page articles caught his eye.

The King in Black
by Willis Bothshine, Journalist

Nearly two decades after the short inglorious reign of Nathaniel Howl, Caliph Browning Howl assumed the Iscan High Throne on a blustery thirteenth of Pash.

The last of the family bloodline, King Howl arrived in Isca fresh from Desdae where he graduated with distinction. Though following in his uncle's footsteps may be the last thing Caliph Howl wants to do, both monarchs did hail from the prestigious Greymoorian academy prior to being crowned.

Now at twenty-six, Caliph Howl faces a multitude of political challenges not unrelated to his uncle's reign.

Dr. Yewl, professor of Stonehavian Politics at Shærzac University says this Howl will face more challenges than any other High King since Raymond VII.

"Unlike [Raymond], who survived the Purple War when tensions between the Pplar and Stonehold peaked, Caliph Howl will have to earn the people's respect," said Yewl. "He will have to secure his authority while everyone is thinking he's the nephew of a categorical tyrant. On top of that, he's the youngest High King in the Duchy's 668 years of independence."

Though opinions polled in Three Cats show a majority favor the Council's dissolution and the reinstatement of the Office of the High King, fears persist that memories of Nathaniel Howl may darken the new king's reign.

Another omen is Caliph Howl's mysterious disappearance immediately following his graduation, an event that has troubled many Stonehavians. New information from an unnamed source in Isca Castle goes

so far as to claim the High King was found only days ago in the company of witches somewhere in the Highlands of Tue.

And while critics assert this means we are in for another dubious
kingship, supporters pass the accusations off as laughable.

"I don't think King Howl was within a hundred miles of Tue. He
wasn't [messing about] with witches any more than Councilor Deuadin
was walking on the moon," said Jeff Tibbs.

Tibbs, an experienced castle historian is conducting a poll on Stonehavian sentiment toward the aging monarchy.

His findings will be published in a subsequent edition of the *Herald*.

"I'm gathering a lot of fascinating data," said Tibbs.

"One anonymous man from Candleshine heard that Caliph Howl
had been crowned and I think his exact words were, 'Kings are for story-
books. Get the Council back's a better choice. That way there's no
throne to fight over.'"

Unfortunately, for Stonehavians like this man, the High Throne continues to cause turmoil. And with the High King's alleged secret trip to
Tue and rumors of a "witch pact" spreading through every pub and
bistro, tension seems inevitable.

Certainly Isca's free-tongued assayers are already arguing.

"Whatever the truth is, we're not likely to hear it from King Howl's
mouth. At least not for the first few weeks of his reign," said Tibbs,
who expects the coming month to be relatively quiet as Caliph Howl
meets with various advisors and familiarizes himself with the routines
of his new office.

"Certainly he'll be out and about, touring the city discreetly and
making appearances at important events. Namely the rededication of
Hullmallow Cathedral in Grue Hill and probably the opening night of
Er Krue Alteirz at the Murkbell Opera House.

"With tensions growing between Isca and Miskatoll few things are
certain except that Caliph Howl has his work cut out for him.

"On a lighter note," Tibbs laughs, "one thing I can't figure out. [The
High King] apparently refuses to wear clothing befitting his office. I
guess [he] prefers stuff that's simply black."

So what can we expect from our king in black? War? Witchcraft?
Only the summer of 561 will tell.

Caliph had eaten his eggs and strudel while he read. He set the tray and
the rest of the paper aside.

Obviously in the sixteen years since his uncle's death, the voice of the press had blossomed under a democratic Council. Caliph didn't mind. It was time people started thinking. And who could blame them for wondering? It was his fault. Running away from responsibility.

He got up and washed in an enameled basin fixed in a washstand in the corner. The pipes in the wall hammered at him as air worked itself out.

Light from the west was creeping in, a great golden blaze that seared the cold gray skies above the Greencap Mountains and ignited the cherry wood moldings and furnishings with exquisite luster. The white floor turned to gold.

Caliph's bedroom was situated so that it looked west and north over the cliffs and walls of the Hold and down on the farmlands and hills and rocky moors. Despite the warming season, mornings in Stonehold remained chilly and damp.

Caliph dawdled. Finally, Gadriel returned.

"Mr. Vhortghast is here, your majesty. He's waiting in the royal study."

"Oh good . . . uh—"

"I'll show you the way," Gadriel said in a warm tone that indicated Caliph's fumbling ignorance would not be faulted. "We will, of course, have it redone to suit your tastes. If you have any particular requests simply mention them to me and I will ensure they are taken care of. Your book buyer is already combing the shops for—"

"I have my own book buyer?"

"Of course."

"All he does is buy books?"

"She, your majesty. And yes. She summers in the Duchy but travels the rest of the year to Pandragor and Yorba, returning with the newest publications in the spring."

"I take it she doesn't like the cold."

They had left the bedroom, gone through several up and down staircases and were now walking briskly under ribbed vaults, heading in a southerly direction. Suddenly they stopped at an ogive fitted with a heavy oak door.

As Gadriel opened the portal a slender man immediately rose to his feet.

Caliph was mildly disappointed. He had been harboring a suspicion that the man from the train platform, who'd called himself Alani, would turn out to be Zane Vhortghast. He had asked the zeppelin crew how they had found him, whether there had been a spy, but no one would give him a straight answer.

As it was, the spymaster looked nothing like the pock-faced man he'd seen under the streetlamp in Crow's Eye.

Caliph did not have time to examine the room before Mr. Vhortghast was at the doorway, shaking hands, smiling and bidding the High King to please follow him for there was much to see and much to do.

As they hurried down the hall, Caliph saw Gadriel look after him with an expression of fleeting paternal concern.

The spymaster was a wiry creature several inches taller than Caliph. He moved with profound grace and was dressed no doubt for the occasion, sporting a luxurious herringbone suit of dark material. His face moved like malformed clay and two dark eyes had been thrust like chunks of pewter into the sockets. Overall, Caliph thought it was a visage that could easily have been hacked from a block of lard.

"It's good to meet you," Caliph was saying. "I hadn't heard of you until this morning."

He had noticed the spymaster's teeth. They were ungodly: strange brutal slabs of gray ivory that had been worked with ghastly results by some dentist on Bloodsump Lane. There were faint glitters in his mouth that hinted at metal pins and makeshift attachments.

"I'm fairly insidious."

Caliph smiled affably. "Really? How insidious are you?"

Mr. Vhortghast grinned. A sight capable of cracking glass. "Sometimes when you're sitting under the chain and you let one drop you get a splash that comes up and snaps you right in the hole. It's alarming but you tend to forget about it almost immediately after it happens. I'm like that. I'm the cold water that makes your ass pucker."

"I see."

Together, they reached the south courtyard where a carriage was already waiting. A Pandragonian man with long lemon-colored hair and skin as brown as chestnuts stood by, wearing an open shirt and roomy pantaloons. He carried a chemiostatic sword on his hip. The green light of the cell in its pommel turned his hand a ghastly undying color.

"This is Ngyumuh," said Vhortghast. Ngyumuh bowed slightly at the waist. "We'll have additional security as we make our tour but you won't see them."

Ngyumuh opened the carriage door for both men and once they were inside shut it again.

Caliph watched the Pandragonian man climb up alongside the driver as the carriage lurched forward.

Vhortghast sat across from him, noticing where Caliph looked and what caught his eye.

"You're a watcher of people," Caliph surmised.

Vhortghast said nothing but looked out the window as they trundled

across the drawbridge, over the moat and into the the Hold: Isca's only independently walled borough.

"Bit of a mess in the *Herald*, eh?" The spymaster looked apologetic.
"But nothing we can't fix."

"What? You mean about the witches?"

Vhortghast nodded.

Caliph glanced back at Isca Castle. The high tower rose like an incredible needle from the midst of half a dozen lesser spires, all of which gleamed
yellow on the west side, slowly melting out of the cool blue shadows in
the east.

"Do you know anything about them?" Caliph asked.

Zane studied him as though gauging whether Caliph was really ignorant.

Caliph threw his hands up.

"Look, I didn't expect to find a pack of women in the middle of the
woods. I'm asking you what you know about them."

The spymaster glanced out the window as they passed the brown dragons of Octul Box.

"Of course I know about them. But the details concerning Shrądnæ
Witches are always foggy. They hide behind layers of deception. If a witch
hunter shows up in Mirąyhr with a valise full of gadgetry for detecting
holojoules, folks direct him, as they're supposed to, toward Eloth where
they know he'll find nothing but gruelocks and death.

"They despise Stonehold for reasons I'm sure you picked up in history
class. But they're more secretive than the Long Nine."

"I see. But that's it? I mean, what do you know about them?"

Vhortghast looked offended as he tapped his fingers on his cane.

"They're loose fish. Soiled doves. They're trained from prepubescence
up to give better spread than the Rose Courtesans in Iycestoke. Is that
graphic enough? A witch in the right position can tie a baron or barrister
tighter with the laces of her stockings than with a length of rope.

"They're a political entity. Once the governments of the north hunted
them. Now, in Mirąyhr at least, the witches are the government. Really,
your majesty. What is it that you want to know?"

Caliph supposed that pretty much covered it. There wasn't much
there that he hadn't heard before. But the thought of Sena doing strange
things, secret things for an underworld organization put a coldness under
his skin.

He looked out the window at half a dozen strange towers in the direction of Temple Hill. Above the pitched rooftops and shanties that clung
like barnacles to decrepit town houses and gray tenements, the towers
rose like bones.

"That's Gilnaroth," Vhortghast waved at the looming stone shapes, "the citizens' necropolis. Anyone who can afford it is buried in Marbolia, the upper crust's cemetery located in Os Sacrum."

Caliph nodded. "Yes that's right, that's not far from Candleshine—I used to live there."

"I know." Mr. Vhortghast regarded Caliph shrewdly.

Caliph frowned. "You seem to know an awful lot about me. I'm told you saved my life several times while I was at Desdae."

"Only three. Three in eight years isn't bad."

"I'd like to hear the details."

The spymaster smiled wanly.

"Well, twice it was Saergaeth—though that's not common knowledge and we have no proof to substantiate it. But he gave up after the second attempt. We sent him a clear message that you were quite safe and would continue to be quite safe so long as you were at school. Those were two and three. The first occasion was actually some stray effort—we're not sure whether it was funded by a government or an independent company."

"I see. And how do you do it? How do you come by your information—?"

"Whispers, gurgles. It's the usual network of filth. Like a sewer system, really." Vhortghast drew a handkerchief from his vest and wiped his hands as though conscious of some asomatous stain.

"The bigger the city, the more advanced the network. Not many people like to work in the sewers and you could say the same about spy networks. There's no trick. Just like a city engineer memorizes the various tunnels and cesspools, I remember the names and places and take note when things change . . . when people die.

"And now I'd like to hear how you gave my men the slip. How did you get out of Desdae without being seen?"

"I went out the attic and down a tree. Maybe your men need better training."

Zane Vortghast smiled.

The sinister towers of Gilnaroth had already fallen behind a series of pubs and restaurants that fronted stores at ground level while upper windows revealed apartments and trendy domiciles of artists and musicians whose wrought-iron balconies dangled with plants and banners welcoming the new king.

WELCOME TO BARROW HILL, KING HOWL read one of the softly curling banners.

"How do they know I'll see?"

"They don't," said Vhortghast. "Mostly it's marketing. Everyone's claiming you patronize their establishment these days. You're the newest way to advertise anything. And artists more than most need to eat."

Caliph nodded with sudden wonderment. He hadn't fully realized his fame. It was obvious that no one really knew what he looked like up close. Litho-slides would make their way into the papers fairly soon but in the meantime they could tell he had dark hair.

Crude renderings of his image had been plastered up in patisseries and clothiers. They looked nothing like him.

THE HIGH KING'S STYLE IS HERE! promised one poster in a barbershop window. LOOK LIKE THE KING!

Caliph's jaw went slack.

"Pathetic isn't it?" asked Vhortghast, "until you realize they're just trying to survive."

The carriage lurched out of Barrow Hill into North Fell, following King's Road to the south.

"Where are we going?" asked Caliph.

"To get you a proper sword."

"I have a sword."

"No, my lord. You have a trusty blade. Obviously it fell on hard times while you were . . . traveling. In any case the monarch's sword is his symbol. I don't care what you wear, but we can't have you carrying around that filthy thing."

Vhortghast seemed so amiably in command as he made decisions that Caliph felt no need to challenge him.

Instead, he looked out at North Fell's market where cheap summer clothing hung in bright racks beneath deeply shadowed arches. Faux jewelry dangled from wire-armed trees, glittering with inane narcissism.

Already the populace was out shopping. There were early vegetables and fruits piled up on tables and overflowing baskets, attracting files and customers. Fresh cuts of meat drizzled blood on the cobblestones and children in grungy dresses and threadbare pants darted through the throngs, pressing shopkeeps for coppers and scraps.

The carriage paused for the stately glide of a chemiostatic streetcar, looming out of a tunnel in the bulwark of ancient bricks to the west and clacking toward Blękton. It left a strange ozone smell in its wake.

"I remember them laying the rails when I lived in Candleshine," murmured Caliph.

The carriage lurched forward and they trundled out of North Fell, rolling into Tin Crow where the buildings were thick as crates, overhung and ponderous with outthrust gables of stone and heavy timber.

Finally, the carriage bounced into Three Cats where the enormous sprawling market of Gunnymead Square hunkered beneath the awesome hulk of West Gate.

A vast haggler's paradise, but there were certain things the determined buyer would have to go east for, into the warrens of Thief Town, Maruchine and (for the particularly adventuresome or perverse) Ghoul Court.

Above the raucous commerce rose the massive bulk of West Gate. Nearly as large as Isca Castle and three times as threatening, West Gate was more like four castles all mortared together with flying buttresses and parapets that bridged over and looked down with solemn warning on Isca's busiest point of entry.

Caliph stared at a clutch of rotting pipes that burst forth from the inner bulk of the fortress and twisted down through bolted grates, ejecting foul sediment and dark gray geysers of foaming sewage.

Children gathered near the gouts, tossing pebbles into the torrent and threatening to push one another in. The carriage stopped.

Ngyumuh jumped down from his seat to open the door. Vhortghast exited first and eyed the crowd. Several soldiers shoved the masses back with poleaxes and truncheons while others clustered around the carriage, forming an impenetrable wall of armored flesh.

Caliph stepped out to the sound of cheers mixed with shouts and a few catcalls. Vhortghast bid him hurry and directed Caliph through a secured inner gate flanked by half a dozen men.

They traveled up a square staircase pierced by windows. The effect was that the immense thickness of the wall was perforated by breathing holes like a child might punch in a shoebox for insects.

"There's going to be a short ceremony here. Just mumble something gracious and we'll be on our way. They're going to give you a sword."

"Who?" Caliph asked.

Vhortghast threw open the final door at the staircase's terminus.

"The military of course." Both men exited onto a windy rooftop, over three hundred feet square and crenellated on all sides. Three stout watchtowers bordered it and thrust themselves even higher into the slowly bluing sky.

A great quantity of giant Nanemen in light armor stood in formation. Silent. Grim. Facial muscles tight and strained as though something crawled beneath their skin. They gripped heavy axes and wore claymores on their backs.

A guttural Naneman salute stunned the air, echoed momentarily. A ferocious shouting choir on the roof of West Gate as the High King came into view.

Caliph felt appalled.

There were a few civic leaders present as well. A handful of barristers and judges and more than half of the burgomasters.

Caliph took his position near the head of the army, following the subtle directions of Mr. Vhortghast. He shook hands and offered pleasantries before a horn sounded. It ripped the air and everyone's attention across the rooftop to where, much to Caliph's surprise, the Blue General marched out of what appeared to be a giant hangar that occupied one of the three towers. Yrisl was accompanied by a platoon of men, most of them much larger than he was.

Caliph could also see that Yrisl was carrying something.

It took over a minute for Yrisl and his platoon to cross the roof. Finally they halted in orderly fashion and Yrisl advanced, stopping just before the king. He knelt, holding a sheathed sword at shoulder level in his upturned hands.

Caliph noticed that many of the former Council were among the assemblage and they clapped with proper smiles as Caliph took the sword.

Some political drivel and an overwrought metaphor about Caliph both taking and becoming the Sword of the Duchy was delivered with halfhearted gusto through an echophone. Despite its volume, the speech seemed unheard by most of the crowd.

Caliph was just about to inspect his new weapon when something truly amazing drew his attention once again.

The vast hangar door through which Yrisl and his troops had come suddenly swelled with an enormous indistinct shape.

Something fierce and slender and huge was gliding from the darkness into the morning light, pulled on many ropes and heavy wheeled carts, drifting out above the rooftop.

The zeppelin was spherical but compressed so that it looked slim and dangerous from the side. Its internal framework protruded through the skin covering the gasbags, slipping out to form long imminent spines. They ringed its equator and flowed in menacing rows.

At least six such elliptical hoops armored the balloon, the longest of the barbs circling only the equator. The spines dwindled gradually toward the crown and undercarriage, looking more like serrated knives compared to the great spikes that sheltered its central girth.

Underneath the gasbag, but no less threatening, hung a cunning saucer-shaped structure like a lidded frying pan turned upside down. It was decorated with longitudinal bands of metal, oval widows and a bouquet of down-thrusting spikes, the longest of which jutted like an inverted steeple from the exact center to the thing's belly.

There were ballistae mounted to its underside as well. Housed in well-greased oscillating turrets. The gasbag was perhaps one hundred fifty yards in diameter and twenty-five in height. Including the spines, the thing needed an inordinate amount of space to float out of the hangar and up above the battlement.

Caliph noticed a six-foot circle of metal riveted to the masonry of the roof. It was scooped out like a socket and fitted with couplings. The inverted steeple that jutted from the bottom of the zeppelin's observation deck sank into this socket with a solid clunk and was secured momentarily by several dexterous men in dark uniforms.

Air horns sounded again and somebody was announcing the High King's tour of the city was about to get underway.

Vhortghast led Caliph to a mechanized lift and from there onto the boarding platform.

Though less than half the height of the high tower at Isca Castle, the view was only slightly less impressive.

Gunnymead Square moved far below like an animal carcass thronging with life. Its paper lanterns of blue and yellow bobbed happily. Its colorful awnings frittered and declined, surrendering only after four hundred yards of unchecked sprawl to the dismal brown tenements of Three Cats.

Clock towers, steeples and belfries confused the horizon with hazy ominous shapes.

"Welcome to the *Byun-Ghala*," said the captain of the airship. Caliph turned away from the vista and smiled, shaking the man's hand. "Right this way, your majesty."

A narrow bridge with railings had been extended from the craft to the tower roof and Caliph stepped off solid ground with an uneasy pit in his stomach. The bridge swayed ever so slightly as a gust of wind tried unsuccessfully to buffet the enormous craft.

Caliph stepped through an oval door frame into a cramped passageway that opened on a small but luxurious stateroom paneled in dark jungle wood. Much different from the military craft that had picked him up in Tue, this space was lit with gas lamps as well as many small windows.

Brandy and cigars waited on a wooden table with a mirrorlike finish while a woman in provocative dress played soft lilting music on a baby grand. Paintings of former High Kings, generals and other nameless politicians hung on the walls. They looked solemn and important.

An open archway led to an outer observation deck, girded with railings and fitted with spyglasses on convenient swivel mounts.

Vhortghast directed Caliph through a paneled door into another room that smelled of fresh leather and wood polish.

Caliph noticed a hulking four-poster bed in the shadows.

From the previous room came the sound of additional passengers boarding, clinking glasses and music. The smell of freshly lit cigars began to filter in.

General Yrisl entered, amber eyes flashing. He gave the spymaster a strange look of disapproval and immediately poured himself a drink.

"I don't want him visible," said Vhortghast as though Caliph were not in the room. He shut the door and then turned, graciously gesturing for Caliph to have a seat.

"I think I'll stand."

Yrisl swallowed his whiskey in one gulp and set the glass down with stinging decorum. "He should mingle."

"No he shouldn't," said Vhortghast calmly.

Yrisl looked on the verge of cutting off the spymaster's head.

"We haven't had a High King in sixteen years. Your agenda is outdated."

"Yours is dangerous," countered Vhortghast.

"Am I even here?" asked Caliph. "What in the trade wind—"

Vhortghast flung his finger toward the other room where the sound of music and conversation barely carried through the door. "That is a dangerous room." He was speaking to Yrisl. When he turned to the High King his voice became restrained and cordial.

"Forgive me, your majesty, but those people, good as they are at being burgomasters and barons and whatever else we let onto this ship, have only one thing on their minds right now."

"Oh for fuck's sake!" cried Yrisl.

Vhortghast raised his palm. "They want to sidle up to you, your majesty, while you are still new and—forgive me—still inexperienced. If they can get you to promise them some kind of favor or action or exemption while you are yet unable to gauge the possible repercussions—" He shrugged. "You may wind up playing favorites without realizing it or be called a liar later on when you try to back out of an innocent and even good-intentioned promise with unforeseeable consequences. Everything you say will make it to the papers."

"Bah!" Yrisl seemed to barely restrain himself from spitting on the carpet. "Caliph Howl handles himself better in a crowd than Jerval Nibbets. Did you read the papers today? If he stays in here he's going to look like a recluse, like he has something to hide."

Vhortghast made the southern hand sign for no. "I understand your point, really I do. And yes I read the *Herald* and several other unofficial publications. I assure you, one week of silence will not hurt his image in the least. If anything it will give the illusion that he is planning for the looming conflict with Saergaeth, devising unfathomable plans. He'll—"

Illusion! Caliph felt incensed.

Yrisl took a threatening step toward Zane and the spymaster fell silent. "If you want to listen to the worm of the underworld, your majesty, that's fine." Yrisl's eyes pinned the spymaster in place. "But his kind doesn't process information like the average citizen. You pay him to think like a criminal and frankly we don't really care what criminals think of you right now. We need a kingship that's open and accessible to the masses, especially with the recent publicity.

"Stonehold is used to a Council nowadays. You'll have to emulate that democracy and candor. They held open forums before you arrived! Debates, for Palan's sake! With journalists in the wings writing down everything they said! If you take that away now . . ."

Vhortghast bit his lip, looking at Caliph and Yrisl with equal anticipation.

"I appreciate your concerns. But I think I can manage," said Caliph. "All I needed was a warning."

Vhortghast bowed graciously.

"Of course. As you wish, your majesty."

Yrisl rolled his eyes.

Caliph adjusted his lapels as Vhortghast opened the door for him. The High King emerged.

The crowded smoky room quieted for an instant. All faces turned to him with a kind of bathetic wonderment.

Caliph could see a few furtive smiles amid the throng, knowing glances cast between apparent partners or friends. He marked them immediately. No doubt there were those with more sinister intentions, hidden behind flawless smiles, but those were a job for Vhortghast's men. The less subtle of the lot Caliph could handle on his own.

"Good morning, your majesty."

Various cheerful greetings rang in Caliph's ears. A young lieutenant general seemed to hold Caliph in particular awe.

Three old men with handlebar mustaches, sporting an array of medals on their chests welcomed the High King with suspicious warmth.

Caliph accidentally bumped into an ugly woman with black hair and a nose like a fin who stood wrapped in fashion. As he apologized, Caliph noticed the debonair but visibly spineless gentleman she clung to. Both of them fawned over Caliph as though he were their long lost son.

Caliph's stomach lurched slightly.

Somewhere below, the coupling had been released and the *Byun-Ghala* lifted off the roof of West Gate and powered east over Gunnymead Square.

Almost at once, the well-dressed herd pressed gently but persistently toward the observation deck and the mounted spyglasses, oohing and ah-hing and pointing at the tangled sepia piles of architecture below.

"How many men does it take to pilot a zeppelin?" asked Caliph, turning to the Blue General.

It sounded like the beginning of a joke.

"Depends on the size, your majesty. This one here is the smallest of three basic designs. We call this a lion. It's small, agile, but not as power-ful as sky sharks or the largest: leviathans."

"And crew size?"

"Sorry. Yes. A ship like this could run with anywhere from nine up to a dozen or so men. The larger ones range from eighteen to fifty."

"How does it run?"

"The engines? They're electric. Off monster chemiostatic cells toward the aft. They funnel air in different directions, over the fins and such. This one has a range of over a thousand miles but the big ones can go sev-eral times that. We'd like to get our hands on solvitriol or the coriolistic technology they have in the south. But so far no luck." Yrisl looked at Vhortghast who seemed not to be listening.

"We're lagging behind," said Vhortghast with thin cynicism. "Shouldn't we be out with the others? Mingling?"

"Absolutely," said Caliph with underscored conformity. Mentally he tacked *you shit* onto the end. Caliph walked out onto the wide balcony that overlooked the sprawl.

Light from the enormous chemiostatic cells could be seen faintly, re-flecting off the spines.

Behind and to the west, West Gate formed a swollen rupture in the city wall, spewing buildings out toward the farmlands and hills like the contents of an overripe blackhead. "That's West Fen," said Vhortghast.

Caliph allowed his annoyance to show. "Thank you, Zane. Isn't that one of Isca's two external boroughs?"

"My apologies," said the spymaster.

Eastward, the sky moved with a grisly ivory color. Between the zeppe-lin and the indistinct haze of the dockside boroughs rose and fell the un-dulant jumble of Maruchine, Grue Hill and Os Sacrum. To the south, the long squamous blocks of Candleshine knitted together like cells under a monolcular.

Caliph remembered Sena standing beside him in the musty lab, her perfume purling up into his face as he leaned forward, pretending to look at pig muscle on the slide.

"There's Cripple Gate!" shouted the woman in black, still clinging to her enslaved husband. She pointed at a pentagonal structure below and fore of the airship. "Where all the beggars go to panhandle. I do hope you plan to do something about them, King Howl. The *Herald* says they're the main cause of disease."

"I find that unlikely," said Caliph.

The woman's mouth opened in mute shock. "Well! The papers are written by scientists, your majesty. And they're poor." She said the word poor like she might have said the word evil.

Vhortghast's eyes flicked to Caliph, scrutinizing him suddenly for any reaction.

"Actually I believe the papers are written by journalists," said Caliph.

The spymaster smiled wanly and tossed back his brandy.

"Disease or no," said Travis Whittle, the burgomaster of Lampfire Hills, "most of our expenditures go to mopping up after them. That's just the way it is. We have eight thousand city police to pay!"

"And Ghoul Court should pay for seventy-five percent of them," said Clayton Redfield. He was the burgomaster of Blękton.

Everyone laughed except Caliph and Zane Vhortghast.

The unpleasant woman was clearly drunk. "I think we should sell them as slaves to the Pplarians or collect them for the physicians to experiment on, not the police I mean but the poor. If we get some useful medicine out of them, it will be absolutely ticky."

"Ticky?" whispered Caliph.

Vhortghast smiled. "Means clever or novel. That dress she's wearing is ticky."

"I see."

The *Byun-Ghala* was churning east and Caliph could see the terrifying black splendor of Hullmallow Cathedral erupting from the chimneys of Grue Hill. The enormous structure utterly dwarfed every other building in sight. Like a diffuse nightmare, the ornamented spires and flying buttresses gave the appearance of a grossly fat, daemonic spider with sky bent legs and a horrid horn-encrusted head.

Caliph endured another hour as they sailed over Lampfire Hills, where Travis Whittle pointed out all the peculiar wonders of his domain but snubbed questions about Winter Fen and Daoud's Bend, the boroughs abutting his south and east borders.

When the zeppelin turned north, Caliph noticed how the pilot avoided the sky above Ghoul Court and churned instead into Maruchine.

Up ahead, rising from what by now had become a monotonous clutter of peaked roofs, six enormous zeppelin towers fumbled like partially exhumed claws toward the stratosphere. An array of other airships could now be seen drifting over Thief Town and Murkbell. They carried huge industrial parts through the dirt-smeared skies.

Malgôr Hangar, however, was a strictly military installation. Built lower to the ground than Hullmallow Cathedral, it was less visible but still ten times the size. It housed most of Isca's zeppelin fleet at the very heart of the city on the border between Maruchine and Thief Town.

Caliph's zeppelin ride had come to an end.

The ship slowed and eased toward one of the six towers. They docked with a disconcerting lurch as somewhere far below ropes were quickly tightened.

Enormous gears and pistons like titanic tree trunks adjusted the dock's elevation, pulling the airship down.

"We'll be bidding Mrs. Din farewell here," whispered Zane.

"Is that her name?" remarked Caliph, watching the woman gather her dress as she prepared to disembark.

"Freja Din and Salmalin Mywr aren't natives," said Vhortghast lowly, "they have strong ties to Greymoor and the Pandragonian Empire—respectively. Both of them would probably like nothing better than to see Stonehold and especially Isca annexed by a southern power."

"They're harmless gadabouts," muttered Yrisl. "Don't let him spook you. They spend too much time at the opera to plan a coup."

Vhortghast curled his lip at the Blue General as though catching wind of something foul.

Caliph's head hurt from trying to see the entire city from the air. He stepped up to a spyglass and peered through its lens at a distant clock tower. Eight-sixteen. Nearly noon. His stomach grumbled.

"Right this way, your majesty."

Caliph didn't even look at who was talking to him. He turned and headed back through the stateroom, stale with the smell of cigar butts, spilled brandy and sweating bodies.

A bridge led to solid ground and a windswept battlement behind which the sky glowered with wisps of dirty rain already falling over Tin Crow and Nevergreen.

Freja Din guided her husband directly toward the shelter of the tower as though frightened by the wind.

"The opera house is just there," pointed Vhortghast, "across the canal in Murkbell. We'll meet them again this evening for the premier of *Er Krue Alteirz*. The High Seneschal will be coming."

"Do we have tickets?"

Vhortghast grinned like a ruined fence.

"The High King donates a sizable sum to the opera. You have the best seats in the house. We don't need tickets."

Caliph was beginning to understand that ordinary rules did not apply to him. He could do virtually whatever he wanted and all but the most outlandish would accommodate him without question.

"I'm hungry."

"You'll want to save your appetite for this evening," said Vhortghast.

Caliph scowled visibly. "Actually I'm starving." The eggs and strudel had been wonderful but hadn't stuck with him past an hour ago.

Vhortghast shrugged.

"We can eat, but you may lose whatever you put down."

"Why?"

"We have some business which I'm fairly certain you will find most memorable—more so than our zeppelin ride and more so than *Er Krue Alteirz*, unfortunately because it is somewhat . . . distasteful."

Caliph's hunger slacked only slightly at the spymaster's words.

CHAPTER
9

aliph never saw the zeppelin hangars of Malgôr firsthand—at least not that day. He heard about them instead from Vhortghast on his way down a crepuscular spiral staircase deep inside the northwest zeppelin tower. Humming overhead metholinate lights illuminated patches of rust and slippery stone.

"Watch your step," warned Vhortghast.

They passed through several well-manned checkpoints before the staircase dumped them into a small dingy tiled foyer with the number six painted in red, barely visible through layers of grime.

They stepped out into a half tube that tunneled north and south. Over one hundred fifty feet wide and seventy-five floor to ceiling, the black-green tunnel burrowed out of sight in both directions, obscured slightly by steam and questionable vapors that drifted aimlessly over the floor. The space was lit by sustained magnesium lights suspended far overhead.

Cones of intense white revealed patches of crud-caked block work, walls befouled in a way that suggested black frosting dripping down the sides of a moldy cake. Echoing reverberations and random mechanical clicking filled the quiet vault with ominous background noise.

Vhortghast pulled a breaker switch. It snapped down with a faint sizzle. From the south, a pinpoint of yellow light flared up in the curtain of blackness and a clattering racket chugged slowly toward them. The yellow light drew closer every moment, seeming to gain momentum until its awkward truth was revealed.

It passed through a harsh white pool thrown across the tracks, taking the shape of a strange mechanized engine with a small front cabin and an enormous swollen canister lying behind it. Like a queen termite it rolled into view. The light on its nose revealed it was number six in some unknown series of stations or contraptions or both. Below its bolted numeral, a heavy framework of ornate wheels, six on each side, connected it to the tunnel's rails.

Behind the front cabin, which was choked with levers and rods, eight additional wheels supported the long iron canister whose paint bubbled with corrosion. Small chemiostatic lights glowed limey and pale in the dark.

The vehicle seized suddenly, squeaking on the rails, disturbing the low waft of steam across the floor. A sour smell filled the air.

Vhortghast motioned Caliph in and threw several indistinguishable rods.

The grotesque contraption lurched, plunging forward into the dark.

"We're under Thief Town now," mentioned Vhortghast. "Headed toward the docks."

Caliph had said nothing during their entire time down the staircase. He didn't know what to say. Finally he tried, "I take it these aren't the normal subway tunnels?"

Vhortghast's reaction couldn't be seen in the dark.

"No. There are the sewers. Then there are the streetcar tunnels. And then there are these. No one knows about these except myself, the dissolved Council, the men who work in them and now you."

"What about the Blue General?"

"Clueless."

"Where in Emolus' name are we going?" The canister-bearing engine was hissing along at a clip faster than a galloping horse. The magnesium lights passed by overhead. Stripes of light and dark flashing. They made Caliph's head throb.

Soon they passed another alcove with the number five stenciled in red paint.

"Have you ever wondered where a city of two million people gets all its food?" Vhortghast's question brought an irrational hysteria to Caliph's mind. "I mean the Duchy of Stonehold isn't exactly huge yet we've got Vale Briar with close to three hundred thousand. Tentinil with another hundred thousand. Miskatoll is what? About four hundred thousand? And then Mortūrm weighs in at sixty-two thousand. In the shadow of Kjnardag that's a lot of people to feed off a landscape too cold to grow decent crops. And those are just the capital cities. Add the smaller towns and villages from Gadramere to Tairgreen and this is a damned densely populated country with some rocky fields and a deep dark sea that's been heavily fished for half a thousand years. If we didn't supplement what our hard-working cotters produce, and what our sleepless fishermen bring in, we'd have hardly enough to feed ourselves—maybe not enough at all—let alone any caviar or isinglass to export."

Caliph's mind tried to guess at whatever Vhortghast was teasing him with, searching for some logical alternative to the spymaster's compelling evidence for starvation.

He's going to tell me we're all eating rats and fungus, thought Caliph.

They passed another empty darkened station with the number two painted on dingy tiles. It flashed in the magnesium lights and disappeared unsettlingly, swallowed up by surroundings unimaginably contaminated and unclean. *Not the place to be discussing creative food sources.*

Vhortghast threw one of the engine levers and the grease dripping machine began to slow.

"All I'm saying is that we have to eat."

Up ahead a brightly lit station with a squad of armed Nanemen in full battle gear lit by pink and blue gas lamps waited unpropitiously. The engine drifted to a crawl and the Naneman soldiers saluted the High King as Caliph stepped onto the platform.

The guards parted as Vhortghast guided Caliph up several steps to an open bay and into a wide hallway lit indiscriminately along its black esophagus with candles and torches and gas lamps and forgotten lanterns.

They passed a wooden chair with a crusted and gruesome jacket hung from its back. Together with a gory hook laid at its feet, the chair composed a sort of mile marker on the interminable walk.

Several metal doors evolved from the gloom but Zane Vhortghast pressed on. Caliph felt only too happy to bypass them. They had small barred windows and offered only darkness beyond.

At the end of the hallway, Zane bid Caliph wait at a pair of double doors similar to the ones they had passed but devoid of peep slots.

He approached a wooden cabinet mounted on the wall under a flickering lamp. Upon opening it he dragged a pair of strange objects out into the light. One he handed to Caliph.

"You may want this," he said without explanation.

It was a leather mask with glass eyes and a strange canister that hung like a proboscis over the mouth and nose. It fit snugly by means of adjustable straps that netted over the back of the head.

Caliph took it limply with a growing sense of unease. Vhortghast turned the handle on the doors and a dull echoing thud sounded as some metal pinion retracted. The doors swung in.

Caliph stepped forward, hesitantly, eyes adjusting to the gloom. At first he could see nothing. Then the stench hit him in the face like a blacksmith's hammer.

The vile, overpowering fume of concentrated piss and sewage choked him as if a bottle of pure ammonia had splashed across his face. Caliph fumbled mindlessly for his gas mask, trying to pull it on before he convulsed.

Vhortghast helped him unsympathetically, tightening the straps that hung off the back of Caliph's head like drooping antennae.

For a moment Caliph concentrated on breathing. He closed his eyes and rested his palms on his knees, sucking odorless air into the close leather funnel around his mouth. After a moment he felt better and stood up.

The room seemed to sway before him. But it was not an illusion brought on by nausea. The room did in fact sway, or rather the contents of the room swayed.

Caliph could see men in headgear similar to his own moving between row upon row of large caliginous shapes. They carried rods and wore seemingly one-piece uniforms and high top boots with cleats. Occasionally they reached out and touched one of the hanging shapes with their rods and the shapes jolted mindlessly in response, swaying on creaking chains.

Caliph felt his gorge rise. A network of pipes along the ceiling knitted in perfect symmetry over the prodigious objects hung beneath them, elbows of black ribbed metal turning down at every cross section, thrusting into the top of huge breathing bulbs of meat.

Like a cattle yard, where butchered animals were hung on hooks to drain. Only these great carcasses were alive and three times the size of a butchered cow. Three heavy chains hooked onto iron rings that pierced their upper portion and suspended each living meat several feet above the floor. They were vaguely the shape of a human heart and the iron rings that suspended them pulled the tissue into painful-looking triangles, like the masochists in Ghoul Court who pierced their nipples and stretched their skin until it bled.

The meat had no head or arms or legs. It had no skin but a translucent bluish white membrane that covered the dark maroon muscle tissue and bulging blue veins underneath. Lumpy patches of yellow adipose clustered in grooves and seams where the muscles joined in useless perfection.

Cable-thick tubing ran from above, bundled together and coupled into various implanted sockets for reasons obviously associated with sustaining dubious life.

Occasionally, muscles twitched or a sudden shudder went through the enormous cohesion of mindless flesh and sent the body swinging in the slow tight spiral allowed by the chains.

At the bottom of the meat, near the more pointed but snubbed posterior, something like an anus spewed filth with peristaltic violence into a square depression in the floor. Urine dribbled or sprayed from some hidden hole proximal to the defecating sphincter, helping to wash soupy piles of shit and blood toward runnels in the floor.

Caliph stood in stupefied horror, trying to digest the scene before him. Thousands of living meats hung in orderly rows throughout the darkened room. Caliph tried to speak through his mask but it was no use.

Vhortghast beckoned him through a side door and then through a secondary door into an observation hall with large windows that looked out on the mindless herd. Caliph removed his mask. The air was tolerable and Vhortghast did the same.

"How do they breathe?" asked Caliph. It was the first of many horrified questions that he raised.

"The tubing supplies oxygen directly into the lungs and likewise removes spent air with every exhalation by means of one-way valves. I'm not sure what the other small cables do myself but I'm sure it's important. The main pipes that run down into their throats carry a kind of nutrient sludge made of ground-up silage and grass and rainwater or whatever else it is in Emolus' name that they put in it. I think some of the other cables help keep the meat healthy, taking the place of exercise. But those boys with the chemiostatic rods help too. They shock the meat all day long, stimulating whatever it is they stimulate."

"We eat that?"

"Every day. You pay a pretty gryph for real beef these days. But not even the butchers know the difference. Only the major distribution points get whole carcasses. They cut it up from there and send it to the markets and meat stores. As the High King you get a choice very few people get: meat or beef."

"Does it . . ." Caliph struggled, "Does it feel?"

"Seems to. But it doesn't think as far as we know. All it's got is a spinal column that runs involuntary muscles and the like. No brain. Think of it as one big chicken breast. No gizzard. No neck. No wings."

"I don't like it."

Vhortghast shrugged with apathy Caliph was growing accustomed to. "Like I said . . . we have to eat. The alternative is grim. The upside is that when Freja Din orders a rare steak before the opera tonight only you and I know what she's really getting."

Caliph found little humor in the truth. "So how long has this been going on? Does all this . . . meat . . . just feed Isca?"

"Gods no. This is a huge operation. Why do you think the secret rail goes straight to Malgôr Hangar? We pack whole carcasses in refrigerated canisters and fly them to distribution points from Vale Briar to Mortürrm. This has been happening for nearly twenty years now. Odds are you ate some meat when you were living in Candleshine."

Caliph nodded.

"I suppose if it killed you it would defeat the purpose."

"Exactly. It's actually pretty tasty. Lean, tender . . . I guess the down-side is that Mrs. Din won't even get a stomachache."

Caliph had an immediate gut instinct to terminate the whole clandes-tine industry. But obviously terminating the industry would mean cata-strophic famine—if Vhortghast was telling the truth, which Caliph felt just as strongly, though unfoundedly, that he was.

"So why show all of this to me?"

"Because you'll see the paperwork, even though it will be itemized as something else and it takes a lot of money to run this place. Now that you know what it is, you won't throw a fit when the quarterly losses are de-ducted from the treasury."

"We lose money on this?" Caliph couldn't believe the growing bad news.

Vhortghast nodded. "Not as much as we would raising cattle in the mountains. But look at the technology! That's not a low-maintenance op-eration on the other side of this glass."

"How . . . do they—er, multiply?"

Vhortghast shook his head and made the southern hand sign for no all at the same time.

"That my friend, you do not want to know."

It had been a day filled with surprises, just as Gadriel promised.

After learning the disconcerting source of Stonehold's protein Caliph had finally gone to dinner. Then had come the dark gaudy maelstrom of the Murkbell Opera House featuring a Pplarian love story about a four-armed sorcerer trying to seduce a young girl into his mansion on the moor.

Following the show, Vhortghast rode silently in the carriage while Caliph stared out at the moving panorama of cubist patterns: shadows and pipes and sickly orange landings where lovers groped or children sat play-ing with dead things they had tortured during the day.

A man with a lantern pushed his wheeled umbrella cart over the slick cobbles.

Finally, they reached King's Road and entered the Hold close to mid-night. The drawbridge was still down, torches guttering brightly, waiting for the High King's return.

As soon as the carriage rattled over, the huge wooden bridge groaned up behind them, securing the castle from anything not brave enough to enter the cold watchful waters of the moat. Amid the silt and spongy bones of former criminals, Vortghast assured him that multieyed creatures sulked and waited.

When the carriage finally stopped, Vhortghast stepped out as Ngyumuh held the door. The Pandragonian watched closely as Caliph left the carriage.

"I'll see you early tomorrow morning," said Vhortghast. We'll be meeting the Blue General for tea in Ironside before touring the armada."

Caliph restrained a sigh. He waved halfheartedly as the spymaster departed. When he arrived in his room, he unbuckled the sword he had been given and let it clatter—unexamined—to the floor. He didn't even undress but opened the west-facing windows that looked out on the hills and fields, letting in the slightly rural sounds of the distant moors.

A fresh wind set his shirt rippling across his back. It made him smile weakly before he turned and fell face-first into bed, knowing this was only the beginning of a very long week.

CHAPTER
10

*T*he wound goes bad. Sena's breathing quickens; her heart is racing. Chills and fever come in tides. Her mind shuts down to protect her from the pain.

She remembers night sweats and the constant taste of vomit. They say the bizarre wound is putting Megan to the test.

The Shrạdnæ Mother comes and goes. Sena hears fragments through the snow of quasiconsciousness. "Septic shock." "We have to move her." "She'll die in transit." "Get the smell-feast . . ."

Sena wants to scream at them to stop. Let me go! Let me die! But Megan cannot conceive defeat. She rips the stitches out, opens up the wound, intolerant of its insubordination. She fills the cavity with numbers and commands the flesh to mend.

Sena passes from cognition back into the void.

TOWARD the end of Pạsh, Sena woke slowly.

Silver hoses hung like jewelry in the air. Black silk enrobed the room. It draped her, fell in valances all around. A ray of diamond-colored light struck her midriff, splashing wetly on the creature making love to her naked waist.

The smell-feast's corpulent red shape had no head. It looked like a scarlet oyster without a shell except for the tendril-like pseudopodia that clutched her abdomen in a hungry embrace. Its peristalsis was slow and hideously erotic.

The silver hoses were for it, pumping in a warm cocktail of drugs and juice. Mindlessly, it fed on the perpetual flow and exosmotically released its waste slime into her blood. Her circulation coursed through the creature's digestive tract, adding to its color. It was using her heart to pressurize its intestines, force the piped-in nutrients into receptacles in its gut.

If the hoses were unplugged the slow horror would reverse several of its pumps. It would shift from regulation to suction and turn its insatiable hunger back on her. But the Sisterhood's iatromathematiques were skilled. The creature's biorhythm was perfectly controlled. Sena found herself both host and symbiote in the coupling of its stringy arms.

The witches watching her with holomorphic eyes were silent as the smell-feast devoured everything diseased, even the bacteria in her blood. Slowly, over days, the creature filled her with medication it deemed waste, hydrating her with excess water from its food.

Eventually, Megan and one of her iatromathematiques entered the room.

"Shh. Be still."

With a needle, they introduced a virulent toxin into Sena's veins. It was poison only for the smell-feast. The creature's mucus reacted immediately, suturing her veins with a kind of rubber patch, a sealed valve that allowed it to withdraw safely from the pounding pressure of her heart.

No more pain. She must have fallen asleep again.

Megan stood over her with a bundle of scrolls under one arm: glowing, Sena realized, not with happiness but with the euphoria of victory.

"It's time you had something to do. Time you started preparing."

"Where am I?"

But Sena recognized the carvings in the walls; the starry fresco smeared eight hundred years ago across the ceiling dome. With the dreamy nocturne playing on the gramophone Sena could be certain they were in parliament.

She sat up, gathering the black silk bedclothes around her. Her head was still foggy and she squinted in the patchy sunlight. "Can I have some water?" Her mouth was dry and she wanted a bath.

"I've brought some things for you to study."

"I'm barely awake."

Megan flicked her wrist at a young girl in a white smock. "Give her some coffee."

"Coffee? I want water and a toothbrush."

Megan scowled. "We know what attacked you in the Highlands of Tue, Sienæ. We just don't understand why. I warned you about the Porch of Sọth—"

"The Porch saved my life. I had a binding . . ."

"A binding!" Megan nearly dropped the coffee that the child had moments ago put into her hand. "Sienæ, you don't stitch bindings to the Porch of Sọth. You can't—"

"It saved my life, Mother!"

"*I* . . . saved your life!" Megan fired. "Ridiculous girl. You're going to get yourself killed with holomorphy like that." She took a brisk sip of her coffee. "The Willin Droul found you, which means you're a pathetic field agent. But you should be safe in Isca Castle."

"I'll leave immediately."

Megan ignored her bitter tone. "We aren't ready yet. You must leave when the timing is right."

Sena's face slumped into her hands. She stared between her fingers as leafy shadows from outside fell over the pair of blond girls stationed nearby. Initiates, about twelve years old, they stared blankly at each other while the breeze levitated their hair.

Megan circled around behind and started helping her with her bra, scrutinizing the lacy undergarment. "That's a bit of black evil, isn't it? Where did you get it?"

"Ghalla Gala, in Sandren. What are your plans? What are we doing in Stonehold?"

Megan hesitated. Sena saw the shadow of her arm rise up and quickly stretch across the floor. The young girls in the room left immediately. They pulled the door shut behind them. It made a dull bang followed by a vast hollow echo.

Megan continued. "We have several agendas. The Willin Droul has resurfaced. Evidenced by your attack. Half-sisters in Isca say an old school is reforming in the undercity. We do not know why. Hopefully you can help us discover this once you are there."

"Who do you have in Isca?"

"Miriam."

Sena sniffed disdainfully. "You aren't sending me to Stonehold just to play cloak and dagger with some smelly little clerics."

"No. But that would be enough," said Megan. "Your inexperience combined with this mystagogic society out of Iycestoke . . . well, they're far more than smelly little clerics. They have preternarcomancers that sleep beyond sleep in warm coastal waters and perceive farther than—"

"If they're so good at predicting the future," Sena interrupted, "how did they get themselves butchered seventy years ago in their own temple? By a general they employed?"

Megan scowled. "We're happy to have some historical proof that they do make mistakes. But the Willin Droul go back. Thousands of years. Discounting them is an old mistake."

"Thousands?" Sena scowled.

Megan began to pace in the spacious domed room, heels clicking loudly. "Yes, well. It wasn't that long ago that the king of Sandren bore the Hilid Mark."

Sena knew what that meant: the mark that shadowed the navel, three dark tendrils reaching upward.

"We wonder if they might be trying to infiltrate the Sisterhood."

"Why would you think that?" Sena thought back to the rag-thing at her cottage and her flesh tingled with cold.

Megan stopped pacing. She faced Sena directly and her eyes burnt like tiny gray stars. She spoke barely above a whisper. "Some of our Sisters have died or disappeared. Wives of powerful men have been lost in the woods, run away with charming highwaymen or, according to the papers, fallen down stairs and snapped their necks."

Her obvious skepticism added a new dimension to the discussion.

Sena raised her eyebrows. Considering the laws of the coven and the inordinate amount of physical dexterity it took to become a full-fledged Sister, such stories (while convincing to the general public) were ludicrous to a member of the Sisterhood.

They must be fearless, thought Sena. The more she thought about it, the more likely it seemed that someone could be laughing.

Through the antiseptic words of a journalist some entity might certainly be able to flaunt that it, or they, had attacked the Sisterhood in their most ensconced locations, beaten them at their own game. By publishing absurd accounts of accidents and capricious infidelity, things a highly trained Sister would easily and doggedly avoid, the enemy could broadcast in words clear only to the Sisterhood: we know where you are. We know how to find you.

Sena imagined the results. It would be like turning off lamps in a vast house. When the undercover wife of a regional lord vanished the very eyes of the Sisterhood would be plucked out of that household. The holdings of the Sisterhood would become darkened and obscure.

Maybe her attack in the highlands was related. Maybe she had escaped what others in the Sisterhood had not. Still, Sena remained skeptical.

"Why are they coming after us?"

Megan pursed her lips. Again she hesitated.

"There is an old book. Lost. Possibly in a shop or private collection by now. It was an item of conflict decades ago between the Sisterhood and the Cabal. It slipped through both our hands and wound up in Stonehold until its owner died. No one knows where it is now."

"So the Cabal . . . the Willin Droul . . . think we have it?" Sena lied well.

"I don't think so."

"Where do you think the book is?" asked Sena.

"Perhaps Stonehold. It might explain why the Willin Droul have resurfaced there."

"So you're sending me to Stonehold to find a book?"

"Things have changed during your illness. As I said, we have several agendas."

Sena felt her stomach pitch, wondering about Caliph.

"A few days ago," Megan continued, "a zeppelin was lost in the Valley of Nifol. Shot down. Certain powers in the south had valuables, priceless valuables on board. Which they believe are being ferried into the Duchy of Stonehold."

"So you've made a deal with them? What does the Sisterhood get out of it?"

Megan did not smile her cunning smile as Sena expected. Instead, Megan's voice cracked, almost quavered. What she said still sounded so pitiless and cruel that Sena winced at the words. "Not yet, Sienæ. Until you've realized the task before you, I would be giving everything away in the event of your torture."

Sena reeled for a moment but recovered quickly. She knew it would be useless to persist so she went down a different road. "At the very least I have to know who I'm helping and what I'm helping them achieve."

This time Megan did smile, albeit unkindly. "For now, all you need know is that we are in league with Pandragor."

SENA spent five days trying to get back in shape. After morning exercise, she sifted through the newest piles of holomorphic research the Sisterhood had compiled in the vast underpitched barrel vaults of parliament's basement.

It was frightening stuff.

Holojoules, the raw malleable energy the holomorph drew from blood and dropped into change equations, represented a quantifiable tally of individual annihilations. At a cellular level the number of sacrifices the holomorph needed was astonishing.

Holojoules were naturally limited to the amount of blood in the holomorph's body. There was an old saying, "You can cast what you can cut," and it always brought to Sena's mind gruesome pictures of the greatest holomorphic achievements realized only through suicide.

Yet, according to the notes in the basement, there was another way, an older way. And the Sisterhood had found it. It was spelled out in meticulous ledgers that Sena read, reminding her of stories she had found at Desdae pertaining to hemofurtum and the dead empires that had practiced it. She imagined white curtains stirred by salt winds, sheltering hundreds of spell slaves that had once slit their snowy skins, collecting holomorphic energy into slender silver ewers.

Vast colligations, as they were called: giant collections of silver vials filled with the fluid to argue reality.

After all, holomorphy was a kind of legalese that focused reason through the lens of the mathematician. Holomorphs were reality lawyers whose logic convinced the world to bend.

The Sisterhood's research covered it all. Sena found slides spotted with various samples of erythrocytes and platelets in stiff paper boxes. She examined them, remembering plant cells under the monocular at Desdae, moving the coarse and substage adjustments. Focusing. Switching through the jumble of parachromatic objectives.

These lacquered brass drawtubes in parliament's basement were equally powerful and gorgeous, sliding on clock oil under the smooth subtlety of half a dozen finger controls.

At Desdae, she had fumbled in amazement at the squirming glowing life. With the soupspoon mirror condensing light through the slide, thylakoids, vacuoles and chloroplasts had lit up in lucent green, magenta and aqueous blue dyes. She had marveled at each level of magnification, then pricked her finger over a fresh slide and watched herself die.

But hemofurtum made self-mutilation obsolete. The nonphysical numbers in the ledger subtracted against themselves to produce remainders greater than zero. They were capable of snatching iron-rich proteins at the moment of flux. Vampirism.

Hemofurtum's central equations revolved around a mathematical loop. It was designed to siphon blood from a source outside the holomorph's own body . . . hold the energy, use some to take again. Its logic was frightening, a kind of gruesome sipping answer to the elusive perpetual motion machine.

Once the reaction began it was up to the holomorph to turn it off. The only limit to the equation was linked to how many pints were available in the vicinity. If the holomorph was willing to siphon or even kill an unlimited amount of people, then the equation's apogee would be roughly synonymous with population.

Sena left the basement feeling awed and sick.

AT noon on the twenty-third, Sena convinced Megan to let her retrieve some things from her cottage in the Highlands. She promised to return in time for her mission to Stonehold.

Sena took a chemiostatic cab toward Jṵyn Hêl[8] where her mother had been burned seventeen years ago. No one would question her going in this

---

[8] I.: The Place of Burning.

direction because no one would dare broach the subject of her mother's death. Juyn Hêl lay close to the Valley of Eloth, close to Tuauch and the hidden Tombs of Aldrŭrn. More importantly, Newlym was on the way. In Newlym, she bought a horse and boarded the only northbound train.

The final stop was Menin's Pass.

The station was actually closer to Ell's Lake, a cluster of brick warehouses and fat, decayed mooring towers for airships out of the Duchy.

Sena left the crumbling platform with her horse and melted through the fog. The Highway of Kafree wasn't part of Mirayhr's official infrastructure. Ruined and bereft, it had been built by one of the north's fallen empires. After sixty miles it forked. The east arm ran slightly north to Menin's Pass. The west drooped south toward Esma.

Despite thick fringes of moss and weed, the stone blocks still formed a remarkably serviceable road. And yet, even with the horse, she guessed it would take her two days to reach the place she had hidden the *Cisrym Ta*.

Sena glanced over her shoulder. Just to be safe, she pulled her sickle knife across her horse's croup. The creature's orchid colored skin bled black, six tails expressing anguish in a squirming mass.

"Shh—"

She spoke the Unknown Tongue and the tails drooped. The beast's withers relaxed.

It didn't hurt to cover her trail.

Shradnæ Witches tracked by numbers, a kind of dead reckoning based on humidity. If Megan was having her followed, Sena's pursuers would use coordinates based on the water memories of her own sweat inscribed molecularly into thin air.

She didn't bother peering for a hidden stalker in the fog. Shradnæ operatives wouldn't be anywhere she looked. The tiny numbers they cut into their corneas neatly tabled the pre-echoes of what they called *blind line of sight*.

Sena was in the Seventh House, merited or not, but had decided against making the cuts. Until now, she'd never had a use for better invisibility than what she could manage as a common thief.

Unfortunately, if Megan had put a tail on her, that wouldn't be enough. She rolled the horse blood into a hemofurtive equation, testing the new concept she'd learned in parliament's basement, and laid a jumbled trail of numbers in her wake. In answer to water memory, she encrypted air.

On her second day in the Valley of Eloth she left her horse to fend, marching downhill from the road until she found a set of abandoned stone huts near a lake. Ragged green thickets grew in profusion along the shore. She hugged the waterline and made good progress. Her side still pained her and she rested often but a gnawing anxiety filled her stomach. Eloth belonged to long-toothed predacious things.

Sarchal hounds, with jaws capable of killing a horse, hunted the wilds. And there were other horrors. Enormous black otter-things with tiny malevolent eyes and twitching ears, long dark muzzles bristling with whiskers and gharial teeth. Unknown numbers of them lay in wait below these northern lakes.

Sena kept her eyes open and moved quickly. The undergrowth gave her no choice but to skirt the shore. Eventually the pebbled beach gave way to a shadowed drop-off overhung with flowering thickets. She could see several large fish, backs like dull battered tin, gliding in the murk below.

She scrambled up a soft embankment and found an animal track that led her back to the water through a garden of cattails that sprang from semisolid ground.

She tread carefully on the shifting sod of what seemed to be floating dirt and vegetation. The rich close stench of metholinate burbled up through black, snot-thick water. She couldn't see four inches down.

After half an hour, breathing through her mouth, the cattails thinned and the track emerged but ended in disappointment.

Sena looked with disgust at a stinking morass of deep feculent mud and squalid pools. Ruby-bellied reed flies darted through the vapor. The mire looked impossible to cross and her trail had given out far from shore.

Her eyes cast about for a way of crossing the muck and landed on a series of large flat rocks. They were east of her, farther out, vulnerable to one of the otter-things but she knew she could leap the distance between them without much strain and decided to risk it.

The hungry flies swarmed, bellies like gemstones. She leapt to the first then the second and in such fashion crossed the inlet.

The insects pursued her until she reached the top of a slide of boulders at the lake's north end. There, the storm front struck relentlessly and a cold freshet of wind swept the flies back down to their reeking hollows by the lake.

Sena worked her way above the skree.

She moved gracefully. She was trained for this.

After three thousand vertical feet and five miles, the spires and dome of Esma rose slowly into view. It was an ancient thing. Ugly and old like a fractured skull.

She checked her watch as the first small drops of rain began to fall.

From here she could see most of the valley in ominous panorama. All around her, the mountains rose in tortured gray piles, blasted back from the valley's pit as if by a synchronized cacophony of screams.

Sena climbed into a flat barren clearing before the desolate temple. Perspiration licked tight curls along her neck.

The whole of Esma had been raised in ciryte, a white rock that held light like velvet. But the closer she got the grayer it looked. Ruinous after eighteen thousand years of storms, if it had not been for the ciryte's extraordinary granite-surpassing durability, the whole edifice would have dissolved like a sugar lump. As it was, great chunks had given way. Unseen blocks and entire substructures had slid cataclysmically down with the skree into the lake.

As if someone had plunged broken femurs into the ground, jagged fragile towers, sundered and hollow, stretched with ghastly luxuriance toward the sky. The ruptured dome, graven and blackened by its own encrusted ornateness, pushed fatly at the towers that buttressed its enormous weight. Almost against gravity it seemed to hold together, bulging and loose, gawping and precarious to enter.

Sena watched swallows float in and out of Esma's orifices. They cast fluid shadows over friezes in the walls.

Inside the immense foyer, leaves and twigs shuffled in the gloom. She entered one of the gargantuan rooms that opened off to either side. In the vaulted space, walnuts rotted in the shadows and the floor had been decorated with inlays.

A vague uneasiness smothered everything. Though the designs were striking, hundreds of long sharp-edged lids overshadowed their beauty. Sunk in the foundations, designed as part of Esma's vast floor plan, over two hundred crypts rested underfoot. Their lids rose, low, oblique and sharp across the spacious floor.

Sena had walked lines from her cottage to this very spot. There were old stories written in the walls of Esma, vague frightening prophecies. But Sena could not afford to be superstitious. She had been desperate. And in desperation she had hidden the *Cisrym Ta* before stumbling down to find her sisters by the lake. Myhr through Pash, when the weather was typically mild, the Sisterhood could be found in Eloth, delving into the past, unearthing things from the ruins near Ryhd Ŭl.[9] Even so, with the rash of thunderstorms, she had almost missed them.

It was just as well that Caliph hadn't followed her here. He would have found the ruins empty.

She bent over one of the elegant lids that decorated the floor and pushed. It ground away to reveal a dark trough. The bones inside had dried and long since lost their odor.

[9] O.S.: Water of Apparitions.

She found her pack just where she had left it, crouched in a corner by the yellow feet. She pulled it out, loosening the buckles.

The crimson book slid smoothly into her palms, leather soft and cool against her fingertips.

"Megan's looking for you," she whispered to it.

Almost reassuringly, the faint howl that only she could hear floated up onto the moldy draft. Outside, the sky flickered. Thunder rolled like a boulder over the Javneh Mountains and sweet-smelling water began to trickle from cracks a hundred feet overhead.

Sena didn't give a damn about Megan and her errands. All she wanted was to open the book. And Caliph remained her best chance of that. *Now Megan actually* wants *me stargazing over his shoulder! And I was worried about fårǫn[10] at Desdae!*

Sena thought about seeing the pages of the *Cisrym Ta*, covered with Inti'Drou glyphs. Secrets larger than the world, like an infinite opalescent mobile hung above her crib, cutting across and out: away from the planet. Past the sun. Past the blackness.

Sena let herself wallow in anticipation for a moment. Then she stood up and left Esma, walking lines back to the Highlands of Tue.

[10] W.: The Betrayal.

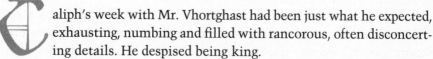

aliph's week with Mr. Vhortghast had been just what he expected, exhausting, numbing and filled with rancorous, often disconcerting details. He despised being king.

He had seen warehouses filled with qaam-dihet seized from drug lords in Thief Town and Maruchine. Stockpiles of munitions. Gas mines and vitriol bombs laid in the bellies of zeppelins. He had returned to Malgôr Hangar for a full tour; seen the armada of brigs and first rates and the only three dreadnoughts in the Duchy of Stonehold, powered by iron sails and mountains of coal and acid.

He had talked with every burgomaster willing to meet, found how each borough squared (as nearly as he could) from the sources at his disposal. He had traveled to every district with the notable exception of Ghoul Court, which (the more he thought about it) seemed less like a borough and more like an independent state.

Caliph had examined tax reports and census reports and toxicity levels from the city well water. He had been shown Bloodsump Lane in all its anathematic squalor under broad daylight without the merciful cover of dark. He had made an appearance at Hullmallow Cathedral for its customary rededication (which happened at the beginning of every High King's reign) to the multitude of gods worshiped in the seething city and shortly thereafter visited Cripple Gate where he had donated a large sum to the Church of the Mourning Beggar that brooked homeless people from Three Cats and Candleshine.

It had been ten days of nonstop secular, religious and image-enhancing activity. And there was only one thing Caliph knew for sure.

The city stank.

Gadriel assured him that it would not last long. Only at the height of summer did the streets cider. That's what Gadriel called it.

"The streets cider," he said, "when the weather turns warm."

Caliph couldn't have picked a milder assessment if he had spent all day thinking. Gadriel's euphemism was actually a total mollification of reality.

What really happened was that piles of garbage stacked between slum buildings generated spontaneous life as hot weather and their own weight started to liquefy discarded foods and mattresses and cans of varnish and bags of powdered paint.

Great heaps wedged in alleys began to ooze and seep. First- and second-story tenants could do nothing but draw their moth-eaten drapes and ignore the squirming refuse that threatened to break through their windowpanes.

The piles could only grow if people on the top floors tossed garbage out their casements or off the roof—which they frequently did. Great armies of flies stirred in the labyrinth of trash, a dual testament to people's inordinate laziness and the fact that the wasteyard in Brindle Fenn was not large enough, even at nearly a hundred acres in size.

To say that the streets cidered was nearly as litotic as saying that sticking one's head into the anus of a cow was not a very tempting thing to do. But what troubled Caliph most was that Gadriel's description seemed less outlandish when it was said within the confines of the castle.

Not all of Isca City was ripe with festering piles of detritus and tatters and offal and sludge. There were enchanting canals in Murkbell, bewitching beauty in the endless arches of Candleshine and Lampfire Hills. Blekton fairly suffocated under the ambrosial pollen of variegated blossoms. There were hundreds of clean streets swept up by men with long-handled dustpans every night, places where (rain or shine) the bricks gleamed with polish. For the rich and fortunate and even for a great quantity of middle-classed citizens, saying that Isca cidered in the summer did not seem a cruel understatement of the truth.

But Caliph had seen the cesspools. They weighed on him as if their great piles of garbage had been stacked in his own bedroom.

While he pondered the slums, Caliph examined the sword given him on the zeppelin deck of West Gate.

It was a marvelous piece. Forged out of tunsia, the blade would actually float on water. It was impervious to the rust and corrosion of weather, which Mr. Vhortghast had joked was good fortune considering what Caliph's previous blade had endured.

Light and quick and sharpened by holomorphic stones to an edge only tunsia could hold, the sword was broad and short and two-handed with a long handle filled by apple-green chemiostatic fluid. It represented the highest achievement in hand-to-hand combat possible north of the Great Cloud Rift.

The cell was good for two or three wallops before it had to be changed out. A beryllium circuit traveling down the center of the blade ended at a silvery point where even a glancing thrust enabled the charged sword to deliver the coulombs capable of deep tissue burns and the vaporization of flesh. A dark whimsical thing, Caliph's chemiostatic sword could produce surreal open or comminuted bone fractures. Paralysis. Thrombosis. Death.

He had never flicked the switch on the pommel that charged the circuit from the cell. There was a safety ring that had to be unscrewed, loosening tension before the switch could move.

Determined not to grow soft and lethargic, Caliph practiced forty minutes a day. The tunsia edge removed the oak necks of practice dummies like a machete slicing through bamboo.

On the last day of Pash, as the city cidered and Caliph pondered the problem of the slums, he received word while taking tea in the high tower that he had visitors. Two young men by the names of David Thacker and Sigmund Dulgensen.

Caliph set his cup down so hard he chipped the saucer. He leapt up and sped down the many staircases to the grand hall. His elation and joy over hearing the familiar names was indisguisable.

As he approached the grand hall he slowed, forced himself to walk instead of run. When he reached the archway he paused. He peered into the vast room where a curtain of light fell from the windows, glittering with millions of dust motes.

There they were, two of the Naked Eight standing in conversant poses near the darkened fireplace. Two of the boys who had shared his misery in the pillory and his triumph when Roric Feldman had gone home in shame.

Caliph flew into the room and fairly danced around them, overjoyed by their visit. He bid them sit before the unlit hearth while they recounted certain professors and Chancellor Eaton and his cane.

Sigmund Dulgensen was a brilliant engineer. He had studied almost nothing else at school and he could tell any listener all the differences between stress and wear and flow meters and load cells and solenoids and calibration.

His hands never came clean.

The tiny grooves around his nails and the whorls of his fingerprints were impregnated with burnt oil, engine grease and other grime. He was a meaty man. Strong. And often sat with a strange humorless smile on his face caused by the emotionless contortion required to chew at the hair under his lower lip.

David Thacker was Sigmund's antithesis even though they shared the same build. He was nearly as large but hopelessly docile. He had taken calligraphy and painting and all kinds of other classes that his friends called useless crap. Caliph wasn't sure what degree David had actually graduated with.

The three talked about virtually everything they had done since graduation although Caliph shyly omitted many details of his journey to the Highlands of Tue.

Even when David asked him point blank if he had gone to see Sena after graduation, Caliph denied it, saying instead that he had almost forgotten about her—that with everything going on in Isca and Stonehold he had more important things to think about.

After an hour of catching up, Sigmund leaned back in his chair and put both hands behind his head, chewing at his beard.

"I can't believe I'm in Isca Castle. How about a tour?"

Caliph chuckled, half embarrassed.

"Well," he scratched his head, "we could do that but we might get lost. I've spent more time out of the castle than in." He suddenly sensed that there was business at hand. "What really brought you all this way . . . through the Fort Line?"

"Jobs," said Sigmund. "I'll be honest, I headed down south a bit and didn't like what I saw. Turned right around and came back up here. Dave and I traveled together."

He pulled a pillow that had been wedged between his robust body and the arm of the chair and threw it at David Thacker. David caught it and grinned.

"Yeah that's right."

"Jobs?" Caliph smiled wanly. "I bet I could find plenty for you to do up here. What kinds of jobs?"

"Writing," said David. "I want to sit around all day and write and get paid for it."

"I want to go into the military," said Sigmund. "Not swords and mines and hacking people up, mind you. I want to design war engines."

Caliph stood up and paced around in a tiny circle.

"I'm pretty sure I can get you both in somewhere. I don't even really know what jobs are out there, but I guess I'm the High King and if there's not a writing job around I'll make one up for you. You can be my scribe or write plays for all I care. I saw the treasury the other day and I think there's enough there to support a couple more salaries."

Sigmund shook his head.

"The Iscan Treasury. That's some serious buying power. What's it look like, Caph?"

"Kind of brown actually," said Caliph, "on account of all the boxes.

But inside the boxes there's a lot of gold. Stacks and stacks of trade bars. There are collections of jewelry and gems. I don't know. I guess it's pretty standard." He threw his hand in the air.

"You arrogant prick!" said David.

Caliph laughed.

"I dunno, sounds ticky," said Sigmund. "I'd be a damned arrogant prick too if I was High King. Get me a chambermaid in a short frilly skirt."

"One-track mind." David jerked a thumb at Sigmund and rolled his eyes.

Caliph shrugged.

"So what else is new?"

Sigmund lowered his voice. "Well, that's another thing I've been wanting to talk to you about. I . . . er, we . . . got our hands on some blueprints when we was in the south."

He gnawed at his beard and looked over both shoulders, making sure they were alone.

"Solvitriol blueprints, Caph. Hard shit. Coriolistic stuff too. Though I'm not sure if I have enough information to make anything coriolistic-wise . . . but solvitriol tech—"

He whistled.

"I've got some theories—some ideas after looking at 'em. Stuff that's never been tried before. I want to tell you about it sometime. Maybe over breakfast or something."

Caliph was too stunned to speak. Solvitriol technology was the unattainable jewel behind Iycestoke's might. Like most power sources it supposedly had its foundations in holomorphy, but everything else about it remained a mystery.

"You've got blueprints?" Caliph whispered. "Here? With you?"

Sigmund licked his lips and repeated the southern hand sign for yes many times in rapid succession.

"It's crazy shit too, Caph. You're not going to believe it—I mean you're not going to believe what it runs on—how it works."

"But how?" stammered Caliph. "How did you get them? You said you went to Pandragor. Pandragor doesn't even have solvitriol tech."

"Not yet. But they were going to get it. We came across this crashed zeppelin—you should have seen it—it must have been shot down by an army of bandits—some diplomatic airship strewn across the eastern ribs of Nifol. All the cash boxes broken open and emptied except for letters and deeds . . . and blueprints. I realized the idiots had overlooked the most important stuff in the lot.

David piped up.

"Iycestoke was shipping their secrets to Pandragor. That's what me and Sig figure. Maybe one of the Three Kings is trying to stab the other ones in the back or needs money."

Caliph tugged his lip.

"And that's not bad reasoning. Probably as good as Vhortghast could manage."

"Who's Vhortghast?" both men asked in unison.

"Never mind. The point is you don't have to be connected to figure things out. I'll bet Pandragor is combing the hills for those blueprints. Yet they can't say a thing."

"Yes!" Sigmund jumped up and gave a shout of unrepressed elation. Several maids and sentries appeared in various doorways, looking worried. "I knew it! I knew you were the right one to bring them to! Set me up, Caph. Give me a workshop, tools, things that need juice to run. I can bring Isca into the modern fucking age."

The sentries and maids melted away at a sign from the High King.

"Do you have the plans with you?" Caliph sounded mildly skeptical.

Sigmund's excitement choked on the question. Caliph could see momentary apprehension flicker behind his friend's eyes.

"Um . . . no. I, ah . . . I left 'em at the hotel."

Caliph looked bemused and clamped Sigmund reassuringly on the shoulder.

"What are you worried about? You think I'm going to cheat you out of something you rightfully stole?"

Sigmund's hesitancy melted into denial.

"I never said that. Of course you're not. Sheesh. We're friends. Why don't I bring them by tomorrow?"

"Over breakfast?" asked Caliph. "They make pretty good breakfast here."

"Sure!" Sigmund beamed at the proposition of food.

David, grown slightly bored, had begun poking around the room, examining the heads of halgrin and gruelocks, otter-things, a sledge newt, mystikoos and a soot-tailed deer. Caliph noticed his distraction and turned the conversation back to more general topics despite his excitement.

"I want to see. I want to hear all about it. Breakfast it is. In the meantime why don't we take that tour—check out the treasury along the way?"

David perked up.

"Sounds good to me."

Caliph summoned Gadriel and the High Seneschal played guide with his usual decorum, uniquely devoid of condescension.

Gadriel's particular charm lay in his ability to exist in a desert of self-imposed sobriety while dispensing a fountain of pleasures to castle guests. His graciousness had no discernable limitations.

As afternoon approached and the tour wound down, Caliph had learned almost as much as his friends.

They concluded in the grand foyer where Caliph instructed Gadriel without prior warning that he would like both men to be employed: Sigmund in the design room of the engineer corps and David doing whatever suited him best.

The High Seneschal acknowledged the king's request with the same graceful accommodation he might have used to bestow a second lump of sugar in his lord's coffee. Then he penciled Sigmund into Caliph's breakfast schedule for the following day since David said he would be unable to attend.

Caliph bid his college friends good-bye and for the remainder of the day endured several other meetings, one with General Yrisl concerning developments in Tentinil and two with the spymaster.

Information came and went from the castle by means of carrier pigeons and surgically altered hawks.

Saergaeth remained quiet. There had been more movement north of Bellgrass. Engine tracks between the Grass Heath and Miskatoll but no threats or engagements.

Caliph guessed he was maneuvering. Positioning his forces. Playing the badger game. Saergaeth hoped that by rattling his sword he might obtain the crown without a fight.

Yrisl advised Caliph that everything was under control. Troops had been garrisoned at Fallow Down since before Caliph's coronation and more had been moved into Fairden's Drop last week. Tentinil herself sheltered a regiment of roughly two thousand Iscan soldiers.

Yrisl then promised to go over military scenarios with the High King later in the week.

Despite his eagerness to share news of Sigmund's blueprints, Caliph remained silent. He felt it would be a violation of Sigmund's trust to say anything just yet.

Instead, he listened to details from the spymaster about a group of thin, sickly looking Pplarians that had been arrested by the watch in Daoud's Bend. They bore what appeared to be a new gang insignia, small dark tattoos above their navels.

Caliph paid little attention to the account. He was thinking about solvitriol power and enjoying the smell of the malt house in upper Ironside.

Delicious vapors trickled northwest across the sky and into the high tower. He was sick of crime and disturbing stories and revolting tours and meetings with despicable people.

Images of huge meats creaking on chains filled his head at night, tunnels puddled with magnesium lights and men in goggles loading vitriol bombs into zeppelin bays. He was sick of intrigue and shifty men whose loyalty he had no way of ascertaining.

When evening came and the meetings were finally over, Caliph ate supper with his servants.

He invited most of the castle staff: laundry, kitchen, cellar, garden, kennel, stable . . . the list was extensive. They gathered in the grand hall where Caliph presented them with a speech, half-composed, half-impromptu, thanking them for their hard work and announcing his great appreciation for all the polished floors and moldings, delicious food and beautiful clothing, lovely flowers and so on.

His silver tongue was in top form and all the heads of staff cheered him stentoriously as though he had promised never to make them work again.

Following supper, he had an unplanned appointment that forced him to take brandy in one of the castle's many opulent parlors with Simon Stepney, the burgomaster of Growl Mort.

After listening to Simon petition for less stringent labor laws and plead for relief from the city's pollution tax (while professing the indispensable value of Growl Mort's factories) Caliph politely accepted a miniature factory made of iron.

The ugly little contraption was bedizened with tiny emeralds in place of windows and contained a chemiostatic cell that made them glow. Caliph felt fairly certain there was some kind of bromidic metaphor going on.

About clean factories and clean power sources.

A hidden ampoule of chemical ink and some sulfate, or so Simon explained, was mixed at the touch of a button and produced a soundless but violent reaction that caused black steam to bubble from the smokestacks and dissipate harmlessly into thin air.

Caliph smiled graciously at the clever but hideous effect and handed the model off to Gadriel for relegation to the hidden stockpile of useless gifts accepted with outward cordiality from the arms of many decades' worth of wheedling politicians.

Then, maintaining decorum despite a throbbing headache and exigent need for sleep, the High King accompanied the burgomaster of Growl Mort into yet another lavish parlor where a dozen other guests had gathered for an evening of chamber music.

Somewhere between the sublime strains of violins, violas and cellos Caliph nearly lost his sanity.

Though the music dripped with gorgeous sounds Caliph could barely stay awake. The recital ended at sixteen-forty, an hour and a half before midnight.

Caliph clapped brightly and thanked everyone before the High Seneschal—who must have seen the king's discomfort like piano wire stretched under his skin—mercifully made an excuse and ushered him from the room.

"I'm terribly sorry." The seneschal began a bizarre apology. "They're usually much better."

Caliph waved off the man's kind but baseless repentance.

"It's not that, Gadriel. The musicians were fine. They were wonderful. I'm just exhausted. If I don't start getting more sleep—"

"Tomorrow morning you will not be disturbed. I swear my life on it. I will postpone your breakfast appointment until—"

"No, that's no good. I need to be there. It's a very important breakfast. Don't postpone it. And don't make the cooks go to any special trouble. I don't want it to seem like an important breakfast."

"Very well." Gadriel paused at the High King's bedroom with a strange look of sympathy. His eyes said something like, twenty-six is too young to be High King. He opened the door and Caliph walked in like a blind man, slowly but straight for the bed.

"Shall I help you undress, my lord?"

"No." Caliph fell like a tree across the mattress. He muttered with his face in the comforter, "Wasn't that miniature factory hideous?"

"Ungodly," the High Seneschal agreed.

"What did you do with it?"

"I had it melted down for sling bullets and given to the castle children for hunting crows."

"Excellent choice. I'll see you in the morning."

Gadriel turned down the gas lamp in the room, opened the windows as was his lord's habit and shut the door as quietly as he could.

THE next morning Caliph waited in the high tower, watching Bilgeburg smolder into another day's work.

Sigmund arrived on time and was admitted by the seneschal. He wore grimy leather overalls that had once been mostly tan and no shirt. As usual, Sigmund's hands looked like he had made a reasonable attempt to scour them and then thought better of it or had been distracted or simply given up.

"How's it goin', Caph?" he asked, slouching into his chair with one meaty arm draped over the back.

Gadriel made a noise of distinct admonition as he set a tray of pastries and tea on the table. Nevertheless, no visible trace of disdain marred the aged butler's countenance and Sigmund would have probably ignored him even if there had.

Gadriel poured each man a cup of tea before leaving the room.

"It goes," sighed Caliph. "And it continues . . . indefinitely."

"Sounds like I'm glad I'm not the High King," Sigmund remarked, scooping up two pastries and shoveling one in. It left a puff of cream at the corner of his mouth.

"I brought a booprints," he struggled while chewing. His left hand set the other pastry down and rooted around in a filthy canvas rucksack slung over his shoulder and down across his waist.

Outside, zeppelins were cruising through the striation of vanilla and oyster-colored clouds. They looked deadly. Like ornately finned fish, duny shinquils and coelacanths, that glinted in the high oblique sunlight from the west.

Sigmund pulled some thickly creased and wrinkled squares of paper out, each folded many times, and set them in a leaning stack beside the pastry tray.

He smacked down the rest of his breakfast, dumped three spoonfuls of sugar into his tea, stirred, gulped and swished.

"Thing is, Caph . . ." he dug at some bread trapped in his molars, "this stuff, this solvitriol mechanics. It's some scary damn shit. It's no wonder the profs at Desdae couldn't figure it out even when they got their hands on that little clurichaun. They even had some extra cells taken straight out of Iycestoke but once you crack 'em open the real important stuff, the stuff that makes the cell work in the first place, escapes . . . like light."

Caliph reached out and picked up the blueprints. He unfolded them with care. He had still not spoken to anyone about Sigmund's claim. He wanted to make sure his excitement was justified before he made the secret official.

On the paper were all kinds of formulae and dimensions. Blocks of information penned in precise handwriting framed by perfect squares and rectangles that hovered around carefully drawn diagrams of tubing and cells of blown glass.

The cells looked similar to chemiostatic batteries but instead of holding acids and holomorphically charged fluid, the cells on the blueprints contained something called solvitriol suspensate.

The glass was not normal glass either—something professors at Des-dae had already figured out.

"What's solvitriol suspensate?"

Sigmund was about to bite into his second pastry. He reconsidered and set it down, folding his hands and looking suddenly solemn.

"That's the scary part, Caph. That's the scary part." He dragged his chair around to sit beside the High King.

"See these caps and tubes and whatnot? These are like chemiostatic junk we've all seen before. You know, conducting electricity from the bat-tery out along a circuit to power whatever it is you want to supply juice to? It's really basic shit. Problem is you lose energy over distance. That's why it's better to light a city with gas. Localized chemiostatic cells can take care of a building if the cells are big enough and you want to change 'em out every couple months."

Caliph snorted.

"Yeah, right."

"Exactly." Sigmund shared the sarcasm. "Pulling bolts on a two-ton chemiostatic cell in a zeppelin is bad enough. I don't want to be the one lugging one out of someone's basement. But what if you never had to change it out?"

Caliph's brow knitted and he bit his lip.

"I suppose you could find a way to drain the battery and add more fluid, enhance the housing so it could withstand a decade's worth of acid and—"

"No, Caph," Sigmund interrupted by laying his hand on Caliph's arm. "I mean what if you never had to change it out?"

"Never?"

Sigmund shrugged. "At least maybe until we're all stone-screw dead and the world's turned into a ball of frozen rock and the sun burns out or falls in on itself or whatever in Emolus' name it's going to do. And even then. Even then . . ." His voice trailed off, insinuating the miraculous possibility.

"You mean these cells are infinite sources of energy?" Caliph's in-credulity showed as he looked at the diagrams.

Sigmund nodded with an expression of gravest formality.

"This is it," he whispered. "The fundamental shit, Caph. It's the fuck-all source. The . . ." he shook as though trying to dislodge words from his body, ". . . the . . . panomancer's dream! It's shadow matter. Not a gas or a solid or a liquid. It doesn't have gravity or normal mass. It doesn't reflect light. It's un-fucking-detectable.

"Remember those rumors we heard in the Woodmarsh Building back in Desdae? About how they froze light in a cloud of gas inside some tank in Iycestoke? Coughed up some old magical mathematical formula for ass-puckering cold and stopped a beam of light dead?"

"Yes. I remember." Caliph shifted in his chair.

Sigmund chewed at the hair under his lip.

"That's it. That's how they found it."

"Found what?"

But Sigmund was too caught up in his own theatrics, his own wonderment to slow down for silly questions that would be answered soon enough. He plunged on, heedless of his friend's new authority as High King.

"Look at this." He rifled through the stack of blueprints until he reached the bottom. "Remember me saying how there was a few snatches of coriolistic tech in these plans—not enough to really go on, but . . . ? Well this stuff down here is mostly useless as far as I can tell, but it does hint at what a coriolistic centrifuge might be used for—besides the academic speculation that it's just a big thaumaturgic reactor that runs off holomorphy to capture energy from planetary rotation."

"You're starting to lose me," said Caliph.

Sigmund held up his index fingers like the goal in a mugball game.

"Okay, let me slow down. What would you do with an energy source that never runs out of energy?"

Caliph shrugged. "I don't know. I suppose anything. The possibilities are . . . probably limitless."

"Exactly. So let me ask you this: What would you be willing to do to make this power source a reality—assuming you had in your service a capable engineer, a man who assured you it could be done?"

"Are you asking for a raise already?"

"No, Caph. I'm not talking about compensation here. I'm talking about you personally. What would you personally be willing to do?"

"Given that I'm not sure what the implications are, that I'm not quite imaginative enough to have already come up with a host of good ideas, I guess I don't know. Maybe if I—"

Sigmund clamped his hand over his own mouth as though damming up his frustration.

"I don't know!" shouted Caliph. "I studied swordplay for Mamre's sake. You're the engineer! Why don't you tell me what I'd be willing to do if I were you, or better yet, just tell me what in Emolus' name you're getting at?"

Sigmund scratched the side of his neck where some wiry hairs poked out above his overall straps.

"What I'm saying is that most folks would and have been willing to do just about anything, including locking their conscience in a box and sinking it to the bottom of the Loor. Damn dark nasty shit, Caph. Something like murder. But this is a brand-new kind of murder, boys and girls. Brand shiny new, like a knife you've never seen. Like some new torture you've never imagined. This is a crime we don't even have a name for because until those cruel evil bastards in Iycestoke came up with the concept of solvitriol power it wasn't even possible to perpetrate."

Caliph looked at the blueprints, trying in vain to grasp what Sigmund was getting at.

"You stopped going to church back at Desdae, Caph, so I gotta ask. Do you believe in gods and shit like that? Do you believe in anything after death?"

Caliph felt himself grow cold and nervous as he had one night in his uncle's house on Isca Hill. Like the time he woke to a nameless hour in that huge house with the breeze whistling under the sash and his tiny body shivering beneath the sheets.

The old trees of the mountain wood had bent beneath an autumn gale while distant chanting rose from someplace far away and tugged with it the smell of a dying sea.

Though his room was dark, Caliph saw the drapery twist by the window and slap against the wall. The servants had gone home for the night. And though some shape of blackness moved within, Caliph knew his uncle had gone abroad and that he was alone in the house on the hill.

Fearfully, he had sat up and looked out the great window, down across the hills and moors. The glass seemed to melt and the geometry of the window to change. And he knew somehow he was looking south—even though his window faced true north—and that the mountains had fallen away and the seas had dried up and a murrey darkness filled the sky.

In the distance, on a great tabletop of stone, danced a group of three whose lean, terrible figures reeled around a crucible of gold. The crucible sent flecks of light up like the residual holomorphic effluences out of Murkbell and Growl Mort.

The figures were blazoned in Caliph's mind because there was one among them whose legs did not bend oddly like a goat's, whose arms were not long enough to drag along on the ground. It was he who laughed loudest of all, yelling something about the numbers of the stars, an unmarked tomb and a series of obelisks that would shatter like glass. His voice bounced through the casement, off the flat plateau that did not exist south of Isca Hill. And then, from the darkness near the window had come a deathly utterance.

"It is him, Caliph. It is him."

The speaker's cold white hand, deformed as a dripping candle, the claw of Marco, his imaginary friend, had rested on his shoulder . . .

"CAPH? Caph are you okay?" Caliph shook his head. "You look a little green. I'm not spooking you, am I?"

"No. I mean yes, I suppose I do believe in gods and life after death and that sort of thing. Wasn't that your question?"

Sigmund nodded slowly.

"Yeah. Anyway. Like I was saying. That's good I suppose. Because it means we don't have to have some big long existential discussion or talk about Ihciva or Ahvêllę or whatever else people believe in.

"We can keep it simple.

"Solvitriol power, Caph. Solvitriol power runs on souls."

For a long time both men sat looking at each other like they had just finished a ghost story on Ilnfarne-lascue. Any minute they expected the other to break the ridiculous solemnity and laugh, point fingers, mock the pale look of terror that painted the other one's face.

"What does that mean?" asked Caliph. "It runs on souls?" He sounded like he was trying to fathom some abstruse physics problem. "It burns them up or something?"

Sigmund's laugh was sad and forced. He made the southern hand sign for no.

"Forget the old myths and tales about creatures that eat people's souls. That's all crap. You can't suck up a soul. Well, I mean you can, but you can't start a soul on fire or digest it or turn it into nothing. It's indestructible. Eating souls is an ass-stupid idea made up by someone who likes to think about impossible shit for fun."

His hand cut a wide sweep in front of him as though brushing away the concept.

"But what's the next closest thing to murder, eh Caph? What's the next cruelest thing you can do to someone?" Sigmund didn't wait for a response. "Lock 'em away in a cramped tight space, right? An oubliette, a shit-hole dungeon where they gibber for months until they go piss-pants insane. That's the next closest thing to murder. And that's what solvitriol power is all about. Plus murder to boot."

"I don't understand. How—"

"No, look, it's so simple. So ball-jerking simple."

Sigmund stood up and started walking around like Caliph sometimes did, in agitated circles. "You have to extract a soul, right? You have to catch it before it floats away to wherever it floats away to. That's a whole other topic of debate better left to priests. What I'm talking about is putting a body in a coriolistic centrifuge. Not a dead body, but a live one. Maybe someone sick or old.

"Then you start the spin. Only the coriolistic centrifuge doesn't just spin off in the dimensions of known physics. We're talking about other dimensions here. Branes. Shadow worlds. We're talking about separating undefined matter from flesh, bones, body fluid, straining off blood and fat. Decanting the soul for Palan's sake!

"Look, you stick some poor sod in the tube, spin him 'til he dies and don't even let him escape. You trap his soul in a holomorphic tube of treated glass before it can slip off to sweet oblivion, plug him into some machine and let him work for an eternity."

For a long time Caliph and Sigmund once again regarded each other with an appalled, almost stupefied stare.

Finally Caliph said, "That's not right."

"No shit it's not right!" Sigmund was off and running at the mouth again. "There's this hierarchy thing going on too. Like you could stick a cat or something in there instead of a human, only your results might vary. Half power or quarter power or whatever. I don't understand how they categorize solvitriol batteries yet but—"

"Iycestoke does this?"

Sigmund looked annoyed at the interruption.

"Yeah. They probably power half the city on it. Like I said, cruel evil bastards. But that's an ochlocracy, right? Why waste medicine on the sick when you can power a city block on 'em dead?"

"And you want me to use this in the Iscan military?"

Caliph's appalled look did not fade. He began to regard Sigmund with a look of horror.

"That's just it, Caph. Like I said you don't have to use people. You can use animals."

"You sick bastard!"

Sigmund glared. "Hold on—"

"I've heard enough!"

Sigmund raised his voice in desperation. "Wait! I told you I had some new ideas based on this. Stuff nobody's ever tried before."

There was an urgent knocking at the door. Caliph didn't even glance at the sound.

"Look, if what you're saying is true, if this solvitriol power comes from murdering life and sentencing it to endless enslavement then I'm not interested in hearing anything more about it. It's heinous, disgusting crap as far as I'm concerned and I don't want any part of it. Gas and chemiostatic cells are just fine by me."

"But Caph—"

The knocking on the door intensified. Mr. Vhortghast's meticulous voice came from without the room.

"No!" Caliph nearly shouted. "Look, Sig. Keep your job in the military. Be an engineer. I'm happy to have you, really I am. But I don't want to hear another thing about solvitriol power. I'm already sick beyond words from the shit I've seen since I took this miserable crown. Let me tell you, the last thing this city needs is another sin on its slate."

Sigmund, visibly angry and frustrated at not having been able to share his vision, glowered in silence as Caliph answered the knock.

Zane Vhortghast stood just outside the room, pressing his fingertips together, looking slightly winded as though he had mounted the considerable staircase in a hurry.

Caliph briefly wondered if he had been eavesdropping.

"Your majesty. I am afraid I have some terrible news." He noticed Sigmund at once. "Perhaps you should be alone to hear this. Perhaps you should sit down."

Caliph smiled quizzically. He tried to imagine what news Vhortghast could possibly know that would upset him more than he already was. Nothing came to mind.

"Mr. Vhortghast." He gestured for the spymaster to enter the room. "Please. I'm sure it can't be that bad. Sigmund is an old friend. It's perfectly fine to tell me here and now. I don't need to sit down."

"But your majesty—"

Mr. Vhortghast's clay-like face twisted into some rare facsimile of regret.

"I'm fine," said Caliph. "What is it?"

"Your father. Your father has been . . . assassinated."

Caliph drew back sharply, wincing. "What? How?"

The unpleasant and grisly details followed and rested in Caliph's mind.

Sigmund, distracted from his reprimand, looked disconnectedly sorry for his friend. He sat quietly while Zane Vhortghast described how Jacob had been jumped the previous night, a sack thrown over his head and knocked unconscious with something like a brick. The assailants had thrown him in the river.

"Sig—"

Sigmund was already headed for the door.

"I'll talk to you later, Caph. I'm sorry. Sorry . . ." He disappeared into the staircase, a fading, sinking mumble of apology and hurried footsteps.

Gone was the recent excitement and debate over solvitriol power. Gone the sweetness of the creamy breakfast pastries in Caliph's mouth.

Outside, one of the zeppelins sounded a piercing low Klaxon, plowing south over Bilgeburg and the ships in the glittering sea. It was carrying factory parts or refrigerated canisters packed with meat or metholinate or coal. The sun had finally risen high enough to reach the bay. Morning crept like something wounded toward afternoon.

Vhortghast maintained a look of well-conceived empathy as the High King swallowed his anger and began calculating even before he mourned . . . calculating his response.

Sena leaned at the window of a dark bedroom over Litten Street, her face tense and solicitous.

Beyond the casement, laughter and song echoed from taverns and all-night cafés. The voices were weird and thin, sounding like wind-tossed cans off Sandren's reeling vertiginous streets.

Sena hadn't been home yet, having hitched a ride with a farmer all the way from the Stones to the ghettos of Seatk'r. That had been yesterday. She'd taken the ancient lift up to the City in the Mountain and stayed the night with Clea. But tonight was different. Tonight, contingencies had forced her into a room at the Black Couch: a lavish and discretionary inn that catered to the one-night stands of the reckless wealthy.

The tang of homemade perfume ruffled through her room. Behind her, the darkness stirred with human irritation as another gust swirled over the bedclothes.

"Sounds like it's picking up." A man's voice came from the bed.

Sena did not answer. Her gaze dipped with mild amusement to where a band of cup-shot youths twirled and swaggered beneath marcescent statues that threatened to topple. The city was splintered with deep fissures and the boys crossed Lôrc Rift on a bridge of antiquated stone.

Sena spun her tiny wineglass between her fingers and enjoyed the architecture. The Ghalla Peaks had been crammed and chiseled by another of the north's prehistoric civilizations, one older and more sinister than the numinous mummified horrors that that had built the Highway of Kafree.

"Why don't you shut it? It's cold," the man said.

He was not Tynan.

"I like it cold." Sena took a sip and set the glass in the open window.

The man drew the sheets around him and turned to face her.

"What are you doing?"

Sena stepped out of the faint blue cast from the window. Her body stooped to gather soft dark shapes from the floor.

"Go to sleep," she whispered. Parts of her were disappearing.

"I thought you were going to stay here for a while—" He sat up, trying to find her clothed body against the gloom.

"You need your rest. You must have been tired tonight—Robert." She said his name as though hardly remembering it.

Robert growled but the door clicked and wind howled briefly through the bedroom, billowing up gusts of Sena's perfumery. When the door clicked again, the wind had blown her out like a flame.

Sena walked briskly, adjusting the black britches and a studded watchman's jacket. She had not gathered her own clothing from the floor.

It's a good fit, she thought. Robert was a very small man—the reason she had picked him out of the crowd. His leather pants pulled tightly across her slender hips.

She smiled as she fancied him trying on her skirt in the morning. Around her index finger swung a heavy ring of city keys that slapped against her palm.

If all went well, Robert would never see her again, and never understand why she had stolen almost everything in his possession.

His cloak, stitched with the city insignia, displayed a winged silhouette against a pink sun.

The do'doc statues were Sandren's most prominent skyline feature and one of several things that drew the tourists. They hunkered on all fours atop their spindles of stone, looking beyond the curvature of the planet with a unified expression of morbid, almost alien anticipation.

Sandren's murky history was the reason she was here. Gimmon Mae had come late to the north. The city's foundations had been laid by the Groull, creatures that flourished and fell long before human tribes discovered fire. Just like men, they had come here for the gold.

But something had forced them to abandon the mines before the ore ran out, a mystery to the archeological society that flourished here. Certainly an invasion was out of the question. Sandren's position precluded siege.

Sena wished she had followed Megan's recommendation to infiltrate the city's archeological society. Her goal tonight certainly would have been easier to achieve.

Still, in the dark, no one would notice that her uniform pinched or sagged a bit in places that made it obviously masculine. Robert's weapons moved against her hips with an easy sway.

She met the concierge of the Black Couch with a smile, mentioning that "the man upstairs" would take care of any residual fees. The concierge checked his register. He eyed her and made the hand sign for yes. Sena headed into the street.

Outside she could smell summer blooms like tender-loin girls: pink-petaled skirts ruffling in the wind. She walked southeast, listening to the creak of queelub cages swinging over Litten Street.

The wind in Sandren was always delicious. Sena could see west now down Windlymn Street and beyond the cliffs to the remote clouds over Tibiŭrn that had smeared like charcoal into night. She felt comfortable here. Not a tourist. Living in Tue had made her part of the city-state and she read tobacco signs and bistro names with ease in several different tongues.

She entered the Aerie: the most extravagant of the rich districts. It was where Tynan's family lived. She had met him this morning at the Merchant's Pillow just above Jdellan's Fountain and told him a carefully abridged version of her disastrous spring.

His corresponding tale had revolved around his own panic at finding her cottage a mess. He had told the police, and a squad of officers had been dispatched. Sena gnashed her teeth until it was clear from Tynan's story that they had found nothing of the secret cellar.

Sena had endured their hour together at the Merchant's Pillow but she could not look him in the eye. The tenderness in his face was unbearable and she understood that for him it was like she had come back from the dead. His affection only reminded her of the deep secret between them, the thing they never spoke of, whose tiny bones lay in the ground at Desdae.

Sena had buckled the coins he gave her in her pack and swallowed hard, forcing a smile.

Later, alone over lunch, she had counted the wealth. He had given her southern scythes. They were worth twice as much on exchange for northern gryphs and Sandren's system accepted both kinds of currency.

They would get her to Stonehold and back again if things unraveled with Caliph.

The dark streets of Sandren wound confusingly behind pubs and town houses. Rose-tinted light bled from deep-set alley windows onto cobbled walls where the smell of blossoms mixed with the sour stench of rotting fruit and garbage: refuse from the never-ending galas of the rich.

Sena swung between wheeled crates of waste and arrived at a narrow intersection sheltered from the wind and glutted with a humid veil of sewer steam.

She swung Robert's ring of keys around her finger and snapped the heavy bouquet together with a clank. Then she fanned them and examined the teeth and relative length of each shaft, trying to gauge which ones might go to standard doors versus large metal gates. She would have only one chance to bluff her way through . . .

Distracted and nervous, she turned down Gullet, trying to ignore the howling in her head. As crazy as she imagined it might sound, she believed the book wanted to be opened.

Crossing over an archaic bridge, cloak billowing in a roaring updraft, Sena thought about Caliph and about opening the grimoire.

Thoughts of Caliph still flitted through her head as she moved into an unlit section of town, gliding through the blackened tapestries of laundry lines and orchid-clustered walls.

Another loud group of young nobles passed her on their way to a party. They saw her city insignia and hid their bottles discreetly behind backs or against thighs.

Sena turned down a narrow street stacked with hives of vented coils. Gauges glowed, tiny featherweight beads inside them tumbled with the flow of gas. She exited at a bright intersection where metholinate lamps flickered overhead, illuminating one of the do'doc statues: a fantastic long-clawed leering beast crumbling into air.

To the south stood a well-lit gate. Frosted bulbs enclosed white darts of flame on either side of the portal, a tall block affair comprised of lofty columns capped with pyramidal stones. The columns framed and anchored ornate grilles of iron that rose thirty feet or more above the level of the street.

Two men in studded watchman's jackets identical to Robert's stood talking about the bets they had placed on the fights in Northcliff Court. They glanced at her as she approached but kept talking. It was time for her to focus.

"Got a report of somebody making noise on the other side of the fence," said Sena as though such an idea were preposterous.

The watchmen chuckled.

"Yeah right. Probably someone's cat gettin' laid."

Sena fumbled through Robert's keys, trying to guess which one fit.

"Hey, you're new," one of the men was saying. His eyes traveled her body. "You see police?"

"Maybe." She winked at him. "What time you off?"

"Seventeen."

"Palan damn these things." She was genuinely frustrated. "I can't keep them straight. Which one is it?"

The guard came over and flipped through the assortment, touching her fingers.

"That one." She guessed it was his best seductive baritone. "GS-Four."

Sena suddenly noticed the tiny digits engraved on the shaft. They probably stood for Great Steps Gate Four.

"Thanks." Sena looked up with an expression that showed her (completely false) interest in him. "I'll be back after I take a look around."

"Hey," said the other guard. "Where's your lamp?"

Sena scowled as though he were being ridiculous. "I'm not going to need one. It's probably nothing. I'll just have a peek and write it up as a stray."

"Suit yourself. Place gives me the creeps even from this side of the bars."

The guard, who was hitting her like bait, offered to go with but Sena convinced him that leaving his post wasn't worth the risk.

He grinned and shut the gate, stopping her one last time. "Take this just in case." He handed a whistle through the bars.

"Thanks." Sena draped it around her neck and turned her back on him.

She went south toward the black cascade of masonry stacked against the mountainside, monstrous and dark like the terraced ascent to some Veyden ziggurat. The city officially ended here. Eight broad terraces rose fifty feet like a giant staircase.

The steps were monumental. Wide and curved to embrace the contour of the mountain, as though the mountain itself had been set on a vast dais. At the back of the topmost terrace, burrowed into the mountainside, the Halls yawned.

Sena could already hear them. Miles of deep vaulted corridor honeycombed the Ghalla Peaks; few were unexplored but their depth precluded frequent visitations. Many now found use as wine cellars or crypts for the wealthy. The Halls were another leftover from the Groull.

Sena moved quickly and soundlessly, scrambling up each of the six-foot steps. Listening to the ominous breathing of the mountain.

When she reached the top she turned and glanced briefly out over the city. Its weltering rooftops and chimney pots formed an eerie black landscape of smoke and domes. Beyond them, through a deep cleft in the Ghalla Peaks, the smoky glimmer of Mirayhr's dusk-burnished lakes still smoldered under leagues of mist.

Sena watched the friendly red lights of taverns and inns flickering with drunken abandon. Behind her, the sheer face of the mountain rose skyward and the low moan of the Halls waited.

She turned and walked along them, unsure of her exact position. Beyond the huge openings, colossal columns jutted mightily from the walls, supporting far-flung ornate ceilings with inconceivable designs. The floors, though smooth for the most part, ran in almost imperceptible rises and slopes of limestone tile. Sena felt a steady gush of warm damp air as she stood near one of the many hundred openings that lined the top of the Great Steps.

Inside, the smallest sounds echoed. Water drops. Even wind. A black shape shifted in the darkness and her hand clutched instinctively at Robert's sword.

" 'S'me lady." A raised palm came out into the starlight as though from behind a curtain.

"Gavin?"

"Yes. 'S'me." The voice of the guide she had hired sounded ridiculous as it reverberated through the empty vault. He was Worian but even Trade Tongue exited rough and half-formed from his mouth. She wondered briefly how he had made his way past the guards.

"Show me quickly," she whispered.

He stood up and brushed off his backside. He looked small and formless, as though a diaper bunched beneath his trousers.

"No light until we are far enough inside," he said.

She followed his footsteps for several hundred feet. When the starlight vanished, the Halls grew unnaturally dark. The air felt pulpy and damp. Gavin produced a book of matches but had trouble getting them to strike. Each spluttering blue streak that snapped ineffectually along the book hiked Sena's tension. *Would the matches run out? What the fuck was he doing wrong?* She counted six tries in the palpable blackness before the candle box finally fluttered to life.

Muttering to himself, Gavin swung the light around and tromped off into the mountain without saying a word. Along the first leg of their journey, Sena noticed more recent stonework. Niches had been carved and then mortared shut, sealed off with marble slabs graven with dates, names and short serious poems.

Gavin guided her through immense passageways that turned back and forth, all of them generally sloping down. Fallen slabs of rock and ribbing lay like scattered bones and an occasional pilaster, loosened by shifts in the mountain and eons of seeping moisture lay sprawled out, having relinquished its lifelong marriage to the wall.

"This way," Gavin whispered. Sena was timing their pace on her watch. She flipped it open again, chemiostatic fluid flaring like an emerald in her palm. She squinted at the chronometer. They had traveled nearly two and a half miles into the mountain.

Gavin's breathing was loud and nasal as though he were growing excited or fearful. Sena followed the dirty yellow bob in his hand another thousand feet, judging a slow but steady descent the entire way.

Neither of them talked.

Finally, though the wide chilly tunnel ran on, Gavin stopped.

"It starts right around here, mostly on the far wall. I want my money before we go any farther." He looked like a blind mole in the rake of light.

Sena tousled her hair. "A little pushy, aren't you?"

"I brought you here. Now I want my money. Maybe I'll leave you here in the dark."

Reluctantly she unbuckled her pack, fished then tossed him a pre-pared pouch that clinked when he caught it.

Gavin opened it and scrutinized the contents.

"This way." He swung the lantern around and stumped toward the far wall. The carvings materialized slowly, picked out by candlelight.

"No one knows they are here but me, maybe. Maybe some others too, I don't know. No one can read them."

Sena crouched and gazed at the ancient writing. *Few can read them,* she amended silently.

A week before the attack at her cottage, Sena had found a reference in the Holthic Scripture, supposedly a translation of a Gringling text made by Yacob Skie before he released his prophetic Roll of Years.[11] One of the clues that originally began her search for the *Cisrym Ta*, the Holthic Scripture also referenced "unholy vaults below the mountains at Nifol" as containing script regarding the *"Red Book."* Sena hoped to find the script, if it existed, and learn more before attempting the books's anathe-matic lock.

Talk with the stonemasons' guild led her to this man, Gavin, who had interred many of Sandren's newer additions to the stockpile of wealthy dead.

"Few know the Halls like Gavin," the guild master had said, "because few spend as much time in them as he does."

The dead languages Sena had learned at school whipped up in her head. Each one poised, ready to dissect the rich field of carvings Gavin's light pored over.

The carvings rose up the wall and down the passage out of sight. Sena recognized them as a form of Jingsade Runic Script, mingled with pho-neticized spellings of what strangely seemed to be Mallic glyphs.

It was an exceptional mix.

Jingsade Runes were indigenous to locales surrounding the Great Cloud Rift; there was nothing strange about finding them here. But Mallic

---

[11] A controversial prophetic text said by some to list every year since 337 W.C. by name. Yacob's Roll ends at 563 "Y.o.T. Sealed Scroll," supposedly marking the end of the world.

glyphs were found only on the isles and in desolate seaside ruins along the southern coasts—never this far inland.

She would need rubbings to take back to her cottage for further study. So engrossed had she become, she barely heard the light grate of metal behind her.

Suddenly, Gavin hurled himself like a block snapped loose from a scaffold crane. As she turned, Sena felt what must have been a long heavy knife strike her shoulder at an angle and glance off the studs of the watchman's jacket.

She fumbled for her sword, Robert's sword, and tried to parry, but Gavin was too close. Head down, pressing her against the wall. His knife slashed gainlessly against her rib cage, unable to penetrate the jacket's heavy leather.

Instinctively she brought her knee up, heard his jaw snap shut with a loose-toothed crunch. A muffled yelp echoed off the carvings and a second plunge of the knife struck the wall just left of her torso.

Gavin smelled of grease and dust. He was small but compact. His weight made her stagger. She felt herself being dragged down and couldn't tell where his knife was. Her fear had given way to anger. Not this. Not again. She brought her knee up once more, this time striking nothing but air.

But Gavin stumbled backward holding his face. Apparently her first blow had done more damage than she thought.

In the tilted light she could see him swagger like the flame. For a moment it looked like he might give up, then suddenly he lunged again, apparently unaware of Robert's sword.

Almost with the motion of a dance step Sena caught him on the steel. His knees buckled. The thick hard fingers that had worked years of stone did grasping motions. With hardly a sound, he fell to the floor.

Sena kicked the knife from his hand. He still breathed in a gurgling fashion.

"Who sent you?" Her voice sounded too loud in the darkness.

No answer.

"Who sent you!" she screamed. But it was no use. The stonemason's life was pooling on the floor.

In a sudden fit she thrust her sword into him once, twice, three times. A spasm shook the body and it lay still.

Sena sank down against the wall by the candle box. She bit back fiercely on her tears. Even trained as a Shraḍnæ operative with the attendant skills of the Seventh House at her disposal, she could scarcely contain the angst over this. Her first time.

"You're a stonemason, not an assassin," she screamed at the corpse. The word assassin echoed hollowly down the vault. The blood on her sword was thick like syrup and seemed to shrink away from the metal, refusing to coat it with an even film.

Who could it have been? Who could have known she had hired Gavin besides the guild master?

The world felt small. Dangerous. The Halls smelled of Gavin's intestines tangled with a cloying sweetness she couldn't name. There was blood on her clothes, on the back of her hand. How had that gotten there? She tried to wipe it off. Instead, it blended into her skin like rouge. Her left hand was definitely ruddier than the other. She felt sick. The smell was making her gag.

I can do this. It wasn't my fault. He tried to kill me. But she knew Sandren wasn't safe anymore. They would find Gavin's body. Maybe. Maybe not. Gavin said no one else had been here, this deep in the Halls. Even so, he would go missing. The stonemasons would remember that she had hired him. A dog would find him, gnaw off a limb and drag it out. What now?

Going back to the Black Couch was out of the question. Robert had no motive for killing Gavin and besides, the concierge had seen her leave, wearing Robert's clothes. The weapon couldn't be left behind. Nothing could be left behind. City detectives would lug iatrophysical gadgetry in to sniff the air. They would analyze molecules. They would dust for prints.

She was beginning to remember her training, to understand how wrong everything had gone. She had made a mess by not planning ahead, not preparing for the contingency that Gavin might have to die. And that was the cardinal rule. Broken.

Rule one: Someone other than you must be available to take the blame.

But there was no one now. No other possible suspect. Sena held her head in her hands.

She muttered in the Unknown Tongue, trying to jumble her molecules in the air. She tried to use Gavin's blood, use the trick of hemofurtum she had learned in Skellum, to muddle her trail. But the air would not obey.

How had this happened? Was Gavin after the book? She had signed a false name when she bought it.

She spoke again in the Unknown Tongue, this time calling for light. Nothing. A third time but with the same word, she ordered Gavin's splattered cells to illuminate the air. Quiet thrumming answered but still no sparkle. No sudden incandescence. Gavin's candle box fluttered pathetically near the floor.

Maybe I'm getting it wrong. But hemofurtum wasn't a complicated skill.

She retrieved her pouch of coins as the blackness beyond the lantern seemed to churn. Something slippery against light sidled just beyond the lens's throw, wrapping around the massive corridor.

Sena let the Unknown Tongue explode from her lungs but the sound echoed away, consumed by the mountain.

She turned back to the wall, closed her eyes, resting her forehead against petroglyphic stone. It felt cool.

Clea's daughter, Jemi, still took a bottle at night. Sena had washed them out in the sink, cylindrical masses of clotted white, heavy and light at the same time, sliding smoothly past her fingers, vanishing suddenly down the drain.

Here, beneath the mountain, the air was like that. Clotted-milk air. Except it was sweet. Like at the Porch of Soth. She could feel it in the Halls. Poised on the other side of rational geometry. The skin of the only dimension Sena could comprehend bulged around its cyst, its cradle. It moved. A pustule that could roam, sliding like a parasite just beneath the cuticle of real. A monster. Pressing. Struggling to reach her. Pushing its formless mass against the locus of an ancient embryonic sac.

Sena had read about them in the small hours at Desdae. The eggs laid between the branes. The cosmic larvae stretching the membrane of physical space, stretching with alien desperation, disrupting temperatures; drafts; the basic outcomes of subtle natural events: like the striking of a match.

Sena's holomorphy wouldn't work.

Whether intentional or an inadvertence of the thing's impossible presence, Sena's equations remained unsolved. The math of the surrounding air had been modified just enough that her formula refused to function.

There were myths of daemons carved into the cathedrals of the north, skeletal men with bat wings and scorpion tails. There were old woodcuts in Holthic Scripture of bipeds with wolf heads and hooves and goat tails and huge selachian teeth. But for Sena, who had pored over superlative manuscripts, piecing together the vague and hideous outlines of these starry nightmares, such woodcuts were amphigoric in the extreme.

Real daemons had no concept of anthropomorphism; would not stoop to assume human shape any more than a biologist would attempt to become a laboratory grub in a dish of rotting meat. *Real daemons,* thought Sena, *ignore our narcissistic renditions of evil. Real daemons cannot be fathomed.*

Sena shook convulsively. Maybe the daemons in the darkness could feel the Inti'Drou glyphs. Like oceanic things drawn to Naobi's lunar glow, certain entities might be compelled toward the book in her pack.

Sena clenched her eyes but she could still feel the horrors behind her. One or several of the Thæ'gn, scrabbling silently in the ether.

Their names were laced with nonphysical numbers and could only be written accurately in the Unknown Tongue. Sena rummaged in her pack, trying not to think of those old words.

ꭙꞔꭙꞑ ꭟꞔ ꭙꞡꞠꞽ ꞡ.[12]

ꭟꞔ ꞭꞠꞾ.[13]

And most dreadful of all: ꞽꞾꞽ.[14]

They were words that twisted in the brain, their pronunciations difficult and the depth of the throaty sounds was lost when translated into Trade.

Slowly, Sena composed herself and pulled a book of blank paper and a box of charcoal from her pack. Like a child in the lantern's halo, she swallowed her fear and began the long task of rubbing over the inscriptions that stretched out into the infinite and eternal blackness below the Ghalla Peaks.

SENA closed out her Sandrenese bank account and converted her money back into gems. City-state police had already been to her cottage once in the past three months. Still, she had to go home. One last time. She left her spare key with Clea and did not say good-bye to Tynan.

When she arrived, she found her cottage more or less how'd she left it with the exception of her missing horse.

"Did you chase away the brigands?" she whispered to Niṣ. Maybe the police had confiscated her horse.

The cat looked at her quizzically with a high-pitched chirp, not even half a meow. It seemed like a vocalized question mark that asked many things at once.

Sena noticed food items out of place. The note on the corkboard was missing. She opened her cellar. *The Fall of Bendain* had been taken and her atlas was left open, a page torn out. Her scowl melted into a charmed smile.

Caliph *had* been here. The papers were right.

No matter that luck had not allowed them to meet. She would be in Stonehold soon enough. A broad smile spread across her face.

---

[12] U.T. Approximate pronunciation: Yillo'tharnah.
[13] U.T. Approximate pronunciation: Thay'gn.
[14] U.T. Approximate pronunciation: Nayn.

She laid the rubbings she had made in the Halls on her table and began picking them apart.

A portion of them originated from chapters found in the Gallin Scrolls. Sena's mother had brought copies of them from Greenwick to the mainland. The copies now belonged to the Sisterhood, but Sena's memory was good. She licked her thumb, pulled out a book on Mallic glyphs and thumped it open.

Referencing it often for the difficult phoneticized Jingsade spellings proved nightmarish since the glyphs were organized by shape and grouped by meaning and the phonetic representations in Jingsade gave her little clue what the glyphs themselves might look like.

Intuition and the fragmentary knowledge gleaned from Desdae were her only guides. Still, she formulated a workable translation and copied most of it into a thin journal she could take with her.

> *What is read will unseal*
> *Twice in bird years.*
> *The times are written*
> *On the Island Scroll that*
> *The skies will open.*
> *Where D'loig strikes*
> *Quietus comes.*
> *And there will be Three . . .*
> *To Inscribe the Final Page*
> *With the numbers of Nen.*

Sena had hoped for more details. She didn't find this vague bit of verse compelling in the least. What she wanted was something coherent, real hints at what waited between the covers of the book.

"What is read? What is red?" She liked the wordplay. She imagined this reference pointing to the *Cisrym Ta*. But the homonym didn't really work in Jingsade.

"Final Page" rang a bell. She had heard that phrase somewhere before. Or maybe she had translated some of it incorrectly. She would have another go at it later. For the moment she was drained.

She shut her journal despondently, gathered up the papers and folded the rubbings in half.

The rubbings went into her pack with the journal. The other notes she took upstairs to the hearth to be burned. As she tossed each page into the flames she noticed how thin Nis looked.

He had been safe here, as she knew he would, but not anymore. He moved cautiously around the kitchen, sniffing the floor with a pecking motion.

Out of habit, she swept the kitchen, ignoring the stains by the door. Then she picked Nis up and left through the broken front door, walking down to the Stones.

From the Porch of Soth she walked lines to a cromlech in southern Mirayhr where she stayed at a village under a false name. She put as much distance between herself and the Stones as she could but it didn't matter.

That night she still dreamt of the rag-thing and of giant spectral shapes coiling in the meadow below her house. She dreamt that starry winds above the Porch filled those ghostly shapes like sails; that they had followed her from the Halls, monstrosities that suffused the sky with close, sweet humidity. They drooled otherworldly secretions, congealing across the Porch and beading on her home.

In the dream, she could feel them gazing at her without true eyes, across dimensions, slavering mouthlessly. Only the weakest of their kind had mouths. The book had drawn them. Maybe Megan was right. Maybe she had drawn their attention by binding one of them to the cottage. But she didn't doubt, with the *Cisrym Ta* in her pack, at some point the Yillo'tharnah would have found her just the same.

CHAPTER

13

Public surgery happened on a regular basis in Tin Crow. When the gutters of Bloodsump Lane ran thick and red it meant someone had gone under the knife.

Body fluids and knots of clotted blood slithered through little eyebrow grates, dumping directly into shallow channels that bordered the street. Sometimes scrubby strips of flesh would snag on the bars. They dangled stubbornly and slapped about in the ichors that issued from crowded moldy buildings.

Sometimes it was a slow steady trickle. Other times it came in waves as though someone were sloshing hidden mistakes out with a mop.

For a silver bek, a gentleman and his lady could purchase tickets and gain admittance, not through the gory back alleys but through slightly more professional front doors where gaslights flared on the names of well-known surgeons and grime was kept to a minimum.

Large panes of frosted glass glowed with snowy whiteness on all sides of Grouselich Hospital's doors.

Nearby, a voluminous glass tube, lit from within, hung beside the brass-lettered names and cast unpleasant patterns on the bricks below. Filled with some clear fluid, through which a stream of heavier red liquid fell, the tube gurgled and hummed.

A line of men and women had gathered, the head of which showed tickets to a bald man with a white mustache and a black suit. He had just unlocked the doors. The line of people shifted. Some watched the red liquid ebb through the tube while others whispered about what speculative horrors their tickets might grant them access on this particular night.

All of them had heard about arms being sawn off, eyes replaced with lenses poured from glass, and the gruesome, mysterious term well worth the silvery price of admission: brain surgery.

Everyone was giddy because everyone knew that unlike the opera, where murders and intrigue happened right before their eyes, this was for real.

Slowly, the line edged toward the doors as the mustachioed man examined each ticket with care. He took them and turned them over, peered down his nose like a jeweler examining diamonds. Finally he made a precise tear in each one and handed it back to the bearer, motioning for them to step through the portal and into the unsettling cone of antiseptic light.

From the front doors, the nervous ticket holders were ushered by a second man down a narrow gray hallway that smelled of chemicals. Lit by clear gas jets in steel fixtures, the hall felt vaguely threatening. A wooden gurney with tiny cracked wheels stood along the left wall. Draped in hospital white, it looked clean relative to the walls. Its position forced the spectators to squeeze past in single file. They made excited idiotic sounds as they passed, asking each other whether a dead body might at some time have rested on that very spot.

A wider hallway of two-toned olive and beige welcomed them on the other side and more transparent gas jets revealed a pair of double doors that admitted the throng to an austere oval chamber with steep stands that allowed them to hover over whatever happened below.

There was no place to sit. Voyeurs had to remain in rank, each one four feet above the other, separated by low metal railings whose topside had been upholstered with padding meant to cushion the forearms. Unfortunately the padding was like everything else, gray and thin and dilapidated. Its cracked surface had either hardened with age or altogether crumbled away.

Below the dim tiers (which were dark enough to cause the ticket holders to stumble and ask each other why someone didn't turn on some lights) the central oval-shaped pit basked—a sort of phosphorescent eggshell color under the glare of magnesium spotlights. As people filed in and the tiers filled up, a door in the pit opened slightly and a man could be heard talking behind it.

"Next week . . . sure . . . just send it over there . . ."

The pit had several tables with shiny metal tops. Dubious cloth bundles had been placed on them before the audience arrived.

A rack of glass bulbs ranging in size from miniscule to grandiose stood at attention. Most of them contained various quantities of some clear fluid, reflecting the spotlights through a clutter of curves. Like strange retorts, their necks were screwed with metal caps fit snugly with a jungle of pink-orange hoses. The flow of fluid could be controlled from various knobs.

Finally the door in the pit swung wide and a man in a white apron, the one who had been talking, came out. A fringe of black hair went around the back of his head from ear to ear but his dome shone like fleshy glass beneath the lights.

Two boys, who appeared to be no more than fifteen years apiece, followed him into the room. All three ignored the whispering crowd. Like debunkers at a séance they unrolled their equipment. Cloth bundles unfurled to reveal an array of glittering blades and forceps. Hooks and sponges.

The crowd murmured excitedly while the man in the apron checked the hoses and then reached down to unstopper a drain in the center of the floor.

A metal contraption in a square frame near the rack of glass bulbs began to hum as one of the boys flipped a switch. Chemiostatic lights flared up like emeralds in the twisted brown guts of the machine. Wires and slender hoses were attached with grim decorum.

Finally the surgeon stepped to the middle of the room and addressed the crowd.

"Ladies and gentlemen." His voice sounded thin and tired. "I am Dr. Billium. Welcome to this evening's surgery. I am sure you have all been warned about the graphic nature of what you are about to witness; therefore if any of you should begin to feel light-headed or ill, please remove yourself from the lecture hall at once. There will be no refunds. You are free to talk during the operation but I ask that you keep all conversations to a whisper. Any more and I will have you removed at once."

As the surgeon spoke a large man wheeled a wooden gurney in.

Everyone gasped except those who had previously been to Grouselich Hospital.

A gray man lay atop the wooden tray like something crammed in a shoe box, arms restfully at his sides. His eyes were closed and his body seemed hairless.

"This man is not dead," said Dr. Billium, "he has been administered vapors by means of a cloth mask. He is sleeping . . . very deeply."

The surgeon demonstrated his patient's insensibility by prodding the bottoms of his feet with a sharp metal pointer.

One of the boys dropped a scalpel into a bottle of antiseptic.

The tension mounted.

In the crowd above, a group of four women huddled together under very deep hoods. They were hardly watching what happened below. They were whispering in the rolling rhyming syllables of Withil.

"Whetoo brithou frumoo Aogi?" asked one of the witches.

Translation was straightforward for those who knew the trick. "Whetoo brithou frumoo Aogi" became: "What breath from Gig?" or, "What did Giganalee say?" The reply spoken by a second witch translated as, "To leave Stonehold. We cannot stay if Megan casts her hex . . . if the Pandrag-onians fail in their negotiations."

There were two half-sisters and two Sisters. All of them were young and pretty though their hoods made facial features practically irrelevant.

The Sisters were both in the Fourth House, a respectable position that had taken them between twelve and fifteen years from the age of six. Their names were Miriam Yeats and Kendra Liegh. The half-sisters' names were completely unimportant. Only one of them even spoke.

"I do not think the Pandragonians will succeed," Miriam said in Withil. She had golden hair and eyes like beads of polished mahogany. "Giganalee suspects they will buy the transumption hex."

Though her skin was Pandragonian, Miriam had been born in Mirąyhr and her only interest in the Empires of the South was finding a way to ex-pand the Sisterhood into them. She had climbed through the Houses with astonishing speed. The Fifth was almost within her grasp. If only she had reached it earlier she might have been a candidate for replacing Megan.

But Megan's eye was fixed on Sena as Miriam and every other Sister knew. The fact that Sena had reached the Sixth House so young reeked of pseudonepotism but when Sena graduated and Megan welcomed her to the Seventh, shockwaves traveled through the north as though a bomb had been dropped.

Miriam had quietly watched Megan's favoritist act as she placed Ais-linn's daughter among the Sisterhood's highest elite. Less than one per-cent of the Sisterhood resided in the Seventh House. Not even Megan was among them. Sena, talented as she was, had not been tried. Her rank had been gifted rather than earned.

"Trans-what? What kind of hex?" asked the half-sister. Her Withil was rusty.

"It's nothing you need worry about," whispered Miriam. She used the slang with expert efficiency, shortening her sentence to three words. A man in a stylish coat overheard it and gave her a curious glance. Miriam noticed him. She didn't need an annoyed or curious bystander trying to decipher her Withil. She smiled at him and, with a fake accent, told him she was Ilek.

The man took her diversion like a compliment and flirted back, a bit too loudly. He got a look of warning from the surgeon. When he glanced back to grin sheepishly at Miriam, she was ignoring him. He adjusted his arm on the railing and focused once more on the slippery scene below.

The surgeon had slit the man's belly and clamped it open under the lights. Subtle movements occasionally rippled through the mass of entrails that packed the cavity, causing men and women to swoon.

Large attendants near the doors dragged them quietly from the room.

"This is the liver," Dr. Billium was saying. "An organ for cleansing the blood." He pointed to a dark shape while the man's life ran through tubing, feeding out from his body into the brown chemiostatic machine. Another tube returned the blood after some dubious treatment, sluicing it back in. Several of the glass bulbs had been hooked up to his arms by means of needles held in place with elastic bandages; they dripped clear fluid through the pink-orange hoses to his veins.

From what Dr. Billium was saying, it seemed that a floating rib and a strange ossified mutant rib from his zygomatic process had grown down into his soft organs and was causing him pain.

The surgeon wiped his hands on his lapels and lifted a bone saw from the table.

"THERE'S something afoot in Isca," whispered the half-sister. "Something strange going on in the Court."

"Unless it has to do with the book, forget it," hissed Miriam. "If Megan is forced to cast the hex . . . you don't want to be here when it happens."

"It will look a bit odd if I let a flock of fifty pigeons loose at once," said the half-sister.

"It can't be helped. You'll be leaving anyway. No one will have time to send an inquisitor. You'll be provided new positions in Wardale or Yorba."

Miriam watched the half-sisters. She could tell their hearts had sunk. They would take their children of course, bundle them up in the middle of the day while their husbands were working. Some would leave a note behind, others nothing.

"But Ghoul Court!" insisted the half-sister. "There's something going on. Something to do with the brickyard . . . and the old brewery. A squad of watchmen were sent last Day of Dusk. They found nothing but I'm sure the Willin Droul are holding meetings there."

Miriam grew interested enough to clarify. "The Vindai brewery?"

The half-sister nodded.

"I'll look into it myself," said Miriam. "But I want everyone else out of the Duchy."

Placated, the half-sister grew quiet. Miriam instructed her subordinates to wait until the surgery had come to its conclusion.

The gray man had endured a much larger incision than was necessary for the sake of showmanship. The good doctor had cut him neck to nuts in order to show off all his vital organs. The poor had no choice. Unable to pay for their own care, they signed papers allowing the hospital to sell tickets to their "event."

He was stitched up and rolled away while puddles of blood dribbled down the drain in the center of the floor.

Sickened and dizzy and strangely elated or depressed, the spectators were ushered out with a definite feeling that they had gotten their money's worth.

From the darkened court, lit mainly by the tube of ebbing fluid, the four witches parted without a word. They vanished into alleys and over bridges, becoming part of Isca's degenerate underbelly, heading off to spread word of their exodus.

Back inside, one of the fifteen-year-old boys began sponging up the rest of the show.

THREE miles through the urban sprawl of South Fell and Thief Town sat the Murkbell Opera House.

Only half a mile from Ghoul Court, the opera house stood among the canals of Murkbell with a kind of gray and sinister splendor. Romantics could approach the opera by boat, poled along the avenues.

There were sections of Murkbell that still stood in rarefied grandeur (the opera house being one of them) and many historians and antique collectors lived in crumbling opulence along the borough's southern stretch.

As the largest borough in Isca, Murkbell had room for diversity. From the black confusion of Vog Foundry—which seemed to crawl out of Growl Mort like something hideous and half-dead—the industrial loll of noxious factories and warehouses full of coal gave way to tenements near the wasteyard in Brindle Fen.

South and west, the numberless network of canals were cleaner, dragging discarded newspapers and empty bottles along their bottoms rather than the sediments of heavy industry. Except for Bragget Canal, which came out of Ghoul Court, the waters were lucid and gleaming and reflected the ostentatious houses of the very eccentric and the very rich.

Like many of the other buildings, the Murkbell Opera House had been built when Isca was young. It rested on enormous stone piers that supported it like a dollhouse on a pair of unseen sawhorses, allowing it to straddle forgotten sewers and vaults that now served to collect most of the city's rainfall.

The capacity of the vaults was sufficient that Isca's sewers had never needed extensive redesign. They sucked floods down an ineluctable network of straws like a fat girl at a soda fountain and pushed them through turbines toward the bay where powerful geysers of odious water gushed into the sea.

The same night the witches met at the surgery, after the curtain came down on *Er Krue Alteirz* and the hundreds of candles in the chandelier had been extinguished, the manager walked the halls of his opera.

Reddish-orange light fixtures cast tangerine glows across walls the color of exotic olives. Russet shadows depended from blackened boxes in the theater walls; frescoes filled plaster ovals across the baroque ceiling.

The masked ladies who sold concessions had gone home. The huge brass beehive with its gauges and pipettes serving flavored soda and whipped coffee had been cleaned out and rolled into a brooding corner. The stage lights were dim. The actors had vanished, scurrying off to various parties held in historical penthouses and rooftop pubs that glimmered across Murkbell's cruel skyline.

Mr. Naylor, the opera manager, walked his empty establishment with keen pink eyes. Like cheap glassy buttons, they seemed as unreal as they were ugly.

He blinked them constantly, wetting them many times a minute as he searched the opera for a dawdling janitor or any other kind of trespasser. He moved with his hands perched awkwardly on his hips, smacking his mouth as though he needed a drink. His tongue was pasty and sticky with spit. His pink eyes were fiendishly sharp.

He stopped to check his pocket watch. It was after midnight. One-something. He didn't bother to tell the exact minutes.

He descended a black stairwell without light and walked stiffly across the ornate carpet of the ground floor. When he seemed satisfied that everything was secure he stopped and stood in the foyer for a long time, listening to the quiet.

Finally he turned and stalked down an obscure corridor that led beneath the stairs. It was filled with buckets and mops and push brooms and bottles of wax. Mr. Naylor unlocked a short door, barely four feet tall, at the back of the passageway. Like a grasshopper folding its legs in impossible compression he climbed into the cramped space, forcing his body down between his legs and bending his neck in such a way that it looked like he had been murdered and stuffed inside. His hand reached out and pressed a square button on the wall then quickly withdrew like a tentacle, afraid of being severed.

The button clicked and a dull banging motor that filled the space with the smell of burnt grease slowly unwound the service elevator on its frayed and shaky cable, sinking Mr. Naylor into questionable depths.

He was quite uncomfortable, the descent excruciatingly slow. He smacked his mouth and waited patiently as the elevator trembled slightly and the banging motor strained.

There was no light. His pink eyes couldn't see a thing.

When the ride finally ended he pushed open a crude hatch, much different than its walnut-paneled twin far above, and stepped into a dark space, grasshopper legs unfolding.

He stood in an immense barrel vault similar to the secret meat rail Caliph had ridden with Mr. Vhortghast. This, however, was better lit with candles and phosphorescent fungus and odd lights that seemed to issue from below the waterline.

Mr. Naylor walked along a cement platform, having picked up a candle box to light his way. He descended some steps into the water and sloshed toward an island of rounded brick that raised its slippery hump above the lake of sewage, shoes instantly ruined.

"Cut that light you muck!" said a voice from the island. It was a hideous garbled voice, barely capable of human articulation. Mr. Naylor tossed the candle box into the lake as if it had been crumpled wax paper from one of the sandwich shops on Freshet Way. It sank almost immediately. The light went out.

A vague stink issued from the darkness at the top of the domed island. Much different from sewage. It stank like rotting salmon—a stench that gripped Mr. Naylor with fear. Perhaps one of *them* had come. One of the *flawless*!

"Lift your shirt, muckety," said the same ruthless voice. Mr. Naylor obeyed. His pink eyes were getting used to the gloom. He could make out dark shapes crouched around the slick crown of the island, buttery with fungal growths. He hunkered down to join them after eyes better than his had found the tattoo above his navel.

Another shape started burping. Hot, reeking blasts erupted noisily into the already close air.

Several eructations followed, resonant and deep. Soon the island was moaning with them, guttural and melancholy sounding. They were like the sounds of strange frogs, sad and pitched. Changeable. Now like something gasping through a reed. Now like great volumes of slow wind yawning through the sewers.

Mr. Naylor knew the sounds traveled for miles. He had overheard a man at the opera telling another man about his singing toilet. How he had felt the reverberations in his ass and leapt up, the *Herald* and his smoke still in hand, looking fearfully into the water as though something might reach out and grab him. "It sang," he said. "Like a drafty window, sort of, but I'm telling you: my toilet sang."

Mr. Naylor pictured the man after several ineffective flushes, watching the bowl continue to vibrate, holding his breath and straining to hear the very faint and secret sounds of the Iscan Council of the Willin Droul.

Mr. Naylor was not participating as much as the others. His weak body could not produce the sounds that the other Council members could. Thankfully, none of the flawless were here tonight. He did not relish the chance of being randomly eaten.

Mr. Naylor did not participate but he did pay close attention. They were telling a story he had already heard about one of the flawless that had walked lines to the Porch of Soth in search of the book. One of the flawless had been beaten back because the book's owner had made a pact with *The Hidden*.

"She has it! She has it!" bellowed one of the black shapes. Its language was not spoken in anything resembling human form, but Mr. Naylor understood.

"How can you be sure?" moaned another.

"I told you, word has come from Yǫloch. They verified the story."

"Yes, but we've heard nothing from them for decades and now they want us to storm Isca Castle? How do they know she's coming here? How do they know anything at all?"

"Those in Ŭlung know. If those in Ŭlung find out we are loath help—"

"We are not loath to help." The amount of phlegm in the voice made it seem like the speaker would choke. "I do not even want to talk about such a thing. We will help. We must help. We have sat useless for centuries and now when word comes, we try to pretend that we know better? Even these brainless mucks are smart enough to listen and obey."

Mr. Naylor took no offense at the speaker's words. His pink eyes could not quite penetrate the gloom.

"So . . . Yǫloch says she's coming. Fine. If they say she'll be in the High King's Castle, fine. But we've already got a muckety in there. Why do we need to organize a raid?"

"The muck is difficult to reach. He has been quiet for years . . . and . . . we don't want to give away our position."

Another of the creatures made a bubbling sound. The equivalent of "Hmmmm." Then it spoke. "I wonder. The opera muck might be able to give us a third chance. Why not let him have a go at getting it for us?" Mr. Naylor grew even more attentive now that they were specifically discussing him. "If she winds up staying at the castle she'll certainly attend the opera at some point and if not, then at least we've got the other two options."

The whole gruesome obscure assemblage seemed to mewl and smack their mouths together as though tasting the suggestion.

"Yes. Yes. That's a fine idea. We'll let the opera muck try his hand."

Finally Mr. Naylor spoke.

"Who is she?"

The creatures chuckled at his expense because he had come late and missed a large part of the meeting.

"Some Shradnæ Witch who's been poking around Yọloch. She found the *Cịsrym Tạ*! Stupid crawler who thinks she can open it and read it like poetry. She has no idea what it means. None at all. We have to get it back and send it to Ŭlung—they'll know what to do."

"What is her name?" asked Mr. Naylor.

"Name? Name? Stupid muck. We don't know her name. But she'll be Sslîạ if we don't get it back from her soon. She'll be Sslîạ to us all if we don't stop her from opening the book." The thing speaking wrung its hands in a horrid parody of human behavior.

Mr. Naylor smiled.

"I'll need her name if I'm going to invite her to the opera."

"Names. Muckety wants names."

The creatures were quite intelligent but they were plagued by their half-states, unable to escape the clutches of madness brought on by too much of two kinds of blood.

"We'll get you names, you muck. We'll get you all the names you need for the crawler with the *Cịsrym Tạ*."

"Wonderful," said Mr. Naylor as though speaking to one of the burgomasters that frequented his shows. "I'll set about it at once just as soon as I know who she is."

Something large and heavy slid into the water. The Council was breaking up.

Mr. Naylor stood and brushed himself off as though doing so might solve the ruinous slime that had soaked into his pants. He turned and began sloshing back toward the platform and the weary elevator.

"Mr. Naylor!" burped the voice from the island. It was the first time it had spoken Hinter instead of the guttural language used during the meeting. The first time it had used his name. "Make sure you are careful on this one. Make certain you are extra, extra careful."

"Of course," said Mr. Naylor. He smiled and continued toward the platform where he crammed himself back into the tiny compartment and rode the banging lightless box back to reality.

CHAPTER
14

The brown many-tiered spires of Isca City slid skyward over a twisting baroque catacomb of lanes and streets. Glimbenders squeezed out of offal-piled nests behind glowing clock towers.

In the evening, they took to the air: mad droves of singular candent eyeballs stitched with fur and bat wings. They tumbled, gracile bits of blackened ash or street confetti into the sky; whirling out from belfries and cupolas and campaniles, searching for stray cats and dogs, quadrupeds of virtually any kind into whose brains they would drive their slug-filled ovum.

In Lampfire Hills, the buildings grew together as in other sections of the city: nine, twelve, twenty stories high. Dozens of flying buttresses and arches straddled the lanes at various heights, passing thrust onto and between buildings, shoring up the city with dangerous interdependence.

A clockwork shop on the corner of Tower and Mark displayed cuckoos and pocket watches, flickering with the bubbly green glow of chemiostatic fluid.

A deep-hooded figure slid past the shop, down Mark Street. It turned east on Seething Lane, left the pawnshops and clothiers behind, walking briskly for the derelict brewery that sulked in the shadow of Ghoul Court's south side.

Miriam stopped under the huge decaying shingle whose paint had erupted in a rash of hives. She could barely read the name: VINDAI'S BREWERY.

She melted into the darkness along the north wall, shedding light like water.

A tangle of pipes extruded out and up from the brewery's sides and roof like fingers come through a meat grinder. The dank alley surrounding the brewery was littered with glass and scuttling refuse that moved torturously in the wind.

She took hold of a sturdy elbow and mounted the wall, careful not to throw her weight in such a way that might buckle or snap the tenuous moorings.

There were faint sounds weltering through the shattered panes of glass. Coiling broken bits of conversation in Trade, not meant to be heard, rose heatedly into the deserted air.

The city was quiet here: only the drone of distant factories and the low, almost unheard hum of far-off conversations mixing with streetcars and footsteps and wind. The collective muffled roar hardly interfered with her ability to eavesdrop on the voices issuing from the brewery's lightless interior.

". . . got away. But not the others. Both dead."

Someone answered. ". . . to be expected . . . not without a price." The voices were passionate and tense as though discussing something monumentally significant.

Miriam's fingertips were the only parts of her hands not covered by supple leather gloves. They searched the window ledge with expert care, feeling for blades of broken glass or loose mortar—any kind of dangerous debris. Her ears had tuned themselves to the conversation going on inside and she could now make out larger parts of what they were saying.

"Once this thing is stripped down I s'pose we'll have the honor of carting it across town in chunks."

The other voice muttered something indiscernible as Miriam found a handhold and pulled herself up into the casement. Her cloth boots had soft tacky rubber soles. They made no sound.

For a moment her body cut a lithe silhouette against the gray gloom of the alley while her eyes struggled to sort the murky shapes inside the building. Miriam had not carved her eyes. There was no way to tell whether the occupants would happen to look in her direction while she formulated her next move. All she could do was minimize her exposure by moving swiftly from conspicuous to hidden.

The element of chance was unavoidable.

Finally she made out a rusted tank. A great cylinder on its side. She leapt, lighted on its top, legs buckling to absorb her weight as soundlessly as possible. Even so, the landing produced a dull hum as the metal caved slightly and reverberated under her weight.

"What was that?"

Miriam opened her mouth and made a sound exactly like a cat. She tossed a shard of glass onto the floor.

"Some tom gone hunting," said the other voice. "Where are you putting these?"

"Pile's over there. Keep the fat ones separate. They go to the housing."

"Fuck off! I know the difference between an anchor bolt and a—"

"Shh—"

Miriam stopped. She had left the tank and now crouched behind a thick staple of black pipe. A broken jar had scraped slightly as her foot touched it. The darkness was nearly impenetrable and she cursed silently that the gray row of squares through which she had come did not shed enough light to reach the floor. The windows served only to outline vague canisters and barrels that had once held grain.

Great bulkheads of machinery and partially scavenged stills occluded her vision. While the glow of a lantern crept around one great black shape and wavered on a slick of oil, it did not reach through the jungle of wheeled bins and other objects that cluttered the area around her.

Miriam bit her lip in frustration.

"Better check it out," said one of the voices.

The sound of some heavy metal tool dragged across the floor. A man's shadow passed in front of the lantern light.

"If it's a cat, I'll give it a new shape." Miriam saw the giant shadow of a wrench swing across the cement and disappear into crowding pools of darkness.

There was something crawling through her hair. Gingerly she reached up and plucked it from the side of her face, tossed it aside without emotion.

She focused on where the searching man had gone. His footsteps echoed slightly, bouncing off countless metal bodies and the huge empty curve of ceiling overhead.

Miriam's pupils had dilated to their widest possible diameter, crying out for any trace of light. She could see a ladder on the side of some tall metal structure. A chute perhaps that emptied into an enormous drum. She reached out for it hesitantly, keenly aware that the level of corrosion in the building made her peril that much greater.

She couldn't tell what surfaces might support her weight and which ones might give way, call her out amid a ragged collapse of gashing metal edges and bars clattering to the floor.

She withdrew her hand from the ladder and melted back behind the tank, moving slowly but persistently away from the last place she had made noise.

Suddenly the beam of a chemiostatic torch cut a wide cone behind her, lime-colored light running over chains and pipes and wires. Miriam froze.

There was a support strut bolted to the wall that helped stabilize the tank. Biting her lip she crouched on it, pulling her feet up so that the torch wouldn't reveal her legs if the man looked underneath.

The green light panned across the wall and up toward the ceiling.

"Shh, you daft prick! Keep that down from the windows. You want someone to see?"

The searching man did not respond but the light dropped and flicked under the tank. Miriam could hear the man getting down on his hands and knees. The light played back and forth, inches below her feet.

"There's nothing back here."

Miriam used the light to her advantage, memorizing every detail of the landscape behind the tank. Then she closed her eyes to advance the process of readjusting to the dark. When she opened them the light was gone and the man had moved away, clomping over crumbling piles of discarded sheet metal and broken glass.

Miriam used his racket to mask her own sounds. She moved quickly and quietly through the dark jumble and into the diagonal shadows of a tall movable rack.

She could now see the lantern and the crouched forms of both men as the second one settled in again beside a large piece of dirty machinery. He switched off the torch.

"Nothing there," he muttered.

"I heard you the first time," said the other man. Both of them were covered in dust and grease. "Put that bar in here and pry up while I loosen this nut, will you?"

The second man thrust a heavy round crowbar into the engine and bent his back. They were dismantling some huge contraption that looked alien to and much newer than the apparatuses of the brewery. They had stacked various parts in neat piles around the floor.

Miriam had no idea what they were up to. She had come here only because the meeting at the surgery had prompted an investigation and additional leads indicated something was happening here at Vindai's.

Her plan had been to nose about. She had not expected to find anyone.

She slunk closer, behind a pyramid of metal drums whose skins of salmon-orange paint fled rapidly spreading patches of corrosion.

"I don't think we'll have to carry it across town," said the first man, going back to their earlier conversation. "But I bet we have to be there to put it back together."

"Yeah. And soon," said the second. "They ain't goin' back for seconds on this one. It's gonna be all or nothing. Trust me."

"You know what burns me?" The first man paused from his work. "I heard they got the opera muck running the first half of the show. I bet he puts little miss in a glass wagon right off, and all our late nights here are for nothing."

The second man tilted his head sideways and scrunched up his face, dramatizing his uncertaninty. "I don't know . . . the engine ain't about puttin' her down. Ŭlung says we're s'posed to hit 'em everywhere at once . . . cuz we only got one chance at it. See, we gotta put the Sslîą in a box *before* she's Sslîą . . . otherwise, there ain't no goin' back. And at the same time, we gotta get the book. So this is a complex sorta thing. Killin' her and stealin' from her at the same time, before there's any warning . . . before the fuckin' bulls know what hit 'em . . ."

There was the sound of some small part falling through the machine and clattering on the floor.

The man cursed, reached for the torch and flicked it on. Miriam faded back behind the drums. She peered between the imperfect slit where they met.

"I can't reach it," said the first man. "Can you lift it up a bit?" His shirt came up and Miriam saw the Hįlid Mark above his navel.

Her plan turned from eavesdropping to interrogation.

The second man took hold of a driveshaft of some kind. "Not there, you clay-brained hedge-pig. You want to bend it? Grab it there, by the frame."

The second man obeyed without rebuttal. Miriam heard him grunt. Veins roped his arms and neck as he cradled one end of the machine in his lap and lifted.

"If you drop this on me I'll—"

Miriam was already moving. She had darted out from her hiding place and slipped up behind the second man, circling his throat with the crescent of her knife. He let out a gasp and the machine plunged down, crushing the first man's arm underneath and pinning him to the floor. A scream of pain rocked the brewery and lifted out the shattered windows into the desolate alleys and dead-end streets.

Miriam backed the second man away from the machine, her sickle knife tugging at his skin. A vicious collar that made it impossible for him to swallow. The first man gurgled in agony, holding to the shoulder of the pinned arm with his free hand.

His eyes were glazed.

Miriam's arms had folded expertly around the second man's head, locking him in with her blade. As she moved him backward away from the machine, she called out to the first man's blood, leaking from his arm like engine oil onto the floor. The Unknown Tongue and the Sisterhood's brand of hemofurtum gathered his holojoules.

She seemed to choke on the throaty sounds that molded the coalescing power.

Then she finished the argument: "⹀𝄫 𝄢."[15]

The air around the engine wavered like warped mirrors at a carnival, bending space into thin or fat distortions. Parodies of its own self. The trapped man screamed as his body began to colliquate and fuse with the metal.

Miriam froze in horror. Her equation was not supposed to do that. She could only watch in stupefied amazement as her formula went haywire, derailing and turning on itself, mutant and rogue and powerful.

Even the man in her lethal grasp went slack as he watched in fascination something grotesque and wild rippling around the machine.

Megan's transumption hex wasn't supposed to have happened yet. But that was what made it so dangerous and why the Sisterhood had pulled all their operators out of Stonehold: transumption hexes leaked unpredictably *through* time. This could easily be a premonition ripple that had seeped backward from the future. Miriam had been expecting repercussions but not so soon, not so violent and random . . . and close. She was the last witch in Stonehold, ignoring her own admonition.

"Where is the book?" she hissed into her captive's ear, trying to ignore the horrifying results of her equation.

"Book? What book? I'm just a mechanic—"

Miriam pulled back on the bladed collar around his neck just enough that it broke the skin. "You know what I mean," she whispered. "I want the *Red Book*. I want the *Cisrym Ta*."

Normally the Willin Droul could not be bought or tortured, but this thin-blooded specimen was different. He was close to human, enough that he could be intimidated through violence.

"You are alone," Miriam whispered, "with a Shradnæ Witch." Her words had a visible effect, ending an assortment of possible games he might have otherwise played. He broke immediately.

"We ain't got it—yet."

"Yet? Then you must know who has it or where it is."

She continued to back him away from the disquieting scene by the engine. The equation had resolved, died down like an over-boiling pot.

The first man was dead. It could no longer be determined where his body ended and the machine began. The smell of burnt hair and flesh was catching up to them, flowing outward from the point of violence.

"It's comin' to Isca Castle," muttered the man. His own blood was wet and sticky on his neck. Miriam took him behind the tall movable rack to-

---

[15] U.T. Approximate pronunciation: "! sh !" (! indicates bilabial or dental clicks, epiglottal plosives and other nonstandard sounds).

ward the tank she had landed on when she had first entered the brewery. She stopped.

"Don't make me ask for the rest," she breathed.

"It's comin' with a girl. That's all I know. I don't know when or how. Sometime soon. We're getting ready. We don't know where it's comin' from. It's just comin'. That's all. That's all, I swear."

"Does the girl have a name?"

"Something with an *S* I think. They said Sauna or Sara. Something like that. I'm a crawler. They don't tell me shit. You know that!"

Miriam scowled. Her heart cooled. She bit her lip as her mind began to work.

"Think harder. I need a name. If you can remember all the parts to that engine I'm sure you can remember a simple name."

"I told you. It's with an *S*. That's all I know. It's like Sema or Suana. I don't fucking know!"

His distress was genuine, on the brink of being pathetic. But his last attempt had solidified a gut-turning hunch in Miriam's stomach, something that sickened her at the same time that it gave her hope.

"Was it Sena?"

"Yeah, that's it." The man coughed. "I swear I ain't just playing along. That's the name I heard. How did you—?"

He dropped to his knees, relinquished from the deadly hold. There was the sound of something landing lightly on top of the tank, then the spring of the metal as it retook its original shape.

By the time the man turned around, Miriam had vanished through the same window she had come through and was running full-out down the alley, turning onto Seething Lane, sprinting down the cobbles, heading for home.

The man swore softly and touched his throat, beginning to formulate a story. Something simple, something he could remember if he was asked to retell it exactly, many times in a row.

WHEN Miriam reached her flat in Maruchine she mounted the iron steps to her window in a winded flurry. She had left the casement open. Cool night air lapped past the tattered curtains, sinking the darkened apartment to a reclusive, somehow impolite temperature.

Miriam had never used the small coal-burning stove that tottered in the corner. She struck a match and lit an oil lamp. Orange light scraped over uneven plaster, revealing a room as exhausted as Miriam after her two-mile run.

She didn't want to believe that Sena had somehow found the *Cisrym*

Ta̧. It seemed preposterous that Megan's protégé could have discovered it and kept it secret when there were so many eyes looking for it, scouring the Hinterlands from here to Yorba.

Maybe Megan had planned it. Maybe she had found the book and given it to Sena to hide and reveal at some later time. A maneuver that would ensure Sena's ascension to the tunsia circlet of Coven Mother.

No. Megan could not be trusted. Not with this particular information.

The realization filled Miriam with fear. She grew sick to think that she was going behind the Coven Mother's back. But she had to be sure. She had to treat the man's words as though they might be true, as though there were no other women named Sena in the north.

Miriam pondered the man she had interrogated. It was always difficult to tell, but she guessed he had told her the truth as far as he knew it. He was a weak link in the Cabal's chain now. If his own order did not discover his treachery, she might return to him, find him again and extract additional information. It was no danger to leave him alive.

Between a dark cage and a ramshackle sideboard cluttered with bottles, Miriam adjusted the lamp flame and penned a hasty note in Withil, using miniscule letters to conserve space on the tiny roll. In it, she warned of all she had learned, the implications and the fact that the Duchy had been evacuated. All the Sisters that could, had gone through Menin's Pass into Mira̧yhr.

Then she rolled the tiny scroll tightly and pressed it into a leather tube.

She opened the cage. Its bottom had been lined with yesterday's newspaper, headlines still shouting with idiot urgency: HIGH KING'S FATHER MURDERED! MISKATOLL TO BLAME!

Two-thirds of the city had rallied around their new king with news of the assassination. In a twisted political way, his father's death had been a stroke of luck for Caliph Howl.

Gently, she lifted the cage's occupant out into the lamplight. She snapped the tube to a permanent clip around the pigeon's leg and then removed a hood that kept the bird blind and quiet.

The pigeon's head had been altered ruthlessly. Its left eye glowed with green chemiostatic fluid that powered a series of small clockwork devices buried in the creature's brain. The feathers had been hacked away at the top of the skull; a square patch of bone was revealed, screwed with a little tin.

Miriam drew a triangular piece of metallic mineral from one of the bottles with a tweezers and set it in a similarly shaped socket in the tin. She pressed it down hard with her thumb until it snapped into place.

The bird shook its head as though infested with parasites. Some itch in its brain that would never resolve.

The cruestone would alter the bird's path; take it to the tower of parliament's Eighth House, to the rookery of Giganalee's discreet hand.

Miriam walked to the window and flung the bird into the night air. The cruestone would goad it; complete a circuit through the cruel device in its head that fired electricity into its brain. It would prevent it from resting. It would whip it relentlessly toward its destination in the Country of Mirạyhr, tiny wires like fiery worms burrowing into what little consciousness it had left.

Miriam hoped she had done the right thing; that if the information she had been given was false, her sense of practicality would be recognized and her disregard for hierarchy overlooked.

If what she had learned was true, only Giganalee could be trusted, only the Eighth House would know what to do. But Miriam understood the risk she had taken.

In case she had miscalculated, her hopes were false. There would be no lenience for operating behind the Coven Mother even with the good of the Sisterhood in mind. Her conduct would be seen as betrayal and faithlessness to Megan's rule.

As Miriam listened to the sound of the pigeon's wings beat into the filthy night, she turned slowly and began to gather up her things.

A foreign ambassador, added last minute to Caliph's itinerary, joined him for dinner. His name was Bjorūn Amphungtạl and he was from Pandragor.

Considering Sigmund's recent disclosure of the solvitriol plans and the death of Caliph's father just four days ago, Mr. Amphungtạl's timing was extraordinary, like a crow settling on a carcass.

Despite the surprise, Gadriel had orchestrated, in a matter of eighteen hours, a phenomenal affair, complete with crisped haunches and baked pears. Hooves wreathed in rosemary folded reverently beneath legs dribbling juice.

Candied fruits capered around bottles of red wine and hot breads added their plumes to the delicious bank of fog.

It was gorgeously barbaric. The piles of food seemed to have been thrown with force onto the sprawling table, but everything had been arranged to entice and overawe. The silverware was gold, the napkins crimson silk, the plates of ancient Pplarian design.

On seeing the room, Caliph was reminded of Stonehold's visceral history. Gadriel directed him toward the highest chair at center, after which all the other guests took their seats.

The room stilled. Caliph made an impromptu speech welcoming his guests and, as usual, thanked the staff.

After that, Gadriel spoke the traditional Hinter charm, making several unclear passes over the food with his hands.

Caliph withheld a smile. The ancient clannish ritual caused Mr. Amphungtạl to fidget and glance sideways at his secretary. When the singsong charm came to its traditional boisterous end, everyone except the foreigners added their voices to the final shouted syllable. An echo that faded like thunder from the hall.

Mr. Amphungtạl jumped a little; then offered a pained smile. The amount and presentation of the food seemed to confuse him. He was new and probably sent as political fodder in case something went wrong. He looked to his neighbors for direction and figured out soon enough that it was a help-yourself affair that required a certain amount of forward behavior.

After dinner, Caliph and Mr. Amphungtal retreated to the east parlor for ice cream and brandy where the Pandragonian's uncertainty was set aside along with dessert.

"We know you have them." One of the key phrases that Caliph realized he would take away from this discussion. It became clear that Mr. Amphungtal's doubtfulness had been left at the dinner table. Now Caliph watched the ambassador's dark eyes glitter, noticed how softly the Pandragonian man smiled when he said, "We're just looking for a way to have a peaceful, low-profile resolution . . . and of course we need extradition of the thieves."

Caliph thought about turning the blueprints over. He didn't *need* them. The only problem was that if he did that, Pandragor would have proof of the crime. And if he failed to turn Sigmund and David over . . . to extradite them . . . the Iscan Crown would appear to be harboring criminals.

Caliph didn't like Mr. Amphungtal's supercilious smile. It reminded him of college, of a certain professor at college who had smiled the same way when he had held a grade over Caliph's head. It was a smile that said, "I'm one up on you, boy . . . and there's nothing you can do about it."

In the end, it was loyalty that determined Caliph's response. He couldn't turn Sig and David over. He just couldn't.

"I'm sorry," said Caliph, "that your country lost its blueprints. I'm also sorry that I'm unable to help." Caliph watched the smile crumble, piling up at the bottom of the ambassador's face as a reconstituted frown. It felt good to toss a pebble into Amphungtal's glassy disdain and see the angry ripples spread out under his face.

It also felt like a huge political mistake.

Sena traveled from Crow's Eye to Null Hill.

She was accompanied from all directions by a throng of black ghostly shapes that crossed roads at night, heading unerringly for the heavy, thick-walled buildings of Skellum whose tiny panes of glass twinkled dissolute and golden. By the fifth, all of them had reached the ancient town.

Sena arrived midmorning and went straight to parliament, passing an enormous sledge newt tethered at the gates. It hissed while its collection of slippery black eyes glinted in the sun.

From there, she passed into the garden where statues swam amid white rosebushes. Large sapphire-tinted butterflies nuzzled the blooms and fornicated indiscriminately.

Sena saw a woman in a lavish costume wandering the yard. On her head was an incredible crown that started as a band at the back of her neck and rose behind her ears, completing its loop at the very top of her forehead. Blades of deep blue metal fanned back as stylized feathers, spreading like an array of ornate knives. The front of the thing sloped down into a graven mask accented with bits of lapis. It obscured everything but her eyes from the cheekbones up.

Haidee had been in the Sixth House only weeks ago; now she was wearing the ceremonial headgear of the Seventh. She returned Sena's greeting in Withil. "Clea's bird brought word that you had gone to Sandren rather than Tue. What happened?"

Sena dropped Niṣ, sensing that perhaps something was wrong. The cat immediately began chasing butterflies.

Sena had known Clea would inform on her and had been constructing a feasible lie based on the Sisterhood's existing paranoia. "I was following a lead. I think it was the Cabal."

"Really?" Haidee was looking at Sena's hair. Sena had dyed it black.

"It washes out. I needed to cut a low profile getting out of Sandren."

"Yes . . . I think we've all heard about the stonemason's body. That's amusing, the Seventh House using that kind of street thief charlatanry? Why not just carve your eyes?"

Sena snorted. She didn't like Haidee's cool smile or the way she carried herself: perfectly erect under the extraordinary costume.

"I don't blame you," said Haidee.

"What?" Sena looked startled.

Haidee clarified. "I don't condone your flagrant abuse of the Sisterhood or your disregard for coven law but I don't blame you for feeling the way you do. It would have been hard all those years, standing in her shadow, having her correct your every move, having to live up to some unattainable mark. Still," her chin dipped indicating a mild reproach was on the way, "I think your lifelong rebellion against Megan is childish—no matter what was done to your mother. Megan didn't—"

"You can stop there."

"All I'm saying is that Megan acted indiscriminately—"

"You're right. Setting your friend on fire *is* pretty fucking indiscriminate, isn't it?"

"I'm sorry," said Haidee. "I should have said *impartial*. Coven law protects us . . ."

Sena whirled. "What are we doing? Why do we need to be protected?

What is our goal anyway? Kill off or seduce anyone with the ability to challenge or discover us? For what? What are we preparing for?"

"We empower women—"

"Oh gods, stow that shit! I'm so sick of our diagrams of self-actualization at the expense of others. You and I both know the Sisterhood's philosophies are just a means to an end. What is it? What is Megan planning?"

"If you had been around more . . . instead of . . . mucking about in the Highlands of Tue, you might already know."

"I was doing research."

"You were supposed to be spying."

"What is Megan doing?"

Haidee's smile leaked across her face, serene and supercilious. "Preparing for war."

"With whom? The Duchy of Stonehold?"

"The Willin Droul, you artless scut. Don't you know anything anymore? You and I used to talk before you left for Desdae with that foot-licking wine peddler from Sandren. Megan may be naïve enough to believe that you didn't give him something in return for your tuition but I'm not. She might even call it pårin if she found out—"

"Which would be correct . . . if it were true. I haven't seen him since I graduated. He was nothing to me."

"So you're saying you went to school for the Sisterhood's benefit? Pårin is for the good of the whole not for the good of the one. Megan should have seen through you long ago—"

"And why is that?" asked Megan.

Both girls whirled. The Shrâdnæ Mother stood within arm's length, curiously obscured until that very instant, positioned at an angle just outside peripheral vision. Haidee went white. Sena simpered.

But her simper deteriorated instantly when she saw the look on Megan's face. Like the look of a pet hound, Sena had expected familiarity regardless of Megan's mood. But this was something else, the look of an animal that had unexpectedly turned on its owner: quiet, uncertain and lethal.

The Shrâdnæ Mother wore a ceremonial robe. It was much simpler than the attire of the Seventh House because Megan, even as Coven Mother, resided only in the Sixth. Her robe's shoulders did not curl up but the fabric had been stitched with shiny threads of metallic blue in an arabesque pattern. Hemmed in black satin, the sleeves fell partly past her wrist, making her fingers look like paws.

Haidee did not try to make excuses. Her apology came quickly and with convincing sincerity. Sena said nothing.

Megan took a drink of something brown and iced and set the glass on the portico railing. She walked toward Sena and embraced her rigidly, leaving an unspoken question floating in her eyes.

"So nice to see you, Mother," Sena cooed.

Megan plucked Nis from where the cat crouched, licking butterfly guts, and began stroking him as if he were hers. "I can't believe the mess you made, Sienæ."

"The Cabal—"

"Shht—not here." Megan glared. She touched Sena's hair like a granger examining blight.

"You grow away, Sienæ. It's not good to live outside the Circle as long as you have."

Megan set Nis down.

"It's temporary. It comes right out."

Megan snorted. "At least it isn't blue or purple or whatever they dye it in the city these days." Megan clucked. "Sienæ, you would look charming if you had no hair at all."

"Thank you, Mother."

Haidee rolled her eyes.

Megan moved back to her sweating drink.

"Come with me, Sienæ."

Her request dismissed Haidee at the same time it left Sena no other choice. Sena saw hatred crawl beneath Haidee's lovely cheeks.

Megan opened a door off the portico and ushered her into a complex of chambers, cool and dim as a cave.

Statuettes stood in nubile poses, gazing across music rooms or onto languid staircases that flowed like syrup from the second floor. A terror bird's head was mounted on one wall. Most of its skull was a six-pound beak, rosy pink fading into dirty white. Fleshy blue skin ringed a set of glassy golden eyes. Sena plopped down in a stuffed chair beneath the trophy.

"How was your trip?" asked Megan.

"Abominable. Muggy—"

"I thought you had a horse . . ."

There was a squat iron canister on the floor fitted with tubing and a tight lid. A chemiostatic cell supplied power. It hissed as Megan unlatched the lid and scooped out a glass full of ice. She poured Sena one of the tall cinnamon drinks and topped it with a straw.

Sena accepted the glass and sipped it greedily, making a fourth of it disappear before she answered.

"I did."

Megan frowned. "You cleaned up after yourself according to Clea but really . . . Sienæ . . . what were you doing in the Halls?"

"Are they looking for me?"

"They were. We provided several thousand gryphs and one night's pârin to the chief constable, I think you know him, last name Hews. He's not an easy man to bribe but he's been aching for this girl we placed a year ago, Autumn? We knew his taste and were hoping to use her for something more sensible. What got into you?"

"It was the Cabal."

Megan raised her eyebrows. "Of course it was! Clea checked. Gavin bore the mark!"

Sena was momentarily stunned by the detail, fearful and embarrassed that she hadn't checked Gavin herself and simultaneously grateful that the facts supported her fabrication.

"Why did you go to Sandren?"

"To close my bank account."

"Why didn't you tell me?"

"Gods, Mother! You know how you are! You didn't even let me get my clothes when you dragged me out of college! But it's *my* money! I earned it. I wanted it." She pretended to sulk.

Megan softened. "Maybe you're right . . . but then what in Emolus' name were you doing in the Halls?"

Now it got tricky. "I overheard Gavin, talking about a meeting with the Cabal. It was supposed to happen there, in the Halls. I thought I was doing the right thing."

"Do you know what the meeting was about?"

"Something about the book."

Megan scrutinized her for a moment. "Tell me how it went wrong."

"It was my fault. I didn't think I'd have to kill him. I didn't plan ahead. I made a false step. He heard me, turned around . . . we never made it to the meeting."

"The Seventh House doesn't make false steps, Sienæ."

"Well, I'm sorry. I'm not exactly that kind of operative, am I? It was my first time."

Megan drummed her fingernails against her glass. Sena knew it was no excuse. She knew the Sisterhood couldn't tolerate this kind of blunder, especially from an Ascendant.

Megan's expression remained soft. "With the Willin Droul hunting us, we have to be careful. There's no telling who to trust."

Sena put her drink down. "If they're such a problem, why not focus on them? Why go to war with Stonehold?"

"War? Who said anything about war?"

"Haidee." It wasn't exactly what Haidee had said, but Sena enjoyed stirring the pot.

Megan snorted. "It's not a war. It's a transumption hex. Pandragor's negotiations with Stonehold have failed. I shouldn't be telling you this, but the Pandragonian Empire isn't paying us for this. It's an exchange of services. They've agreed to help us with the Willin Droul . . . help us locate the book."

Sena tensed. *Wouldn't you die,* she thought, *to know I've already found it! It's sitting in my pack six feet in front of your nose!*

"What's a transumption hex?"

LATER that night when Sena had wriggled into the doll-like allure of the Seventh House's ceremonial dress, painted her eyes black and her lips red and pulled the sepaled mask over her head, she sauntered into Deep Cloister with a mounting sense of dread, ignoring the propositioning looks she received from her Sisters.

She had hidden the *Cisrym Ta* carefully. She knew her belongings could be rifled at any moment.

The great hypostyle of Deep Cloister sat inside the enormous courtyard made by parliament's wings. Deep Cloister was a circular collection of pillars holding up a slightly conical roof.

Sena wove inward through the columns. They were positioned in such a way that no clear line of sight extended to the interior and even daylight choked after forty yards.

Thorn apples grew in profusion throughout Mirayhr and the Sisterhood had gathered leaves earlier that day. Now they boiled them, brewing a drink that promoted visions.

Some had already become sick. Others laughed and ran screaming that they were flying and that the darkness above the columns had dissolved into sky—a sky that flamed and spiraled with brilliant sinister hues of green.

Sena sipped the beverage shoved into her hands and made her way to the center where Megan was already calling loudly from atop a dais of ashen slate.

The Sisterhood responded with unified shrieks of holomorphic formulae. Though the cacophony must have floated far above parliament and filled the streets of Skellum with terrifying echoes, whatever dissidents might have heard stayed well away.

"Tonight we call on the Faceless One." Megan's frail voice lifted from the dais. She held an ornate staff of metal and bone, riddled with tubules and hoses and bundles of wire.

Ghastly and slender, the staff glistered. Tiny gem-like windows revealed its center was filled with chemiostatic fluid. From a distance it looked like glowing chrysoprase decorated its grotesque length.

It was not a Shradnæ implement. This thing had come out of the south. *Out of Iycestoke,* thought Sena. *Or more likely Pandragor itself.*

Wires trailed from the staff's base across the dais to an arcane machine comprised of coils of ydellium tubing that phosphoresced faintly, drawing energy from shifting mile-thick slabs of atmosphere.

Like a gruesome mechanized god, the bulky creation produced strange arbitrary sounds: ticks, knocks and creaks as the fluid that filled the tubing expanded or contracted. Tiny valves occasionally exhaled uncanny spurts of vapor, pouring a pastel shroud of halitus out and down across the dais, cloaking Megan's feet in icy tendrils.

Like a tuning fork, the staff had begun to hum, the blades of bone to resonate and slice through air somehow thick as cooking fat. Maybe it was just the thorn apple drink. Sena set hers on the floor and watched in fascination from beside one of the ubiquitous columns.

Megan was speaking in the Unknown Tongue.

Sena's throat went dry as the numbers behind the words and the meaning behind the numbers rose in a distorted spiral through the displaced roof and into the sky.

The tuning staff sang an oscillating, bone-shivering sweetness, a keen, a razor cutting, a howl, a bone-shattering sledge, a feather tickling. The sound induced spasms, sudden vivid nightmares that Sena could never after describe.

As Megan raised her staff, the throng of witches poured blood, the Sisterhood's own blood, into the argument. Hemofurtum . . . but willingly, consciously.

The Unknown Tongue poured from the assemblage, fortifying the math: "ᘓᘐ ᘕᘎᘅᘎᘊ ᘏᘈ ᘅᘐᘋᘈ! ᘓᘐ ᘕᘎᘅᘎᘊ ᘏᘈ ᘅᘐᘋᘈ!"[16]

Witches jackknifed, clutched their stomachs. They vomited blackness. What came out of their mouths did not hit the floor but purled upward like ink gouts in water. Winding skyward. Imbuing the spinning green clouds.

Convulsive twitching gripped their bodies, arrhythmic shudders that

---

[16] U.T. Approximate pronunciation: "Quem sah-aydl-ntah hkdlim!"

sucked from inside their chests. Their arms, legs and heads flailed like marionettes. A surreal paroxysm of extraordinary violence.

The very substance of space and dimension quailed, undulated, air sluggish now and even thicker, like sewage. Like curdled milk. Rippling and heaving. Solids bled into vapor. Vapor solidified. Liquids became plasmodia—mobile and sentient. The stone columns began to seep into the sky, drooling up like candles melting from the bottom, gravity reversed.

Sena tried to flee but the air rebuked her, heavy and suffocating. Warm pudding. Her arms lengthened. Melting candy. Honey drizzled across the vacant roof.

She clutched a column. It was cool and empty. She fell inside and tumbled up its vacuous length. Not stone. Soluble as gas. Maybe she was vapor. Maybe she didn't exist at all.

The tuning staff's wavelengths broadened, as though its own substance were being altered, vibrating at a lower frequency. She couldn't hear it anymore. She could feel it.

Shut it off! she thought. *You stupid fucking beldam! Shut it off!* She staggered into pudding again, somersaulted through a thicket of black empty columns.

As if in answer to her unspoken demand, there was the faint sound of stone shivering from hundreds of miles or alternate dimensions away. Something came apart beneath a sonic blow. Shards blew. Ricocheted off walls and underground passageways.

Then the machine faltered and the tubing on the staff broke loose under enormous pressure, frequency, vibration, sound, hoses whipping. They left wakes of vapor like white millipedes in air.

Sena couldn't see it except during the split instant when the air returned to normal and the Sisterhood fell to the ground. The women's retching ended as pillars reverted to solid stone. Sena had made it out of the hypostyle.

But in the real world, the summer breeze had grown thick and cold like it sometimes did by the Porch of Soth, like the black nitrous air in the Halls below Sandren.

The clouds over the hypostyle were spinning in a tight whorl and the huge columns shone with ghastly, almost invisible halos.

Sena had to crouch against the wind or be blown over. As she fought, a fetid reek began to fill her lungs. Electricity pulsed overhead. Her robe shredded along strange geometric lines, like paper torn along a crease. She realized her boots were lost, possibly entombed forever in one of the columns, only when her bare foot came down on something cold and wet. Sena saw a salamander lying in the grass.

Its wet skin flickered in the nearly constant lightning, looking pale and ghastly. Its head was crushed open and it stank. Slapping noises struck down all around her in the grass. Frogs, salamanders, even fish falling from the sky.

Screams lost in the storm. Women running this way and that. Some curled into balls in the grass, arms thrown over their heads.

Hail.

A blast of wind picked Sena up and dragged her over the lawn. She clawed her way just lee of a garden statue, listening to the faint tinkle of breaking windows overhead.

Great white chunks of ice bounced in the lawn, seeming to pop up out of the ground. One of the hailstones struck a girl in the shoulder. *They are falling. All of them . . . are falling.*

This is a transumption hex. Using numbers. Taking Grū-ner Shie: the Faceless One, from one place? To another? Sundered distant stones. Stars that form a prison. Far beyond the Nọcrịpa.

I am drugged.

I am falling.

Ϭʜᴇ Key

Ϭhere are legends that fabulize the first time the Cịsrym Tạ
locked itself, just after Davishok and the Rain of Fire. Sena
reads them at Desdae. She discovers how the Tamaraith, that
legendary Ublisi, was forced to unseal her own book in the aftermath of
a terrible disaster. A terrible mistake.

While the pipes from the boiler stir Caliph's dreams she examines an
unusual account from a general turned historian who lived nearly a century ago. In it, he provides his own translation of inscriptions he supposedly found in the Jungles of Ḳhloht that tell how darkness came to Sọth.
He can't present the carvings to the ISSA,[17] he says, because they were
lost along with most of his gear in a Veyden ambush.

No one takes him seriously.

A week of ridicule in scientific journals ends with the mass murder of
a sect of priests that investigators say financed his expeditions. He flees
back to the jungles and though pursued, is never apprehended.

Sena glosses the cutting and turns to another of the man's manuscripts which details (again by unsubstantiated translations) the Cịsrym
Tạ's lock. She skips halfway down the page.

". . . LAST inscription makes it sound like a woman at a restaurant checking the time, waiting for the man that never comes. With disuse it with-
draws into sulking; it has to be coaxed again with a sign of fidelity, a sign
of unwavering commitment. Because there is no key."

THERE has never been a key, reads Sena. Nor are the lock's tumblers
rusted from neglect. They are rusted from use. According to his account,
which Sena copies word for word, the holomorphic lock drinks blood.

It is bizarre. And it gets worse, a bathetic bit of recipe seemingly con-
cocted by someone who knows nothing about real holomorphy.

Sena laughs when she reads it.

---

[17] Iycestoke Society for the Study of Antiquities.

It is sentimental garbage. She begins to side with the general's critics. He is a sham, a homicidal huckster selling trinkets from the jungle.

But then she reads the other clipping.

A story from a journalist out of Stonehold whose story had been republished in an anthology. It recounted a woman's complaint, filed sixty-one years before, about a man, her lover, who had assaulted her, cut her. Sena is captivated. The dates, the names of those implicated cross-reference easily with something else she knows: the only account of the last person to open the Cisrym Tạ.

She goes back to the general's recipe and copies it precisely. Her mind is spinning.

In the darkened library something besides Caliph's breathing makes noise, a sudden itching in her ear. She turns but there is nothing.

Sena re-reads what she has copied.

1 ampoule of thy true love's blood taken by theft.
1 ampoule of thy own blood taken with silver.
1 hunk of dead man's hair taken only in spring or autumn time.
1 ampoule of water blest in the church of Thool.
2 leaves of Trindixahht and meat of the tantun nut.

A STRANGE *argument follows whose numbers, even to Sena, make little sense. She has read it many times since Desdae. Its meaning has grown. She recognizes part of it now as a form of hemofurtum. She carries it in her pack with the Cisrym Tạ.*

The morning after the hex, she washes the black out of her hair and leaves Skellum. The Sisterhood is in disarray. Megan is ill, sleeping with a smell-feast. Sena tells Haidee she is going to Stonehold to spy on the High King in accordance with Megan's wishes.

No one argues or tells her it is unsafe.

Haidee arranges for an electric cab to take her as far as Jụyn Hêl.[18] The starlines there will take her to Stonehold.

FROM her tower window, Giganalee watched Sena go. She had not approved of Megan's decision to sell a transumption hex to Pandragor. Such holomorphy was unpredictable and Giganalee felt certain that the Pandragonians could not even fully understand what they were buying. It would make Stonehold forever dangerous as the effects of the hex seeped through time. The Duchy would be beaten repeatedly, at random intervals,

[18] I.: The Place of Burning.

as if by a blind giant wielding a maul. The devastation would be indiscriminate and unprecedented. Regardless of misgivings, her duty to the Sisterhood was to advise, not control. The Eighth House did not engage in politics.

Giganalee trudged across the room and sat in her throne like a dead thing, claws clutching velvet armrests, head balanced like a skull, trying to see into Sena's future.

Hours passed. The Eighth House did not sleep while she dreamt of red skies and death. She could not catch the shapes, could not pause them in their flight. They soared like scarlet clouds across the murrey pitch, recreant shapes wheeling to turn south; they tried to get away. They were hideous and malevolent as they scooted before the weather, fleeing something far more ominous.

All at once, Giganalee's eyes opened.

The sallow, oily light of dawn slipped through the windows, shearing off around the shape of a bird.

Giganalee dragged a broken tooth across the back of her hand, tearing skin like tissue. She muttered in the Unknown Tongue as her blood broke through the fragile, liver-spotted flesh.

The pigeon came to her, charmed.

It was ugly and in poor health, ragged from mountain winds and weather. It had not been as fast as the Pandragonian albatross that had delivered word of Mr. Amphungtal's failed negotiations.

Giganalee clutched it and carried it to her workbench like a piece of wood. She laid it on its belly, forcing the legs down. With her other hand she pulled a jeweler's screwdriver from a rack of delicate tools.

Using the flat edge she pried the cruestone from the socket in its skull and dropped it into a bottle on the nearby shelf. Then she flipped the bird over on its back and, with a pair of tweezers, pulled the coiled message like a clock spring from its housing.

Her eyes were old and cloudy. Her collection of ornate magnifying glasses lay scattered throughout the room. She shoved the bird into an enormous cage and locked the door.

When she found a lens, she studied Miriam's note under the ochre window light, reading the miniscule Withil with ease. Then she stuffed the paper into her mouth and chewed it to paste, swallowing it like a lump of phlegm. She laid her glass on a small stand near her chair and frowned.

Miriam had done right. She was brave. Brave enough to be Coven Mother someday. Yet Giganalee faltered in her thoughts. After all, it was too much to believe.

How could she have missed it? How could the Eighth House not have seen? If the book had been with Sienæ, it had been in Skellum, within parliament's walls!

How could she not have felt it? How could she not have known?

Giganalee felt fear trickle through her iron insides, cold and unfamiliar. There must be some mistake. Sena could not have found the book. Or could she?

The Eighth House had read legends of the book hiding when it did not want to be found. Giganalee retreated to her chair and uncoiled the tubing from her hookah. She lit it and sucked long cool tendrils of smoke through the water. The facets of the giant spinning bottle caught light, threw different colors across the orreries suspended from the ceiling and encouraged her to dream.

No.

She could not move. Miriam's intelligence must be wrong. If the Eighth House moved without proof, the Sisterhood would stumble, sensing the uncertainty of its leaders. She had to wait. Even if Sena had the book, she couldn't open it.

Giganalee frowned. Sena knew nothing of love.

With twenty-six boroughs and thirty-six square miles of sprawl, Isca City was easily the largest city north of Yorba. Its population exceeded two million and Caliph had more to keep track of.

Keeps and towns with ancient names like Clefthollow and Coldwell slugged against nature, scuffling through mist and cold and marshy fields. They had their own industries and rulers and local villains. Caliph wondered how he could be expected to compass his own section of the Duchy, let alone the other four.

With Saergaeth's threat, Caliph's time for planning was attenuating. He had to know what to do.

Now.

Word had come from Prince Mortiman in Tentinil that the town of Bellgrass had signed a treaty with Miskatoll. Saergaeth's wine-colored flag was creeping south. Great fuming engines scarred the south-sloping plains between the Fluim and White Leech rivers, pressing the prince's borders like a giant thumb at the edge of a blister.

Saergaeth needed Bellgrass because it gave his engines access to the swath of land between the rivers. They rolled south and west out of Miskatoll, heavy metal tracks tearing up the soil, plumes of black smoke and pounding echoes shivering in their wakes.

Willoch Keep had also surrendered without a fight. Without actually attacking, Saergaeth was making headway.

The White Leech was his new border. It fortified Saergaeth's position as much as it hamstrung his further progress. There were few fords capable of accommodating war engines and the prince of Tentinil had taken measures to ensure that nothing crossed the river. He had mined both banks with vitriol explosives and positioned troops to overlook the fords.

For the meantime, Saergaeth's advance ground to a halt, hobbled by defiles his engines could not manage. But Caliph knew it wouldn't last. The metholinate shipments out of the Memnaw had stopped.

He knew with enervating certainty that Saergaeth's zeppelins, which ordinarily transported canisters of gas, were being busily outfitted for war.

Caliph had stockpiled what metholinate Isca had, rationing use with an iron hand. But stingy allocation of resources would not win the fight . . . and it was making the populace uneasy. There were already demonstrations in Gas End. People didn't want to fight their own countrymen, let alone a national hero like Saergaeth Brindlestrom.

People wanted light, hot water and gas to cook with. They didn't want to fight the man who controlled the supply. Saergaeth and Miskatoll, by virtue of the metholinate industry located on the edge of the Memnaw, controlled the largest fleet of zeppelins and war engines in the north. In order to export the gas, airships were needed. In order to protect Stonehold's primary resource, thousands of troops were under Saergaeth's direct command. Miskatoll had an endless supply of gas and men, both of which had now been turned against the High King.

It hadn't been anticipated because the Council hadn't actually believed Saergaeth would turn traitor. And even if they had, what were they supposed to have done? Confiscate the zeppelins that the metholinate industry—that Stonehold itself—required to survive? Pull thousands of troops out of Miskatoll and leave the mining facilities denuded of protection?

No. There hadn't been a way to prevent this mess. Saergaeth had known his position; he had certainly used it to his advantage.

Caliph had sent one of his three dreadnoughts to guard Tentinil by sea. The enormous ironclad ship with its pounding engines had smoldered out of Isca Bay the night before last, taking with it two thousand sailors including the two brigs that escorted her.

Most of Caliph's light engines were already in Tentinil. But if he sent more, Saergaeth could have a fleet of airships prowling the skies over Isca, and Caliph with little left to shoot them down.

Caliph felt pinned, unable to maneuver. He had to keep his engines close to the city, which meant he had to face the brunt of Miskatoll's mechanized onslaught with infantry.

Flying his own fleet of zeppelins out to meet Saergaeth wasn't an option. Isca's military boasted forty airships including the *Byun-Ghala* and several older, less reliable models that were practically tethered to Malgôr Hangar.

Even the most conservative estimates placed Miskatoll's fleet at one hundred strong, including fourteen leviathans.

Caliph sat in the royal study, moving his eyes from the window to stare blankly at a map of the Duchy varnished to the top of the low table in front of him.

Gadriel lounged across the room, leg crossed over his knee. He seemed to be counting books on the study shelves. An oil lamp spread the room with pearly radiance and shadows that wavered in the corners.

Caliph had left the windows open so they framed the dark steeples and ancient gables: strange creatures watching the sea. "Gadriel, what were you before you were seneschal?"

The other man stopped his count.

"I was an intern, your highness." His very proper gray beard and moustache twitched as he spoke.

"That's quite a synopsis."

"I've liked your wit ever since your arrival, King Howl. You have a particular economy of words that I admire."

Caliph leaned back in the cushioned divan and folded his arms. The light wrinkled across the rich pillows that, like him, seemed to brood.

"I don't enjoy being king."

The seneschal looked worried. "Is something wrong?"

Caliph smiled. "Nothing I could blame you for. But I feel like I'm running with a blindfold on."

"Nonsense," said the old man. "You've already got the hang of it."

Caliph made the southern hand sign for no.

"It's bad luck that I took the crown during so much strife."

"Forgive me, your majesty, but your coronation was the cause of the strife and therefore inevitable. It's good that we have a king now. A Council may run economic affairs well enough, but for war, a king is best."

Caliph frowned. His eyes went out of focus. "What is happening in Tentinil? I should be out there, touring the field."

Gadriel took a small snuffbox from his pocket and rapped it lightly with a knuckle. "I've given word to let you sleep in."

Caliph forced a smile.

"Shall I have anything sent up?"

"No thank you, Gadriel." Then the careful, quiet exit, the seneschal barely allowing the door to click so as not to disturb—even Caliph's thoughts.

Caliph lay back on the divan, staring at the molded ceiling. Most of his thoughts were stillborn, hardly worth Gadriel's care.

Yrisl knows how to fight a war. If I give all military command over to the Blue General maybe it will be better for the Duchy. I've got all my life to learn how to be king. No sense trying to pretend I know what I'm doing during such a critical time.

Exhaustion crept over him. He gazed from the edge of consciousness at the ceiling, eyes drooping, in and out of a dream. In the dream he was tapping on his desk, trying to explain something to Clayton Redfield about not regulating the sale of religious artifacts along the Avenue of Charms. Temple Hill was screaming their approval. He was tapping with a silver pen to make his point, tapping, tapping on the polished desk. Tapping. Caliph woke up.

There were two doors to the High King's study. One opened inward on the castle. The other opened out. The outward one was a thick oak and metal-studded thing that screened the room from the battlements.

He sat up.

After a moment the tapping came again, outside of the dream. Soft. Insistent. He stood slowly. A guard?

He waited.

It sounded again, barely audible through the thickness of the portal.

He walked, dumbfounded, to the door and slid away the bolt. An assassin? *I could be so lucky.* With well-oiled silence it opened and Caliph peered before him at the empty moonlit parapet.

To either side, the crenels looked down into deep courtyards. Naobi glowed fat and white, a reptilian eye wreathed in green. Stillness covered everything. The clear balmy night seemed devoid of sound. Not even cricket song. The gardens lay too far below.

Caliph took a half step out. He stopped. A heady sweetness lingered on the air. A whisper from behind the door. "Caliph?"

He turned slowly.

She stood in the shadow of the arch that sheltered the seldom-used portal, all but her face masked in darkness.

Caliph's eyes burned her image into his brain. Hair, silvery-gold and short. Her eyes were worlds of blue.

Fear filled him instantly. Had she returned to finish what the witches in Tue had failed to accomplish? Was this a trick? But her eyes communicated a silent apology; a sincere vulnerability, real or imagined, that made him want to hold her and protect her.

His tongue lay ignorantly at the bottom of his mouth. His head might as well have been severed for the all the help it was in determining what to say.

Almost cautiously, as though afraid she might vanish, he reached for her face. As his fingers touched her, her lips twisted into that familiar smile that both mocked and tempted him at the same time.

Caliph couldn't help himself. He attacked her. She gave way easily, kissing him back, letting his emotions come out.

"I guess you're glad to see me," she breathed into his ear.

They fell apart. A test fit after two years. But their bodies had remembered, had conformed to each other with aching familiarity.

"How—what are you doing here?" He felt inebriated. A tailless cat stepped out of the shadows and marched into the castle as though inspecting newly conquered territory.

"How am I doing here?" She laughed softly. Her shoulders lifted then fell. Her voice was husky. "Feels all right to me."

Her lashes slipped. Lazy. Blue planets eclipsed. Only the corners of her mouth turned up. It was a well-practiced look. One that Caliph supposed had sent many men into short-term madness.

Caliph came at her again.

She was shocked by his eagerness. Of all things, this had been the one she least expected. Not from quiet, lethally rational Caliph Howl.

His hands ran over her like the fingers of a votary, leaving no line uncaressed. They traveled from wrist to ankle, drawing her up, off the parapet, off her feet, inside the castle.

Like walking lines, she moved without sense. Caliph carried her away, cradled her. A pearly light flickered in darkness. She was disoriented. She struggled free from her clothes, desperate to be rid of them.

Caliph had turned her arrival into something wild. It was better than she had hoped. It was necessary. It was urgent. She felt herself let go of the controls, let go of the premeditated steps, the calculations she used with sex. It had been a while.

Sena bit her lower lip. Her mind slipped away as the catapult fired. She was floating . . . drifting . . . in an ocean of stars, stuttering again . . . zoetrope spinning.

In the morning, the light lay crisp and white across the rich crumpled sheets of the High King's bed. Sena had no idea how she had arrived in this room but by the look of the sheets she must have been awake at the time.

Her memory fogged with feelings that pulled her mouth into an amazed and contented smile. Caliph was nowhere to be seen.

White marble flooded the floor. The four-poster bed she had slept in was carved from cherry wood with tall spindles at every corner. In the center of the room a gleaming enameled tub stood steaming on short recurved legs. It crouched like a fat cat above a plush colorful rug.

Several wardrobes, a desk and a chest all sat at attention. They were crafted from imported woods, carved laboriously and stained deep red tones. On the walls, tapestries of inestimable value curled with the outside air.

Leaning back, she gazed up at the ceiling which comprised a vaulted affair whose ribbing floated from pillars in the four corners and met at a recessed oval where some artisan had done a fresco in the dome. It showed a cherubic youth with black wings descending from a sunlit cloud aiming a bow at an innocent-looking rabbit. Archaic lettering around the fresco read in Hinter, *there is purpose in death.*

Her journey had certainly been worth it. She had walked lines to an abandoned cromlech on a low hill amid fog-draped mountains. Surrounded by dark, worn-down stones and brambles, she had used her sickle knife to cut her way through.

Relying on road signs and other travelers for directions, she had taken a road south and after walking several days she had finally come to Isca.

She had seen it in the distance: the mighty wall, the city pouring smoke. Blue-gray worms from a hundred chimneys had bent beneath the castle spires, everything caked in evening light.

Inside the city, a sea of people had sloshed against walls and buildings. Sena had been surprised at the chill twilight brought and the women in long coats who wore next to nothing underneath, showing skin and multiple belts around tightly circled hips. Shouting boys had torn through the crowd, dragging dead things on strings attached to poles. A gypsy with a beard had scowled and offered her toothpaste from a tray just before a huge man pushed past, nearly shoving her into a lamppost.

Sena had seen shops for tobacco and unicycles and soap. Mechanized cars and strange creatures moved through tunnels in the walls. Metal boxes on pulleys carried regular deliveries on wires strung across the street. Clotheslines garroted gargoyles. Iron strangled brick. Windows slid up and down like teeth. People screamed and bartered and talked about war.

A door opened somewhere and Caliph stepped out from behind one of the tapestries, breaking her reverie. She heard him thank a servant and shut the door. In his hand, he carried a copper kettle that he emptied directly into the tub.

"Plumbing problems," he said and looked around the room as though making sure everything met with his approval before coming to stand somewhat shyly near the baseboard.

"I thought you might want a bath. No one knows you're here." He glanced at the ceiling where she was still looking at the fresco. "Yet."

"What did you do to me?" She climbed from the sheets and walked shamelessly to the tub.

Palms up, silent, he felt suddenly uneasy, almost bashful.

"I don't even remember what you like for breakfast. I don't know if you're staying. I don't know . . ."

His words trailed off and he walked to the window. From behind he heard her slide into the water.

"I didn't come here just to have breakfast," she said lightly.

"What then?"

"Caliph, you think too damn much. You always have. Relax. I'm here. I came here for one reason. You."

Her words surprised herself. She sank up to her neck. "Nice scar, isn't it?"

Caliph came over and sat down by the tub. "What do you mean?"

"My scar. You didn't notice it last night?" She pulled herself up so he could see.

He put his finger on the pink line.

"I missed you."

"I could tell." She grinned. "I didn't expect treatment like that. Thought you might even throw me out. You've got better things to do now than think about me." Suddenly she sat up straight. "Where's my pack?"

"I put it over there." He pointed to where it hung on the back of a chair. Nĩs lay sleeping on the seat. She slipped down again until her chin touched the water, feeling relieved.

"So—" Caliph tried to start any kind of conversation, "nearly two, two and a half years now." He nodded. "I came looking for you and found your cottage. I guess that's where the scar came from?"

"You would have followed me to Eloth, wouldn't you? You found the note."

Caliph felt hot with embarrassment. He hated that he felt so syrupy over her. It had never been the same for her. Never sloppy. These feelings were supposed to be gone, dead with time. But their revival was wonderful, sweet, heady, almost dizzying and lined every inch with fear. *What if she goes away again?* He felt half-tricked, half-cheated at his own enamoredness.

"How did it go? Your search for that book?"

Her eyes lit up. She whispered even though there was no one else in the room.

"I have it. It's here."

"What happened at the cottage?"

A knocking sounded from the door behind the tapestry. "Your majesty?" a servant's voice called from just outside.

"Don't come in, I'm bathing," Caliph shouted.

"Majesty," Sena whispered playfully. "Do I have to call you 'majesty' too?"

"Shh—" Caliph scolded.

She rolled her eyes. "They can't hear us."

Caliph stood up and rummaged through his wardrobe.

"I'm not so sure about that. Regardless, we have to find some clothes for you."

"What's wrong with mine?"

"As difficult as it may prove to be, we need to make you look like a serving boy. The last thing I need is added scandal."

"Sorry to inconvenience you." She splashed.

Caliph turned toward her. "You know I didn't mean it like that. It's political bullshit, nothing else." He stopped and frowned. "How in Emolus' name did you get inside?"

Sena's lips puckered at one corner. "You opened the door."

Caliph snorted. "I mean the grounds. No holomorphy?"

She shrugged. "Maybe . . . just a little."

"Then maybe you could get out the same way you got in. I mean, I can get you some breakfast first—"

His tongue was moving faster than his mind. He came up short.

"Thanks. I'll just eat and," she waved her hand around, "banish myself." But her voice sounded far from offended. "What are you worried about? You're the High King. You can make love to whomever you wish." She turned over in the water and beckoned him with a finger. "You don't really think I could pass for a serving boy, do you King Howl?"

He walked slowly back to the tub.

"It could be done, I think." His voice sounded as though he were actually thinking about it. "It would take some work."

Sena's soapy hands reached up for his ruffled lapels. She pulled him down. The water in the tub rose suddenly, flowed over the lip and wet the tasseled carpet all the way through to the floor.

AFTER her bath, and another session on the High King's bed, she got dressed. Caliph threw a huge hooded cloak over her and escorted her from the castle.

She could tell his charade fooled no one and guessed he wasn't the first king to ferry women. When she was safely on the city streets, he told her he would meet her at a stone marker south of West Fen beyond the city walls.

His plan was bizarre and ill-thought, something completely unnatural coming from him. "I can't have you just show up in the castle. I'll escort you out and then meet you someplace. Then I can bring you back in."

But she didn't argue. He wanted her. That much was clear. And for the time being that was all that mattered. She took a cab to West Gate and left the city, following Caliph's directions.

Without the urban sprawl, Isca framed a new world of mountains and bogs and land by the sea. It brought back memories of her childhood in Tenwinds. Her crotch ached pleasantly. She climbed a low green tor west of Isca, again following directions, waiting for Caliph to show up. While she waited, she tossed the possibility of being honest around in her head the way Nịs played with prey.

For an instant she thought about telling Caliph the truth. *But what was the truth?* And how could she tell him if she didn't know?

She quickly set the idea aside. The formula for unlocking the *Cịsrym Tạ* explicitly said that his blood must be stolen.

She paced back and forth near the stone of Mizraim, waiting for Caliph, arguing internally.

She had never felt this way before. But was it real? Or was she simply deceiving herself, forging false feelings for Caliph in an attempt to find a rare ingredient?

No, she thought, this is love. Mawkish and ridiculous and inutile. Her hopes soared. An ampoule was not so much. Caliph would not die from it. But it must be stolen. And at the right time.

She had to wait. Wait for autumn.

But she felt it now!

She kicked the stone of Mizraim in her frustration, worried that her feelings might fade with the leaves. She began to panic, tempted once more to regard the strange ingredients as mundane superfluities unrelated to the true mathematical workings of the spell. As the temptation rose, so did a gibbering madness at the back of her head, a cold upwelling that quickly swept the notion away.

She had not come for Caliph. She had come for the book. When she had met him in the library that first night in Desdae he had sent shivers through her. She had decided later, after verifying the recipe several more times, that he was the one for the equation—if she ever found the grimoire.

She leaned against the stone and stared down at the strange city. Morning fog sagged in the lowlands and distant shouts ricocheted through the gray patched-over brick of West Fen. She was an interloper, a foreigner. And yet the book's howl seemed to quiet in this land, to give her respite from the urgency to open it.

"Yella byũrn," she whispered with derision. *This is not my home. Once this is over I will not be able to stay here.* She knocked the back of her head against the stone as if to dislodge the fantasy.

For a long time she thought of nothing. She cleared her mind and stood enjoying the clean damp smell of the upland. A mile away the city groaned in discordant unison, like some massive abomination in the agonies of birth.

At the edge of West Fen, breaking from the jagged edge of farm machinery piled against three-story buildings, an enormous black horse trotted into view.

For Caliph, traveling alone outside the castle was not only pointedly stupid, but also difficult to achieve. Yet he had managed to slip away.

He called a greeting in Old Speech.

"You hardly look Hjolk-trull." She crossed her arms and stood with her head tilted toward one shoulder.

He reached down, extended his hand to her.

She took it and pulled herself up onto the pillion.

"That's all right. What's a Hjolk-trull?" he joked. "Did you know I stole your horse?"

"Did you know I'm a witch?" It had to come out sooner or later. She couldn't live at the castle and hide her books, her study, her passion. He had been to the cottage, to her hidden cellar. *He* had *to know!*

"Crossed my mind," he said.

She settled behind him and spoke directly into his ear. "That's quite a headline: HIGH KING IS WITCH-FUCKING HORSE THIEF. Where are we going?"

He shrugged. "Somewhere. I think it's time I looked around in some old places." The warhorse lurched up the tor's heathery slope.

"I suppose I'm one of them?" Sena said. "Your old places?"

"Old friends," he corrected. "First we try to hide our relationship, now the verbal sparring. Are we going to do acrostics next?"

"Mmm—" Her lips were warm against his neck.

Caliph's horse worked into a canter, claws gouging the ground beneath them. The rhythm reminded Sena of the night before.

They rode up a tor and down through some boggy runoff below the mountains. Then up again into steeper foothills. Both of them had to duck their heads as Caliph guided the animal under venerable trees and onto an overgrown road.

"Are we going home?" Sena asked.

Caliph nodded.

Up ahead, a mansion loomed out of the elms and maples. Its towers disappeared as the horse took them through a tunnel of rustling branches. The towers reappeared when the tunnel opened before an imposing house built more like a fortress. It smelled like the woods. Pollen. Spores. Warm damp greenery and rot.

The great sweep of lawn tossed waist-deep grass, weeds mostly. Everything gone to seed. Ivy had taken over the structure. The chimneys looked like strange leafy sentinels standing in a row.

"Has a little character, does it?" Sena said. The blank windowpanes screamed at her. Several had avoided the vine's complete strangulation. She watched a white squirrel run along a sill gripping a nut in its mouth.

"Just like I left it," Caliph joked. He urged the warhorse into the clearing that had once been his front lawn.

Sena looked back over one shoulder then the other, trying to see a series of large statues set around the edge of the estate. They were enslaved by vines, nearly unrecognizable amid the trees. One seemed to be a seraphic form holding a broken sword, weeping green lines down cracks in her face.

"Where do they lead?" She pointed to the right at a few white traces of stone that led deeper into the woods.

Caliph felt an unsettling wash of memory.

"Family graveyard." He dismounted and, as he tethered the horse to some unruly bushes by the front steps, his boot hit something fragile, a cracked earthen bowl stained with the stuff of his nightmares.

He stepped over it, went up the steps. The fortresslike doors, bound in black iron, sprayed intricate metalwork before his eyes. The hinges depicted dead-eyed deer, wolves and wild pigs. They looked ready to take the hand of anyone brazen enough to reach for the knocker.

Sena stood in the weeds, looking up at the windows with rapt fascination. Spectral towers and hooded gables reached up, conjured pictures of Caliph as a brown-haired boy staring out from the panes. There were departures from normal geometry in the spires and turrets. Sena recognized anomalous angles, unsettling yet subtle differences in the thrust of the eves.

Obviously, when the great necromancer had moved in, he had altered the architecture slightly to accommodate his profession, changing space to enhance the dimensions on which his many windows looked. It was a marvelous achievement, one that Sena had tried to accomplish in her own cottage.

"Come on," Caliph called from the top of the steps.

The spires seemed to bleed into the sky.

The doors' lock had been long broken and Caliph pushed them open, revealing an empty foyer with a grand staircase and rotting paneled walls. Leaves and animal droppings littered the floor. Something that had been chewing on the timbers above the ceiling stopped its noise.

Sena sniffed the wet air. "It's like the trees have come inside," she said, "guests to a long-expired party." A sapling grew through the floor of the pantry. It reached for a sunlit hole in the ceiling. She watched Caliph's eyes roam the shapes of the empty alcoves and broken banister.

"The estate was auctioned off to nobles to put me through school after my uncle died. I'm not sure what happened to it since then."

He took one step up the stairs and stopped. "Funny. I don't feel like being here anymore."

Sena glanced through wide doorways to the right and left. To the right, mildewed plaster sagged precariously from the kitchen ceiling. Much of it had fallen to the floor by the hearth, crumbling to its raw ingredients of lime and sand.

To the left, spider-infested dining halls, parlors and rooms without discernable use burrowed away under great beams and blocks of stone.

"Why did you come back then?"

Caliph printed his name in the dust.

"It seemed like I dreamt it. I wanted to come back, you know? See if it was real. I guess I wanted to show it to you. Nothing from my childhood seems real anymore." He chuckled. "I had this imaginary friend. Marco." His voice grew thick and slow.

"He talked to me at night, told me stories of kings and war and death. Always death." Caliph nodded outside. "He lived in the graveyard."

Sena's face showed a curious mix of sympathy and morbid fascination.

"Then I found out he was real."

"Real?"

"My uncle was an extraordinary holomorph." Caliph rubbed dust from his fingertips.

His childhood had consisted of this house, his uncle and the few servants on staff. When he looked around, fragmentary images of Cameron, the dream-man, strode through the cankered passageways and grim parlors.

As usual, the memories were muddy. He knew that the family had chased his rogue of a father off, and that his mother had remained here with her parents.

Then came the unfortunate dinner, an event he had no recollection of. And after that, or so he had been told, his uncle had come out of the south, claiming both the estate and Caliph: a diaper-wearing toddler.

He knew the house must have changed with his uncle's arrival. There must have been a time when the banisters were polished to a golden sheen and bright-colored rugs and vases gleamed in the light of the tall mullioned windows flung open to the sun. But Caliph could not remember such a time or any time when this huge hollow house had been decorated in anything other than black tapestries with strange designs and dark woods imported at tremendous cost from jungles in the south.

One autumn, Cameron had walked out of the woods and come to live with them. It felt bizarre now. Where had Cameron come from? Why had Caliph's uncle taken him in? Caliph remembered the kites and the toys that Cameron had carved on this wide stretch of lawn. With Cameron in the house, the nights seemed less dark and the shadows that moved without caster shrank slightly.

But then Caliph's memory fumbled. Cameron had left. There had been a long journey in the middle of winter and Nathaniel had locked the house on the hill as if never to return. After that had come the white marble floors and the blood and Cameron's voice as the two of them descended that long rope into darkness.

After the darkness, he had no memory whatsoever until, like walking through a doorway into a brightly lit room, he realized that Nathaniel was dead. Cameron had searched for and found Caliph's father. With Jacob and Caliph's reunion, Cameron had disolved into the north and never returned.

Jacob took Caliph to Candleshine, a crowded modest borough that pressed Isca's southwest wall.

He had done the best he could but he was never prepared to be a father. He did not have the tools or the experience. He put Caliph in a local school run by the Sisters of the Second Moon and brought him home on weekends to continue where Cameron had left off—teaching him how to wield a sword.

"We should go. I feel like an idiot out here. I'm supposed to be a king managing a war."

"Wait." Sena sat down by him on the stairs and struggled free from her pack. "I have something to show you."

Her supple fingers loosened the buckle and pushed past a change of clothes, her diary and a few other odds and ends. Deep at the bottom she gripped the cold soft skin of the *Cisrym Ta* and hauled it up into the light.

Caliph stared at it in shock. His hand touched the filthy crimson leather then drew back as though bitten.

"Where did you get that?"

Sena set it on her knees. "It turned up in an old bookshop."

"This is the book?" Caliph whispered in disbelief. "The one you talked about?"

"The one I told you about in the attic before I left Desdae." She nodded.

Caliph stood up, stunned.

"This was my uncle's book!"

"I know."

IT was a long time before Caliph spoke. "So . . . you were after me for that?"

"What?" She scowled.

"What do you mean, what? Obviously you knew. What now? Interrogate me, find answers about my uncle you couldn't find anywhere else?" He took a step away.

Sena's face felt like it was burning. "What are you talking about? You think you're the only one who can open your uncle's book? You know what your problem is? You think everyone is out to get Caliph Howl and you think you have everyone under your thumb. No one crosses Caliph Howl," she mocked, "or he crawls away to get even."

It was the half-truth that made it sting. But Caliph saw beneath her anger. He could read the desperation behind her attack, recognized it in the way her eyes almost trembled at the very tops of her cheekbones.

He raised his hand and looked away, speaking in slow distinct syllables. "You. Do. Not. Love me."

"I don't love you? Where in Felldin's Grace did that come from?" She picked up the *Cisrym Ta* and stuffed it in her pack. "I've never heard the words come out of your mouth." She stood up, preparing to leave.

"And why should they have come out of my mouth?" Caliph shouted with a voice of indescribable fury. "You want me to admit what a fool I am?"

The sound so surprised her that she almost sat down.

Caliph's unfettered anger, while shocking, teased her sense of play.

"I am sitting in my past talking about ghosts while my country is at war!" he roared. He turned and kicked the door so fiercely the antique hinges at the bottom gave way. It sagged inward with a groan, threatening to fall on him.

Caliph jumped back in surprise.

Though partly appalled by his temper, the mysterious tantrum caused an emotion to flicker through Sena's stomach that, while she could not name it, made her smile. Maybe it was because she had tried so many times at school to make him angry on purpose, to see how he would behave, and this was a kind of belated conquest.

When she finally spoke, her voice had attenuated. She used a quieter, more sincere tone than she had ever used with him before.

"I'm not the one who brought us up here to wallow in the past."

His black eyes whirled around and locked on hers.

"I didn't come to Stonehold to use you like a stick for the fire either," she continued. "No. I don't love you, but if it makes you feel any better this is the closest thing to love that I've ever had."

"Wonderful. Terrific . . ." His voice trailed off.

Outside, the warhorse gnashed its teeth and snapped half a dozen tails at flies, oblivious to the difficulties its riders were having. Caliph cleared his throat. "I didn't mean to yell."

Sena's lips curled with sly humor.

"In two years I never saw you get that excited—I mean not like that."

He ignored her and gestured to the *Cisrym Ta* now hidden in her pack.

"Why did you want to show it to me? You can't open it?" In her anger she had given her secret away.

"I said—" she began.

"You said, 'You think you're the only one who can open your uncle's book?' So what? What kind of book is it?"

Sena bit back on the argumentative words that instantly came to mind and replied guardedly, "No one really knows—except maybe your uncle and he's out back talking with tree roots."

W hen it came to his uncle's book, Caliph averted his thoughts as much as possible. It had popped out of Sena's pack like a horrible toy, but that was in the past now. It was just a book. Nothing more. He felt foolish for having gotten so angry over it.

He took Sena back to the castle and introduced her to the staff. He made it clear she was to be extended the same entitlements he himself received. Although he stopped short of formally labeling or defining their relationship, the staff had experience in this sort of thing. They didn't ask maladroit or indelicate questions.

Instead, Gadriel enlisted a squadron of tailors. They descended on her with compliments and measuring tapes and imaginations vivid with her enviable body italicized in cloth. Armed with cropping blades, they threw themselves into piles of luxurious fabric, bolting out lavish styles that swelled ten wardrobes nearly overnight.

Caliph stood in awe as the castle adjusted like a calculating machine.

Several astute personages in uniform took frenzied notes on little pads of paper as they pried information out of Sena. What were her favorite authors? Colors? Musical tastes? And so on.

Did she like fur, leather, diamonds, gold or silver? Did she color her hair? Did she eat meat? Did she bathe in the morning or at night or both or several times a day?

Feminine articles materialized from inscrutable locations. Perfumes and mirrors danced in glittering array. Bouquets and extra toilet tissue unfolded in the water closet on the fourth floor. Huge men hauled additional furnishings out of every direction. Chiffoniers and towel racks and folding screens. Soaps and creams and porcelain fixtures with floral designs.

It happened at remarkable speed, like a theater crew changing props until Caliph felt certain the whole event must have somehow been anticipated, prepared for and orchestrated on cue.

He could tell that Sena was dumbfounded. She looked at him with a sudden vague comprehension of the myriad resources at his command.

For a moment the old question nagged him, bothersome but easily dismissed. Why she was with him was a riddle he probably didn't want solved anyway. But then, pondering his own unarticulated feelings for her was only slightly less daunting.

Not so long ago, he had thought up all kinds of elaborate lachrymose metaphors to describe their relationship. But the truth was simple. She was his bag of qaam-dihet. And he was like any of the old men in ruinous plaster dens along the sea, fingers clenched protectively over the instruments of addiction, choosing to ignore the inevitable.

With Sena, he thought, it was as if someone had created her to bait him. As though his every impulse had been known to her builder. He comforted himself with the mean-spirited detail that even though his heart ached, even though he had stumbled through the Highlands of Tue in search of her, one fact remained.

She had come to him.

Regardless of motive, that single truth assuaged his ego.

Later in the afternoon, Caliph left her in Gadriel's care and followed another of the castle stewards toward an unscheduled but urgent meeting with Mr. Vhortghast.

The spymaster had arrived from the field with intelligence and he met Caliph on the zeppelin deck of the castle's vast east side. A gray lion, fully outfitted for war, menaced the platform, tethered to a sixteen-story mooring mast and anchored to the coupling in the middle of the deck.

Mr. Vhortghast waited at a metal railing, looking out at the gray snarled sky over Ironside while men in black uniforms scurried in the background. Caliph joined him.

A flock of birds took flight with a mournful chyrme, twisting in a helix like gnats over Temple Hill.

"Fifteenth of Dusk, Pash. A zeppelin goes down in Nifol. Probably bandits. They miss a set of sensitive schematics. Blueprints. Manuals on solvitriol power etcetera. Pandragor technically owns them but recovery teams find them missing from the wreckage. Do you know anything about it?"

Startled by the question given almost without preamble, Caliph pawed nervously at his chin.

"By your tone I take it something's happened?"

Vhortghast shrugged. "Not yet. I've got some men on it. We know emissaries from Pandragor showed up in Skellum, if you can believe that . . . at parliament. I don't like the thought of the Pandragonians cutting deals with Shradnæ Witches."

"Why are you asking if I know anything about it?"

"I don't know," said Vhortghast. His lips seemed afraid of the hideous gray teeth beneath them, peeling back and exposing them to view. His pasty, fictile expression was unreadable. "I'm sure you have other employees that give you information."

Caliph didn't. Not this kind of information. He wondered if he should.

Vhortghast clenched the railing with both hands and watched birds cavort through plumes of smoke.

"There've been some strange occurrences in the city. Unexplained . . . holomorphic . . . kinds of crimes. All the Shradnæ agents that we know about—that's only two by the way—that we've been watching . . . have disappeared."

"And you think it's related to the blueprints?"

"No. My first guess would be that it has to do with the war. The Witchocracy is pulling agents out of harm's way."

"Out of harm's way? Isn't it their job to be in harm's way?"

"Not these. The agents we were watching were what the Witchocracy calls half-sisters. Who knows? They might even have been decoys. We never even interrogated them."

"Then I'm not following you. What does this have to do with the blueprints?"

"Maybe something. Maybe nothing. But a Pandragonian official, no name, you know how it goes, claims they traced the blueprints here." Zane fixed Caliph with a piercing stare.

Caliph's throat thickened.

"So I thought I'd ask," the spymaster's tone was the closest thing to friendly banter Caliph could imagine, "if you'd heard anything about it."

"No," said Caliph. *Why am I lying?* "But if I do, you'll be the first to know."

Vhortghast studied him another moment then looked away. "Fine."

Caliph couldn't tell whether Vhortghast's "fine" meant that he knew. Maybe he understood that Caliph wanted the secret kept secret, reading between the lines, understanding that yes, Caliph knew all about the stolen blueprints but that Zane Vhortghast's job was no longer to ask questions about them. Zane Vhortghast's job was to ensure the information didn't leak. Caliph hoped, against serious doubt, that this was the case.

"You've taken a mistress . . ." Vhortghast said it with something between cynicism and bored acknowledgement. "The same girl you were . . . involved with at Desdae?"

As if you didn't already know, Caliph thought savagely. He did not respond, a course that had the desired effect, eliciting mild but nervous discomfort in Mr. Vhortghast.

The spymaster laced his fingers and amended his comment with, "She's quite a catch." He then turned to the zeppelin looming behind them. "I'm headed for Tentinil. Tour the field. That sort of thing. I'm sure General Yrisl will want to coach you on some plans."

The spymaster's tacit disdain for the Blue General showed like wood grain through shallow coats of diplomacy.

"I want you to stay in the city," said Caliph suddenly. "Help me formulate some ideas regarding Ghoul Court."

Vhortghast scowled. "What kind of ideas?"

"I want to assume control of that borough."

The spymaster looked stunned.

"Your majesty, now is probably not the time to allocate resources—" He stopped. Caliph's eyes had slashed out like claws. "But I'll get some men on it."

Caliph's glare shifted from Zane Vhortghast to the seething Iscan skyline.

"This city will not tolerate a sovereign criminal element. I want to personally oversee Ghoul Court's submission to law, inspections and regular patrol—just like every other borough. If we're at war, we can't afford a safe haven for spies at the very center of our city, wouldn't you agree?"

Zane Vhortghast was quick to answer yes.

Ghoul Court, the age-old cesspool, had been ignored for decades because its problems (while ugly and deplorable) had never seemed to spread. The Court drove fear like a wood splitter into every watchman's chest.

Patrols went in organized in boisterous, blundering packs: easily avoided by discreet thieves, smugglers and nascent, highly mobile factions. Usually hard and fast, the raids consisted of fifty or more heavily armed men with a squad of iatromathematiques serving as medics and backup. Such large-scale busts were infrequent and orchestrated mostly to satisfy Travis Whittle.

But when the raid was over, the watch removed themselves quickly as throngs of shadowy, ragged shapes encroached, congregating in smirchy alleys. Watching. They held pipes and boards driven through with eight-inch nails, swung makeshift weapons in crude but adequate grasps.

After a raid, the watch was always left with the distinct feeling that it had been tolerated, indulged by some sinister power that oversaw the balance, placated with a victory before being herded slowly and methodically back toward the border.

Terrified and infinitely outnumbered, the police would stumble toward Lampfire or Maruchine or Murkbell with their prisoners in tow, lugging sacks of contraband and evidence.

Gasping, they would burst into less formidable streets by Bragget Canal or Seething Lane where the old Vindai brewery crouched. By then, the shapes had vanished like cockroaches into jumbled masonry and sub-floors.

Zane Vhortghast didn't object to Caliph's reasons for cleaning the Court. What he objected to, thought Caliph, was the amount of sheer effort and resources that the job would entail.

CALIPH took a late lunch with Sena in the high tower, watching zeppelins plow the sky. Filthy brown clouds marred the pale expanse over the Iscan Bay like dark spots on the achromous fur of a beast. The sky growled and rumpled with extraordinary speed, its weather promising treachery and destruction.

Airships glided into hangars. Those still aloft had little hope of landing. They buoyed like spiny fish from the city's tendrils and headed west, propellers thudding, cutting thick slabs of air, moving out of the storm's path.

Gadriel served an epicurean assortment of exotic cheeses, fruits and breads accompanied by slender glasses of comet wine. While the wind fumbled and creamy tatters of cloud slid around the tower, obscuring the view for moments at a time, Caliph and Sena picked at their food.

"These came for you," said Gadriel. He laid a few envelopes on the table before going to build a fire on the hearth.

Caliph opened the daily totals for what dwindling metholinate still wheezed through Isca's miserly distribution pipes. A sinking feeling tugged his stomach down into a point of unbearable gravity, like a child pulling on his mother's shirt. Caliph looked taut, etiolated and shiftless.

The numbers on the paper, though large, had already condemned the city to the greatest energy crisis it had ever faced.

Caliph blotted the sudden perspiration that collected on his forehead with the back of his sleeve and chewed his lip fiercely as he stared at the immutable columns. The numbers paralyzed him.

"What is it?" asked Sena.

"Gadriel, schedule me a meeting with Sigmund Dulgensen."

"Right away, your majesty."

Sena scowled as she sipped her wine. "Sigmund Dulgensen? From Desdae?"

"Yes."

"What's he doing in Isca?"

Caliph filled her in briefly, omitting sensitive information about crashed zeppelins and stolen blueprints.

"Better make it tomorrow afternoon," he said to Gadriel, tossing the paper aside. "At least an hour—maybe two."

"Do you still want to meet with the Pplarians?" asked Gadriel.

"Shit. I forgot about them."

Gadriel mused. "I can move them to—"

Caliph signed no several times. "I can't put them off. Last thing I need is a bunch of insulted Pplarian ambassadors who think I'm too self-absorbed to—"

"Pplarians," cooed Sena. "Did you see *Er Krue Alteirz*?"

"Yes. Completely randy. About a pervert with four arms—"

"They're on their way from Vale Briar if I recall," said Gadriel.

"Yes," agreed Caliph, "and I don't doubt that my punctilious neighbor has already filled them with a host of doubts."

"Who?" asked Sena.

"King Lewis. The King of Vale Briar. He's . . . something else." Then to Gadriel, "Keep the Pplarians. Schedule Sig whenever you can." He moved to the next envelope in the stack: an embossed and gilt pouch whose vanilla flap he opened warily, apprehensive of more bad news.

Inside was an invitation to the Murkbell Opera House, cordially inviting the High King and his lady to a show the following month.

"How in Burim's name does gossip travel so fast?"

"That's Isca," Gadriel said, standing up and brushing himself off before the roaring fire.

"What are these numbers?" Sena had picked up the sheet of paper with the metholinate levels and momentarily scrutinized it before laying it aside.

She moved from the table to a divan where she crouched, digging her toes down between the cushions and glaring impishly at Caliph while the seneschal inquired what they might want for dessert.

"Nothing for me, thank you." Caliph put the invitation back in its envelope and tossed it to Sena. "Do you like opera?"

She opened it and read the golden script in Hinter.

"Who's Mr. Naylor?"

"The manager of the Murkbell Opera House, my dear," said Gadriel.

Sena flipped the invitation over with an incredulous look.

"How does he know about me?"

"The same way everyone knows about you. Blatherskites and tattlers from West Fen to Growl Mort. But I've taken up enough of your time.

What would the two of you like this evening? Swordfish? Stuffed game hens?"

"Steak," said Sena.

Caliph's stomach turned. "Only if you butcher the cow. We have cows here, don't we?"

Sena looked at him disparagingly as though he had begun foaming at the mouth. "Caliph, what kind of absurdity—?"

"No, look, I just want it to be fresh." He panned his hand before him. "That's all. Butcher it tonight or I won't eat it."

"Caliph—"

"Trust me on this—" He glared at her.

"It's no problem," Gadriel assured. "Believe me, my dear. There are far stranger idiosyncrasies than liking a fresh cut of beef. I am only too happy to accommodate this one." His jovial tone smoothed the ruffled air.

After he had left the room Sena turned to Caliph with a kindly-explain-yourself expression on her face.

"Trust me. You won't eat a piece of meat in this town unless it's been raised and slaughtered right here in the Hold."

"Why in Emolus' name—?"

"I don't want to talk about it. I don't want to fight. Just please—"

She relented and curled close to him, looking again at the sheet of numbers. He hadn't seemed to want to discuss them. Under the yellow storm light, a sudden gale pounded the tower and droplets like glittering topaz stippled the glass.

"Fine," she whispered with mock sardonicism, cupping her hand over his crotch. "I could use some fresh meat."

THE next day was the nineteenth of Hleim. Caliph met the Pplarians in the castle aviary where vast windows framed a rain-drenched and glutted city view. Enormous bunches of vegetation coiled against the glass, rising like blackened pythons from the floor.

A patio near the windows allowed the visitors to marvel at the sinister horned towers of Gilnaroth clawing out of Barrow Hill. East of them, the distant ornate town homes of Blekton dissolved into streamers of incense pouring out of Temple Hill.

When they threw their vision across the miles, the Pplarians found smoking skeletons in Ironside's shipyards, sparked by the desultory stars of remote chemical welders. Beyond that, the dwindling brown piles of variation in Bilgeburg and Thief Town interfused with far-off Murkbell in a sort of sepia twilight near the wharves.

As Gadriel entered with a tray of refreshments, a zeppelin surfaced like a whale over Barrow Hill, skin painted to advertise malted cereal. A flock of blackbirds covered its spines.

"Have you seen *Er Krue Alteirz*?" asked one of the three Pplarians at the table in slightly broken Hinter. He took his striking violet-blue eyes off the airship and glared hospitably at Caliph.

The Pplarian's name was Klǫ. Even seated at the table he seemed to tower, wrapped like his fellows in a traditional kạsh and, despite the balmy weather, clad in loose heavy robes of dark, perfumed, yak fur.

Klǫ had very short blond hair that covered his milk-white scalp like peach fuzz. All three of them were tall and slender.

"I have," said Caliph. "It was very interesting. I understand that the villain is based on historical—"

"Yes," Klǫ took over, "the sorcerer, he . . . came out of the west . . . long ago. It is a true story . . . originally. Made grand by opera." He laughed as though something were very funny.

Caliph smiled. "Your people have a great history."

In unison the Pplarians gave a strangely charmed reciprocal smile that twisted their mouths oddly. Caliph had spoken in White Tongue.

Klǫ leaned forward. "You sound like my younger brother when you speak our language! How much do you know?"

"I studied a bit at college in the Kingdom of Greymoor," Caliph explained.

The Pplarians nodded their heads.

"You must have learned from a Pplarian," said Klǫ. "Your sound is very natural."

"I learned from a man named Gilban Tosh. He lived in the Pplar for many years."

"Yes." Klǫ nodded. "I have heard of him." He drew one of the tall purple drinks from the tray and sipped it. Overhead, crows and orchid-colored rylfs disturbed the air, flitting furtively through stiff tendrils of unnerving vegetation. Gadriel had left the room.

Klǫ's first councilor was also his wife. She looked almost exactly like her husband except her eyes were piercing lavender and her bosom stretched the scintillating fabric of her kạsh.

"How do you feel about your uncle?" she asked with straightforward curiosity that she seemed to find perfectly appropriate.

"Yes," said Klǫ, "we are very curious about him."

Caliph inhaled deeply and wondered, *What in Emolus' name has Lewis been telling you?*

"My uncle was not a popular man for many good reasons. I don't think about him. It's a shame the people of this country had to be terrorized while he was High King."

Klɷ's wife looked deeply empathetic.

"You poor boy."

"Nâsa," her husband scolded her mildly, "he is the High King. He does not need our sympathy."

"It's fine," said Caliph. "I have to deal with the past, just like everyone else." He offered them a sincere favoring look. "How was your stay in Vale Briar?"

"Lovely," said Nâsa. "Though your subordinate Lewis is not to be trusted." She seemed unaware of how her statement changed the dynamic of the conversation.

Caliph tried to maintain his calm, pleasant demeanor.

"Really? Why do you say that?"

The second councilor, another woman named Vtî, gestured with slow grace toward Ironside's harbor.

"He keeps ships from Mortūrrm."

"You are different than we heard," said Klɷ. "Your subordinate said you had a charmed tongue that hid a wrathful heart. I enjoy these bird gardens."

He looked overhead at shadowy forms darting near the glass.

"We do not have such things in the Pplar. Your cities are amusing. I always think that you must be very afraid of being out of doors."

Nâsa smiled, her lavender eyes intense.

"King Howl would find our country no less strange. Isn't that right?"

Caliph demurred. "I'm sure it's breathtaking." He wanted to get back to the topic of King Lewis but didn't know how. The Pplarians' manner of speech made him feel like he was still trying to communicate with them in White Tongue.

"It is," affirmed Klɷ as though feeling the need to stress an otherwise empty compliment about his homeland. "The giant yak," he touched his robe, "wanders the snowy waste." He talked with his fingers, indicating a vast expanse of land. "Have you ever been to our country, King Howl?"

Caliph had studied Pplarian society. It revolved around large nuclear families—the most important element of their government. They were fiercely tribal and loyal but there was little fighting between the tribes. He also knew them to be extremely brilliant with technology. The way Klɷ talked, it sounded like they all lived in huts around campfires. Caliph knew that wasn't the case.

Once, long ago, the Pplarians had attempted to enslave the Nanemen, driving strange ships across the Dunatis like ivory water beetles.

Despite their advanced technology, it had ended badly for them.

The Nanemen had chased them back, had stood in the hills below the Healean Range and by their eyes and tongues hurled the heads of fallen Pplarian warriors into the sea. The rumbling echo of their war howls still trembled in the mountains.

Stonehold was not a gentle place.

Slowly the war had scabbed over, healed by medicines and ointments, amethysts and silver. Traders had bridged the gap, obliterating years of bloodshed with commerce and goodwill balanced on a slippery stack of money.

"No," said Caliph. "I have never been to your country. Perhaps one day. If I survive this war."

Nâsa reached out and touched Caliph's hand comfortingly.

"It is a difficult time for you. We know. But we will acknowledge this new government in Isca. We will acknowledge the throne of Caliph Howl."

"Yes," said Klọ. "You are a good heart, like family. We cannot send you help in this war, but perhaps there are weapons we have that you could use. Not much, but we will send you some."

Caliph felt disoriented by the strange metaphor, as though he had just been adopted without his knowing it.

"That is very kind of you. I will accept whatever help my friends can spare."

"It is not much," Klọ said again as if not wanting to inflate Caliph's hopes. "But it is some."

Caliph's mouth dropped open in horror.

Something had wriggled beneath the Pplarian's kạsh. Klọ noticed and drew his dark furs together like a woman startled by a man staring at her cleavage. Caliph didn't know what to say.

Nâsa patted him reassuringly on the back of the hand. Her eyes looked crazed despite the gentle expression on her face.

"It happens sometimes," she said. "It's a throwback to the old days, when the blood was cleaner, when we had mingled less with your kind. Don't worry, Caliph Howl, it was not your fault."

Klọ stood, still holding his robes together. He forced a pained, embarrassed smile.

"She is right, King Howl. Do not worry. I will send some weapons. I like you much better than your subordinate Lewis—and these bird gardens are . . . remarkable." His violet-blue eyes nearly glowed.

The meeting ended suddenly as the three Pplarians rose, bidding him good-bye in White Tongue.

Caliph stood and walked them to the door where Gadriel had been waiting. As the High Seneschal took over, escorting the foreign dignitaries back through the castle, Caliph's mind replayed what he had seen.

The kạsh was a one-piece strip of fabric several yards long that, when worn correctly, fashioned a suit of sorts, winding around the chest, over the shoulders and down the back to complete in a kind of brief underwear tied at the hip with a tassel. It was from beneath the single band of bright cloth that covered Klọ's upper chest that Caliph had seen the strange movement.

The fabric had undulated suddenly and something small and freakish had clawed its way into view. A tiny humanlike arm, no bigger than a caterpillar, topped by an infant's graceless clutching hand. It was white and rubbery, the size of Caliph's pinkie. Flailing. Twisting free of the kạsh's tight bindings. Squirming for an instant like a grub whose tail had been sutured to Klọ's left serratus anterior.

Then Klọ had drawn his robes together, perfuming the air, hiding the mutant limb under layers of heavily scented yak fur.

Caliph stood in the shadowy aviary, listening to winged things rustle through the plants, staring out the vast windows flecked with dry urine and birdlime.

The zeppelins prowled over Ironside, ubiquitous and sullen. He listened to his breathing, smelled the ammoniacal fumes of the birds.

"Well," he whispered to himself. "That went well—I think . . ."

THE meeting with the Pplarians had been much briefer than Caliph anticipated; it left him plenty of time to meet with Sigmund Dulgensen.

He took the *Byun-Ghala* from its new home in the hangars off the zeppelin deck and plowed east over Temple Hill, passing the delicious smell of the malt house to the south.

In Ironside, hulls rose like whalebones from outspread keels as workers reinforced the wood with steel. Chemical welders sparkled amid the shadowy strakes and stanchions and partially plated bulkheads.

Men crawled through a jungle of beams and cables, black as the steel they worked, feverish to outfit warships in case Saergaeth attacked by sea. They ignored Caliph's zeppelin as it neared a mooring mast over the Glôssok warehouses.

From here, Caliph could see the huge lacy arches of the aqueducts that ringed the bay. He left the airship for the military labs secreted in Glôssok.

A body of armed men wearing barbuts and black leather armor accompanied him.

He met Sigmund, who had gotten word the High King was on his way, in an observation room overlooking the factory floor. Caliph ordered everyone else out.

"How's old Caph holdin' up?" Sigmund grinned. His hands were black and slippery past the elbows.

"I'm holding up."

"And the funeral?" asked Sigmund.

"They cremated him in Fallow Down," said Caliph. His voice was thick and monotone. "They flew him in on a zeppelin. He's sitting on the mantle in the grand hall. I guess I haven't wanted to deal with it yet. I tell myself I'm too busy."

Sigmund sighed and nodded softly while looking at his shoes.

"But that's not why I'm here."

Sigmund looked up. "I hope I ain't fired."

Caliph chuckled. "No . . . no, but I . . . I've been doing some thinking. I want to give you another chance to explain this solvitriol stuff to me. Please tell me you haven't told anyone about the blueprints."

Sigmund's face, despite layers of carbon and grease, had already lit up like a welder's torch. "Fuck no. I ain't told a soul. What do you want to know?"

"We're running out of metholinate. Saergaeth's cut our supply from the Memnaw and we're . . . well, I guess you could say we're close to being fucked."

"How much gas we got left?" asked Sigmund, chewing on his beard.

Caliph heaved a sigh and pulled his hair away from his forehead with one hand.

"Not much. You've probably noticed the city's pretty dark at night. Most of the streetlamps have been locked off. We can last another month. Maybe two depending on the weather."

Sigmund grunted and draped his massive arm over the back of his chair.

"That ain't a lot of time, Caph. I've got blueprints, manuals, yeah, but I ain't never built this shit before. You changed your mind about kitties goin' zip?" He spun his finger in the air to mimic a centrifuge.

"Give me a break," said Caliph. "I know you've been tinkering. You must have some of it worked out by now—and no, I haven't changed my mind. It's still disgusting. But frankly . . . well . . . it's no worse than most of the other travesties I've seen lately." He bit his lip and shrugged. "I guess we'll kill some cats."

Sigmund chuckled in a vague noncommittal way and took a tin of tobacco from his overalls. He packed his lip and scowled at the taste of burnt oil.

"Yeah, I guess I can't fool you. I've been tinkering. It's slow going though. I've kept most of my calculations in my locker, got a few tentative mechanisms in there too. But I can't do much more on my own."

"You won't be on your own. I'm going to put you in charge of a classified department. You can have as many engineers as you need. As much space as you need. Nobody talks. Not to anyone. Everyone reports to you and you report to no one but me. How does that sound?"

"Fuck yeah."

"What do you need?"

Due north of Isca the land blistered. Mud pots glopped and farted. They spewed white putty, silica and clay, like liquefied plaster. Beyond them, the green Fields of Gora sprawled inward toward Fallow Down from the sea.

At Fallow Down, Hitchsum Bridge crossed the White Leech where it swung wide and swift toward Borgoth's Noose before cutting back into Bittern Moor and slicing south of Bellgrass. The bridge crossed half a mile of gray chop with a wide flat field of sun-bleached paving stones.

One of only three bridges that could support the weight of Saergaeth's war engines, it had been fortified with artillery, wired by demolition teams in case of a sudden assault. Overhead, the only war zeppelin Tentinil laid claim to cagily patrolled the area.

Its captain had good reason to be afraid.

Mushrooms of orange and green smoke blossomed on both banks, drifting like jellyfish on the breeze. Both sides launched chemical bombs from growling engines that stalked the rivage. Most hit nothing but dirt.

Roric Feldman had come down to fight, accompanied by a House Guard named Garen and a handful of men. He had convinced his father to let him ride one of three engines patrolling the bank.

It took twenty men to operate a light engine and fifty for the big heavies (yet to be seen on either side of the conflict).

Like its zeppelin force, Tentinil had only one light engine. The others had come from Isca, rolling north weeks ago. They guarded the bridges while the remaining Iscan machines stayed behind, shepherding the city from zeppelin attacks.

Roric's father was loyal to the High King. He would have locked his own son in the pillory had Roric so much as extolled a single virtue of Saergaeth Brindlestrom.

But the war hadn't gotten very bloody—yet. At least not here. And Roric didn't even consider this fighting. As far as he was concerned, his allegiance to Isca was a technicality.

He was a voyeur, watching the plumes of poisonous smoke erupt with boyish glee. He stood on the deck of the Tentinilian engine, a small flat space bounded by a single guardrail.

There were two decks stacked on top of each other, connected by a short series of metal rungs. Heavy armored doors swung open from either deck to allow access to the cramped, dark, hissing guts of the machine.

Its lower bowels seethed with fulgent coal. Huge swing gears thrust themselves in roaring grease-spitting revolutions. Massive chemiostatic cells pumped blazing green blood through mechanisms linked bewilderingly to brass and steel fixtures on the pistonlike parts of groaning hydraulics. Gauges measured temperature, flow and speed.

Four great triangular arrangements of toothy wheels pulled the engine forward, laying down a never-ending metal ribbon of blunted blades. The entire engine lifted upward and backward like a boot. As the shift drum turned in some deep sealed transmission, the monster lurched east down the shore, flinging out briquettes of tread-shaped ground.

The thing was heavily armored, riveted and brown with age. A clutch of heavy pipes jacked backward off the bulkhead behind the decks, coughing blackness into the air. Gun cradles housed massive gas-powered ballistae that fired steel spheres filled with pressurized vitriol mixtures.

Roric stood on the top deck, twenty feet off the ground, whooping as the artillery popped from the ballistae and hurtled across the river. On the other side, a violent concussion rent the ground.

Detonated mud and shrapnel twisted outward like sound. A plume of green mist ripped upward like an irate ghost, screaming silent molecular death to anything in its path.

Garen stepped out onto the deck, gripping the railing to keep his balance on the bucking, grated floor. He offered Roric a leather mask with a canister snout.

Roric thanked him at the top of his voice. He wondered briefly what it would be like to ride one of the heavies.

Saergaeth must have known better than to waste effort on the bridge. Although he was miles away, his troops returned volley with what looked like bored fear, vaguely conscious that one of the canisters might hit them directly.

They didn't even aim except in haphazard fashion, eyeballing coordinates and guessing at wind. There was no point. They knew the bridge was wired. Even if they melted the Iscan engines, the demolitions team would ensure they never crossed.

Besides, Fallow Down was the last bastion of Iscan power north of the river. An entire regiment of men still rebuffed the attack as Saergaeth struggled to secure the muddy ground.

Roric wasn't worried. His father had moved a battalion across the bridge, stationing them on the south side, and although he had returned to the town for additional supplies, the danger was minimal.

For some reason, Saergaeth wasn't pushing very hard. After Bellgrass had fallen, the renegade king seemed to pause, unwilling to spread himself too thin.

He's waiting, thought Roric. *Biding his time until his zeppelins are retrofitted for war.* By that time, Roric planned to be somewhere else.

North of the river, over the steep wooden rooftops of Fallow Down, a storm was bloating. A great horn of cloud curved out of the sky, white and gleaming on top, black and treacherous underneath. It spiked down into the ground like a massive rooting claw.

It had developed with savage speed, tumefying out of nowhere.

Roric felt the urge for a better view. As his father's son, he laid claim to more clout than approval but when he asked the commander of the engine to gun the machine for higher ground his request was accommodated with surprising pliancy.

The light war engine hunched forward as it tore up Dürmụth Hill, providing a decent view across the river toward the south of town.

Trees shattered into pulpy pink blossoms, ripped into hirsute shreds by the huge stuttering tracks. Birds and panicked soot-tails bolted from their hiding places as the machine powered east toward the summit. It hunkered forward on strange scorpion joints against the grade.

A lone gruelock that had been lurking in a tree swung into a deep ravine before Roric could shoulder his crossbow. Its black furry body swept gracefully through the branches, several arms moving at speed, unaccustomed but shifting nevertheless quickly from the role of predator to prey.

When they hit the summit, the engine relaxed to a chugging idle, flexing its body back into its usual shape.

Garen and the commander stepped out onto the top deck with Roric, removing their gas masks in order to talk.

"Good view," said the commander. He had to grimace to keep his teeth from chattering with the machine's pandemic vibration.

Fallow Down had turned into a tactical maze. All the noncombatants had crossed the bridge south into the High King's lands or tramped north to side with Saergaeth.

It was the age-old ugliness of civil war: father against son, friend versus friend. The town's layout spread old stone and rusty fingers in starfish multiplicity from a central square. It looked squalid and gray, oppressed by the blossoming cloud.

Roric snapped open his spyglass. Despite the jittering of the deck, he could see troops in the streets and snipers with crossbows patrolling rooftops. To the west, beyond the range of engagement, Miskatoll's light war engines continued to scud along the bank, occasionally sending a glittering emerald arcing over the river to lift in a puff of poison on the south side.

The Somber Hills tumbled morosely to the north, already black and sodden under the shadow of the storm.

"He's toying with us," said the commander. "He won't cross here. Clever bastard's worked through the mountains. Bendain's Keep is under siege."

Fear leaked like treacle down Roric's spine. Kennan Keep was next in line.

"He probably wants the whole string of keeps as zeppelin stations," said Garen.

As the men speculated, Roric's understanding unfolded. If Saergaeth controlled the keeps in the Greencaps, he would control the lowlands as well. His enormous fleet of zeppelins could then pummel the open plains at their leisure and retreat into the crags like dragons to roost.

"If Caliph Howl ain't building airships like Mathias Starlet, he's going to be serving steel wine in Isca."

"That's true enough," muttered Garen.

Roric marveled. The fact that Saergaeth was outwitting Caliph pumped a quiet, petulant, albeit vicarious sense of victory through his veins.

"What the fuck is going on with those clouds anyway?" asked Garen.

All three men gazed at the horn-shaped storm whose hook had bled in swizzled patterns toward the river. At first it looked like the sky had gone rampage-wild. Weltering in frenzied tumbling gouts like a pot of boiling milk hung upside down.

The chaos defied gravity.

Foaming snub-nosed lumps of vapor pushed toward the ground and then retreated, sloshing back into a sky that shuddered like pudding.

Variegated layers of atmosphere burst like invisible pillows, scattering sudden snow. The three men would have cursed if they hadn't been so surprised.

Despite the sudden cold that rolled across the plains at subsonic speed, the air wavered and danced as if through a mirage of heat. Something vast rippled across the sky like momentary circus glass, bending the clouds, warping the structures of Fallow Down like brown kelp.

Across the river, Saergaeth's engines seemed to shiver in the cold, wobbling and trembling like metal bees on honeycomb.

Roric stood at the edge of miles of warped space. It was as if the very air were melting.

The snowfall rolled and veered erratically as though hesitant to fall. Hovering like ash. A shadow six miles in every direction passed over the ground, sliding from the Somber Hills toward Fallow Down. It cast the town in purple umber and dyed the river muscles black.

The entire sky thrashed madly for an instant, flailing as though seen through the bodies of a million glass eels.

The entire crew of the engine, from gunners to coal-throwers to the navigator on the bridge, had crept out onto the decks or pivoted their turrets to watch the display.

It felt to all of them as if there should have been some nightmare sound accompanying the untoward air. But there was nothing. Just the cold and the quiet. The atmosphere burst with slippery invisible grotesque modulation. It flexed. Rolled. Then suddenly it stopped.

The shadow evaporated as if the cloud casting it had dried up. The darkness dwindled. The strange convolutions of atmosphere smoothed without a trace.

"Fuck thunder!" whispered the commander.

Saergaeth's engines had disappeared. Fallow Down, the entire mile-and-a-half-wide sprawl of town—everything north of the river, was gone!

Roric remembered his father and screamed.

AFTER fifteen minutes of heated debate and speculation over whether the phenomenon had indeed reached terminus, Garen and the commander agreed over Roric's insistent wail that they might as well throw dice. Nothing either one of them could say made any sense in the face of such an aberration. So they decided to take pity on Roric Feldman and risk an investigation.

The light engine smashed down the north face of Dürmuth Hill at top speed, crashing through bracken, spitting out flinders and destruction in its wake. When it hit level ground the gears shifted and the treads gouged fresh earth, flinging clods as the machine barreled toward the bridge.

Roric wiped tears from his eyes as he clutched a gas-powered crossbow to his chest. He was shaking with horror, disbelief and utter confusion. Garen stood behind him on the deck, holding a bow of his own. The howling pound of the engines made any kind of conversation impossible.

As they reached the bridge, the treads clattered dolorously and maniacally over the stone, creating such a racket that Roric hung his bow on a steel strut and plugged his ears. It took little less than a minute to cross the half-mile bridge.

What greeted them on the other side would go down as one of the strangest discoveries of the fifth century. And the strangest part was that there was nothing there. Nothing to catalogue. Nothing coherent to sift through.

Roric clambered down the two sets of rungs and leapt to the ground. He scoured the area with his eyes, looking for remains.

Remains?

What remains? he thought brokenly. There was nothing! The ground in every direction had been pulverized to fine gray powder. Granules actually. Tiny hollow nuggets like blistered pewter. Miniscule ball bearings. Some were fused in clumps. Some were slightly larger, the size of a sparrow's eye. Roric lifted a handful and let them trickle through his fingers, ugly leaden beads, freezing to the touch. His fingers ached immediately.

There were still traces of snow, melting rapidly as the summer wind swept in, displacing the anomalous front.

Roric searched for anything. A filament of blackened straw, a splinter of wood or the blasted fragments of bricks poking out of the sweepings. But there was nothing. Not a grain of wheat. Not a beetle wing.

As he disturbed the tiny spheres with his hand Roric had noticed the awful withering stench seeping from the ground. It nearly gagged him and he stumbled backward, dropping the bubbled pellets in disgust. He perceived a trace of diversity in the destruction. Here and there the scrap of widespread disintegration had hardened into a grisly yellowish-gray-green and purple crust. It looked like molten slag had cooled into thin metallic plates, pocked and cratered and ugly.

Roric wept and cursed and kicked about, sending up large clouds of noxious invisible fume. The swath of obliteration centered on the former town and swept its ruin west along the rivage. It had encompassed Saergaeth's war engines and left nothing behind. Even the zeppelin was gone, dissolved instantly in air.

Roric kicked in the dust, heedless of the choking stench. His rage did not diminish when the vapors overcame him, and he began to gag and heave. He crouched, gasping, spewing vomit from his nose and mouth.

Garen and the commander had donned their gas masks. They seized Roric and dragged him, despite his spastic kicking, from the field of dull glittering beads.

Back near the relative safety of the idling machine where the air was less toxic and infused only with engine smoke, they laid Roric out on the deck. His eyes were weeping clear mucosa and slimy bile dribbled from his chin and nose—but he was breathing.

"You dumb fuck!" whispered the commander. He turned his attention to Garen. "Next time he tries a stunt like that, I leave both of you behind."

Garen nodded and snapped his fingers in front of Roric's clouded eyes. The commander went inside and ordered the engine to back up and head for the bridge.

When Garen looked at Roric, his face took on a barely discernable expression of compassion.

BACK on the other side of the bridge, the commander joined the other two engine crews at the HQ pavilion and met the lieutenant colonel of the battalion overseeing the bridge, the five-man demolition team that had wired it and the two knights serving mostly as military advisors.

By the time Roric was breathing well enough to sit up and look around, a fierce argument was already underway.

"We do not, repeat, do not blow the bridge without imminent threat," the lieutenant colonel was saying. His face flushed and strained and his eyes flashed from one man to another as he tried to bring the others under control. All of them were formidable professionals.

"That's not imminent enough for you?" One of the knights threw his arm in the direction of the disturbance. That's what they were calling it. *A disturbance.*

"Imminent threat of enemy crossing," finished the lieutenant colonel. "We have orders. And that wasn't the enemy. We don't know what that was!"

He was shouting in the knight's face, a brave and rash thing to do. Spittle was flying. He flung his hand toward the sky. "You think blowing the bridge will stop that if it comes back?"

The knight did not back down. "Do I look like I give a fuck? We have mass casualties. You've got less than a thousand men left. Our zeppelin's gone. Most of our supplies were in that town. This just became an indefensible, tactically dead position. What good is the bridge without Fallow Down?"

"You're not authorized to make that decision!"

"Whore-shit!" fired the knight. "Decisions like this are why I'm fucking here. We aren't FNG. Our orders were to protect Fallow Down which—by the fucking way—is gone!"

Knight was a throwback term to the days when there was no such thing as chemiostatic power. They were outfitted for the severest kind of contingencies, trained to deal with being cut off, outnumbered and surrounded in hostile territory. Knights were more than one-man war engines. They were seasoned veterans and this one's name was Stroud; he impressed Roric Feldman. He wore heavy brown armor that lifted from his shoulders, arms and back in gracile stingray spines. Despite being made of heavy metal, the armor looked anatomically like plates of bone.

Roric had never seen a suit of it up close. Holomorphically tempered glass bulbs filled with luminescent green liquid squeezed between disks in a virtual spinal column of choratium. He knew the metal was tough as steel but slightly lighter in weight. It oxidized like aluminum; the film that covered it protected it from further corrosion even though it looked identical to iron rust.

Roric's eyes followed flexible metal hoses with glass couplings. Chemiostatic fluid flowed to certain regions of the armor: powering shoulder joints, heating or cooling abdominal plates below the cuirass and the fauld.

Stroud towered over the lieutenant colonel as he argued about the bridge. Roric held his tongue. He knew the lieutenant colonel's rank still gave him the edge.

"I'm about ready to kick your ass, soldier! Your position here as tactical liaison is finished! Are we clear?"

It was a dangerous line to go but Roric saw the knight nod. "Yes, sir."

The lieutenant colonel's face was splotchy—mostly from fear. It had taken every ounce of his authority to regain control under the extraordinary circumstances.

"We don't know what happened out there," the lieutenant colonel shouted again, this time to everyone present. "Whatever it was, it happened to Miskatoll's engines and troops as much as it did our own. Odds are it was some neutral force. It could be weather for all we know."

"Weather my ass. That was witchcraft."

Stroud's opinion was popular. Echoed mutters of "holomorphy" flapped around the open tent. No one wanted to stay and guard a haunted bridge much less a place where they had seen the fiber of reality twist and snap like a shaken rug.

The sudden stillness north of the river and the faint gray plain that most of the men had seen only from a distance had demonized the region.

Less than an hour ago everything was normal: as normal as ordnance exchange on the front line could be. The danger, though extreme, had been categorical, comprehensible, able to be planned for.

But now, even though no trace of the enemy force remained, a host of unclear suspicions beset the men. Everyone wanted out. Now.

"FB!" shouted the lieutenant colonel.

A thin man in light leather armor whose straps flapped from tightly cinched buckles and who still wore his gas mask pushed up like a bizarre hat on the top of his head had been waiting for the call.

He had pulled a hooded bird from one of several cages. It perched on a stand at the ready. The falconer's hand was poised, clutching a pen, ready to scribble the words on a tiny roll of paper.

As the officer dictated, the falconer wrote. When he was finished a cruestone was snapped into the hawk's exposed skull through a hole in its hood. The FB then removed the hood and turned the bird loose. It flapped madly for the Iscan High Command, blind, driving powerful muscles toward release from the fire that filled its brain.

The lieutenant colonel had made his decision. Roric hoped secretly that it was the wrong one, that Saergaeth's tactics would not be hampered.

"Fire the bridge!"

It was the decision everyone wanted. But the lieutenant colonel had made his point. He could have had it either way. He had not caved in to pressure. He had not buckled under Stroud's verbal barrage. It was his decision alone. He had considered the pros and cons, measured the tactical advantages of a bridge versus a barrier. He had removed his ego from the scales and everyone in the pavilion knew it.

The demolitionists turned and headed for the bank.

Roric watched them go with mute nausea. His eyes burned. His stomach felt like it had turned to slime, liquefied by the caustic stench of the wasteland. He held his head in one hand and sobbed brokenly.

The lieutenant colonel ignored it.

"All right soldiers, saddle up! SOP! We move for the Noose in under twenty!" He began barking.

Everyone moved but Roric Feldman. He sat on a field trunk holding his head.

Garen stood beside him with his hand on his shoulder. He had already called for a medic twice. No one was coming. Roric's tears were diminishing slightly. He was clutching, pulling himself together.

"I remember when I was a boy," he hissed. "My father talked about the blight." He wiped his nose and eyes on his sleeve. "Do you remember it?"

Garen nodded. "King's Rot," he said stiffly.

"King's Rot," said Roric. "Only seen during Nathaniel Howl's reign."

"That was different," said Garen softly. "White mold on the ground . . . smut in the fields—"

"Was it?" Roric hissed. "Was it different? Maybe it's the same only worse. Maybe this is Howl Rot."

Garen seemed to swallow with difficulty.

"What are you going to do?"

Roric rose shakily to his feet. "I'm going back to Kennan Keep," he whispered. "I'm going to ensure Bendain's Keep falls to Saergaeth. I'm going to make sure this war turns out right. I'm telling you so you can transfer your fealty to another house," said Roric. He looked away.

It was an outdated rubric, a formality extended to an honored member of one's personal guard. It had been done in days of old as a way of allowing the warrior class to disentangle themselves from political crisis—leave before the assassins arrived, disavow any ties to a doomed line. It was a courtesy. A final charitable act.

Garen looked toward the bridge just as the wires went live. Heavy steel charges filled with hülilyddite flowered, as yellow and bitter and poisonous in their eruption as the acid that gave them life.

Blocks of white stone cartwheeled amid catastrophic debris made weightless by the transcendent moment of concussion. Small bits of mortar and chunks of broken rock turned into deadly projectiles. Nuggets of bridge fell like hail in profusion.

An amber-gray cloud drifted west with the wind, a haze that once connected two sides of a river.

The demolition team knew their business.

"Lord," said Garen softly. "There are no other houses to go to."

Roric looked at the captain, startled, suspicious.

"You mean to—?"

"I mean to serve the Duchy of Stonehold," said Garen with simple candor. "And the Feldman House . . . to its end."

A ripple of doubt clouded Roric's face for a moment, then disappeared as he saw that Garen meant what he said. He felt like weeping anew but didn't.

"All right . . . all right." He looked at his shoes, nodding ridiculously as a father might nod to his son, allowing him to accompany him somewhere dangerous despite his better judgment. "If that's what you want." He cleared his throat of the last trace of the burning fumes. "If that's what you want . . ."

CHAPTER
19

Some claimed Ghoul Court was a pornocracy without the reach of Isca's city watch. It was the lair of people who made their living off atrocities: parnels, hippospadians and magsmen. Blink-fencers hawked stolen eyeglasses in the street while small-time crooks distributed cigarettes loaded with powdered aspirin.

Pavement nymphs performed services up against the moldering foundations of huge brick warehouses or in congested alleys where flying buttresses provided shelter from the rain. They painted their faces with colorful designs meant to ward off the bortghast rumored to haunt the corner of Knife and Heath.

Flesh-tailors from Bloodsump Lane arrived promptly for abuse at the hands of their masters. They lolled in green-lit second-story dens, staring from odd angled positions where they had fallen into chairs and filthy beds. For hours they would look at grungy plaster surfaces where flies and roaches outmaneuvered gravity, tasting the walls for flecks of organic spew.

Zane Vhortghast was a common specter here though no one called him Zane. In the Court he went by Peter Lark, a minor manipulator of the threads. He led a charmed life despite his disconcerting connections to thugs and underworld guilds. If anyone paid him enough it was known that he could produce a body like magic, floating in the Bragget Canal before dawn the next day.

He wasn't a big fish but he wasn't a guppy either. He passed with disturbing anonymity through the Court. Only those that knew him classed him as a dangerous man. But that was the spymaster's desire, to go unnoticed while still being "plugged in."

Zane kept a small apartment in the Court for show. He never slept there but took some time every month to embellish the charade.

He kept a pile of rumpled sheets on an iron bed frame and a partially dissolved bar of soap in his shower. The soap had cemented itself to the tray and seemed morose, surrounded by exposed pipes and tiles the color of toilet bowl stains.

A half-drained bottle of Pplarian whiskey sat on the floor by the bed.

There were some fake time cards from one of the factories in Growl Mort, a change of clothes, a worn-out toothbrush and a knife that looked like it might have once been used for murder.

Zane looked out from his balcony. It was barely large enough to accommodate him standing.

The sun was just slipping into a drunken red-faced coma behind heavily decayed buildings to the east. The sky was pink as nockstress flesh by the time little orange squares began to flicker in the darkening walls and edifices that pressed the street. People lit candles and oil lamps, moving light from room to room.

The streetlamps remained ornate blackened scepters. Metholinate to Ghoul Court had been rationed, said the papers. In reality it had been turned off.

Zane felt the indignation boiling just under the surface. The population wouldn't stand for it much longer.

Just the previous week, a man had tried to tap in under the street to siphon his own supply. He was smoking at the time and the explosion had thrown him through the bricks. He came out of the tunnel, through the street and into the open air, popping up like toast.

A team of city engineers had come in to fix the damage, guarded by a squad of five knights in full battle gear. That was something new. Not even the hardest criminals thought about tangling with the knights. They were quite possibly the first outsiders not to leave in fear.

Zane Vhortghast knew they wouldn't be the last.

Caliph's plan for cleansing the Court would see action soon and it would not be a gentle clean.

Part of Zane bemoaned the time he had sunk into the Court. He would lose most of his contacts to prison or they would become casualties of the raid. On the other hand, if it worked, it meant he would not have to invest any more time chasing phantoms.

From his balcony, Fifth Street extended north like a latrine. Great peaked canisters, water towers and grinding engines squatted on rooftops like deformed metal goblins. They muffled the desultory moans emanating from windows with sashes thrown open to the night.

The struggling cries of Ghoul Court's diverse clientele issued lustily through the thick humid air. Zane imagined their sweating bodies for a moment wrestling in the dark, enduring the hot weather as they worked out anxieties linked to the encroaching war.

A bottle broke in an alley and someone screamed. Three dark shapes trampled across the street, carrying clothes and other plunder.

A knock sounded at the paper-thin door. Zane turned and crossed the room in four steps. He opened it, revealing a hallway that was darker than his room and smelled far worse.

"Hey Peter." A skeletal lad with mad black hair and deliberate scars up and down his arms stood wavering on the threshold. He had a birdcage in one hand. "Got yer tweet."

Zane jammed his hand into his pocket and pulled out a handful of coins. He squeezed them meticulously, pushing them out between his thumb and forefinger one at a time into his other palm.

"Three gryphs is robbery."

The dizzy man smiled and loosely extended his hand.

"Yeah, well, you know any other bird-duffers?"

"Plenty."

The man sneered and gave Zane/Peter the cage.

"Don't spend it all on sweet red," said Zane.

The man made an obscene gesture in reply and stumbled off into the dark.

Zane closed the door and locked it out of habit. He turned up the oil lamp on a small badly beaten desk and pulled off the cloth covering the cage.

He swore.

It was a pathetic sight. The pigeon was black from soot and badly torn as though it had been stuck in and then ripped out of a chimney pipe. The chirurgery had been preformed ruthlessly and recently. Blood still caked the feathers all around the excised flesh. The skull was pink and the bird cried piteously.

Heartless as he was, cruelty to animals was something Zane Vhortghast could not stomach—which was why he ate the insensible meat produced under Thief Town as opposed to beef, rationalizing that meat wasn't really an animal. It was more like plant life that grew in the dark. More like fungus.

He swallowed a lump in his throat and set the cage aside in disgust. He wondered if the thing could even make the flight. It was a long way. Farther than he himself had ever traveled.

He had to hurry. He had been sweating it out waiting for the duffer.

Tonight was the twenty-fourth of Lüme, the night the High King was taking his tart to the opera. Zane had promised to be there when they arrived, overseeing the security detail assigned to the building.

He took the note he had composed earlier and opened the cage. The bird went hysterical. It didn't have a hood. It thrashed about, terrified, clawing and pecking at his gloved hand. He was forced to grab it by the head to cover its eyes. The duffer hadn't even given him a tube.

Cursing violently, Zane struggled to get a tiny scroll case wired to its ankle. He then inserted his note and grimaced as he pressed a black crue-stone into the metal clip screwed into the creature's skull.

He took it to the balcony, hoping it could still fly.

Carefully, gently, with ridiculous indulgence, he set the thing on the floor. It took off at once, flapping back into the room, crashing into walls and lamps in its confusion.

Zane winced and swore. He leapt about, trying to corral it, waving his arms, herding it toward the open sky. For a moment, he wondered if the chirurgeon had been ripped on something when he performed the operation. But then the fire in the bird's mind finally seemed to consume its confusion. It stopped its self-abuse and wheeled toward the balcony. It sped out, up and away into the skyline's brown glow.

Heart pounding, Zane Vhortghast let out a long sigh, vowing to find the duffer and the chirurgeon when he had spare time.

With only twenty minutes to reach the opera, the spymaster leapt out his balcony window, landed deftly on a steel drum and hit the bricks running.

As the sky clotted with stray vapors and shadowy things, the *Byun-Ghala* departed Isca Castle. Its huge pulsating propellers powered it out across the striated murk. Miles of bruised atmosphere and city enmeshed, twisted together in a surreal tangle of deep maroon and deviant structural black. Lights twinkled far below, white-gold and tiny.

From the observation deck, the wind smelled clean and cool despite the humidity. Sena had never flown before. She was giddy with delight.

She wore a formal décolletage, indigo with tiny diamonds down the kick pleat. One of many choices given her by the army of tailors and dress-makers, it accentuated her movements by design. Her entire back was bare.

She had explored every cranny of the zeppelin, seen the huge bedroom and made a flirtatious joke before dragging Caliph quickly out onto the observation deck. It being her first ride, she was unwilling to miss a moment of the view.

The airship plugged east, great flaps of skin pivoting, guiding it out over Ironside, over water. It slipped into the darkness above the bay and turned south, providing a rare romantic view of the city, a deception caused by dusk.

Sena rested her head on Caliph's shoulder and gazed at the distant lights and smoldering industrial stacks of Lower Murkbell. Growl Mort gave off a volcanic glow that turned the heavy vapors erratic orange. It came home to her again with considerable poignancy that the man who ruled the city, who ruled everything she could see was standing right beside her. The most powerful man in Stonehold.

She looked at Isca.

Caliph looked at her.

She felt a tremor in her resolve that frightened her but gave her hope at the same time. She had to wait for autumn. For the lock of a dead man's hair. The book was breathing at the back of her head, at the back of her neck, even though she had locked it up in the rolltop desk in Caliph's bedroom.

She shivered. Not from cold.

Tonight was the debut of a local writer's opera that would run concurrently with *Er Krue Alteirz*, alternating weeks to finish out the season. The *Herald* had proclaimed it a stunning success for a first opera and avidly encouraged attendance. But then, the Murkbell Opera House owned part of the *Herald* and independent publications had been noticeably less flattering.

The *Byun-Ghala* headed inland, crossing Bragget Canal, mooring at an over-elegant spindle of steel and stone. The spindle poured down like molten slag into a nexus of canals where lamp-lit gondolas set out for a luxurious fifteen-minute cruise through the baroque darkness of Murkbell's upper south side.

Discreet operatives, along with the High King's elite personal guard, secured a moving perimeter around the king and his mistress.

Some were discreet.

The musclemen ruthlessly accosted or otherwise blocked pedestrians with chemiostatic nightsticks, giving no explanation when they either turned people away into side streets and detours or when they suddenly let them pass again as the perimeter moved on.

Caliph and Sena glided down the lapping black canals, passing buildings of fantastic age, sliding under fabulous bridges carved with winged things. Through inundated avenues and drowned forgotten alleys, the gondolier poled them. Floating. Lost amid a dizzying agglomeration of decayed fantasy in brick.

Square mooring columns jutted like blackened fingers from sloshing boulevards smeared with nighttime reflections of distant, multicolored lights. The blue and orange lanterns on the boat cast their halos over stone, blazoned cheerful glimmers along dreary piers and culverts.

Wind bothered them.

It rocked the lanterns and swung the light through tunnels, up massive pylons of stone and steel cladding. It illuminated brown monochromatic graffiti.

Suddenly they emerged from the extravagant squalor as from between artificial cliffs. The boat scudded spryly out of a flooded byway onto a lake behind the opera house.

The huge gabled building startled Sena. It loomed like some gray-caped hulk with orange-magenta eyes, lights on for elitist guests who gossiped and smoked and drank champagne in thickets by the doors.

Gas lamps and streetlamps clustered like magic wands, bundles of glass bulbs throwing abalone light across the cobbles, utterly defiant of the metholinate shortage.

Caliph grumbled when he saw the waste and made a mental note to bring management into line. As the gondola touched the pier, a body of guards was already waiting. They held the curious rich at bay. Vhortghast was among them, looking winded. His pale skin glistened. Caliph wondered where he had run from.

Political icons and others who routinely basked in the illustriousness afforded them by the High King's sodality were of course let through. Clayton Redfield was among the few who strode confidently past the sour-faced wall of bodyguards.

Caliph intensely disliked the sense of profound segregation, the illusion of elevation—the utter pomposity. He wanted to call out to the ogling nobles, *What are you staring at? I shit just like you!*

The guards moved as the High King moved, shifting the perimeter as if by smell. They were no less attuned to his movements than a cloud of flies circling the eyes and mouth of a cow. The wealthy parted in gleeful tides, calling out as he and Sena passed, complimenting his choice of apparel—the same mundane black he always wore—as if it had been the newest style.

Caliph waved graciously and made sure Sena managed the stairs in her heels. She smiled and pinched his arm.

The Murkbell Opera House enfolded them.

It was a sea of formal attire. Perfume and pomade. Awash with red lights and the smell of whipped coffee. Perfectly dim. The atmosphere exuded opulence and a frenzied exchange of erudite artistic sensibility.

Gorgeous paintings and draperies soaked in the costly incense of exotic tobacco while men exchanged brand names, prices and offered each other cigars.

After Clayton Redfield had finally agreed to enjoy the show for the third time and summarily faded into the crowd, Zane Vhortghast led the High King to his private box.

A blushing young woman handed Sena a pair of opera glasses despite the box's nearness to the stage. The girl informed her that she could use them to examine the superior craftsmanship of the costumes or the precise expressions on the actors' faces as she chose.

Caliph raised his eyebrows incredulously and studied the program that had made its way into his hand.

As the mournful sounds of violins being tuned wafted from the orchestra pit, two huge men positioned themselves just without the High King's box. They scrutinized and menaced the hall. Their twins lurked inside but hung discreetly back, watching the theater with mechanical attention. Vhortghast himself monitored surveillance from a straight-backed chair that gave him a wide view of the audience below as well as the boxes spaced around the elaborate walls.

Most of the women in the audience and not a few of the men used opera glasses to snatch better glimpses of the royal couple. Girls with fishnet pantyhose and feathered tails and bras distributed fanciful drinks in impossibly tall glasses or whisked empty ones away.

Below the royal box, in aisle three, a soused nobleman groped his friend's wife and fell over a row of chairs, creating a small fracas. He promptly disappeared in the arms of three burly ushers and the tittering waves of conversation resumed as though nothing had happened.

"I liked the Minstrel's Stage better," whispered Caliph.

Sena smirked indulgently. The preceding weeks had been hard on both of them.

At first, Caliph had chuckled when he read the note drawn out of the hawk's tiny canister. Then he had reread it. Then he had reread it again, disbelieving. Finally he had begun to shake and whisper and pace the floor and scowl. What could it mean? he thought. *Fallow Down has disappeared.*

By fast horse and private zeppelin, the adventuresome had already gone out and returned with firsthand accounts of the devastation. There was no keeping it a secret.

The fickle papers had minted every kind of lie and theory they could dream up. Laws passed under the old Council ensuring freedom of the press remained unchallenged though barbs enough to fill a dozen quivers had been hurled at Caliph by several fearless periodicals offering special biweekly editions (or seditions as those loyal to the High King liked to call them).

Caliph had juggled all kinds of meetings with military personnel and worried burgomasters and journalists who constantly overstepped their bounds.

He wanted to go out and see the thing for himself but his advisors forbade it. Round trip, it was nearly seventy-five miles out of the way, and those were precious hours to and from Tentinil better spent in Isca directing operations from a central seat of power.

Caliph had departed on the fifteenth for Queen Guerrian's funeral (the prince's mother had died in her sleep) and returned late the same night by zeppelin. He leapt off the *Byun-Ghala*, and dashed to a late-night meeting like the operator of a mad machine racing to throw switches in an effort to regain control.

Then came the second blow, more devastating on a personal level to Caliph's reign and even more confusing to his supporters than the news that Fallow Down had disappeared. It brought the castle down to a deathly hushed still as the staff read the *Iscan Herald* with utter disbelief.

Some woman had come forward with details. She claimed to have known Sena for many years and felt it her duty to inform the Iscan people of the truth behind the High King's new mistress.

Sena could still remember the headline and the opening paragraph of a two-page story.

High King Court's Witch
by Nick Glugh, Journalist

As if the Iscan people needed more bizarre news another report rocked the foundations of King Howl's fledgling reign when a woman identifying herself as Miriam Yeats came forward with an accusation that the new High King's mistress is a Shraȼdnæ operative. This, just scant days after the tragedy at Fallow Down, an event critics are calling a holomorphic holocaust, once again casts the specter of suspicion over the Iscan Crown . . .

The fact that Caliph had blown it off entirely only made Sena's sense of guilt more profound. He wouldn't even consider arresting the journalist for slander—who had gone into hiding after the story created a sensation. There were rioting protesters near Octul Box: something that had never happened before.

But Caliph dismissed the suggestion of his advisors to retaliate by naming names. They had dug up the college degrees of every politician in Isca, ready to publicly announce those who had gotten a grade in holomorphy from any university in the north.

Instead, Caliph held a press conference and told the journalists the truth.

"Yes," he said. "She's a holomorph. She studied holomorphy at Desdae—just like I did." He refused to answer any question directly as to whether holomorph also meant *witch*.

"No . . . no I won't change the laws pertaining to witchcraft. As far as I know, the women sentenced over the past several years weren't even tried on the grounds of witchcraft but as spies for treason."

It had been a long conference. Caliph had been raked over the coals afterward by the same newspapers that had backed him two months ago when his father died. The same newspapers he allowed to exist.

All he had to do was give the word and the city watch would raid. He could fill West Gate overnight with editors and journalists and have their bodies swinging from chains over the castle just as fast.

But instead of engendering gratitude, the fact that Caliph didn't crush his critics under a mailed fist made them all the more brazen.

The more sensational rags published all kinds of outrageous speculation. He was going to set up a Council of witches to enslave the population. He had been charmed by Sena and was now her puppet. He wasn't even human. He was some creature who went around in disguise, advancing a ridiculous list of ghoulish designs.

"They're entitled," Caliph said blithely. "It's actually quite amusing. They're incessantly creative. And don't worry," he whispered one morning while they were still in bed, "you're quite safe here in the castle."

He was right. His actions, while they didn't win him any favors from the tabloids, had cemented his staff to him. His graciousness to the maids and his refusal to be waited on hand and foot along with a charming tongue-in-cheek way of coping with the "world out there" (as he called it) had so enamored the inhabitants of Isca Castle that after the initial shock of the headline they scoffed and promptly burnt the *Herald* on the grand hall hearth. Thereafter they boycotted it entirely.

By Gadriel's command, Caliph's daily edition was the only edition allowed on the castle grounds.

The burgomasters were nervous. But they bit their tongues. Caliph's charm had a way of reassuring them in ways they found difficult to explain. Clayton Redfield had told him to his face, "We don't know how . . . but we know you'll eventually make things right."

Caliph didn't know how either but his notoriety seemed indistinguishable from popularity. The large boisterous opposition ensured his every public appearance was scrutinized by the masses. But those occasions only reinforced his image as an absolute gentleman and a very good-looking one at that. If he was sinister at all, the women of Isca found it irresistible.

Thus, there probably wouldn't have been any catcalls at the opera even without the small army of bodyguards capable of smashing any fearless critic into paste.

Tonight, Caliph and Sena had promised each other not to talk about headlines or critics or war. Next week began a new month, the month of Streale with a new set of pressures and goals (cleaning out Ghoul Court among them). Tonight was separate. Tonight was only for them.

Caliph handed the program to Sena and rolled his shoulders back, trying to relax. The lights had dimmed and chronic talkers squeezed in a few last words before climbing over the laps and knees of the tactfully irritated toward their seats. Stage lights flared. Brilliant luminous cones flooded the deep crimson folds of curtains that loomed beyond the orchestra.

The show was about to begin.

Icy tendrils of white vapor crawled out from beneath the curtains. A deep vibration of drums had begun resonating from the pit. Suddenly all the lights went down and the curtains swept back, tearing up vortices of mist as they collapsed into the wings.

A man in a pillar of light stood center stage, hand extended overhead, fog pouring in around his feet. Stylized props of leaning cemetery markers, dripping vines and ruinous mausoleums crowded the gloom. His clear tenor rose in a solitary wail of grief as he slowly swept his arm down toward a headstone at his feet.

What followed was a captivating descent into the man's tragic loss and unconsummated love for a fiancée that appeared on stage only in the form of a ghost who drove him laconically toward avenging her murder.

By the end of act two, when the curtains came rushing back together for intermission, the audience also had the vague unsettling notion that she was also driving him to suicide.

Caliph rubbed his eyes. They were dry and tired from staring.

"Better than *Er Krue Alteirz*?" asked Sena.

Caliph yawned. "Surprisingly so. Do you want anything to drink?" Ten minutes before the break, the warm rich smells of the concession stands had begun percolating through the stuffy theater air.

"No. But I need to pee."

"Shall I get you anything?" asked Vhortghast, leaning into Caliph's left ear. "I'm headed for a coffee."

Caliph made the hand sign for yes. "Well, if you're going, I suppose something to keep me awake would be fine. Thank you, Zane."

The spymaster left the box and snapped his fingers subtly at one of the two guards in the hall. He deftly indicated for him to follow Sena to the bathrooms and ensure her safe return.

Vhortghast held the curtain aside and affected a very shallow bow as she exited the box. Though his appearance horrified her, Sena smiled at the spymaster before heading toward the privies. She held her clutch in both hands in front of her waist, taking shortened graceful steps, constrained by her gown.

The huge guard shadowed her every step of the way.

She got several looks, mostly from jealous women. One leering man got a foot too close and found himself pushed by an enormous outspread palm effortlessly and unapologetically into a wall. The affronted gentleman whirled and opened his mouth to complain but thought better of it and snarled mutely instead.

The guard wore a chemiostatic sword on his hip and several throwing knives in a bandolier across his ornate leather breastplate. Outside the women's closet he stopped and glowered at his new post.

Sena went inside and passed a row of filigreed oval mirrors interspersed with gas lamps clad in pink fluted glass. Cherry wood stalls housed overhead tanks with delicate pull chains and dainty porcelain bowls festooned with floral pink.

A gaggle of women primped and gossiped. Some, who had been discussing the High King's mistress, went abruptly tranquil a moment too late.

They stared at her for an instant before either offering pleasantries or snubbing her altogether.

Sena entered a stall and did her business. The silence in the room had spread and become more uncomfortable than if they had just packed it in and whispered. She flushed and walked out. They were staring at her, or pointedly not staring at her. All of them had gone totally silent.

Sena washed her hands and patted them dry.

Just before she left, she turned to the silent throng and said, "Whatever you're thinking . . . it's true." Then she pulled open the door and stepped back into the hall.

There was a scream.

The huge guard appointed her by Zane Vhortghast reached out and roughly jerked her behind him. His sword ascended from its scabbard like a star. His great muscled body plowed through people like sheets on a laundry line.

Sena couldn't see what was going on. The hall boiled with arms and legs and trampling falling people piling for the stairs. A woman in a frenzy came at Sena from the side, unintentionally crashing between her and the guard. The guard responded automatically, grabbing the assailant by her hair and tossing her back the direction she had come. Whether out of confusion or indignation, the woman charged again and Sena's bodyguard punched her in the face, sending her to the floor with a broken nose.

He took Sena's hand and dragged her like a child through the crowd. Frankly, she felt like a child. She allowed herself to be led. She didn't have a weapon. She didn't *want* to be a Shradnæ operative. Since the Halls in Sandren, she didn't dare to trust herself. *No!* Caliph's bodyguards were well trained. She would let them take charge. As the huge man pulled her forward, her legs couldn't keep up and she heard the narrow dress rip. Instead of coming free she stumbled. Tangled in the tube of satin.

Vexed by the slowdown, the guard noticed her dilemma and paused to reach down. He tried to tear out the kick pleat. It was an error.

When he crouched and turned his back on the mass of people something struck him from behind. He dropped to his knees with a chilling look of surprise.

Sena saw a tall thin man behind the guard, a slender stiletto in his hand, ugly pink eyes intent on her face. The guard had dropped his sword, slumped forward, sprawled out in the hall.

A sudden chunk sound, followed by the pink-eyed man's head doing an abrupt forward nod, jarred Sena from her trance.

A crossbow bolt had entered Mr. Naylor's head from behind and ruptured his forehead. He looked like an apple on a skewer. Sena followed the trajectory back to the box where one of the other guards cradled a light metal crossbow in his hands.

The truly horrifying part of it was that Mr. Naylor did not go down. His head popped back up and he looked around despite the gruesome trauma.

His distraction was momentary. The hand with the stiletto lunged for Sena. She launched backward off her toes, avoiding the knife but impacting an elderly man with a cane who had been shuffling in bewildered circles right behind her. The codger tipped over like a chair and Sena tumbled over top, landing on her back with her buttocks on his head and her shoulders on the floor.

It was too crowded to be graceful and her clothing was still an obstacle. By the time she had gotten to her feet, she had managed to pull off her high-heeled shoes. She looked up at the pink-eyed man just as a second guard tackled him from behind.

Mr. Naylor went down like a sled under the momentum of the flying guard. He slid across the carpet, crushed down and howling with rage. It looked so painful that Sena nearly screamed with disbelief when the guard was lifted up on the back of the rail-thin man like an enormous pack.

Mr. Naylor turned around, his head transfixed with metal, his arms pinned at his sides, a great pink rug burn trawling down the middle of his face. Despite the man encumbering his back, his powerful grasshopper legs moved him with ease over the fallen bodies toward Sena.

A second crossbow quarrel struck the opera house manager in the chest. This one took him to his knees. But the guards had no interest in anything other than getting the High King's mistress out of the opera house unharmed.

The man riding Mr. Naylor's back let go, grabbed Sena and pulled her toward the spot where Zane Vhortghast was motioning to a window.

The stairs were choked with people. But there was more to it than that. Sena saw why the spymaster had herded them toward the casement. Two other tall thin men with glassy strange-colored eyes were closing in on their position. The newcomers had bald heads and open mouths and seemed by their strange exaggerated motions to be climbing across the level floor, clawing at the air with arms in a bizarre mantis-like posture.

One of the guards pulled his trigger and a crossbow bolt plunged into the lead creature's shoulder. Another bolt from the second guard pierced its head. Neither one slowed the thing down.

Like in a nightmare, the monster took hold of the quarrel in its face and pulled it out, tossing it aside carelessly.

Zane Vhortghast was shoving Sena through the window while his men drew their swords and engaged the seven-foot scarecrows in desperate melee. One had powered up his chemiostatic sword and touched the enemy with a vital thrust. There was a flash. The creature shivered as fire darted from its skin both where the electricity entered and from the explosive wound that appeared instantaneously on its foot.

Its ankle ruptured. The tibia burst through like a whitened spike. Still the thing came, walking on the knife-like point of its destroyed leg, dragging its foot behind.

The guard tried to power up his sword again but the superhuman hands were upon him, long thick fingers lifting him in a vise-like grip. The creature tossed him aside, searching for Sena.

Zane Vhortghast took one last look at the fearless almost-human-thing behind him before following Sena out the window. A fire escape clattered down in switchback fashion to a small wooden dock where Caliph, having been dragged off against all effort, stood furious but relieved to see her safe outside.

More men had pulled up in thin slender gondolas at the rear of the theater. They hauled Sena and Caliph on board as something thin and powerful emerged on the fire escape above. Crossbows thumped and a cloud
of bolts converged on the creature, filling it like a pincushion. It fell from
the metal stairs and landed brokenly at Mr. Vhortghast's feet.

Sena thought she saw something pale and large jackknife with lethargic grace below the dark water as she passed from the dock into the boat.
It vanished before she could get a proper look.

"There's something down there! There's something in the water!"

As she spoke the second gondola jerked sideways, throwing men in
flailing profusion and great splashing blossoms of foam. The boat capsized
and promptly began to sink.

"Out! Out! Out!" shouted the spymaster. He grabbed Sena's wrist and
pulled.

Caliph made a dangerous leap and hit the dock. Awkward. Bashing his
shins against the planked edge. He yelped and cursed. Someone pulled
him to his feet and shoved him toward a two-foot cornice.

The tremendous foundation from which the building sprung poked
above the waterline, a vast slab that extended just beyond the dimensions
of the opera house proper. It formed a ledge all the way around the lower
extremities of the structure and allowed Vhortghast to goad Caliph
through the darkness around the north side.

Caliph would have none of it. He was fed up with being steered around.
He turned and shoved his way powerfully back to the dock, taking hold of
Sena's hand. By what dim light there was, she looked remarkably col-
lected. Her face was unafraid.

Together they stepped out onto the lip of the foundation, following an
impatient spymaster north then west to the building's front.

A retinue of operatives had pulled the royal carriage up to the water-
front. Unfortunately, there were now so many people milling around that
they had little hope of using it to get away.

On seeing the spymaster and the High King picking their way along the
north face, big men with cudgels began to clear a path. They gave a mighty
push and when they met resistance they swung away. People went down
in rows, crawling and scrambling to escape the very determined, exces-
sively short-tempered royal guards.

The High King and his beleaguered party stumbled into a small clearing made by their brutality.

"Get inside," said Vhortghast. It was not a kind request.

Caliph piled in with Sena, growing more and more frustrated. He hadn't
had time to think since the commotion erupted in the theater.

He had been sitting, glossing over the remaining acts, estimating time on his pocket watch.

When he looked up, a tall thin man had somehow appeared in front of his chair. He must have dropped from the box above, Caliph thought with amazement. The two men lurking in the shadows had burst forth, grappling the intruder as Caliph's seat overturned. A chorus of shouts had gone up from the audience below, a sea of fingers pointing toward the tumult.

What is happening? Caliph had thought. *Where is Sena?* Vhortghast had appeared suddenly, without coffee. He had dragged the High King from the box while other menacing shapes were closing in.

It had been a blur.

Caliph had gone out the window only after Vhortghast's insistence that Sena was already safe.

The spymaster had lied to get him moving.

Outside, men had encircled the carriage with swords and nightsticks. The carriage was rolling. The men were forcing a path through the mob. The carriage creaked on its springs. Its wheels clattered on the cobbles as they picked up speed.

Something hit the backside of the compartment and Caliph held his breath. There were shouts. Violent sounds. Caliph wondered if at any moment another of the thin men would reach around and scrabble at the window. He waited—but it never happened.

Caliph reached out, held Sena closely as the horses gained momentum, pulling them out of Murkbell, into the terrifying geometry of Thief Town, toward the hopeful safety of Isca Castle.

Fenwick Bengello is found amalgamated with the drive assembly of an engine smuggled out of the Croustate Brickyard near the middle of Hleim. His flesh is fused so completely with the output shaft that tendrils of muscle and skin have slithered through the lube passages, wrapped around the drive pinions and gears like roots. After a single failed attempt to cut him free (when their saws hit bones like steel) the city watch decides to bury Mr. Bengello's remains in a criminal cemetery south of town.

The only way they can finagle him into the coffin is to lay him face-down, twisted around and clutching the shaft. No one comes to see him anyway.

His business partner, Jacob Vindai, who until recently held the deed to the abandoned brewery, turns up in a repair shop on Vhodâsh Street, decapitated, mouth filled with nuts and bolts, head sunk in a barrel of used oil.

The city watch is dumbfounded. Recent attempts to steal machinery have left a trail of curious murders seemingly without motive.

Investigators from the watch add it to ledgers crammed with unsolved crimes waiting for a lead.

DURING the hot midsummer evenings, while the city ciders, strange rag-men carry bundles out of Maruchine, out of South Fell, sticking to the backstreets of North Fell, crossing into Barrow Hill. Some pull handcarts. Some carry baskets. They blend, cryptonymous, brown and overlooked. They tote washers and piston rings in their pockets, lug pulleys, chains and valves in canvas sacks. Connecting rods are hidden in flowers and withered potted plants. Their pilgrimage is sedulous. They do not relent. They go to Gilnaroth.

The ruinous multitiered cemetery dubbed the Citizens' Necropolis chokes on its own brickwork. Dense and barren and inconceivably decayed, the bewildering monuments thrust aberrantly above hard-packed clay.

The mausoleums of the poor are dead slums, crowded just like the tenements of the living. Some are broken open and spilling apart. Raised yards of cement are fenced with wrought iron as if there are feuds, disputes and challenged boundaries: placed there to keep the neighbor's dead children out.

The ragmen pick their way over the course of many days, going back and forth, bearing engine parts like holy relics through a menagerie of absurd stone. They are not frightened by the awful maws of open charnel houses or the low piles nesting just inside. They are familiar with death and blend in, even here, where stacks of crumbling tombs fill the sky with colors like rust and urine streaking bone.

The ragmen drift north toward the crest of the cemetery, wading through patchy ugly weeds that flourish like pubic hair. The crypts around them fairly rocket skyward, visible above the walls of the Hold as enormous charred leg bones overspread with renegade tuberosities, held together purely by virtue of their weight.

The ragmen ignore them.

A low crouched tomb of blebby moldy-white, cracked and peeling and filthy in its mortarless crannies draws them like a magnet.

They come at odd hours, make counterfeit gestures of reverence or grief. A ludicrous display. No tomb so old has such devoted visitors let alone ones capable of remembering the deceased.

The ragmen place their flowers then shove bags into the open hole, ripped open by grave robbers long ago.

Deep inside the black corruption of the body niche, a shaft opens and drops straight down through the hillside. A rope and pulley installed in the middle of the night allows for bundles to be lowered through the shaft. The ragmen come and go from the tomb, passing engine parts to cohorts deep below.

Then, just as silently, they leave Barrow Hill, avoiding the trendy cafés and chocolate houses along King's Road where people sing late into the night, bohemian music bubbling and tinkling from saxophones and plucked or hammered strings. The ragmen hear the gaiety and shrink from it, fading away from crowds of people whose hair glows obscene colors under paper lanterns and colorful bulbs: purple, orange and incandescent pink.

Back through North Fell, through South Fell, plotting a course through the tangled shadows of Hullmallow Cathedral into Maruchine, the ragmen return home. They dissolve like fog into the arched mélange of Ghoul Court.

By the twentieth of Lüme, the Cabal of Wights has rebuilt the engine and swapped new parts for the drive assembly the city watch laid to rest. They are ready.

There are good reasons for the elaborate plan. The sewers of Isca Castle are detached from the sewers of Isca City except for very slender culverts barely large enough to admit rats. One main line extends east out of the castle grounds, burrowing under Incense Street and the military yards of Ironside.

Countless grates and guard posts secure it, make the High King's toilets virtually impregnable.

But when the foundations of the city were first laid, Isca Castle was planned on what is now Barrow Hill and a gigantic septic pit was dug and later covered over when the surveyors changed their minds.

The empty tank remains far below the graveyard. A drain field additionally helps to suck excessive water away—preventing the kinds of grisly landslides that occasionally plague Marbolia, the cemetery of the rich.

A lateral tunnel from the Barrow Hill septic tank runs north, pouring into what would have been the Barrow Hill castle's main line to the sea. When the site was abandoned, this second vault was sealed off except to the east where water collects under the graves, sluiced down through narrow pipes into the labyrinthine channels under Temple Hill.

Thus there are two sewer systems sequestered and forsaken from the rest of Isca's gurgling conduits. They are entangled and fight for space like two tarantulas below the hills but at no place do they ever intersect or intersect the rest of the city sewers.

A thieves guild once toyed with the idea of a base of operations in the Barrow Hill tunnels. But they are so inaccessible and so prone to sudden flooding that the guild reconsidered and settled Thief Town instead.

The powers in Ghoul Court rediscover them and fathom a use.

A tall gaunt man oversees operations in the dark. He has pink eyes like Mr. Naylor. On the morning of the twenty-fourth, long before the Byun-Ghala is set to leave Isca Castle for the spindle in Murkbell, the engine sparks to life.

A maul, head covered every inch with teeth, begins chewing methodically at the north end of the tunnel, pumping up and down. It rips chunks of rock away and kicks up heavy dust.

The gaunt man seems capable of ignoring the choking haze. His associates, who are crawlers—more like Fenwick Bengello—are forced to retreat up the southern tunnel toward Gilnaroth.

Several others like the leader watch the machine. They pamper it and make adjustments as it edges relentlessly north. Due to mechanisms that lock the wheels in one direction and a great anchored tail off the back, the engine can only advance into the wall. The toothy maul dissolves inches of stone in minutes.

It takes only seven and a half hours to eat through ten feet of stone.

Finally the barrier between the castle sewers and the necropolis sewers burst in, caving slightly under a fine rain of debris. The thick stench of raw sewage gobbles hungrily at the dry cloud of dust.

Long-legged men in striped suit pants and overalls and other various occupational costumes clamber through, disregarding the fumes. They begin sniffing their way through the tangled pools, searching for a hint of cleaner air.

They have an inside man. Someone who knows they are coming. This has been prepared and rehearsed as carefully as the show Caliph and Sena sit watching.

From slick black tubes and catch basins, under baffles and hoods and around garbage-clogged weirs, the man-things hunt fresh air. Like Mr. Naylor they clamber through small spaces. They pass grinding pumps that move scum and sludge into deep containers that gel with slowly thickening sludge cake and lime. Walls, lumpy white and griseous with coagulated fat from the castle's kitchen seep into chunky waste below.

They pass a grit chamber thronging with mycophagous creatures that pause in their filthy reverie to listen to the man-things clamber through. The creatures twist back and forth like grubs rooted in fecal chowder, wavering blindly at the intruders.

The man-things ignore them. They stalk onward through the pitch black, now and then banging their heads or shins on odd projections or hidden chunks of fallen stone. They seem oblivious to pain. Their eyes are no better than Mr. Naylor's but they can decipher vague radiations.

Without a trace of light, they are only partially blind. They catch a hint, a whiff. Lose it. Search in repetitive back and forth swathes; sniff and catch it again.

Finally.

The faint sweet smell of blossoms trickles on a downward draft, sifting pollen through circular grates overhead. The lead man claws upward. He fumbles at the grate. It has already been unlocked. He eases it up and sets it aside.

A short vertical culvert above the first grate supports a secondary grate just a few feet overhead. It too is unlocked. With a faint creak and muted thud the grate opens trapdoor style onto a plush crop of perfectly manicured grass.

The sheltering arms of a black mulberry normally help conceal the

grate in the sumptuous gardens. Now they cloak creatures hauling them-
selves up into the courtyard as across town Caliph and Sena leap into
the carriage, making good their escape.

The man-things spread out quickly and quietly. One lurks at an adit
until a pair of sentinels walk past.

The creature waits, biding its time, emotionally detached from its goal.
Then, at precisely the most favorable moment it casts its long sinuous arms
out and pulls both men deep into shadow. Before they can scream, iron-like
fingers burke them with savage efficiency.

The strangled corpses are pulled into corners behind bushes and
sculpted shrubs.

While their fellows at the opera are bent on putting an end to the Sslîq
they fear, those at the castle advance relentlessly through the courtyard,
searching for the book and putting an end to any sentry in their path.

CALIPH and Sena had gone slack in the aftermath.

The carriage rumbled past Gilnaroth through Barrow Hill to King's
Road and turned north into the Hold. By the time they reached the castle
gate, the terror at the opera house had been replaced with nausea and exhaustion.

As usual, huge gears began to turn the instant the High King was inside, pulling up the drawbridge, locking the castle down on its island for
the night.

Vhortghast leapt from the back of the carriage before it had fully
stopped. Since the metholinate lamps had been shut off, torchlight licked
the edges of the vast court where governmental buildings crowded. He
opened the door and helped Sena and Caliph clamber out.

A quad of soldiers crossed the yard heading in formation toward the
east gardens. Their leather cuirasses and barbuts glared as facets of the
armor turned in unison from the light. Despite their presence, something
felt strangely wrong.

The carriage driver was quick to bid everyone good night. He had not
asked what had gone on inside the opera. With a curt tip of the hat, his
nervous meaty hands whipped the horses toward the livery.

Caliph glanced back in the direction of the gates. It was three hundred
yards to the drawbridge from the center of the south bailey. He felt
strangely isolated.

A courthouse and a row of statues shone green in the sultry night.
Crickets chirped. The last queelub of the season flickered in a stately stand
of maples to the west. After dusk, when the visitors had signed out, the
small village of governmental edifices became austere and chilly, like

monuments in a park. Even with all the night noises, the humidity seemed to stifle sound.

"Why are the lights out in the kitchen?" asked Caliph. The bank of mullioned panes west of the foyer usually glowed all night.

The spymaster scowled. "I don't know."

A lone cicada screamed from nearby.

"Everything is fine," Caliph soothed.

Even so, Sena felt her skin prickle.

Zane led them toward the front door, up a steep staircase, across another miniature drawbridge to the lavish foyer decorated with tile and statuary and lit by gas. Vhortghast rapped. The glazed door was unlocked.

They stepped inside.

A short extravagant hallway flickered with amber glass on either wall. Lit by candles in hidden guardrooms, the narrow colorful panes covered arrow slits; the paneled ceiling: murder holes. Isca Castle had not been in danger of siege for so long that its defensive architecture had been concealed with more aesthetically pleasing fixtures.

At the top of a second staircase, the grand foyer engulfed them like bits of food under domed glass. To the north, the great staircase curled down from the second story, ending at the foot of one of several pillars that framed a series of four lofty arches to the grand hall: a room that currently glowered in darkness. Other doors led to guardrooms, the kitchen and the east wing.

The silence was interminable. Sena's thoughts reduced to the book hidden in Caliph's bedroom. The emotional impact of the orchestrated ambush at the theater and now the empty abandoned corridors of the castle were sinking in, fomenting into panic.

Vhortghast said something soft and unintelligible, probably because the wrongness of their surroundings was also affecting him.

"I'm going to have a look," said Sena.

Zane hushed her savagely but she ignored him. They had made enough noise coming up the stairs that any unfriendly ears in the nearby rooms would certainly have heard. Caliph looked at her apprehensively.

"I'll be fine. Trust me." She pinched him and slipped away, moving up the stairs.

Caliph nearly cried out, almost pleaded with her to come back, but he didn't. The oppressive quiet in the castle seemed to crush his ability to shout.

Zane had drawn a long knife from his belt. It curved away from his forearm like a claw. He was circuiting the foyer. Checking doors. Peering into various rooms. He let Sena go without a word and Caliph realized suddenly that the spymaster's only responsibility was to the High King's safety.

Caliph swore and headed for the grand hall, determined to turn on some lights.

"Your majesty—?"

Caliph didn't answer. Like at the opera house, he had had enough. He strode into the darkness and immediately fell over a large obstacle. Three bodies lay in a low pile, obscured by the darkness of the archway. Caliph scrambled up, stifling a shriek. His fine suit was smudged with blood. Zane pulled him back, picked up a sword from the fallen guards and handed it to him.

Caliph's terror was burning off as his anger mounted. He would find whoever had done this.

SENA had always lacked confidence in her abilities as a Sister of the Seventh House. Her accelerated ascension and keen awareness of her unfair promotions had resulted in timidity and self-doubt.

In crisis, she often choked.

But the dangers she had faced since spring had begun to chip away at her insecurity. She had survived two, possibly three attempts on her life if she counted tonight—though that was a bit premature. She had moved the *Cisrym Ta* through Skellum under Megan's nose.

Her diffidence had begun to crumble.

Without shoes, without a weapon, she slid from the great staircase into the blackness of the upper hall. To the west, the white marble and tall windows of the grand hall's second story chilled the air like a solid cube of ointment. Leaf shadows twirled and danced in swaying rhythms across the floor. She headed east toward the High King's bedroom, up another set of marble stairs.

When she reached the fourth floor, she had yet to see a guard. A post, flooded with yellow lamplight, revealed a game of cards left in midplay. One chair rested on its side. There were no other signs of struggle. Coins still stood in little stacks or lay in piles indicating ownership and the unclaimed pot. A switchblade had been left beside one man's winnings. Sena snapped it up in passing and drifted down the lofty passage to the west.

By now, her evening gown was in shreds. The kick pleat had continued to tear. What few diamonds were left hung from threads. Her movements were fluid, unrestricted.

The paneled walls marched west.

Great vases and indistinct statues twisted up in menacing shapes.

Dozens of candles petaled the walls with daylily orange while orchid-colored shadows leapt from side tables and potted trees.

Sena slid below a bank of mullioned palladian glass, keeping to the darkest part of the passageway. Not even twenty feet in front of her, the High King's bedroom doors hung open. Narrow, ornate and twelve feet tall. Like most doors in the castle, they swung on four hinges: a moving piece of wall.

A gruesome splatter on the wood paneling beside the doors looked purple in the light from the window, like someone had hurled a bottle of milk at the wall, bursting its contents explosively—only the liquid wasn't white.

Sena could smell the faint cloying reek of bungled wetwork. Like a slaughterhouse. The gagging stink of burst entrails.

At the door she stopped and listened.

Silence.

She had just set her muscles in motion, building momentum to dart from the shadow under the window to the shadow of the bedroom, when a tall thin man walked out from the narrow crack of blackness.

Sena pulled up short and diverted her energy into a spin that planted her shoulder soundlessly against the north wall. Still in shadow, she rested at a forty-five degree angle to the man-thing's flank.

The tall creature stretched its fingers and glanced around as though tasting the air. He looked frustrated. One of his hands dribbled gore and his sleeve flapped heavy and red. He must have been seven feet tall. Bone thin. White saggy flesh hung from his neck and hollow deep-set eyes glittered with pink light.

His clothing was a mess, spattered and crusty with mud and foul-smelling sludge. Partially dried clods of night soil had fractured and fallen away from his pant cuffs, leaving a trail as he walked down the center of the carpeted hall.

Sena saw an opportunity. She could dart out, slip up behind him, plunge her knife into his kidney, pull it out before he fell, draw it deeply across his throat. She had been trained for this. She had practiced the movements like a dancer in the gymnasium at Skellum.

But something sat on her instinct to kill. Intuition perhaps.

She waited.

A second man emerged from the High King's bedroom. Equally filthy, equally gaunt and horrifying. His eyes were more orange; more amber, like little nuggets of petrified sap. He too was speckled with blood and sewage. A third and fourth man exited the bedroom. They were shorter and carried weapons. They wore gas masks around their necks like bulky chokers.

Sena consoled herself on the fact that she had waited. None of them carried bags or packs. None of them carried anything besides the two with broadswords. They looked ridiculous, like people that had been at work and suddenly gone insane, leaving customers at the counter to embark on some blood-soaked impracticality. They looked thoroughly psychotic. Thoroughly deranged.

None of them carried the *Cisrym Ta*. Nor could they have hidden it, as big as it was, in their vests or suit coats or tucked it discreetly under an arm.

If not the book then what? Why would men like those that attacked them at the opera ransack Caliph's bedroom within the hour?

Sena drew blood from her palm. She whispered an equation to stanch the wound and used the remaining holojoules to throw a glamour down the hall.

From the far end, a light glimmered. Her own voice laughed lightly. Echoing. Two indistinct figures passed south around the door frame, shimmery and fumbling. Like inebriated lovers stumbling off to fuck.

The pack of four men set off at once, headed for the illusion.

Sena crept around the door and vanished into the bedroom. Despite the jungled darkness, she could tell the entire chamber had been destroyed.

The mattress was ripped open. Feathery guts disemboweled and scattered over the corpses of what she estimated to be half a dozen castle guards. Formerly magnificent wardrobes were virtually torn apart, broken into as though they had been searched for secret parts.

Chairs and trunks were splintered. Slashed cushions exuded cotton like tissue dribbling from open wounds. Even the fireplace grate had been uprooted, cast aside and the ashes excavated carelessly as if by an unruly dog.

Sena turned to the rolltop desk. It had been shattered. Broken ink bottles and papers where distributed without consideration. The drawers were emptied and tossed aside.

The *Cisrym Ta* was gone.

Sena gasped.

She held her stomach. She looked at the exact place she had left it. Defiantly, as though she could bullwhip reality for misbehaving, she pawed through the nearby refuse. From fast-flowing undercurrents of thought, she drew up a bucket full of aching icy acceptance that she would not find it.

As the slow realization began to sink in, anger seemed amphigoric. She couldn't alter what had happened. But what now? How could she get it back?

Her thoughts leapt to the four men that had left the bedroom just before she came in. She tried to remember clearly. But second-guessing herself was useless. She knew none of them had carried the book.

She couldn't think. The *Cisrym Ta*'s absence filled her mind like a
yawning chasm. Years of legwork sifting information, clues, rumors and
outright prevarications had been wasted. As if she had been sculpting a
masterpiece for the past four and a half years and some vandal had come
along with a sledge.

Sena couldn't breathe.

She sank down amid the ruined room, stunned.

I have to leave, she thought. *I have to follow the men.* Nothing else
made sense. There was nothing else to do.

She jumped up and bolted from the room, sprinting down the center of
the hall, sticking to the narrow strip of carpet that swallowed up the beating of her feet.

She hadn't even grabbed a pair of boots. She had no time. The men had
already disappeared.

CALIPH heard the sound of fighting. It echoed strangely through wood
and marble halls, faint shouts that hinted at profound urgency. The clang
of ringing steel like a bell. He did not wait for Zane.

He tore off down the hall, sword in hand, looking for a place to stick
his boiling rage.

As he ran, the sound grew louder. He could hear yelps and cries and
strange inhuman grunts. After turning several corners left and right he
barreled directly into the fray.

He had come up behind the enemy. A group of guards to the west held
their ground against a trio of tall thin men nearly identical to those Caliph
had seen at the opera. The guards were cut off. They faced the man-things
head-on, sword to hand. They saw Caliph appear on the far side but they
couldn't reach him.

Caliph sailed into battle. He had arrived with such velocity that his presence went unnoticed until he had already run one through. The broadsword
Zane had handed him slotted neatly into the center of the creature's back,
made its legs to go pliant.

Caliph drove the sword out through the belly and wrenched it back,
pulling it from the terrible wound before the creature fell sprawling to
the floor, its spinal cord severed.

Caliph turned and set upon another savagely. His sword struck the rib
cage but seemed to glance as if from glassy steel, turning the sword in his

hand and nearly forcing it from his grasp. His recovery was awkward and slow.

The men, cowering and nearly beaten, rallied. They rushed forward, taking advantage of the hole Caliph had created in the enemy line. For a moment, the man-things thrashed and floundered as the soldiers surrounded them.

But the thing on the floor was still crawling, pulling its useless legs behind. It reached out huge hands and pulled one guard's feet out from under him.

The ghastly mouth opened to reveal a picket fence of yellow teeth. It bit ruthlessly through the guardsman's leather, eliciting a scream.

Caliph lost his footing as the half-paralyzed creature lurched around the floor. He reeled backward, crashing into the west wall and heading for the carpet.

Blades were glittering with their own vibrations as they struck and glanced off the strangely deflective hides. The creatures' clothing had been hacked away. Ragged and snarling they endured a hail of blows.

The guards hewed with all their fury but only one stroke in three drew blood.

Caliph looked up to see one guard's sword turn aside so abruptly that it struck another guard and cut him deeply on the upswing. It chopped through his pectoral muscle, up into his armpit, deep enough to sever the subclavian. The man screamed as a fountain of red burst from his arm, an unstoppable rhythmic torrent.

Another blow landed on the man-thing's hide and Caliph watched again in horror as the strange mechanism of its armor swept the stroke aside.

It was miraculous to see all the strength and momentum of the guard, focused in a falling edge of steel. It bore down on the creature's unprotected flesh, intent on parting skin from bone. But the thin tissue did not resist. It gave to the blow like limp sausage casings filled with barely enough water to make them buttery along internal surfaces. As though fluid rather than muscle lurked just below the epidermis. The skin sank and traveled in a ripple along the bone.

The force carried laterally, following the length of the creature's arm. When the sword had moved a foot or more along the skeletal frame of the monster it must have met the smooth ramp of an inhuman condyle like a toboggan going off a jump. The weapon went flying back out harmlessly into space. Caliph sat where he had fallen, stunned.

His fascination was broken by the thing on the floor flinging itself around on powerful arms. It was trying to attack him.

Caliph snarled and adjusted to his new understanding of the creature's anatomy. He stabbed instead of slashed. The sharp point punctured the creature's chest, darting between ribs, deep into a lung. The thing gasped and recoiled.

"Stab them!"

His men, grappling with faint understanding, obeyed. They brought one to its knees almost immediately with concerted thrusts.

Zane Vhortghast had finally appeared. In actuality, he was less than twenty seconds on the High King's heels but much had happened in the intervening moments of melee.

He fell on the back of one of the creatures, driving his knife down with anatomically educated precision. Despite the violent thrashing of the creature he managed to bury the weapon in the thing's heart on his second attempt.

There was one left. Caliph met its eyes and pulled his sword across his own hand, using his blood to power something raw and brutal he had heard long ago in his uncle's house. The Unknown Tongue gurgled in Caliph's throat as the monster fell toward him, murderous fingers spread.

The creature hit Caliph with force. It plowed into the High King and sent him sliding back across the marble floor, skidding on guardsman's blood. His men looked on in horror, certain that the creature's fingers had torn through Caliph's body like steel cables.

Slowly, friction took hold in the stiffening smear of gore and the two bodies agglutinated, coming to a viscid stop.

Everything was still. The creature moved slightly but very strangely as though something were inside it. A bulge moved around like a large mole burrowing just below its skin. With shock, the bewildered guards realized it was Caliph's fist, pushing up from below as against a flimsy membrane.

The creature gave a gurgling scream and seemed to roll sideways like a bag of jelly, slipping off Caliph to flatten against the floor.

Caliph stood up and stabbed it with his sword. The sack of skin popped with a liquescent slurp. The sudden abruption of tissue spilled a tide of gray-and-red fluid out from the amoeba-like blob, issuing liquefied bones and body fluids all across the ghastly floor.

Zane wiped his blade off and looked around, barking orders to whoever was still alive. Outside, alarm bells were finally ringing, calling scores of sleeping guards into the fray.

Lights blazed in the south bailey. Caliph stood up, slightly stunned. His formula wasn't supposed to do that. Something had gone wrong with the math. New sounds turned his attention from the holomorphic aberration. He didn't have time to think about mutated spells. Glancing out a window he could see hordes of armed men pouring from virtually every direction. Some were still pulling on armor.

Green chemiostatic torch beams cut the dark. Tall man-things lurched from crevices in the architecture of the castle, hopelessly outnumbered. They went down under the merciless onslaught of dozens of men.

Trumpets blared. The parapets swelled with running soldiers. Archers with gas-powered crossbows riddled indistinct fleeing forms with enough bolts to add many pounds of weight.

The corpses of the enemy landed in ponderous piles of ruination, splashing into fountains and beds of blue petunias.

Caliph headed downstairs and back out to the courtyard in an effort to help.

The powerful beams of the magnesium lights on the zeppelin deck were turned down into the east gardens. All the gas lamps on the castle grounds burst into hissing blossoms of life.

Suddenly, an army had appeared. They ransacked every shadow, pitiless and angry.

Search parties were organized. Staff sergeants barked commands to their squads. Out came the knights.

They had taken time enough to put their armor on. They stalked into the yard, hackles up, seized chemical torches from the hands of confused and sleepy servants and conducted grumpy solitary investigations of the castle grounds.

They asked statistical questions while they rummaged in bushes and flower beds. "Who fucked this up?" "How many dead?" "How many expectants?"

Groups of guards followed in their wake, feeling virtually invulnerable.

A man-thing made the mistake of leaping out at one knight who then proceeded to blast the creature with a chemiostatic flail the heavy spiked ball of which, being tipped with beryllium, delivered an awesome blaze of light as it turned the creature's skin to ash with a jolting explosion of electricity. The knight stepped on the creature's twitching body and walked on.

It took less than four hours to completely scour the castle and the grounds. Altogether, the sentries and knights found and dispatched thirty-seven intruders, half of which were noticeably more human than the tall thin creatures with the slippery skin.

They laid them out in the south bailey in a long row. The losses to the castle garrison unfortunately surpassed those of the enemy.

Forty-two soldiers had been killed. Mostly by strangulation and mostly by surprise. Caliph got word while he was in the south bailey that Sena was safe but (for reasons lost in the relay of information) utterly inconsolable. He would go to her soon. For now, the fact that she was safe was enough.

They had turned off the magnesium lights after the grounds had been declared clean but Caliph decided to make one last circuit of the gardens before going inside. While men began tossing bodies in the beds of steam wagons and making trips to the gate, Caliph walked into the darkened easterly courtyard.

He wasn't really looking for foes. He was simply trying to sort out the madness of the evening.

Who or what were these gruesome creatures? How had they gotten inside the castle grounds? What had they come searching for?

He turned off the path, brooding over the unanswerable questions. He had told his men to haul the bodies to West Gate for autopsy by government physicians first thing tomorrow morning. He wanted to know, from a dissector's point of view, everything there was to know about their physiology.

As he walked along the courtyard wall he noticed a sudden movement in the dark. His heart froze. He opened his mouth to yell for help, but stopped when he realized the figure was not tall and thin but bulky like a bear on its hind legs. Nor did the figure appear intent on escape. Rather it picked its way carefully across the garden, glancing furtively over its meaty shoulders.

Apparently it had not seen Caliph. Caliph stopped, fearful to watch, fearful to look away.

The figure held a key in its hand, the key that had unlocked the double grated entrance to the sewers under the mulberry shrubs.

The figure fumbled, glancing around as it bent to secure the portals it must have opened earlier that day—the portal through which Caliph realized the enemies must have come.

Caliph flattened himself against the courtyard wall, breathing slow and quiet. He heard the key turn in the lock, leaves rustle. After another moment, the figure appeared on the courtyard path, still nervous, smoothing down its clothing, checking over its shoulder time and again.

It headed for the torch-lit archway beside which Caliph was pressed. Caliph held his breath.

As it walked, the figure's fretful manner dissipated quickly. It whistled, thrusting its hands into deep pockets, moving into the cone of light.

Caliph gasped. It was all he could do to stay silent and hidden as the traitor, whose face was plainly visible, strode smugly toward the castle entrance, confident his actions had gone unobserved.

After the footsteps had echoed into silence, Caliph waited another five minutes before moving.

Finally, muscles aching with tension and stress brought on by heartbroken disbelief, he crept counterclockwise through the courtyards, stealing through the tumid darkness with fumbling uncertain steps, taking pains to approach the castle doors from a direction seemingly disconnected with the place and moment of the crime.

Caliph sat in the dark of his bedroom despising David Thacker. He still couldn't choke it down, that his old friend from Desdae had sold him out. His anger was rogue, displaced, confused. Had he done something to earn this perfidious crime? Could he have somehow slighted the quiet writer who studied composition and novels and diverse fields of criticism? Had he made some trespass against David that his own calluses made invisible?

He thought back to their afternoon in Grume's, where they had seemingly drunk to the camaraderie between them. Had it all been a façade? Had there ever been any true friendship at all?

Caliph had no answers. All he had were questions and the feeling that reality had somehow changed for him more drastically than any holomorph could ever manage with all the holojoules in the world.

One thing was certain. David Thacker had plans of his own.

Caliph had returned from the courtyard to find Sena soulsick and wretched. She equivocated on telling him the reason but eventually it came out that her book, Caliph's uncle's book, had disappeared.

Caliph repressed an intransigent impulse to scold her. He paused and his face tightened. He wanted to shout that soldiers had died tonight—a great many men and women had died tonight and would not be going home to their families, to their friends. He wanted to rouse her, tell her it was common sense that people's lives were far more important than any book. He wanted to ask her where her head was at, that all she could think about was some worm-eaten incunabulum.

Instead, his face relaxed. "Are you sure it's missing?"

"Of course I'm sure." Sena looked insulted.

"Let's have a look."

Sena sighed. She followed him to the fourth floor. With the gas lamps on, the room looked even worse than it had in the dark. Investigators from the watch had come and gone.

They had jotted down clues before letting the servants in to clean. The dead guards had been wrapped up and taken away. All that was left was to sort through the jumble of annihilated objects.

Wheeled bins of feathers (some white, some red and sticky) mingled with splintered wood and ceramic shards. The bins overflowed, waiting to be carted away while men and women on the night shift sorted through the rubbish.

Unfortunately, most of it had already been consigned to the trash.

"Where did you last have it?" asked Caliph.

"I put it in the rolltop," said Sena, "right the—"

Her words died.

The desk was broken open and emptied but on its top, under the array of tiny useless drawers and slots, below the arced groove that until recently had held the interlocking slats that made its clutter presentably discreet, sat the red book.

Sena's stomach flipped, then twisted like a wrung-out rag.

"Looks like it's here," Caliph deadpanned. "Maybe you missed it?"

Sena mumbled something barely intelligible.

"Yeah. I guess I did." Her bloodless lips parted in astonishment. But she didn't believe her own admission. She knew what she had seen even in the dim light.

Maybe one of the servants had found it under the bed or in a corner and replaced it. But how could they have known where it came from? How could they have known where it belonged?

She looked around. They were stacking everything worth salvaging in neat piles by the hearth.

When she asked, they affirmed that none of them had touched it.

"That's where it was when I came in," said a young man.

"Are you sure?"

"I guess so. I was the first in after the inspectors left."

Somehow the news did not surprise her. She picked it up with nerveless fingers and took it with her as Caliph tugged her from the room.

They went to one of the guest bedrooms for the night. Caliph couldn't sleep. He sat on the edge of the mattress in the dark.

Sena locked the *Cisrym Ta* in a chest at the foot of the bed. Despite the evening's events, now that it was safe, she felt almost totally relaxed. She sidled up to him in the dark and wrapped her arms around him from behind. She could feel the heavy hot incubation of his thoughts, the sullen plotting going on inside.

"What is it?"

Caliph exhaled: something between a grumble and a sigh. *What is it!*

Are you blind? Isca Castle has been attacked! I've been betrayed! People are dead!

Out loud he said, "Are all . . ." he wanted to put it more delicately but gave up, "Shraḍnæ Witches trained in . . . subterfuge?"

Sena held her breath, wondering what he would say next if she answered either way. Finally, she said distinctly, "I am."

Caliph let out a sigh of relief. "Then there's something I want you to do."

SENA hung in the blackness of a narrow corridor, wedged against the lofty ceiling. Legs spread. One foot braced on either wall. At five-foot-ten her legs were barely long enough to achieve the feat. She looked down at the tiled floor twelve feet below.

A gas lamp in a stone recess flooded the bottom half of the passageway in capricious opal light. Her stamina was extraordinary but by the time the sentry finally arrived at the door opposite the gas lamp her legs were quivering.

Sena watched him knock at the door. He waited, scratched his ass, muttered something she couldn't make out.

The door was thick. It muffled any sound from within. Sena bit her lower lip and concentrated on maintaining her position.

After a few seconds the door opened.

David Thacker peered out from a dimly lit room. The sight of the sentry discomposed him sufficiently to qualify in Sena's mind as a confession of guilt. He tried to cover his dismay with a yawn.

"What is it? What's wrong?" asked David. Sena could tell he was not accustomed to lying.

"Nothing, sir." The guard had straightened. "There's someone at the gates for you. We told them it was after curfew but they insisted. What with the craziness tonight we can't open the gate. You'll have to take a boat across the moat. You can meet 'em in the Cracked Agate just across the square."

"What?" David was obviously skeptical. "Was it a man or a woman?"

"Man," said the guard. "I guess. I wasn't actually there when they came calling. Just delivering the message, sir. The High King happened to be at the gate, I guess. Said you were a friend and it would be okay."

Sena watched terror welter under David's cheeks, ripple behind his eyes and vanish.

There was no visitor of course. Caliph had dreamt it up to lure David Thacker away from his room. But by the look on his face, Sena guessed a man that fit the guard's ambiguous description did in fact exist—a man that might (in David's mind) have actually come to call.

"Let me get my cloak."

"I guess your visitor said it was urgent," the guard replied.

David froze midstep, half in and half out of the room. The fear in his eyes had turned to absolute horror. "Did he?"

He reached around the corner and pulled a thin summer cloak after him. He put it on quickly and patted himself, checking for essentials. He locked the door and tugged the handle twice before shambling timorously down the hall after the guard.

Sena waited. Her legs were at the end of their endurance. She listened carefully. Only when she was certain did she snap her legs shut and distill, soundlessly to the tile floor.

The guards made regular rounds even here among the guest suites that honeycombed the castle's west wing. She had to work fast.

Caliph had warned her that David Thacker had been granted a request to change out his lock. He was supposed to have given a copy of the key to Gadriel, which he had never done.

Sena had already palmed a torsion wrench and two different picks. She set one in her mouth, biting the tang like the stem of a rose while she slipped both the wrench and a snake pick into the keyway.

As her mind adjusted to the lock, she drew the pick, feeling it pop past the pins. She noted the stiffness of the springs and counted them without applying any torque to the wrench. There were five.

She began to work.

When she gave it clockwise torque the lock stopped dead, counterclockwise she felt it mush. She pulled the torsion wrench down ever so slightly.

It was like fucking, just the right amount of tenderness and force.

Pin two set first. She heard it rattle, felt it give against the snake. She upped the torque and felt pin three go next. Obviously the holes had not been bored straight.

There were guards just around the end of the hall. She could see their shadows reaching monstrously from the flicker of a torch. They weren't talking much and she couldn't risk scrubbing the lock. They weren't in on the deception and if they heard, despite her status as the High King's mistress, it would be a bust.

Pins four and five went together under the double tips of the snake. Almost there. Pin one came last. Or did it? She tried the wrench. The plug refused to spin.

"Yella byūrn."

She had false set one of the pairs.

At the end of the hall the voices picked up. The shadows leapt as the men began to move. Sena's heart did not skip. Her self-confidence was growing.

She withdrew her tools from the lock, jumped, jumped again off the wall and in such manner attained a remarkable height. Again her legs spanned the corridor.

Two sentries stepped chuckling into the intersection thirty feet away. For a moment they glanced down the long empty hallway where David Thacker's door was one of many.

To them, the corridor was empty. They stopped for a moment, sharing some coarse anecdote before shuffling on their way.

Sena dropped from her split position, hidden by perspective against the darkness of the ceiling. Once again, she began to work the lock.

Pin two crossed the sheer line first. She flicked it with the pick and heard it rattle. Yes. It had set correctly. Pin three went next but different than before. She increased torque and scrubbed. Four, five and one set and the plug turned.

That is, it turned one-hundred-eighty degrees and stopped. In an amateur mistake, she had forgotten to place the flat of her pick in the bottom of the keyway. Pin three had a spacer. It had dropped out. She traded the snake for the hooked rake in her mouth. Carefully she fished the spacer from the lock, catching it in her palm.

David's key was not likely to work when he came back. He would know someone had been in his room. Sena bit her lip in frustration. Oh well, there was nothing for it now but to go on. She turned the wrench, spun the plug, hit three-sixty and the bolt popped back.

The door opened.

Papers littered the room beyond. Segments of a novel, bits of poetry and pages from a play scattered across a desk, a bed and the floor.

A writer, Sena mused. A coiled radiator on one wall could have offered heat from the boilers if the season had been later, but the metal pipes were cold. A wardrobe, a desk and a bed did a good job of limiting walking room.

Sena stepped carefully, making sure she disturbed nothing.

David had been gone nearly ten minutes now. She checked her pocket watch under its own green glow. Unfortunately she didn't really know what to look for.

Caliph had told her what he had seen and how he suspected his old friend from Desdae had let the creatures in from the sewers.

A key then, thought Sena. *That's where I'll start.*

She went through the pockets of every garment in the room. Empty.

There was, however, a locked coffer in the bottom of the wardrobe squatting beside several pairs of shoes. It was padlocked which was good since she had three different skeleton keys that fit most warded locks made in the north. She got it on her first try and flipped the lid.

Inside were several disturbing things.

One was a letter.

Mr. Thacker,

    A writer with vices seems such a stereotypical tragedy. I couldn't help but notice your name in the Herald *as one of several artists come to stay at Isca Castle. Nor could I help noticing your name on the ledger of a truly unsavory bordello in Ghoul Court just the other evening. One should generally use an alias whenever blackmail could be an issue.*

    I propose we meet, unless your qaam-dihet habits are something you wouldn't mind your longtime friend Caliph Howl finding out about.

Yours truly,
Peter Lark

The note had been crumpled as if its owner meant to throw it away and then changed his mind, smoothed it out and tucked it in the box.

Beside the note was a little brown pouch, a bloody scalpel and a stained sponge. As Sena had supposed, when she checked the pouch several lumps of deep crimson material rolled into her palm. They were vaguely cohesive like brown sugar.

A small effigy carved from polished black stone rested beside the paraphernalia. Shaped like a stylized ink spatter, it gleamed, bulbous at the center with exaggerated pseudopodia radiating out. Rather two-dimensional and disk-like, a single grotesque eye had been graven on its bulging middle.

Sena's skin went cold. It was the icon of the Willin Droul. Ten to one odds David Thacker also bore the Mark. Sena had no wish to touch the horrible little carving.

Several other items demanded scrutiny. A key (likely capable of opening the garden sewer grates from what Sena knew of keys), four rows of gold gryphs stacked in columns ten coins high apiece (which she was tempted instinctively to take but left alone), and finally another letter: this one from Chancellor Eaton dated in the spring of this year.

What it said was both gracious and embarrassing. Sena felt herself flush. Apparently David Thacker had graduated without a degree.

The coffer was the mother lode of dirty laundry, a treasure trove of bones. Sena almost felt humiliated for David Thacker (it was more than enough, way, way more than enough to destroy him) until she remembered the black icon and the key and the forty-two men and women killed in the siege.

She shut the box and locked it and tucked it under her arm. She had what she needed. She headed for the door.

Caliph's plan had two outcomes depending on what Sena found. If she found nothing, she was supposed to leave the room undisturbed, return to the guest bedroom where they were temporarily staying and report. But if she found evidence, she was to remove it and bring it to Caliph who would then assess it and determine whether or not to order David Thacker's arrest.

There were no protocols for policing the Hold. Within the castle, the High King's word was absolute.

Sena reached the end of the hall and turned the corner, listening for noise. It took her by surprise when, without warning, an iron grip seized her by the elbow just above the joint.

The pressure was exquisite, focused and educated with regards to specific points of pain. She dropped the coffer with a tumultuous clatter and tried unsuccessfully to whirl.

Whoever it was had an expert grasp. He had her by the thumb and elbow now, tugging on her opposing digit in directions it was not meant to bend.

"Move and I'll break your arm."

Sena whimpered under the brute force.

Mr. Vhortghast stepped out from the shadow.

"My lady," he said with a perfectly courtly tone. He did not remove his hands. "What oh what are you doing?"

"Why don't you ask the High King?" she spat.

He released her. "Theft is still punishable by removal of the hands," said Mr. Vhortghast.

"Fuck off, you whey-faced freak."

"Tut. I'm sure this is a misunderstanding." His voice was smooth as cream but he glowered at her. "We'll resolve this in the morning." He moved to pick up the fallen box.

"Resolve it now," Sena demanded.

Zane Vhortghast rolled his eyes. "You mean to tell me the king is still awake and that I should disturb him in his room?"

"Yes. That's exactly what I'm telling you to do."

The spymaster scoffed.

"Or you can have it your way," Sena fired, "and I'll be sure to let him know what happened. He's expecting that box."

Zane's face was taciturn and tranquil. But his pause told Sena he was considering. He wasn't stupid. He knew she slept with his employer.

"You're remarkable, aren't you? Very well, I'll accompany you to his majesty's room."

"Let me carry the box," she said.

He thrust it at her.

Sena took it with a sneer.

They walked in silence, passing guards who didn't dare glance sideways at the unlikely couple. When they reached the room currently servicing the High King, a small unit of guards saluted Zane.

Zane raised his hand to knock. Sena smirked and simply walked in.

Caliph pulled on a robe when he saw the spymaster. His eyes absorbed everything in an instant: the coffer in Sena's hands, the tension in her face and Zane Vhortghast trying to look nonchalant.

"Hello, Zane." Then he turned to Sena and nodded at the box. "What's this? What did you find?"

"David Thacker," her voice was soft, "I'm sorry, Caliph. He's . . ." She handed him the box and the skeleton key to open it.

AFTER he had gone through every article, Caliph pushed the container aside, feeling sick. He handed the key to Zane who was still patiently waiting to hear what was going on.

"That opens the sewer grates unless I'm sorely mistaken."

Zane took the key and frowned. "You're suggesting the assailants came from the sewers?"

Caliph nodded.

"Impossible. The castle sewers are independent of the city sewers. The only way into them that doesn't drain out of the castle is by a main line that's locked and regularly patrolled. We've had no disturbances. It's impossible that . . ." His mouth stopped working as he began to ponder more creative ways.

There were certain prisoners in West Gate with tattoos identical to those found on the bodies tonight who had been caught trying to steal heavy machinery. The Croustate Brickyard had filed a report. All of it began to form a fuzzy picture in his mind.

"Impossible?" asked Caliph. "Let me tell you what's impossible. I have forty-two dead men and women. Forty-two grieving families I have to address tomorrow without any excuse for our incompetence. Now I swear—" His voice began to rise.

"Forgive me, your majesty," Mr. Vhortghast crooned. "I'll have a thorough inspection of the sewers completed before dawn."

"Arrest David Thacker." Caliph seemed to collapse as he said it. He sat down on the edge of the bed, utterly bereft.

"Right away, your majesty. On what charge?"

Caliph waved faintly at the coffer. "Qaam-dihet for now. Maybe treason later. And find out who Peter Lark is. I want to know what this letter is about."

"I will conduct the interrogation myself, your majesty."

Zane Vhortghast left the room.

Sena felt dirty. She had never actually used her skills in this way. Pårin and fårσn were innocuous choices compared to sentencing a man to death. And death, she felt certain, was what David Thacker would get.

THE basics of interrogation were simple. The first was to capitalize on the stress of capture or, in this case, arrest.

David Thacker was thrown headlong into a filthy concrete cell. He hurt his shoulder as he tried to break his fall. Zane Vhortghast watched from a dark room behind a pane of glass while three men roughed him up. They shone lights in his eyes. Then they introduced him to the first of many stress positions.

David Thacker kneeled on a cement floor, ankles crossed, hands behind his neck, a sandbag on his head.

Zane Vhortghast entered the room.

"Do you own a key to the grates in the east garden?" asked Zane.

David was already crying.

"No."

"This isn't yours?" Zane held up the key from David's box.

"No. It must have been planted."

"Planted? How do you know where I found it?"

"I don't." David sobbed. His face was awash and gleaming with snot and tears under the lights. "I just assumed you must have gotten it from somewhere."

Zane ignored the useless statement.

"Do you use qaam-dihet?"

"No. Only sometimes." Under the lamplight, David's sleeves had fallen down. His arms were crosshatched with an ugly pastiche of scars.

"Who is Peter Lark?"

David froze with fear. "I don't know. I swear I don't know." The other men in the room took notes while Zane asked the questions.

"Obviously he knows you. There was a letter in your box. Did he tell you to unlock the sewer grates?"

"I told you, it's not my key."

"So it's his key, and you just agreed to unlock the grates for him?"

"No. Peter Lark's got nothing to do with the sewer grates. That's something totally different."

Zane smiled at the sweet sound of truth.

"Really, what does Peter Lark have to do with?"

"Nothing. I don't know. I never saw him but once and he wore some disguise."

"Who did you open the sewer grates for?"

"Fuck off!"

But the spymaster knew that David's knees were already aching and his arms had gone numb. He was patient. "Who did you open the sewer grates for?"

It was to be a long night of games at which David Thacker could not win.

Roric Feldman was a traitor. That was the news Caliph heard on the first morning of the new month.

A hawk had come streaking into the spires of Isca Castle like a stiletto. Its dark streamlined form shot out of a blinding dawn.

General Yrisl was the first to read the note, which he then took directly to the king.

Messieurs,

Our boundaries remain ominously intact. The enemy refuses to cross the White Leech River. It remains a cold glittering line between the loyalists and the dissenters. Unfortunately, the mountains now belong to Saergaeth Brindlestrom.

Regretfully, it is my duty to inform you that Kennan Keep, governed by Lord Roric J. Feldman, has sided with the enemy. There is neither time nor space for me to detail his treachery here. Suffice to say, Forgin's Keep remains our last position in the Greencap Mountains.

I respectfully request that you muster a legion as our front grows. I will position one army at Coldwell and the other at Borgoth's Noose with the hope that we maintain our hold on Menin's Pass.

Else when winter comes we find ourselves cut off from the outside world.

Yours Sincerely,
Mortiman Tentil
Prince of Tentinil

Caliph sank into his chair.

"Can we spare two armies?"

Yrisl shook his head. "Tentinil already has five thousand active duty spread along the front. Even if the prince calls for a muster and adds his to ours we'll wind up with a thin legion. Two armies of about four and a half thousand men."

"Remind me what we're up against."

The general leaned forward with his elbows resting on his knees, hands hanging limply toward the floor.

"The whole north is with him. That means Mortūrm and Gadramere and a total of about seventeen thousand infantry compared to our fourteen. We have eleven light and seven heavy war engines to spread across six thousand square miles—all the heavies are still in Isca. Meanwhile, they have all their engines at the front. Something like eight heavy and a dozen light minus what we guess they lost at Fallow Down. All of that wouldn't be half-bad if their zeppelins didn't outnumber ours by more than three to one. And as you know, that's Saergaeth's game.

"He pressed us to the river and dug in. Now he's using the river as an easily maintainable line while he secures the keeps in the west as bases for the fleet of zeppelins he's retrofitting day and night back in Miskatoll."

"What about King Lewis?"

Yrisl snorted. "The intelligence the Pplarians gave us can't be substantiated but personally I think you'd have better luck convincing a leper to spare change."

"So he won't help, but let's assume he does. Assume we can convince him."

"At the very best he'd give you four thousand infantry and a hundred knights. You can count Vale Briar's zeppelins on one hand."

"So it's the zeppelins that will kill us."

Yrisl nodded. "It's just a matter of time."

Caliph signed off on the order for a muster. As the fountain pen scratched across the paper, Caliph felt a terrible premonition.

"Do you think I should tour the field?"

Yrisl tilted his head with a pained expression and gestured as though the matter were highly debatable. In the end, his answer was simple. "No. I wouldn't count on Saergaeth to move before fall when the leaves are gone and there's less cover in the woods for our troops to hide. He'll want maximum visibility. Stark contrast for the bomb sites. Men and machines will stand out even better against snow.

"Our morale will hold. No sense putting you in danger."

They avoided the topic of Fallow Down as they talked. There simply wasn't anything to say. Nothing new had come to light and all the papers printed were the speculations drawn by scholars who struggled for the limelight by claiming expertise in some tenuously related field. In truth no one knew what had happened to Fallow Down.

No one but Sena.

IT had been particularly difficult for her to contain her rage when Miriam had gone to the papers in an effort to dislodge her from the castle. Obviously the Sisterhood suspected something. They were turning against her. But she was cut off from them now, with no way of knowing what they knew.

All she knew was that Megan's hex was working. Finally. A month after the transumption hex, Fallow Down had disappeared. The Pandragonians were getting what they paid for . . . though they had yet to deliver the book to the Eighth House.

Holomorphy had become unpredictable as Grū-ner Shie's influence adjusted numbers in the natural world. Vog Foundry had erupted in fungus, great mushrooms sprouting from the holomorphic energies in the furnace. Bilgeburg had nearly shut down. It was in the papers. Things that relied on holomorphy were turning wild. Vog Foundry had hacked out the fungi and gone back to pure coke. Factories adjusted. Chemiostatic power still seemed safe. Sometimes holomorphy worked just fine. But people were crumbling. They took their money out of banks. They stocked up. They stole. There were fires burning in Blekton. And Sena didn't blame them. They relied on the papers for answers and the papers had no answers.

How could they? How could any of the journalists propose that some entity outside rational geometry was trying to eat them?

In reaction to Fallow Down people grieved and shouted in the streets. They wrote poems and articles and threats against the government. Some found purpose and friendship in the lonely urban wasteland by forming groups and posting flyers. They latched on to the tragedy in a peculiarly maudlin way that made less sentimental folks acutely uncomfortable.

Then there were the crasser lot, people without any direct link to the immense loss, whose lives and tiny close-knit circle of friends had been spared any lesson in privation. They grew tired of hearing about Fallow Down and thought up vulgar rhymes and pseudonyms, perhaps as a way of feeling strong in the face of horror, perhaps because they were simply ignorant. But even minority opinions, no matter how outlandish or cruel they seemed, found representation in the thronging streets of Isca.

"Fallow Down the vanished town," some said. Others shortened the grim nickname to *Fallen Down*.

Sena marveled that Megan's hex had actually cracked the prison. Like a histrionic felon scrabbling at the bars of his fabricated cell, Grŭ-ner Shie was groping, casting arbitrarily about for anything within reach.

It was not a question of corresponding angles, of physically reaching through a crack. It was a question of hypothetical geometry, of warped space drooling into many different places. A question of imaginary time.

If it had been otherwise, if regular laws had obtained, there would be no Duchy left. If Grŭ-ner Shie had been able to see and designate its motions, what had happened at Fallow Down would have happened everywhere at once.

Instead, the incomprehensible thing reached out into different dimensions, into different times. It pawed through optional reality.

Sena didn't bring it up because there was nothing anyone could do. She understood the danger. It was only a matter of time before the fumbling throes of the otherworldly entity struck Stonehold another lucky blow.

Sena's mind felt numb. She could only handle so much trauma before her brain shelved the mechanism that processed fear. The horror didn't exactly go away. Nor did the tension or the stress or the endless hours of waiting before she could try to open the *Cisrym Ta*.

But it was boring horror. Like being confined in a very ugly room that she wanted to paint over. After a while, the anxiety faded and only nausea remained.

To stay numb, she read the papers. The near constant sensationalism had become so familiar that she was beyond being shocked. Instead, it had the reverse effect. The headlines seemed to scream: Chaos is everywhere! Remain calm! Everything is normal!

She moved on to the gossip columns where, at first, it was beguiling to see her name in print. Then she grew bellicose, then phlegmatic and finally entertained.

It was like living an alternate life without any memory and reading about it later. For the sheer amount of information they printed, she thought they would have had to ask her opinion, filled up stacks of notepads.

Now she understood that in order to oblige the insatiability of the masses, fabrication was required.

The High King's witch.

That was what they called her as they speculated about why holomorphic energy was going wild. Some second-string journalist had coined the phrase. It was catchy enough and able to be pronounced (by the lazy) in an effortless breathy gust. It had stuck.

After finishing yet another defamatory article about her life, Sena tidied up breakfast and returned to her bedroom . . . his bedroom . . . their bedroom.

It had been thoroughly restored and partially redone. A new ceramic tub decorated with hand-painted roses had been hooked up to pipes from the boiler and sat elegantly in the center of the floor. New carpets, furniture and a massive ornate half-tester stood in state around the room.

Light from the western windows diminished as the sun raced east like a gymnast jumping over the castle toward the sea.

Sena took out the *Cisrym Tạ* and ran her fingers over it. She lay on the bed and stroked it. Heard it whisper. Legend claimed its vellum pages derived from stillborns. The notion pained her vaguely.

Nịs appeared and leapt up onto the bed. The cat sniffed her, sniffed the book and then retreated. Sena closed her eyes and tried to imagine what she would find inside. Wonders. Miracles in ink.

THE second piece of news Caliph heard was that David Thacker had been interrogated with mixed results, most of which indicated he knew less than anyone had hoped.

Zane Vhortghast showed up in person with this trivial bit of information and seemed to hover in the room.

Caliph expressed his desire to go and speak with David personally, a desire Zane keenly discouraged.

"You're an old friend. Regardless of how you interact with him, a familiar face will probably console him—and thereby compromise our ability to—"

Blah. Blah. Blah, thought Caliph.

Finally the spymaster left.

Caliph decided to visit David.

He grabbed a bite and went to his next appointment. The autopsy report out of West Gate, hand delivered by Dr. Baufent, the physician who had performed the procedure.

She was a short powerful woman with graying hair and a healthy complexion. She wore the red trench coat indicative of her career. Her apparel and her demeanor reflected a no-nonsense mentality. Just like the instruments she used, her remarks were concise and painfully direct.

"They haven't any brains."

That was the first thing out of her mouth.

"What?"

"Their heads are empty. Apparently they've enough tissue in their spinal columns to do the thinking—which would explain a variety of nonlethal wounds I catalogued to the glabella, occipital, temporal and other bones of the skull. On top of that, the bones themselves are not only extremely dense but also pliant. These creatures must be capable of absorbing incredible external force. My question is why?"

"What about the others? The men who wore the gas masks?" Caliph was as horrified as he was enthralled.

"Yes, they seem to be less whatever it is that their taller thinner counterparts are. More human if you will. They certainly have brains. Which brings me to the other curious thing. In the tall ones there are vestigial organs one would expect to find in . . . well, fish. Cirri, pyloric caecae, that sort of thing. The initial data would seem to indicate that our tall thin friends are actually only chips off the old block—not a race unto themselves. Like breeding a horse with a donkey, you wind up with a freak."

"So you're saying what? Humans are screwing fish?"

Dr. Baufent simpered at his vulgarity. "I don't know what's happening, your majesty. Cross-copulation on the scale it would take to create hordes of these creatures seems unlikely."

"Then what do you suppose?"

"I never suppose anything." Obviously she read the papers and chose to dislike Caliph Howl. "I'm still running some tests. I'll let you know more when I do."

During their conversation Caliph had assimilated quite a bit of additional information. Dr. Baufent's report detailed the existence of mucus glands beneath the skin which she said would help reduce friction and proliferate the phenomenon the guards had experienced: weapons striking glancing blows. It would also protect the creatures from various forms of bacterial infection. A list of iridophores and xanthophores and other discoveries followed in a twelve-page dossier.

Caliph shook Dr. Baufent's hand and thanked her for her time. After she left, he tossed the report aside.

He climbed the stairs to the high tower and stood alone, looking at the sea.

Meaningless skirmishes along the river and consistent losses in the mountains defined the war that he was losing.

And, thought Caliph, *to top it off there was Roric Feldman . . . which I suppose serves me right.*

The door to the high tower opened and closed.

Caliph did not turn around. He heard Sena sit down.

Sena looked at him. The reflection from the glass made his face gray. She remembered sitting in the library at Desdae, watching him read.

"Do you love me, Caliph?" She felt immediately ridiculous after saying it.

He nodded, the worst kind of answer she could imagine.

"Someone's here to see you."

"Someone always is," Caliph replied dryly. The waves soothed him.

Sena stood up and moved toward the door. "He must be related to you. His last name is Howl."

Caliph whirled. "Where is he?"

"Where do you think? The grand hall."

Caliph's heart began to beat again. He kissed her lightly and hurried down the steps of the tallest tower in Stonehold.

CAMERON stood gazing into the fire, watching blue worms of flame eat the white and pink undersides of a log.

"Cameron?"

The man bowed.

Cameron seemed to step out of Caliph's head, turn around and look at him. A figment turned to flesh and blood. The dream-man's tan looked burned-in, weather-beaten brown. His thinning blond hair was still in the ponytail Caliph remembered. Cameron's waist seemed to have grown but not out of proportion. He had a powerful presence, not much taller than Caliph, but with a build that far exceeded the younger man's lean musculature. Cameron's blue eyes were exactly as Caliph remembered them.

"You seem smaller," Caliph said.

Cameron chuckled. "You don't."

"My father's . . . well, I didn't think my note to him had been read or, if it had, maybe he didn't have time to write to you before . . ."

"I know." Cameron nodded sympathetically. "I took my time getting here. Stopped along the way. Talked with soldiers on the move." He rubbed his chin. "I wasn't all that sure about coming back—lots of ghosts here for me."

"I suppose I can relate. Please, sit down." Caliph pulled a rope and told the servant it summoned to bring wine.

"I'd just like some warm milk." Cameron smiled. "Myrrh feeds me what she calls secrets—strict diet and wine upsets my stomach nowadays."

"Secrets?"

"Supposed to help me live as long as," he glanced around and whispered, "as long as your kind." A ghost of a smile crossed his lips. He leaned back and rubbed his knuckles. "I think she's far too optimistic. Besides, it feels like I've been around longer than these walls and I could use the rest."

Caliph sat down and interlaced his hands.

"I don't—really know what to say." He searched furiously. "I hardly remember Myrrh—not to mention anything about you."

"I don't suppose you do." Cameron's blue eyes went back to the fire. "What do you remember?"

"I remember kites."

Cameron laughed.

"I remember sparring," Caliph continued. "I remember the little wooden figures you carved for me. The halgrin was my favorite. I still have them." He shifted as though momentarily uncomfortable. "I remember some brown fans . . . police swords . . . holding on around your neck one night. I think there was a battle."

Cameron shifted uncomfortably. "Yes. I remember all of that."

"Where did that happen?"

"Right here. In this castle." Caliph sat farther forward as a silent indication for Cameron to go on. "Your uncle was High King. Of course you know that. When he took the crown he took you with him, leaving the house on the hill and moving up here to the castle. I was no longer in his employ."

Cameron glanced at the doorway. He had noticed a woman's shadow had come to rest there. She was obviously listening.

"Inadvertently I was the one who helped your uncle get the crown and once certain matters came to light I took it upon myself to correct the mistake—part of that mistake was leaving you in his . . . care."

"You stormed the High King's Castle for me?" Caliph said it as though this one realization were enough. In all the years of doubting, when his father's whereabouts were typically unknown, when he had been locked in the ascetic halls of Desdae like something forgotten and alone, before all of that, in a place he had not remembered, the man in front of him had stormed the High King's Castle for one reason. For him.

"Well, I had some help—"

The way Cameron said it in his slow simple voice assured Caliph that it was true. The impossible odds of creeping into Isca Castle, where the guards took their duty as a sacred honor, both excited Caliph's imagination and caused another ripple of worry as he remembered the night of the opera. It was hard to believe only two days had passed since then.

"You knew how to get in because you served the High King, didn't you?"

Cameron nodded very slowly. "I was the Blue General once."

"Who did you serve under?" Caliph's hunger for the cloudy details had been whet.

"Caliph, I'm sorry. I . . ."

"What is it?"

"Well . . . it's just that . . ." Cameron let out a long breath. "I suppose it doesn't matter. You have a right to know the truth. And if you think I'm crazy, what's the worst that can happen? I'll go back home and you'll go on managing Isca."

"Why would I think you're crazy?"

CHAPTER
23

A small door opened into the massive hall and a servant came in with wine and a pitcher of steaming milk. He served the two men and left without a word.

"After Nathaniel poisoned your mother . . ."

"What?"

"He poisoned your entire family, Caliph. He had to. For the house. For the crown."

"I thought . . . it was bad food."

"It was very bad food."

"But . . ." Caliph tried to sort time. Things he remembered and things he had been told combined in an indistinguishable pile of maybe-facts. "I get the chronology confused. It's like I don't even know who I am." He had so many questions he wanted to ask. He picked one at random, a particular day that jumped out. "I remember a winter morning; we left on a trip. Where did we go?"

"That was the Year of the Crow," said Cameron. "The morning we left for Greymoor. I woke your uncle and he made a dash for the fireplace. Incontinence forced him to use whatever was close at hand. We were going to Desdae which seemed ridiculous to me. Heading for a library in the Kingdom of Greymoor just to reach some old books in the dead of winter. But Nathaniel was compensating me for the danger.

"That was also the morning I told him I was going to quit. Stop being your tutor. His thin lips always puckered when he got annoyed. Looked like a cat's ass just above his chin."

"I don't remember the trip. What happened? Something went wrong . . ."

Cameron nodded. "Yes. Something went wrong." His eyes glazed with what looked like a uniquely dire memory. "We should save that story. I'll tell you . . . but let me fill in the holes first."

Caliph nodded. "We could start with you coming to the house. Uncle . . . hired you as my tutor, right?"

"After a manner. Do you remember the day he introduced me to you?

You were a downcast little boy then. Standing near that enormous black fireplace decorated with Niloran carvings. And your uncle talking. 'Cameron, this is Caliph. Chin up, Caliph. Fools look at their shoes.'

"Time was muddy for me back then. We used to play on the lawn."

"Fly kites," said Caliph.

"Yes. You got one stuck in a tree once."

"I remember."

"That was the same afternoon you took me where you used to play. Do you remember that as well?"

Caliph had a vague recollection of sculptures behind the arms of trees, filing away. They burnt pale pink in a sinking sun. So bright. More like molten glass than stone.

"Umm—" Caliph pauses. "You want to see?" and after Cameron's affirmative nod, "Come on, I'll show you."

His eight-year-old legs begin a mad dash for the statue-marked trail and Cameron hurries to keep up.

A formerly well-kept path shows disuse and overgrowth. Saplings spring up in the middle of the trail.

"Doesn't anyone come here?"

Caliph shrugs. "No one ever has. Sometimes I play down here with Marco."

"Marco? Who's he?"

"My friend."

"Does he live in the city?"

"No. He lives out here."

"Out where?" Cameron looks around. There are no houses, roads or signs of habitation. Just forest and fallen leaves.

"I don't know." Caliph bounces along, stopping to overturn rocks and tug at leaves. "He shows up when I want to play."

The dappled sway of woodland shadows grows faintly chill. The darkness pulls more closely beneath venerable elms. Caliph can tell that Cameron feels unsettled.

Ahead, gleams of white polished stone lean this way and that, moved by shifts in the ground.

The area is not very large. Only a score of markers jut from uneven soil.

"You come here to play? Do you know what this place is?"

Caliph smiles and regards Cameron with obvious amusement. "Are you scared?"

Cameron clamps his hands together.

"It's just not the normal place to play. That's all."

Caliph climbs a hillock and surveys the sleeping kingdom with sly reverence.

"What's wrong with it?"

"Oh, nothing. So this Marco, he comes to play with you here?"

"Sometimes."

Caliph leaps from the hillock and runs briefly toward a pair of doors set into a nearby hillside.

"Wait! Don't!"

But Caliph doesn't listen. He climbs the vines over the façade, smiles and looks back out of the corner of his eye, expecting Cameron to give chase.

Instead, Cameron shrugs and begins to walk between the stones. It looks like he is reading.

Suddenly Cameron falls to his knees. He seems frightened. He begins to scream. "Where is a spade?" He is shrieking, whirling. "Get me a spade!" He begins tearing at the clay.

"I REMEMBER." Caliph nodded. "I remember you started digging with your hands. I think I ran away."

Cameron didn't smile. "Think I'm crazy yet?"

"No. I want to hear. I want to remember."

Cameron eased back into the cushions. The shadows seemed to take him in and make it easier for him to talk.

"I studied your uncle. Even after he died. His name pops up a lot in places you might and might not expect. I had to . . . study him. Sort out what happened in that house."

"I have dreams of that house."

Cameron nodded. "So do I."

Suddenly Caliph wasn't alone in the house on Isca Hill. Someone else had been there, with him, seen things, dreamt terrifying dreams. "Tell me what you dreamt."

Cameron didn't answer right away and when he did, he took the long way. The slow way. The same way he must have come to Stonehold, with every word prepared.

"I'll get to that. First let me tell you about your uncle."

"Filling in holes—"

Cameron nodded. "Nathaniel planned his ascension to the High King's throne for a reason I still don't fully understand. Something more than simple ego . . . more than power. He was almost successful at doing something I think might have sealed the Duchy's fate.

"At seventy-three years, most of his life had been spent in preparation.

"He was born in Stonehold. Left his family in the Duchy and traveled to Greymoor to study. After his graduation, he made a solitary trip to Twyrloch and when he came back—alone and nearly dead—he was carrying a book.

"Apparently its latch required a loathsome bargain to unlock. He had just accepted a position as professor at the High College when he took a sudden leave of absence.

"He traveled back to Stonehold. Lived in the house on Isca Hill while his sister's family went away on holiday to the south.

"While they were gone he charmed a girl. Told her the house was his.

"He used her blood to open a holomorphic lock on the tome."

Caliph blanched. "How do you know this? It doesn't sound like something you read in a book."

"Because he told me. He bragged about it. The old man was a letch. Anyway, after that, he said he went back to the High College and contented himself to study—for a time.

"Seems the older he.grew, the more frenetic he became. Sensed his time was running out. He took sabbatical in the west-most hills of Stonehold, following a wisp of legend.

"He found something in the hills. In the mountains around the Lost Dale. Something he jotted in his notes. Notes I saw while I lived at the house.

"Something about the Navels of the World.

"It was a place he could go. A place that would let him live until Yacob's Roll ran out. But it was also hidden. Cut off. Nathaniel could never hope to access it. It was a place he would have to commit murder to enter. Someplace close at hand."

Caliph looked around. "You mean here? In the castle?"

"I think so. I believe that's why he needed to be king. And so his real plot began. Over the course of two decades, through poison and holomorphy, he eliminated his own kin to the point that he alone stood in line for the High King's throne.

"But too much coincidence would damn him from the crown. So Nathaniel devised another way. A special way to kill the king."

Caliph hadn't touched his wine. He leaned forward, eager to hear more.

Instead, Cameron handed Caliph a piece of paper.

Caliph took it and unfolded it, not understanding what it could be. On the page was Jacob's handwriting. He read it quickly, twice. One section jumped out of the page.

*No one will remember. No one will recognize you after so many
years. The boy loves you. He has always loved you more than me.
You can give him perspective. Explain the footsteps he's following. I
wouldn't ever ask if he hadn't requested it himself. Please . . .*

" 'No one will recognize you'?" asked Caliph. A picture was beginning to
form.

"I was tricked in the snow. A bad storm. The High King was on maneuvers in the Fort Line. Nathaniel must have had it planned." Cameron's
eyes were haunted. "The royal guards weren't in uniform. Bundled up
against the snow. I thought they were bandits."

"But how?"

"I don't know. Mathematics. Twisted possibilities and time. Your uncle
was an exceptional holomorph. Which brings me to the final truth. The
reason you'll think I'm crazy."

Caliph waited patiently for the secret to be revealed.

"You remember Marco?"

Caliph's throat tightened on the name. All he could do was nod.

Cameron's broad shoulders quivered slightly as he spoke. The muscles
in his face strained to control an involuntary spasm in his jaw. "I do too.
One night." He shook his head. "The sooty darkness covering the floor. I
listened like a child for whatever woke me.

"Everything was silent. Everything was still and cold. I remember I
looked out into the hall first. Through my bedroom door there was a lone
candle. Deformed and melting.

"I listened to the absence of noise. Turned my head slowly, sensing
something there. Watching me. Something soundless. Without the noise
of breathing.

"That's when I saw it. In the smudgy purple of my own room, the
thing in the darkness."

Cameron paused, apparently horrified at his own words. Eventually he
forged on.

"His face was white, like wax—hanging eight feet off the floor. A black
brimmed hat hid his eyes. But it was the grin I remember most! Fierce.
Predatory. Laying bare a set of teeth. Interlocking canines that seemed to
laugh without noise.

"Then it fell backward, the whole phantom, like an anchor, vanishing
into the shadows at the corner of the room. It made the drapery ebb like
ink.

"I've cried for you, Caliph, when I've thought about you, rocked in
your cradle by that man. Sung holomorphic lullabies by the necromancer

on Isca Hill. His rhymes struggled from your nursery on their own, made nightmares lurch around the yard.

"You asked me which High King I served. I served King Raymond VII."

Caliph sank deeper into a numbing chill. "But. That. Was . . . 1397."

"The highest form of holomorphy charged the house on Isca Hill. So high that no one, not even the Shrądnæ Sisterhood, dared to move against him. I am a product of Nathaniel's art."

Caliph shook his head.

"I'm the figure box in math books that can be drawn but not built. Nathaniel built me. The capstone of his achievement. The success story that followed his failure with Marco Howl's ancient, mutant corpse. He needed someone good with a blade. Someone who could cut through a group of the king's high guard. He found me in the pages of his own genealogy, brought me back to become a nameless, faceless assassin.

"And you are something like my great, great, great, great grandnephew: Caliph Howl."

Caliph sat in a stupor. The winter morning they had left for Greymoor snapped back to him with clarity now.

CALIPH *is playing in the yard when Cameron and Nathaniel exit the house. They look cross with each other. Caliph comes running up to them with a small shout and jumps to the top step.*

"Caliph, settle down," Nathaniel chides.

The three of them pause on the front steps while Nathaniel fiddles with something under his cloak.

Caliph traces his fingers over the massive oak portals with iron animals that stare straight back when Nathaniel turns his key inside the lock. Snow lands on their iron snouts and dusts the steps.

Nathaniel produces an earthen bowl of some steaming liquid he has sheltered beneath his cloak. He holds it by the lip with two fingers and swirls it gently as though it is a wand.

A smooth sheet of fluid breaks over the lip and falls, splattering deep crimson across the stone. It melts the feathery flakes at once, drinking them into itself.

Nathaniel traces a three-stroke design in it with the toe of his boot and says something in the Unknown Tongue. What is left of the clotting fluid in the bowl, he places in front of the doors and with a deathly thin smile walks out into the falling snow.

"When will we come back?" asks Caliph. His voice sounds oddly muf-

fled under the swirling flakes. He stands on the steps looking down at the warm fluid with casual interest.

"I told you not to think about that," Nathaniel snaps.

Caliph crouches down and touches the puddle lightly with one thumb. He holds it up for Cameron to see, a dark red oval on his young skin.

"You shouldn't touch it," Cameron says softly.

Caliph shrugs and jumps down the steps with one heroic leap.

"Why? It's just blood. We're all going to die. It's unavoidable."

Nathaniel's laugh echoes through the snowy forest near the yard. "Speak for yourself, boy."

"I DON'T think you're crazy," Caliph said slowly. "I wanted to see you—" He forced himself to spit it out. "My reasons have changed for needing to see you. I guess . . . I suppose . . . I needed to remember. Everything is wrong. My uncle, my history, this war . . . I don't like being king. I'm not even sure I like who I am."

Cameron sipped his cup and winced. The milk was still hot. "There, you see? The Blue General can be wounded by hot milk."

Caliph was glad to chuckle, anything to break the awful oppressiveness of their previous topic. "There's a lesson there, I suppose."

"Mmm." Cameron nodded and swallowed. "The lesson is . . ." He held his cup aloft. "That the world is made up of very small things. This conversation for instance."

He took a somewhat more cautious sip. "If you don't like being king, run away."

"What?"

Cameron nodded. "I'm serious, run away—you're king, what are they going to do to you? It's a small thing. A little choice you wake up in the morning and make. Pack a sandwich, walk out the gates and head in any direction you want. I did it once."

"I can't believe this is the advice you're giving me."

"It's not advice," Cameron corrected, setting his cup down with a clink. "It's the way it is. You can just as easily stay. Every day you have the same choice, leave or stay. Either way, do what you have to. Don't run this kingdom because you feel the weight of a million sheep farmers on your back. They will survive with or without you."

"Tell that to the ghosts of Fallow Down."

Cameron picked his cup back up. "Tell me, do you think you could have saved them?"

"I had no idea such a thing could even happen. It's completely beyond anyone how or why—"

"That's right. This kingdom will go on living and dying with or without you. Those farmers beyond the city wall are just as much alive as you are and they have their own ideas. They don't sit around hanging on every word the High King speaks. A country is made up of millions of people who do what they please. They can manage. Buying. Trading. Feeding themselves."

"They depend on me for protection."

"They depend on the king—whoever he is," Cameron said bluntly. "Not you. If you left tomorrow there would be a new king. This kingdom will not fold up and blow away if you walk out that gate. These people are too stubborn for that."

"You think I should go?"

"I am telling you that nothing in this life is big enough to imprison you. You decide." He downed the rest of his milk. "Who's the girl?"

The shadow in the doorway drew back, then paused.

Caliph did not see it and asked, "A servant didn't see you in?"

Cameron poured himself another half-cup. "An armed squad of soldiers saw me in. The woman I met in the hall was no servant."

Caliph sank back into the cushions with a faint sound.

Cameron cleared his throat. "Never mind. The High King's business is his own."

"No, it's all right. The whole city's gossiping. They think I'm as bad as my uncle. According to rumor we prowl the graveyards at night and mate in the mausoleums when Lewlym is full."

Cameron smiled and nodded as if this too were news he had already heard. Caliph wondered if Cameron had taken his time coming to the castle so that he might arrive armed with every bit of gossip, already informed of how the Duchy squared.

"She seems . . . pleasant."

Caliph picked up his goblet and took a sip. "Her name is Sena. She's dangerous. And I love her." He tilted his goblet all the way back.

Cameron smiled faintly. "Love asks no questions. But a king should. If you decide you want to be king."

"Gadriel would like you," Caliph mused. "The seneschal," he explained. He pressed the cork into the bottle.

"He must like balding goatherds." Cameron grinned.

The shadow in the doorway slipped away.

One of those interminable midsummer months without holiday, Streale came in swullocking and threatened more heat before autumn finally drained it like an insatiable leech.

Beneath smazy yellow skies, the city continued to seep fermenting juices from its cracked and crusted hide. Strange urban smells lifted with the trill of popple bugs from city parks crammed under aqueducts or wedged between museums and tattoo parlors.

The economy crawled along like a half-butchered thing, cowed and wounded by the encroaching war. Grocers ran out of canned meat and powdered milk and chemiostatic torches. Construction workers abandoned the skeletons of new buildings whose funding had gone slack.

Despite the unrest, Sena needed to get out of the castle. The Hold was still relatively safe. She dressed in simple clothes and took a full purse of money.

Accompanied by two watchmen in casual attire she sampled fruits, pawed through racks of outlandish clothing and drank coffee at a chocolate house on King's Road.

On a whim, maybe to spite Megan, she decided to try one of the bright dyes she had seen in cafés and bookshops in Octul Box.

There were pinks and flame orange-reds and deep purples to choose from.

After a stylish cut she settled on blue, just a stripe. When the beautician was done a single whip the color of sky lashed from Sena's crown down along the side of her cheek. It matched her eyes perfectly.

Just a few more weeks, she promised herself. *Then I'll put away this nonsense and open the* Cisrym Ta.

She couldn't explain how it had disappeared and reappeared any more than she could explain how the Willin Droul knew she had it. Everyone assumed the attack on Isca Castle had been an attempt on the High King's life, an effort at a coup. But Sena knew the real motive behind the onslaught and her knowledge made her danger and her fear hugely personal and close.

If she hadn't been unbearably weary of the castle she wouldn't have risked the outing in Octul Box. But she *was* weary. She needed this.

Humid warm and strangely sweet, the smells of pollution cloyed in alleys trickling away through the Hold where fourteen-year-olds bragged about theft, sex, violence and their evasion of the law. They carved at their egos with knives, whittled heroic icons of themselves from the flesh of their rivals.

They ogled Sena like meat.

Sena's Hjolk-trull heritage kept her physically analogous to their age. Somewhere between nineteen and twenty-three. Not that it mattered. She turned plenty of heads regardless of age.

The boys followed her all day, slipping over walls, staying a safe distance from her bodyguards.

She watched them furtively as she went about her shopping. The papers had brought them to her attention. Some called them lice; Sena could tell from their bold propositioning stares that they did not read the papers.

They sculpted their own myths from words taken out of each other's mouths, fashioning from a crude alternative lifestyle something legendary and remarkable. *Worm gangs.* Their language was an arrogant gutter dialect of Hinter mixed with Trade. She could hear them making catcalls.

The stories in the papers were linked to her, which was why she had taken notice. They described how the worm gangs stalked the paths of the streetcars behind terminals servicing the District Line, where rails squeezed through dangerous territory.

By the end of Lüme their bodies had started to surface at an alarming rate. Behind sagging warehouses and fences, where fans spewed hot greasy exhaust from rathskellers and sleazy bistros on the Line, the bodies of Isca's next crop of highbinders had begun to pile up.

The *Herald* also claimed that when the watch found them, they usually made no report. It was part of a conspiracy theory: letting the carcasses melt in with the rest of the city's refuse, a kind of victory said the *Herald*; some vague proof of a self-destructive and deviant lifestyle.

These accusations against the watch pointed up through the food chain at Caliph Howl . . . and Sena. Professors of subcultural anthropology had reported their findings in a school-run, politically boisterous sheet published at Shærzac University in Gas End. But the professors weren't content with small scale distribution. They took their story to the *Herald* and cried murder: a distinction not endorsed by the city watch.

Now the *Herald* was labeling the homicides with bold letters at the top of the second page: BARRAGE OF HATE CRIMES AGAINST INNER CITY

YOUTH. There were demonstrations on campus that accused the High King's witch.

NO WITCHCRAFT EXPERIMENTS! shouted poster boards. The students and faculty compiled all kinds of debatable evidence that slithered loosely into one of several favored conspiracy theories.

Popular opinion in Gas End had begun to wane and chants of *No War!* and *Council or Saergaeth!* echoed across the south greens of Os Sacrum.

Sena finished her shopping and returned to Isca Castle troubled and tired.

ZANE Vhortghast had suggested making an example of the loudest mouths, but Caliph adamantly refused any kind of censor. He knew the claims were baseless and therefore ignored them despite a growing host of accusations.

Mr. Vhortghast, however, would not let it rest.

He knew something had to be done. The city was getting out of hand and with war creeping south along the mountains, and a gathering of nervous burgomasters watching Isca Castle, the spymaster had taken matters into his own hands.

Dressed his best and brandishing a cane, the spymaster had paid a visit to each of the executive editors, publishers and chairmen of the six main papers . . . at their homes.

Zane Vhortghast knew them all on a sordid, personal or compromising level. Shame, avarice and fear were well-worn tools in his hands and knowing which ones to use when and on whom comprised the bulk of his considerable expertise.

"I'm not asking for complete censorship," Mr. Vhortghast would say in a reasonable tone of voice as he poured himself a drink. "Just a bit of discrimination."

And then, in the corner of the room, something would quiver and nod its head in lamentable deference.

Fanatics who refused to capitulate, like Dr. Frezden, had accidents that underscored, in red, the importance of adhering to new journalistic standards.

By the end of the first week of Streale the demonstrations in Os Sacrum hadn't lost their pitch but papers citywide were suddenly casting Caliph Howl and Sena Iilool in a much more empathetic light.

Caliph, unaware of the circumstances responsible for the change in tone, read the *Herald*—utterly bemused.

* * *

ZANE Vhortghast was a busy man that week. He closed up shop in Ghoul Court and let slip that Peter Lark had gone south, searching for greener pastures.

The apartment building he had lived in conveniently burned to the ground, taking the landlady (who had seen him without his disguise) with it to a stinking, smoldering grave. A bird-duffer and a half-slopped chirurgeon also met seemingly unrelated accidental ends.

With the coming cleansing of the Court it was Zane's last chance to tidy up. Caliph's raid would be no less than devastating and there was little use in being diplomatic anymore.

CALIPH talked with Cameron and Sena in the evening, exhuming additional childhood stories around the darkened fireplace in the grand hall. The city remained candent long into the evening while buzzing metal fans sucked humid shadows into the castle, across the faces and legs of the chatting friends.

After dusk they decided to go for a walk on the upper parapets. Caliph relished these spare hours because the days were so busy.

Caliph leaned heavily on the battlements, exhausted. He talked about his visit with David Thacker while Isca's mythic nightscape did little to comfort him. Chimeric gears and water towers enmeshed steepled roofs and smoke. With Sena and Cameron, he watched the city's slow dark rhythm of streetcars and zeppelins evoke to the sounds of bells floating out of dreamholes on Incense Street.

It hadn't happened on the day he wanted it to. Things had come up. But by the ninth Caliph had finally made it down to the dungeons.

There had been a hearing, a jury, a verdict and so on. It had happened quickly in a system without the possibility of appeal. No one was surprised when one of the papers offered a litho-slide that showed the traitor's face and the brassy headline: FRAT BOY GETS DEATH.

The *Iscan Herald* was superficially more tactful, its caption debatably less sensational: MORE BAD NEWS FOR KING HOWL. Both papers were careful to downplay the relationship between the High King and his former friend. They gave Caliph the benefit of the doubt.

Strangely, the same image of David Thacker had made its way into the hands of every major columnist and hatchet man the city over.

Caliph recounted his journey to the dungeons as he walked around the patio. The humiliation, the close, fetid air shuddering with moans and broken sobs. Unidentifiable scratching sounds and insane gibbering in the dark.

"It was awful. Some of those people have been down there since before I graduated Desdae."

He recalled how those sane enough had pled for mercy, how others swore and spit and how several bone-thin crazies on seeing him had palmed their genitals and danced.

He had breathed through his cloak in an effort to stifle the smell. Despite the horror, it was only a short walk to David's cage.

When he arrived he looked around, confused, wanting desperately to be mistaken, to find the unscathed face of David Thacker somewhere else.

Caliph set the lantern down and fairly crumpled to his knees before the effigy of his former friend. All his anger abandoned him. He began to sob, a dry-throated hysterical silence that dredged out his soul.

David had lost a great deal of weight in ten days. His hair was clumped and tangled up in dirty tufts. His face and neck were swollen and rife with untrimmed growth, a merciful actuality that helped disguise his beaten purple skin.

A huge black mouse hung like a sack under his right eye and his left hand was bandaged in a way that indicated missing parts.

David's voice crackled like paper.

"Caph . . . Caph . . . is that really you? Is it that bad?" David touched his own face in a gentle vain way. "You're the king, right? You can get me out of here. I'm sorry. I didn't know what I was doing. I got . . . I got tangled up in . . . the wrong sorts of people, I mean. I just . . ."

He was breaking, beginning to mewl.

"I just want another chance. Just one more chance, Caph. Caph?"

Caliph held his head in one hand. He knelt before the cage, face heavy, eyes clenched tight. He had internalized his sorrow.

David gave up trying to speak. Maybe he could see that quite possibly something was about to happen in his favor. He bided his time patiently.

Caliph was brokenhearted at the sight of his friend. It was true. At a word, the coop would open, his friend emerge, ready to be nurtured back to health. The bruises would fade, the swelling subside. All could be forgiven. All mended. A second chance seemed an easy thing to grant.

"Caph?"

"What did you do?" Caliph whispered without looking up.

"Caph." David's voice was pleading. "I . . . I don't know. I messed up. I already told them everything. The jury said I'm . . ." An additional question, unarticulated but understood, issued through the bars. *Aren't you here to save me?*

Caliph couldn't look at him.

"Gods Dave, look what you've done! Did you have it all planned? That first day? The day I met you and Sig in the castle?"

"Mizraim, Emolus, fuck no! I didn't know. I didn't have a clue. It's like I told them, Caph. I'm a sleeper. I'm a crawler, a nobody. This tattoo doesn't mean shit . . . most of the time."

Caliph looked up and saw David pat his stomach. His eyes were red where they weren't black. They gushed an unremitting effusion of sticky tears.

"Show it to me."

David lifted his shirt. An ugly little curlicue of ink flared above his navel, utterly nigrescent in the poor lamplight. Caliph had not been told about this.

"What does it mean?"

"Mean? Caph. What it means is that I'm branded. I was branded when I was twelve. How could I possibly have made a choice like that when I was twelve? How could I have known then that it would come to this? I'm a sleeper. Expendable as toilet paper. One use and pull the chain! I don't even know enough information to keep from being tortured."

"Who did it to you?"

David's voice filled with hope. "I don't know his name. Some guy, tall, pale face, really messed-up teeth. Crazy as a shithouse rat. I think he broke my ribs, Caph."

"I mean the tattoo. Who gave it to you?"

David slumped against the bars, crestfallen.

"Cabal of Wights. Only I'm not them anymore. They cut me loose like a sturgeon on a three-pound line."

"Who are they? Some cult? Why in Emolus' name would you join—?"

"Yeah, some cult! Some bad-ass, sacrifice you to the oyster-god cult! I don't even know where they're at. I'm the fringe on the lunatic fringe! We're dry-bottom boys. They don't tell us shit. I went for eight years not hearing a word, Caph. I swear. Then I meet a man in the street. I could tell right away he was one of the mucks. He was following me around King's Road by the bistros. Tall, thin. Showed me his tattoo and said I was activated. But all he said to do was make sure the sewer grates in the east garden of Isca Castle were unlocked by noon on the twenty-fourth of Lüme. I swear. I swear I didn't think that people were going to get hurt."

"Then you didn't think," snapped Caliph. "And you're a bigger fool than I thought. I took you in! I gave you money, a job, a place to live!"

"I was twelve—"

"Fuck twelve! How old were you when you unlocked the grates?"

"They would have killed me!"

Caliph was shouting. "And I couldn't have protected you? Inside the castle? You provided them their only way in!

"Forty-two dead! You! You killed them! And now I'm supposed to what? Bail you out? Throw clemency in the face of my judges, the jury, the families of the forty-two soldiers we buried middle of this week?"

David rested his forehead on the bars. He chuckled softly.

"Do you remember our freshman year? When we bunked with Roric Feldman?"

Caliph nodded.

"Roric used to say the damnedest things," whispered David. "He used to say to us, *'Boys, if you fuck a sheep, what's done is done, you have to shear your kids.'* I guess I fucked a sheep, Caph."

Caliph's heart went limp and cold. He stood to go.

"Caph, wait. I know . . . I know you." He bit back on more tears. "I know you can't . . . save me. But don't leave me here. I'll do anything not to spend my last hours down here."

Caliph sighed. When he looked at David, trembling, emaciated, holding his butchered hand, he wanted to shout at the guards, call them over with the key, tell them bathetically to let his friend go free. He believed David's words were true, that he hadn't thought about the consequences of unlocking the grates.

Still, the fact remained that after it was done, after it was over, David Thacker had not come bawling like a baby and thrown himself on Caliph's mercy. No. He had relocked the gates to cover his ass. He had hidden the truth. He had lied.

"You've told Mr. Vhortghast all you know?"

"Yes." David's eyes shone pleadingly.

"Then I guess we're done here."

"Don't leave me. Please . . ."

"Guards!" Caliph shouted.

"Please, Caph."

The soldiers from Gate One came trotting.

David's other hand reached out through the bars, catching Caliph's fingers. The touch was warm and soft. A writer's hand. Unused to heavy labor. "Please, Caph."

Caliph didn't look back.

The guards led him away.

As he recounted his experience Sena shivered. Cameron looked away across the black twist of city far below.

What have I become? Caliph thought. He knew that it was a question like David's unspoken question that neither Sena nor Cameron could answer.

FOUR days later Caliph went to visit Sigmund Dulgensen.

Sigmund was appalled by David Thacker's end, but not in the same way as Caliph. Sigmund didn't have either the time or inclination to leave Ironside and talk about his loss. He and David Thacker had been proximal friends. Put any physical distance between the two of them and it was like they forgot one another existed.

A pot of coffee steadily lubricated the snarled calculations of solvitriol power. Sigmund was making headway. He assured Caliph that the lab's security remained airtight. No one knew about the experiments. He looked giddy to plunge into a full account of his progress.

"I'm set up with a prototype, Caph." Sigmund's eyes were red but exuberant. "Take a peek at this."

He pulled out a slender glass bulb haloed in iron, fitted with sockets or prongs at either end. He set it before the High King.

Caliph gazed at it for several moments, unable to speak. Like a chemiostatic cell the object glowed, but not green or citric yellow. It was not harsh or garish or easy to describe. Unusual pastel colors phosphoresced, crawling behind the glass. They rolled and ebbed along the iron bands, across the polished tabletop. They writhed, mucus pink or yellow ruffling into delicate shadows of lavender and powder blue. It was startling, mesmerizing to watch.

Caliph picked it up. It was cool, like a chilled wine bottle and tingled in his fingers like the back of a wooly caterpillar. He almost dropped it in surprise.

"What can it do?"

Sigmund was already chewing on his beard.

"Power a sword indefinitely. Power a fan, an ice maker, a conveyor belt—" He scratched the side of his face. "Whatever you want. Current generated is DC which means we can't put it through a transformer like they have in the south or carry it very far, but you could hook it up to machines, wire it into a small string of streetlamps and guess what? They'll never burn out.

"Enough kitties have gone whee to power a couple city blocks so far. I've got 'em stacked in racks down in the lab along with the adapters necessary to plug 'em in for electric lights and shit like that."

Caliph nodded, still marveling at the tube of shifting light.

"Now here's something that'll really bake yer noggin. Come with me."

He led Caliph down a metal staircase into the gritty squalor of the lab.

Huge machines stood rampant, bolted to the floor. Bizarre geometry un-folded like industrial plant life. It moved on heavy hinges by hydraulics or pressurized gas.

Caliph noticed the rack of additional solvitriol cells Sigmund had mentioned. They scintillated against the wall, a pale rainbow of ethereal colors.

"You must have found a lot of stray cats."

Sigmund shrugged and led him toward two giant anvils of grease-blackened steel. They stood opposite each other, fenced off by chains, and separated by an empty groove of space.

Like great metal shoes, the anvil-shaped things had been anchored to the floor with massive bolts as well as huge reinforced posts driven many feet into the foundations of the building.

"It's mostly solid forged like the bulkheads for the *Hylden* but each of these were specifically designed to take the strain."

Caliph heard an ominous creak deep in the floor.

"This was our prototype containment housing since the blueprints didn't go into what we should do if we managed to separate. Now we've got something better."

As usual, Caliph was lost in Sigmund's racing dialogue, trying franti-cally to make sense of parts Sigmund left unsaid.

"Contain what? Separate what?"

Sigmund pointed toward the anvils, anchored to the bedrock beneath the building. More creaking sounded from deep in the rock, speaking of enormous forces exerting against the bolts and posts. Caliph still couldn't tell where the strain was coming from.

The empty field of space between the anvils rippled with darkness.

"And what's that?" asked Caliph, pointing toward the void.

"Mother of Mizraim, Caliph—what did you hire me for? Solvitriol power, man." He slapped Caliph in the chest lightly with the back of his hand. "Souls. Remember?"

Now caliph saw them. At the center of each anvil a tiny window of pastel light gleamed fitfully from a bubble of glass embedded in the steel.

"Remember how I told you I had some ideas. Stuff nobody else's ever tried. Well, we built a cold tank like they used in the south to freeze light. That's how I managed to separate one. I mean that's how I managed to split a soul . . . in half."

"What?"

"Yeah. It's crazy. You get your arm cut off but not part of your soul. Fucking difficult. Splitting the unsplittable. I ain't a priest but according to the blueprints souls have . . . high viscosity and they're independently self-attractive—magnetized to their own unique structures. Shit. They're indestructible.

"Anyway you can trick 'em out for a few seconds with devastating cold, plasma diversion I call it, when the attractive charge goes kinda limp. Bottle 'em up like soda pop and put 'em in the containment housing. Whoa! Watch out."

A shuddering creak went through the cement floor.

"We're going to have to hook up a big-ass crane to pull these little chums apart. Stress fluctuates between the two housings with active torque and an attractive force of not less than twenty thousand tons. That means the little bugger inside the glass—which is holomorphically un-breakable by the way and extraordinarily expensive to make—is actively trying to twist 'round on the bolts, swivel the housing on a path of least resistance back to its other half. We made the mistake of fusing the glass cells with the metal housing in this model. Anyway, not bad for a stray calico, eh? Meow.

"Now check this action out. Here's housing number two."

Caliph walked toward a table with a strange device on it. A disk of black metal housed a solvitriol cell on either side, back to back, in little cages that allowed the glass orbs containing the souls to turn independent of the metal housing.

"The whole thing's made of tunsia but still not as expensive as that huge contraption over there. See this tunsia plate here could probably support almost a dozen tons of force applied to one side but that's not what's going on. What's going on is the thrust of both cells pushing against the plate from both sides with equal force. They actually keep each other trapped and the bulbs are free to spin."

Caliph watched the cells revolve slowly, grinding with immense pressure against the tunsia plate between them. They seemed to growl as the soul fragments turned their prisons against the metal disk, furious to undo the division.

"They can't try alternate directions," said Sigmund, further explaining why the second housing worked. "They don't have any power beyond the holomorphic glass. They can spin the cells, but the attractive force between them isn't a choice. They're not consciously trying to meld. It's just some kind of transdimensional physics, some law that says split souls beeline for one another." He lifted the plate and spun it in his hands. The soul fragments must have adjusted instantaneously to his sudden dynamics, never pushing in a direction other than toward their better half.

"What you're looking at here could be modified, rigged with springs and other power cells, wired up and housed in a solitary casing. What you're looking at here is the fundamental heart of a solvitriol bomb."

Caliph stood speechless, waiting for Sigmund to go on.

Sigmund smiled. "Yeah. What you do is create a mechanism that allows the two orbs to come together, a hole in the plate or an inclined plane or some shit like that. You can roll 'em toward a point of contact with hydraulics or . . . well I haven't got that part figured out just yet. But once the glass touches it's over. Absolute attraction." He rapped the plate of tunsia. "This is quarter inch. But even holomorphically tempered glass isn't going to hold split souls a sixteenth of an inch apart. Attraction between the fragments increases to a kind of snapping point. That's where you get your explosion.

"Over there," he shook his hand carelessly at the steel anvils, "you've got twenty thousand tons of attractive force. Here," he rapped the plate, "you've got grundles more."

"How big?" asked Caliph. "How big of an explosion?"

"Well . . ." Sigmund seemed to whine as though he had misled Caliph's imagination. "It's not an explosion like you're thinking. It's a ripple. Like take this beaker for instance." It was filled nearly to the top with water. He took the top of a bun left over from a day-old sandwich and brushed a rain of tiny dark seeds into the beaker. They formed a carpet along the surface of the water. "Like I said, I ain't no priest, but let's say them little seeds is us, suspended in some spiritual layer we can't even detect. Along comes a solvitriol bomb." Sigmund let slide a thick drop of water from his finger over the beaker. It fell with a plop, disrupting the surface tension of the fluid, shaking the seeds like beetles from a rug. They fell, floating down into the bottom of the beaker.

"See, the seeds don't get blown up. You don't feel it when a solvitriol bomb goes off. Buildings don't break apart and go somersaulting through the air. There isn't any discernable shockwave. But everybody. Everybody falls down." Sigmund, shirtless in his blackened overalls, scratched his meaty arm while chewing at his beard.

"Some invisible inexorable tide comes in and washes your soul out of your body like a mussel from its shell. And you're dead. You're meat lying on the bottom of that beaker, nothing left to hold you up," said Sigmund. "That's what solvitriol bombs can do."

FOR a while Caliph and Sigmund shared industrial-strength coffee mixed with brandy from Sigmund's flask. They stared at the tunsia plate separating immeasurable opposing forces and listened to the foundations creak beneath the lab.

"What's that dark ripple between the housings?" asked Caliph.

"The path of attraction," said Sigmund. "You can't see it in the smaller housing because the cells are just too close together. But it's there. Displacing light. That's all it is. I've been trying to find a way to predict how the cells will spin their housing so I can use the path of attraction to calculate some kind of endless cycle, you know . . . like a perpetual motion machine. But it's still too dangerous to try."

Caliph nodded. He asked all kinds of questions. What the attractive force measured at a distance of one, two, even three miles. What the ethereal blast radius of a solvitriol bomb would be. Sigmund had sketchy answers but promised he would do the calculations and get back to him in a couple days.

Their conversation eventually turned to David Thacker.

"I would never have pegged old Dave as a traitor," muttered Sigmund.

"Nor I," said Caliph.

"I suppose when you gathered up his things you found the second set of blueprints."

"What?"

"Yeah," said Sigmund. "I had David draw up a copy of the plans in case . . . well . . . in case you weren't shooting straight." He shrugged. "I just didn't want you thinking I was planning something behind your back. It was just a safety net, that's all."

Caliph frowned and broke into a sudden sweat. He pushed his alcoholic coffee away.

"I had . . . I had David's room searched. He didn't have any blueprints, Sigmund."

Sigmund laughed. "Sure he did. I told him myself to hold on to 'em if . . ." His voice trailed off.

"All he had was a box of creepy papers and a stack of forty gold gryphs."

"Gold?" Sigmund was incredulous. "David was broke as a toilet pipe in Kaoul. He couldn't afford socks!"

"So he sold the plans," said Caliph.

"Unbelievable."

"The Pandragonians know," Caliph said. "They know and I bet they now have proof that we have access to solvitriol power."

"Ideas who the buyer was?"

Caliph stood up.

"Yeah. I'll see you in a couple days."

* * *

WHEN Caliph returned from Glôssok and touched down on the glowing zeppelin deck, Nịs was already dying.

He saw the poor cat from across the vast expanse of concrete, lying on its side, the hazy whirring shape of a glimbender hovering over it. He ran, tried to chase it away, but the thing had already ejaculated its larva deep into Nịs' brain.

By the time Caliph crossed the deck, the furtive hairy eye on wings had gone, darting into the night.

Nịs lay breathing quietly, his life force winding down as the hungry slugs squirmed inside his skull.

Rolling in a bath of their own digestive acids, the glimbender grubs would make short work of their host. After they'd eaten the cat's brain they would spin silken cocoons inside the cranium, gestating for a month or more while the fur and skin moldered away. When they hatched, they'd come fumbling out of eye sockets or through the jaw.

There was nothing to be done.

Caliph called for Gadriel who summoned Sena to the deck. When she arrived, she wept and paced and stroked her dying pet.

Caliph tried to comfort her but she was inconsolable. Gadriel knelt with a tin of tissues at the ready.

Slowly, Nịs' breathing thinned out and settled into strange seizure-like quivers that served no respiratory function.

At last the animal stilled.

A wire seemed to burst in Sena's brain, like a violin string popping at a concert. She reeled as from a blow, crumpled to the deck and into a deep lethargic swoon from which neither salts nor shouts could rouse her.

Caliph carried her to their bedroom and summoned the physicians. They came, hooded and robed in red, carrying bowls and scalpels and hypodermics made of glass. They checked her breathing.

They tried ammonium carbonate mixed with perfume for the third time—risking poisoning. They tried cool rags and gentle slaps about the face. Finally they gave up.

"She's breathing. There's not much else I can say."

One of the physicians drew an ampoule of amber fluid from his robes. He filled the barrel of his syringe and pressed the plunger, adjusting the fluid to the level of several units etched in glass.

"This is a mild stimulant that should work during the course of the night."

He slipped one and a half inches of twenty-gauge steel into the flesh of her shoulder. After he withdrew, he taped a cotton ball over the red pearl that blossomed on her skin and motioned for the others to leave the room.

"Have her watched. Keep her warm. If her breathing becomes irregular, or she doesn't wake in the morning, call me back. Call me back either way and I'll do a checkup, make sure everything's ticky."

Caliph nodded and the physician left.

Once he had gone, Caliph covered Sena with a comforter. Servants issued into the room. They brought coffee.

"I'll take loring tea," said Caliph, "with cream."

The servants glanced at each other awkwardly until Gadriel pushed to the front. He looked as if he meant to protect them from something. The seneschal straightened his collar and forced a smile. "Unfortunately we're out of loring tea, your majesty. But I do have several . . . northern roasts here . . . to choose from." He bit his lip. "Perhaps you wouldn't mind sampling some of our local finest . . ."

It hit Caliph in the face that Saergaeth had blocked lines of import to the Duchy. They were cut off from the south . . . from the rest of the world. Caliph swallowed the fact slowly and then chuckled. "Of course. Loring tea isn't what I need tonight anyway. Brew me a strong cup, any one you want. I'll try them all." He clamped Gadriel on the shoulder and walked over to the bed, where he listened anxiously to Sena's breathing.

When the second hour bells tolled mournfully from Hullmallow Cathedral four miles away, Caliph summoned Mr. Vhortghast to the chamber.

Sena's breathing was regular and deep as the spymaster entered. Caliph felt annoyed that Zane never looked disheveled or tired or disoriented even in the middle of the night.

The spymaster wore black tweed and a purple ascot that made his clay-like complexion absolutely livid.

"I want you to find Peter Lark," said Caliph.

"David Thacker knew virtually nothing about him, my lord."

Caliph started to raise his voice then quickly controlled himself. "I don't give a—I don't care. Find him."

"I'll put some men on it. What's the sudden interest?" Dark glints of metal flashed from the spymaster's dove-gray teeth.

"Mine," said Caliph. "My personal interest."

"Of course. I'm sure we can turn something up before long."

Mr. Vhortghast left.

All Caliph could think about besides Sena's health was the second set of blueprints, David's stack of gold and the note from Peter Lark.

Around three in the morning one of the maids encouraged him to go to bed. She said she would take over. Caliph thanked her kindly before banishing her from the room. He paced the marble floor beneath the fresco in the ceiling, glancing at Sena's face and the stripe of bright blue she had put into her hair.

His head was full. Saergaeth's stranglehold on Isca seemed complete. He would wait a little while; starve the seat of government; terrorize them; ensure morale was at an all-time low. And then Saergaeth would come south, across the moors, riding the winds in a zeppelin army vast enough to darken the sky. "When the leaves fall. When the snow flies," assured Yrisl, "he will be coming."

Caliph envisioned the rain of chemical bombs and steel harpoons and cannonballs made of stone. Even with Sigmund's brilliant mind . . . even if we can get a solvitriol bomb to work . . . we haven't got a method of delivery . . . we haven't even got time to test a soul-bomb's success.

He pondered the dangers of widespread disruption.

What if the ripple effect Sigmund described traveled beyond the desired range? What if my own troops fall victim to a solvitriol bomb?

Sena awoke in a sour mood. Her head hurt. Her familiar was dead. Light from the western fields splayed through tall windows with the dawn hovering, gray and pink above the bed.

Caliph had fallen asleep in a chair. She touched his dark curls with faint affection but he did not stir.

Unaware of the agonizing watch he had maintained, she slid from the sheets and went to find the place they had buried Nis.

She found Gadriel first in the grand hall dusting trophies amid shafts of light. He mentioned the start she had given the entire castle. After a semi-tense conversation she followed his directions to the place the gardener had set her cat on fire. A carefully raked pile and a ceramic jar in the north garden bespoke the ceremony that had gone into the immolation.

Obviously the animal's relationship to her had occasioned this strange effort at decorum. She understood it had to be done, of course. Fire was the best way to guarantee destruction of the glimbender larvae.

Sena looked on the jar with faint stirrings of emotion that ranged all the way from parallels to her mother's fiery end to whether the cat had ever truly liked her.

She wasn't heartbroken. Her hysteria the night before hadn't been about endearment. She was saddened, but not as saddened as she had been frightened of the inscrutable repercussions the cat's death might have on her mind.

As her familiar, the animal had allowed her additional noetic space to calculate holomorphic formulae. Although she hadn't often used the extra processing power of the creature's brain, the pain that gashed the soft tissues inside her skull was deep and real the instant Nis had died.

Ever since getting up this morning she had been unable to suppress the repetitive urge to touch her forehead and examine her fingertips for blood. Of course there was none. Her wound was internal.

Maybe I'll be fine, she thought. *Maybe with the exception of last night, everything will be fine.*

* * *

S ENA left the city.

The moment she did, a strange sense of relief enveloped her. She took her sickle knife, her pocket watch, a bottle of water and her empty pack. Beyond Isca's soot-fouled walls the reach of machines fell abruptly short, amputated by the Duchy's green mélange.

She was free of the grinding gears, beyond the black vomit of urban architecture. And the war front was still over fifty miles away. People were trickling away, burping cars loaded with personal belongings, headed for the Fort Line and safety.

Beyond West Fen the road turned to clay, hedged with thickets and sloughs. Marshy ditches, resonant with biting insects and glutted with sludge as thick as cow sprue, instigated clutches of weeds that spread their hot-sweet smell along the road.

She passed cottages where people shot up like ancient gnarled stumps from benches in the shade. Their fists clutched newspapers from the city in grips familiar with loss. There were children. Babies crying and raucous games in the grass. Everyone capable of hard labor had melted with the morning into acres of corn or barely or rye.

Sena relaxed as she walked. She thought about Nathaniel Howl. Ever since Cameron's arrival she had been collecting stories. The old man fascinated her for reasons beyond his connection with the book.

She had jotted down a few of the anecdotes Cameron and Caliph had discussed, the ones that truly unnerved her, like the time Nathaniel had taken it upon himself to explain sex to his six-year-old nephew.

"His fingers were so thin," Caliph had said. "They did this slow together-apart, together-apart motion that interlaced with a whispery sound as the knuckles brushed against each other. He eased back in his rocking chair and said, 'Caliph, men and women are like honey and muffins. Put the honey on . . . it melts right inside the muffin. Love is like that. Sweet and warm and sticky. It's hard to get off because it gets inside.'

"Then he gave me a hand-illustrated book, inked in red and blue and skin-pink . . . mostly skin-pink. He patted my head and said, 'Love is a good thing, Caliph. It's what even old men like me want.'"

Sena envisioned Caliph poring over love positions by age six. She couldn't tell if her affection for him was growing. She tried to convince herself that it was. Mostly she just felt sorry for his childhood.

Nathaniel's character conjured vivid crazy images in her head, roaming the halls of the House on Isca Hill as Cameron described, marking up the frosted windowpanes with designs he drew with his fingertip. "Ha, that's a little blossom, yes it is. Little frost rose on the window. Cold,

cold." He rubbed his hands. "Lovely little flowers everywhere." She could hear him in her head, babbling.

She continued along the road, looking for round stones. They were easy to find.

Once, the Dunatis Sea had filled all of Stonehold, a prehistoric saline slab that crushed the hills under gradients of darkness many fathoms deep. Back then, the Duchy had been a black icy waste of glacial sediment and mollusks and mud. Sloshing against Kjnardag's feet, licking at the mountains' boots, the great sea had retreated slowly, pulled into the Duchy's pit over epochs like a slavering beast on chains.

Sena glanced north where High Horn filled a quarter of the sky. The sight of its eternal snows glaring through the ragged humid thatch of summer sent a dissonant chill up her spine.

She stopped and dabbed her forehead with her sleeve, knowing for some time now that she was being followed. *It's time*, she decided. The last cottage was a half-mile back. Her pursuer would make herself known.

Sena turned abruptly into an untilled uphill stretch of meadow and vanished from the road. Disintegrating posts screened the weed-choked field from a soggy ditch. Split and crusty with thallus, the posts barely sustained a rusted string of barbules and broken wire mesh.

She dissolved into the bracken, knowing that the sounds of popple bugs and katydids would mask her movement. Her sickle knife was out. Her eyes fought for glimpses through snarled coils of cockle vine and stymphalian grass. She ignored the predacious ephemera flashing through the weeds. A huge beetle, banded black and rotten orange, landed on her hand. She let it be.

From the road came the faint sound of a single person clapping in applause.

"You're very good, Sienæ. Very good . . ."

A woman's voice helped pinpoint the noise. Sena stayed hidden in the grass. She could see a blond woman standing on the road, sickle in hand, gazing vaguely in her direction.

"I only came to talk," said Miriam, slipping into Withil. "Muthiroo fritou uviroo hirou gorloo.[19]"

Right, thought Sena cynically, *I'm sure she does.* She scanned the road for others.

As if able to read her thoughts, Miriam called out again in Withil, "I'm alone, Sienæ. Megan didn't send a qloin. As if she ever would. I know the Willin Droul are after you. The Sisterhood can help. Come out and talk to

---

[19] W.: "Mother frets over her girl."

me. I'm obviously no threat . . . to the Seventh House." She added Sena's rank like a reluctant concession, as an afterthought.

She watched the weeds intently. Miriam turned as she spoke, scanning the ditches in every direction.

But Sena wasn't willing to risk a confrontation—yet.

She pricked her finger deeply for a legerdemain that distorted the air above the road. The Unknown Tongue trickled from her lips.

Miriam must have felt the subtle shift in temperature. Must have guessed that trickery would follow.

Sena's voice came out from the weeds, speaking in Withil. "I didn't really like your article in the *Herald*."

Even though she had been waiting for a response, Sena's voice obviously startled Miriam, who regained her composure quickly and continued to turn as she spoke, guessing correctly that Sena had holomorphically masked the origin.

"Sienæ . . . you saw the hex . . . you know Fallow Down is only the beginning. Leave this place. Come back to Skellum—where it's safe."

"I doubt you're concerned about my well-being, grūrda.[20] You've probably poisoned Megan with your suspicions."

Miriam smiled. "Are you guilty of something?"

Sena scoffed. "I'm the High King's witch. Don't you read the papers?"

"That's pårin. Megan sent you to Stonehold. No one's accusing you of fårǫn. I'm sure you—"

"I'm not using him," said Sena hotly. Her anger was real. "Go back to Skellum. Send a qloin if you like. I'm not coming back."

Sena crept forward. By the time Miriam had turned around again, Sena stood in full view at the edge of the untilled field, glaring. The sight forced Miriam to take several steps back.

Sena walked forward. Careless. Unafraid. Miriam stumbled.

"This is my country, now," said Sena.

Miriam looked surprised, like she had lost her train of thought. There was not enough blood on Sena's finger for her to use.

"Tell the Sisterhood I am my own witch. Tell them I intend to stay here."

"The hex—"

"Does it look like my holomorphy is suffering? I *will* break Megan's hex. I will bind what stones remain. I will patch the holes Grū-ner Shie is floundering through. I will undo this thing. I am not your Sister anymore."

---

[20] O.S.: Animal baby. A mild slur that flexes to a variety of contexts.

Apparently Miriam had nothing to say. Maybe she even believed that Sena wasn't bluffing, that she was capable of doing all the things she said.

"You have it then . . . ?" Miriam whispered in reverential awe. "You've found it?"

Sena gave a crooked smile. "Found what, grŭda?"

Miriam trembled. "The book. The book for binding gods."

Sena hesitated. There was danger in being overly sure. If she admitted, if she confessed, the Sisterhood would send more than a single qloin. She hadn't even opened it. Confirming Miriam's accusation would be folly, so she demurred.

"If I had the *Cisrym Ta* why would I bother hiding from you?"

Miriam's face revealed an inner struggle with the logic Sena posed. She seemed to hang between two presumptions as Sena backed her down the road.

Sena stopped. She raised her arm and pointed her sickle at the other woman's heart.

"Leave Stonehold . . . while you can. 𐤀𐤋𐤉𐤕 𐤏𐤆𐤂𐤅𐤊𐤔 𐤀 𐤉𐤋 𐤀 𐤂.[21]"

At the sound of the Unknown Tongue, patterns of darkness rolled over the ground like clouds covering up the sun. Sena had split her finger open again by discreetly tugging her thumb along the tip of her knife.

The limited illusion that she chose was that her body turned into shadows, blending with the patterns on the ground.

A semisolid darkness remained in the place where she had been, holding Miriam's eyes fixed while Sena darted south into the field by the road.

MIRIAM was left to catch her breath in the aftermath of the well-wrought glamour. For the first time in her life, she respected Sienæ Iilool. Up until today she had never squared off against Megan's girl. She had never seen firsthand the precision with which Sena wielded the Unknown Tongue.

Any witch could throw a glamour and adjust its output with different numbers in a string. Flaws in the glamour happened when the equation got cluttered with variables that hadn't been properly reduced. It was the difference between saying something loquaciously and keeping it succinct.

Brevity made a glamour urgent, lucid and exact. Wordy castings added ambiguity and room for doubt.

Sena's had been exquisitely efficient, pared to the bone, fitted pre-

---

[21] U.T. Approximate pronunciation: Dlimehnayi-oan dlore.

cisely to flex the muscle of a particular effect. Her illusion preyed on Miriam's mind. She was held in thrall by the sudden fleeting shadows and Sena's meteoric evacuation of the road. Like a murder of crows had been wheeling overhead, the shadows on the road wove and flickered. The grasses bent in a sudden gust. A menacing black shape hung for a moment, a Sena-shaped daemon in the air.

After the glamour passed, Miriam realized her heart was pounding in her chest. Yes. She respected Megan's protégé intractably now. Sena's voice filled the weeds with threatening whispers.

The day was young. There couldn't be a better time.

Miriam turned southwest, quickening her pace, and headed ďˑ for Menin's Pass.

SENA darted through the field, making for higher ground⸏ as much distance between herself and Miriam as she could ⸲ ⸲e her glamour allowed.

After a sweaty and difficult climb she reached a second di⸲ road from which she could look down across striated crops and solitary farms. In vast breathless panorama she saw the Greencap Mountains reaching north, High Horn floating in a distant haze and Isca smoldering quietly at the edge of the sea.

The road she had reached wound among the foothills of the Healean Range. The mountain woods leaned out like scaffolding from the precipitous incline to the south, threatening to fall across her path. Above them the Healean Mountains soared next to vertical, a harsh savage escarpment of serrated stone.

Sena recognized an approach a quarter mile to the east where a rutted trail turned uphill into the woods. It was the same trail Caliph and she had ridden many weeks before: the trail to the ruined Howl Estate.

Still shaken from her confrontation, Sena glanced behind her. When she reached the shady tunnel it provided marginal relief. Dappled light floated over the disused path. The trees muttered, boughs creaking.

After little more than ten minutes she reached the yard. The house sat, pouting hatefully amid a riot of weeds.

Sena felt a powerful aversion to the windows. It seemed abnormal that children had not hiked up here, thrown stones and broken the innumerable panes. As she began her circuit of the property, from the corner of her eye, she imagined movement in the glass, at any given window, but every time she turned, there was nothing there.

The building was a motley, mortared, pitted mess. The walls heaved up with obeliscal angles that veered imperceptibly as they wrestled with the sky. Like a fortress or a gate, the hulking structure gave Sena a strong impression that it was holding back untold things, plugging a defect or a wound in space, bulging slightly from decades of strain.

Sena worked her way behind the house, passing through a rusted iron fence. Amid the elms, mourning cloaks fluttered near the statues in the vines. High-pitched, late summer insects echoed off the stones, screaming an alarm.

This is the spot, she decided. *I'll build the monument right here.* She kicked at the weeds tentatively, gauging the amount of work it would take to clear a spot of ground. She emptied the few stones she had collected from her pack.

It would take many trips for her to be ready by the first of Thay.

Although she had no desire to enter the house, she spent the afternoon surveying the extensive property of the estate. She found several property markers in the trees a hundred yards behind the gazebo.

When the sky turned gold she headed back to Isca. Fantastic fears followed her all the way from the yard.

Only when she reached the tertiary road that dwindled through the foothills did her phantom pursuers leave off. They were invisible. But she could feel them staring at her from the shadows of Howl Lane.

Figments, she mused, tousling her hair.

SENA made it to the castle just before curfew as the gatehouse bells were ringing. She hurried across into the tunnel and took a coach to the keep where Gadriel admitted her at the foyer and offered to take her pack. He mentioned that Caliph had already gone to bed.

Tired and sticky from the day's exertions, Sena headed upstairs, longing for a bath. She met Cameron on the steps.

"Evening." He smiled.

"Evening." Sena smiled back. "You look like you're leaving."

Cameron shrugged. "Yes. I think it's time I went back to Nifol . . . to my wife. Autumn's almost here. I don't want to get trapped in the snow."

"You could take a zeppelin . . . or . . . I guess not." She had momentarily forgotten Saergaeth ruled the west.

"Hate flying." He smiled.

"You'll take breakfast with us in the morning?"

"Already said my good-byes to Caliph. I'll be gone before dawn."

She didn't know why she wanted him to like her, but she did. She ridiculed herself for it but still, she *wanted* to meet whatever criteria he employed. Ever since eavesdropping on that first conversation, she had wanted fervently to be good enough for Caliph in Cameron's eyes.

Cameron said good night and continued on his way.

Inexplicably dejected, Sena climbed the stairs to Caliph's bedroom and drew herself a bath.

aliph found out about the metholinate lies on the eighteenth of Streale. Ever since seeing the bouquets of glowing gas at the opera house, he had been nervous.

Lodged deeply under Ironside, the city's metholinate reserves resided in enormous pressurized metal caverns. Before Saergaeth cut the supply, zeppelins from the Memnaw had bellied up to spindles in Ironside and pumped the precious fuel down twenty stories' worth of pipe, through nozzles and gauges into the reservoirs.

Based on readings taken from monitoring facilities in the nether basements of Glôssok Warehouse, Caliph received a weekly update on exactly how much gas was left.

Worried and too impatient to wait for the weekly report, Caliph went to Glôssok on the eighteenth in the company of two knights. He surprised the guards at the measuring station who looked positively terrified at seeing him there. They took him to the gauges so he could see for himself the dwindling supply.

But when Caliph reached the dials, to his confusion, he found the metholinate levels higher—much higher—than the numbers in his reports.

He interrogated the technicians, demanding to know how such an error could have been made.

Terrorized, they stood mutely, shuffling through sheets of figures and looking to one another for something meaningful to say.

"Are these gauges correct?"

"Y-yes, your majesty."

"Has any metholinate been added to the tanks?"

"No, your majesty."

"Then what in the crue-blistered memory of Burim is going on here?"

The technicians seemed to forget their eminent degrees. They fumbled for answers even when Caliph demanded their names.

"Arrest these men."

The knights obeyed.

Furious and bewildered and at the same time relieved at the discovery of three more months' worth of gas (even if the restrictions were lifted) Caliph had the technicians interrogated while he returned to Isca Castle to ponder what it could mean.

Why would someone falsify the readings on the reserves? To panic me? Trick me into a sudden ill-planned offensive against Saergaeth? Doubtful. It was too improbable to hope for. But if not, then why?

For weeks, the reports had been coming out of Ironside, each one carefully contrived. An appalling though plausible level of depletion had been meticulously depicted. An orchestrated plunge of critical numbers that cried out urgently: *the city is starving!*

Unless . . .

Unless someone knew about the blueprints!

The only reason Caliph had changed his mind and sanctioned the solvitriol project had been because he believed the city was on the brink of gobbling up the last remaining cubic feet of metholinate in its stores. Someone had duped him. Someone had known.

But who besides Sigmund . . . unless Sigmund had talked? Who could benefit—specifically—from solvitriol power?

He imagined Simon Stepney, the burgomaster over Growl Mort who had given him the statue of the factory.

No. That wasn't the right question. The right question was: *who might benefit from proof that the Iscan government was conducting solvitriol experiments? Someone who wanted to sell the other set of blueprints! Someone who would send government lab notes to a potential buyer as proof of product! What about blackmail?* Or, thought Caliph with sudden clarity, *what about someone who was truly, honestly loyal to the Duchy? Someone who knew I didn't want to give Sigmund the go-ahead . . . someone who knew a false crisis would prod me into a course of action that (even though I found distasteful) would ultimately save the Duchy?*

Caliph felt sick. He paced around his room trying to figure out who might have been able to discover such sensitive information. The pile of names dwindled quickly. He sat down in a high-backed chair to think.

WHEN Sena opened the bedroom door she could see instantly that something was wrong.

Caliph looked up. "Hi." His voice was soft and expectant. "How's your head?"

Sena touched her forehead where the pain of her familiar's death still ached occasionally. "I'm fine."

She could tell by the way he asked that he wanted something. At first she thought it was sex. They hadn't made love in two weeks. But as she came into the room and shut the door, she could see by his expression that wasn't it.

He whispered, "I have something . . . a favor to ask. I'm not sure if it's the right thing to do. It could undermine . . . a lot of things."

Sena said nothing. She walked over and sat down beside him, looking at him intently. She had never seen him so nervous.

Caliph reached out, as though to reassure himself, and touched her fingers.

"What?" she coaxed. "What do you want me to do?"

Caliph looked around the room as though paranoid of peepholes or vents capable of conducting sound.

"I—want you to . . ." He couldn't seem to get it out. "I want you to find out everything there is to know about . . . Zane Vhortghast."

THE spymaster came to Caliph's room the following evening looking paler than usual. He took a seat only when Caliph bid him to do so and adjusted the ascot beneath his vest.

"I heard there was a discrepancy in the metholinate reports." As usual, Zane's expression gave nothing away.

Caliph was standing at the windows, looking west into a colorless sky.

"Yes. I had some technicians arrested. I was hoping you could shed some light on this . . . what with your numerous connections."

Zane remained cool.

"Unfortunately it's news to me, your majesty."

Caliph turned and met the spymaster's fearless eyes.

"I was afraid of that. I have suspicions of my own."

Zane grew genuinely interested. He leaned forward in his chair and asked who.

"Simon Stepney," said Caliph with an air of strange mystique. "He and Ben Nagrüth would both have a vested interest."

Zane nodded slowly, as though weighing several things on the side.

"That's good thinking. I should check into them . . . both."

"I want you to go tonight. Personally. I don't want any blood or threats. Not until we know something for certain."

Zane smiled. Caliph had to look away.

THE lock to the spymaster's quarters was much more difficult to pick than David Thacker's had been. It didn't have a master key and there were several serrated drivers that tended to false set.

Sena took her time, knowing that the spymaster had been sent across town. She managed to have it open in under a minute and a half.

The spymaster lived in an attic suite atop a cluster of town houses in the bailey's western quarter. Because of this, Sena had the option of going in through one of many windows. But in the end she opted for the front door since it afforded her protection from the parapets and the eyes of several hundred sentinels on their rounds.

Sena found it difficult to tell why she was here—doing this again. Maybe there was a twinge of guilt. Maybe she enjoyed the danger. Her motives were like the obscure shapes that now surrounded her.

She shut the door behind her with a quiet clunk and set about her task. A chemiostatic torch flared in her hand. She flicked its lime-colored beam across walls devoid of personality. Shapes appeared in fractions, disembodied textures in a hollow tenantless abyss. Here the fabric of a chair. There a spot of wood or porcelain or the crooked shadow of a light fixture, flexing like a pedipalp.

She moved efficiently.

She sifted through the drawers of several desks, checked the closet and the space beneath the bed. There was plenty of room for just one man— most of which had gone to waste.

Dormer windows spilled Lewlym's purple light like brandy across barren spacious sections of the floor. Knots in the wood made faces in the grain, grinning stupidly at her.

Three contiguous rooms comprised the suite, linked by six-paneled doors. Having searched the first two chambers thoroughly, Sena tried and found the last door locked.

She shot the beam of her torch into the keyway and saw something that disturbed her. A set of pressure-sensitive wards. Although the correct key wouldn't disturb them, her torsion wrench and rake undoubtedly would. What the wards might trigger, Sena couldn't tell.

She decided there were other ways to get around the door and opened a nearby window.

The ledge was tricky. Overhung and pinched by the dormer eaves, at first there seemed nowhere to go. Sena stepped out, boots scraping on pigeon shit and stone.

The wind was warm and full, like a membranous balloon against her body. She clicked her torch off and stowed it in a utility belt around her waist.

Gripping the sandwich of boards and shingles that composed the eave, she leaned out into the night, seven stories off the ground.

Nearly level with the castle walls, she could see faint black figures floating along the parapets across a gulf of moonlit air. Some carried flecks of light. All of them carried crossbows.

Looking more like a gruelock than a woman, Sena launched her body from the ledge. Her thighs and knees swung up like a grapnel and hit the steep shingles of the roof. Below the eave, her torso jackknifed. Her body held the edge of the roof like a vise between her belly and her legs.

She nearly lost her balance, went nose-first toward the ground, but her hips anchored her on the gable's gritty slope.

Impossibly she clung, gasping. Her center of gravity skewed. She should have skidded down the shingles or plunged to her death. But her movement had been quick and for an acrobat, energy equaled mass: weight that pulled her through the rotation of the move.

Dark and indistinct, she unfolded along the gable's edge, a blemish of blackness curling into stone and wood.

Once she had pushed herself to safety she drifted above the roof's smooth lines toward the adjacent gable—the one whose window granted access to Zane Vhortghast's final room.

Her silhouette balled, extruded and swung like taffy into the murky triangle of shadow beneath the second gable's crest. The guards on the parapet trundled on, undisturbed.

Once more hidden from their sight, Sena knelt beside the pane. She couldn't see inside the room. She had glass-cutting tools in her belt but she noticed something even more useful hanging like a mud wasp's nest in the apex of the eave where a family of swallows had secured a little home.

She stretched and groped delicately about the warm gauzy interior until her fingers discovered life. She took two chicks from the nest, one she buckled gently into a pouch on her belt. The other she decapitated with her sickle knife, wincing slightly at the murder.

She squeezed. Blood poured from its open neck as from a tiny sponge. The holojoules sang and Sena whispered, hemofurtum, syllables that bent the fabric of the glass. She moved through the window, into the room, leaving only a vestigial blemish where the glazing closed behind her. Luck was on her side. Grū-ner Shie's influence had not altered her formula in the least.

This was Vhortghast's study.

She clicked her torch and found a cache of money stacked atop a desk. The drawers contained documents pertaining to various matters insignificant to her task.

After fifteen minutes she heaved a sigh and stopped to rest.

The room was clean.

She clicked off her torch. Lights had come up in the other room, a sheet of fulgurate yellow shot under the door and across the floor.

She could hear muted voices and the distinct clunk of someone shutting the apartment's front door.

". . . not bad . . . better at the Crowing Bistro in Nevergreen . . ." A man's voice percolated through the wood, muffled and nearly unintelligible.

A second man's voice sounded spirited but tired.

". . . that what . . . nobody . . . awful."

Sena crept to the corner of Zane's considerable desk. A pillar of darkness filled the center of the yellow light streaming under the door. Someone on the other side was fumbling with a set of keys.

"I . . . ever . . . profusion of ungodliness. It's a fucking shame." The lock turned, the door opened and a figure hewn from backlit darkness stood facing Sena's hiding spot, talking as if to her. Sena heard the baby bird in her pouch make a faint tentative scratch.

"Anyway," the man was saying, "with progeny like that what can you expect? He's like a," he paused, searching dramatically for words, "like a . . . libelous milk-livered cheese curd."

The second voice came from behind the first man, out of Sena's sight.

"What the fuck is that supposed to mean? Libelous?"

The first man spread his hands as though appalled by his companion's stupidity. "Libelous . . . it means you talk shit about somebody. You know, like libel, like they take you to court over. You're supposed to be a criminal!"

"Yeah, I don't enjoy this aspect of the job . . . unlike you. I've got a wife—"

"My condolences."

The man in the doorway reached inside and groped around the wall.

Sena heard a slow hiss and then a pop as a single gas lamp lit. Ensconced on the wall near the door, it cast enough light to jeopardize Sena's position and she eased back into the dark, peering through a crack between a wastebasket and the desk. For the first time she could see most of the room as one unified tapestry of texture and shape.

Bookcases lined the walls. Several stuffed chairs and a potted plant occupied space on a tapestry rug before the windows. It was sparse like the outer rooms, lacking a certain believable quality, as though it had been staged.

"Just hurry up, will you? Ol' Zane's dust-bugger is probably getting antsy. Southern piece of gorabi shit!"

"Hey, shut up!"

Sena's heart skipped a beat as he said it, thinking he might have heard the sudden fit of tiny scratching in her pouch. The additional light and voices were agitating the chick. "You obviously haven't been around long enough to know Mr. Silent's just like Vhorty. They both like to catch you off guard."

Sena saw the man's eyes pause and scrutinize the room. When he seemed satisfied that the study was indeed empty he continued.

"If you're smart, which you're not, you won't say anything derogatory . . . ever."

"There you go again with the words. Didn't you just call the boss a cheese curd?"

"Shut the fuck up."

The outer door opened and a third voice, a smoother voice with a southern accent, curled into the room.

"What's taking?"

The man in the doorway found a new sense of urgency despite his nonchalant reply. "I'm hurrying. I'm hurrying. Sheesh. It ain't like we're going to meet her holiness at Hullmallow." He walked into the room and headed for the desk.

Sena edged quickly backward, making very little sound. Rather than crawling underneath and cornering herself under a piece of furniture she kept the desk between herself and the man.

The outer door clunked again.

"Is he gone?"

Sena heard the other man's smile. "No."

The man in the study took the chair from behind the desk and rolled it across the floor to the bookshelves. He then used it as a stepladder to one of the shelves and from there stretched out and opened a square in the paneled ceiling.

Sena saw him fumble with some items before he took what he wanted from his pocket and stashed it in the ceiling. He closed the panel, jumped to the floor and brushed off the seat of the chair before rolling it back behind the desk.

Good. Now hurry along, thought Sena.

But the man did not hurry. When he reached the doorway he stopped. There was a click from the outer chamber. A strange thunk and he slumped face-first into the doorway between the rooms.

The same click and subtle hiss preceded the sound of a second body falling to the floor—one that Sena could hear but not see. Then she heard the smooth voice with the southern accent speak in sardonic soliloquy, "Good night boys."

Sena crept from the desk, realizing she had to get a glimpse of the unseen speaker in order to make sense of what had happened. She peeked out despite her instinct to remain hidden and locked eyes with a brown-skinned blond-haired Pandragon that she had seen once before in Mr. Vhortghast's company.

Bad luck alone had allowed them to see each other across a landscape of murder. Sena hardly noticed the bodies.

Ngyumuh held a gas-powered crossbow in his hands. He aimed and fired in an instant. The quarrel burst through the corner of the desk creating a blossom of splintered wood, the tip of the bolt looking like a deadly metal pistil. Sena wheeled across the floor.

Ngyumuh's bow auto-loaded from a clip into the gentle magnet of the groove; its tank of pressurized gas drew the string automatically on an internal gear beneath the lock plate. He leapt over one of the men he had killed and burst into the study, keen on Sena's trail.

The light from the wall fixture flickered over the wooden floor. His eyes took in the body of an infant bird, fresh blood spattered across the boards. Something hazy blurred the bookshelf for an instant. Something out of focus slipped along the wall. Ngyumuh pivoted and fired.

The bolt lodged itself in the spine of a book, riving a dozen chapters of some classical tome. Then the trademark grip of the Shrądnæ Sisters encircled his neck from behind.

The sickle knife, sticky with birds' blood, lightly scored his throat. Sena's whisper sounded almost inside his ear.

"I'll kill you with a twist."

It had a strange sexual connotation that must have scared Ngyumuh. He set the bow on Mr. Vhortghast's desk at her request and tried to keep from swallowing—an action that would certainly deepen his already oozing cut.

"Why did you kill those men?" she whispered.

Trained as the spymaster's personal bodyguard, Ngyumuh must have also known what she was capable of. He tried to buy some time with words.

"What's it to you?"

Sena pushed the handle of her sickle knife counterclockwise so the razor tip of the crescent made a sudden puncture wound beneath his left ear.

"I don't ask questions twice and you don't ask questions at all. Clear?"

Ngyumuh, despite his best efforts, swallowed and worsened the gradual filleting of his skin.

"Yes. Eh'ajyo ogwôg.[22]"

"I speak Gnah Lug Lam, ngôd ilôm.[23]" She cut him again.

Ngyumuh winced but finally gave himself completely to her fatal embrace. Even an elbow or sudden kick to her groin wouldn't guarantee the encircling blade didn't open his jugular as it left his throat. He had no choice but to capitulate.

"Yehw ikeslud ninglas-dey?[24]" she hissed into his ear. "If I have to ask again—"

"I'm cleaning Mr. Vhortghast's house," Ngyumuh said in the Pandragonian Tongue.

Looks more like you're making a mess, thought Sena. "Under Vhortghast's orders?"

"Of course."

Sena nodded toward the bodies. "Who are the curs?"

"Operatives with memories."

"You're talking a lot without saying anything."

Ngyumuh smiled despite his pain. "We both know I'm not going to talk."

"We all make choices," Sena said.

That was it. She ended it with a ratcheting of the crescent. He gasped once and clutched at his throat before dropping to the floor. Sena suppressed her morbid fascination. She stuffed her feelings and rummaged through Ngyumuh's clothes.

In his vest there was a pouch of coins and a cruestone for a pigeon's head. Hurriedly she cast another charm with Ngyumuh's gushing blood, cloaking herself in a powerful hex of bent shadows and distorted light.

The sight of battle in the gas-lit windows had drawn soldiers from the lawn. She could hear the heavy double tramp of armored boots coming up the stairs.

In one smooth motion, the distortion that was Sena floated up the bookcase, opened the panel in the ceiling, drew out the contents and curled like a draft of chilly air, slipping out between the sentries that were filling up the room.

---

[22] G.L.L.: "You lost little girl."
[23] G.L.L.: Shit head.
[24] G.L.L.: "Why did you murder those curs?"

CHAPTER
27

Across town, Mr. Vhortghast was making preparations. He had guessed that his plot had been discovered.

He had not gone to Growl Mort but to a tidy apartment he kept in Winter Fen. A two-room flat with a tiny closet in between, the apartment maintained a northern view of the symmetrical slums of Gorbür Dąyn.

Zane was too practical to be upset. It hadn't been his plan to lose his position or to cause the High King direct harm. Now he realized Caliph's reign was coming apart. He was flailing at his enemies, hoping by luck to connect with one.

Good luck, thought Zane. *I have other business opportunities in the south.* He had gathered all his critical paraphernalia to this final stronghold, his most secret of several lairs.

I'm actually glad not to have to spend another winter in this fucking deep freeze, he thought. The almanac had promised there would be an early frost.

He sorted through a stack of papers on a side table near the hearth. With the installation of the boiler in the basement the chimney had been sealed, but Zane had renovated it once again for use. As he sorted, he tossed various pages on the fire.

A cage by the window held a hooded hawk: his return carrier of a message from the south. Against all odds, the mangled pigeon he had released had crossed a thousand miles to its destination—intact. The reply was sitting on the table, waiting to be burned.

Mr. Prüntergast,
    Messieurs Vôlk, Kranston and Croft are quite impressed with your offer. No doubt you have sent similar propositions to every government within flying distance—judging a lack of adequate carriers from the disposition of this recent bird.
    Be that as it may, we are prepared to go ahead, despite obvious

reservations associated with lying closely as we do, just across the gap of Eh'Muhrūk Muht.

I will arrange for a coffer of scythes to be registered under your name in the Capital Depository on the Avenue of Lights.

As I'm sure you're aware, there are several different empires tangled up in this debacle and maintaining transparency has become a matter of the highest concern.

Should secrecy be compromised, there will be other metals waiting for you.

Once again, our desire has always been for nonwritten communication in this matter. Please accept our apology in asserting our inability to reply to further correspondence of this nature.

Sincerely,
Msgr. Pratt

Vhortghast tossed it on the flames just as the sound of rapping echoed through the room. He pulled a knife and went to answer the door.

The chain allowed him to snatch a glimpse of the corridor. He expected the landlady with an envelope for the rent.

Instead two small children met his gaze. One was licking a sweet from a stick, his face blackened with gooey grime. His (presumably) sister also held a treat but she was slightly older than he, less focused on the yellow-green confection dripping down her hand.

They stared up at him from a hallway strewn with papers, dirty mattresses and junk.

"Mister," said the girl. "Are you 4-A?"

"Yes. I don't want the paper."

"I'm not selling papers." She blinked at him, doe-like and matter-of-fact. "There's a mister in the lobby wants to talk with you."

Zane scowled and motioned at their treats.

"And he gave you those if you delivered the message?"

"Yes. He's nice."

Her brother nodded his head and grinned ridiculously, showing little rotten teeth.

"It's a little past your bedtime, isn't it? What does this nice man look like?"

"He's uhm . . . don't have no hair," said the boy suddenly, patting his head with the treat. Little gobs of goo clung like lice nits to his wispy scalp, making it stand up in places like bundled thatch.

"He's bald?" Zane looked to the girl for confirmation.

She made the hand sign that it was so, giving away that she had ties to the south.

Zane knew no one by that description. He didn't unlock the door. "What are your names?"

"I'm Dotty and he's Moo."

"Those are pretty names. I tell you what. I have some treats right here in my flat. I'll give them to you if you do something for me. Okay?"

"Okay," they said in unison.

"Moo, go downstairs and tell the man I'll be right there. Go now. Hurry along." The boy took off on stubby legs. "Dotty, I want you to stand out-side the door and if the man comes up the stairs, I want you to knock as hard as you can. Then I'll give you some treats. Okay?"

"Okay."

Vhortghast smiled and closed the door. He had no idea who could have found him here. One thing was certain. He had to get out—fast. He turned to finish destroying his documents and noticed suddenly that one of his windows was open.

He spun with his knife.

"Ah-ah-ah." Another voice in the room warned him against trying anything daring.

A man in dark simple clothing stood across the room holding a strange southern weapon aimed generally at his chest.

"Who are you?" asked Mr. Vhortghast, quickly mastering his fear.

"Just an old man passing through." The voice was a raspy haggard tenor. He looked a year or two past fifty. He had bright steel-gray eyes that never left the spymaster's face and a shaven head that revealed early liver spots and wrinkles behind his ears. A thick, exquisitely trimmed goatee of powder gray bunched around his mouth and when he talked, the man with the weapon moved his face in an almost kindly way . . . as though speaking to grandchildren seated on his knee.

Mr. Vhortghast said nothing. Already he was bored.

"Name's Alani."

Zane became un-bored again. His eyes grew wide for an instant as the name registered against the brief list of those he feared.

"Alani out of Ironwall?"

The old man shrugged. "I'm not from Ironwall. Like I said, just passing through."

Zane's mind slid the pieces into place. "Are you working for Saergaeth?"

Alani smiled. "Nonsense. Saergaeth Brindlestrøm is a fool."

Zane slowly set his knife down and reached for a chair. "Mind if I sit down?"

"Yes. Yes I do."

Zane stopped and turned ever so carefully. "What's that you've got there? A nidus?"

The weapon's mouth was like a box without a lid. Inside, a honeycomb of tubules housed several hundred darts fashioned from surgical steel. Like a hive of metal wasps, waiting to take flight.

The stock was made of wood and cradled a canister filled with compressed gas. Several switches determined whether pulling the trigger released one, ten, twenty or all the darts at a time. Vhortghast knew from the casual way Alani aimed the box that they were set to unload en masse.

"I heard you were in business for yourself these days," said Alani, ignoring the other man's question.

Zane shrugged. "You know how it goes. Catch as catch can."

"Catching quite a bit from what these old ears can hear."

"I'm not a traitor," said Zane.

Alani almost seemed to snicker. He made a symbol briefly with the hand that held the stock, something only men of their profession would understand. "That's like saying there's only one shade of blue. What did you do? Set that kid up with a buyer?"

"Why? Can't you figure it out?" Zane was growing tense. "Or did you just decide you wanted a cut? You're like a fucking sarchal hound stealing a carcass from a pack of poor defenseless wolves."

"Actually, since you've effectively put yourself out of business up here I thought I might give my résumé to the High King."

Zane Vhortghast couldn't help but laugh. "You've got to be kidding. If you came back to this town—" His laughter dribbled off. The possibilities, the real possibilities formed moving pictures in his mind. "Mother of Emolus, it'd be like a god walking into town—wouldn't it? Former grandmaster of the Long Nine playing spymaster to the most controversial High King in the history of the Duchy? But I still can't see it. From the stories they tell, you were never one to get so comfortable. What's in it for you?"

"I'm an old man now. I'd like to settle down I suppose."

There was knocking at the door.

"It's the kids," said Zane. "They can't find you in the lobby. I promised them treats."

Alani nodded toward the door. "Unchain it and you die." His voice was so matter-of-fact the meaning of the words seemed hard to recognize—a threat like poison dissolved in wine.

Zane understood.

This was someone on par with his level of thinking, his level of planning. A peer. He almost felt flattered to be entertaining a guest like this. He opened the door and looked down into Dotty's face.

"Mister—"

"Get out of here," said Zane. "If you knock again, I'll take a kitchen knife and cut your little hand off." He shut the door. When he turned around he saw Alani going through the stack of papers on his table, nidus still aimed in his direction.

In the same instant, several things happened all at once.

Zane dove and grabbed a chair. He lifted it like a body shield and charged his adversary. The nidus went off with a concussive hiss and multiple popping sounds.

Heavy pointed pins of steel filled the air, tearing through wood and fabric and plaster.

Zane Vhortghast screamed.

The nidus fell to the floor.

One of the chair legs caught Alani in the chest.

Knives flashed.

The older man moved with astonishing speed. Though aching and winded from the blow to his ribs, he quickly divested Mr. Vhortghast of his knife.

The spymaster was in no condition to fight. Already torn where the nidus's scores of missiles had caught him in the shins and elbows and shoulders, perforating his flesh wherever the chair had been unable to protect him, Zane hurled himself toward the open window. He rolled out onto the fire escape and slid down the metal steps, fumbling in his own blood.

ALANI winced the moment he tried to follow. The chair had bruised something inside. He stopped and watched the former spymaster stumble into an alley and peal away through the slums of Gorbür Dạyn.

The old assassin paused to catch his breath. He had suffered many similar injuries during his long career. He knew how to wrap his ribs. He picked up the papers on the table and left the stolen nidus behind.

Now, he thought, *we'll see if Caliph Howl was worth all this trouble.*

wo days later the hot weather broke suddenly with a crack of thunder. Lightning stumbled over rooftops, through revolving voluted gears while the gutters slithered with mating things.

Alani told Caliph almost everything. He found that he was well remembered from the train platform in Crow's Eye and gained an immediate audience. He made it clear that Peter Lark and Zane Vhortghast were interchangeable names, watched carefully as Caliph paged through the notes he had salvaged from Zane's apartment. The papers Sena had taken from Zane's office rested in a second pile. Together it was enough to be useful.

The new High King wasn't giddy. He talked little. When he spoke, he didn't make puerile exclamations, or ask pleadingly what they were going to do. Instead, he sorted through the papers without a word, separating them into different categories. It was a wealth of incrimination, a fragmented, fortune-forging plan that had spiraled beyond Zane Vhortghast's control.

Lightning seared the sky just beyond the window, splashing harsh light into Alani's eyes. The paneled walls vibrated in rumbling aftermath.

"It looks like we may be in trouble here," said Caliph.

Alani reached into his vest and pulled out a pipe. He lit it; the flame sizzled and flared under his cupped hand. He nodded but did not speak.

"Tell me again why I find myself the beneficiary of your . . . services," Caliph said.

Alani lingered before answering. He looked out at the rain. In the south, he knew that warm dry weather was probably baking the land, even at night, gently. His aging skin and bones remembered that southern climate with longing. But everything about the north resonated with him: the shortening season, the turning of the wind each fall.

And the snows . . .

Stonehold was the end of the world, far from the endless summers of the south. People were real here. They knew what it was to lay up stores, to watch the mountains for an early frost. Such a wonderfully haunting landscape, Alani thought. So filled with life because the season of death was only ever a season away.

"I have a vested interest in the Duchy of Stonehold," Alani said softly after the interminable pause.

Caliph indicated with casual, friendly ease that Alani's answer was not good enough, that he needed more in order to believe.

"I was born here." Alani invested each word with soft-spoken meaning.

Caliph frowned. "A broom."

"I beg your pardon?"

"A broom," said Caliph. "That's what belongs in your hands. You were a janitor at the High College. You nearly caught us in the stables at Desdae."

Alani smiled and watched the memory spread like light across the High King's face. "Correction, Mr. Howl, I *did* catch you. And it's good of you to remember."

"That was the last time," said Caliph. "That was what made me steal the clurichaun."

"I know," said Alani.

Caliph sat back, stunned. "I can't believe I couldn't remember your face."

"You were preoccupied. Under stress, the memory tends to slip."

"I took a caning because of you."

"A clever political move. I was impressed."

"So you didn't work for Zane?"

"No. I had a private interest in you. Four years as a janitor, watching you finish school? That should convince you of my interest in the Duchy."

"But why?"

"Because I'd heard about you. I came to check in on the future ruler of my beloved country . . . to see if you stacked up."

"And if I hadn't?"

Alani waved his hand. "You did. Which is why I wanted you on the throne. I still do . . . but you seem to be at a disadvantage for the moment, and I think I can help."

"You told the Iscan Council where to find me. That's why a zeppelin showed up in the Highlands of Tue. And that started my problems . . . with the witches."

"No, your majesty. You are to blame for your problems with witches. Not me. If the zeppelin hadn't shown up, I think you might have stayed in that pasture . . . permanently."

Caliph considered for a moment, then made the sign for yes. "Fair enough. Maybe you *did* save my life. Now tell me how you intend to help . . . and . . . I want details."

"Well, your majesty. As I'm sure you're aware, Bjorūrn Amphungtạl is still in the city."

Caliph tugged his lower lip. "Okay, but I'm sure the blueprints have left the Duchy by now."

"Which doesn't concern us anymore," said Alani. "You have your own set. You don't need them. The blueprints aren't our problem anymore."

"Then what's our problem?"

"Our problem is Pandragor getting involved in our civil war. Vhort-ghast knew about solvitriol power. He wanted it for the Duchy. And he manipulated you into starting a program by staging an energy crisis.

"But he *didn't* want war with Pandragor. My guess is that he thought you were too inexperienced to handle the situation and took the reins himself. Look at the documents here." Alani sorted through the papers and pointed out one in particular. "You can see what happened. He co-erced David Thacker into selling him the blueprints. Then he turned around and sold them to the Pandragonians for a small fortune. But that's when things went wrong.

"Saergaeth Brindlestrọm started negotiating a new deal with them, luring them out of Vhortghast's pasture. They already had the blueprints and must've seen you as someone they wanted to replace."

Caliph scowled.

It was clear that Pandragor was intent on helping Saergaeth win the war: not that Saergaeth needed any help.

For the next several hours the room grew dark with Alani's counsel. The draperies sagged inward, trapping sound in mournful heavy folds. Even the lamplight seemed lacquered: little snails and lockets of light held in stasis by the darkly polished wood. The two men leaned together, scavenging from the paper bodies Vhortghast had left behind.

Alani smoked. The soft pop of his lips against the pipe stem punctu-ated their dilemma.

"I'm damned any way I go, aren't I?" said Caliph. "There must be half a dozen nations that know I have solvitriol power. If I move ahead with development, the Duchy becomes a potential threat to them. We invite attack, sanctions . . .

"I could sign treaties that I won't proceed with solvitriol research . . . allow inspections—"

"And ensure losing your own civil war," finished Alani.

"And ensure losing my own civil war."

Caliph's echo was quiet and resigned. "It's the only edge I have against Saergaeth."

Alani nodded as he smoked.

"Alani—or should I call you Mr.—?"

"Alani. Just Alani."

Caliph barely smiled. "Your altruistic endeavors—"

Alani wagged his finger. "It's nothing that preposterous. I told you." He laid his pipe aside and adjusted his old hands, folding them across his lap. "I am not a charitable individual, King Howl. This is more than patriotism. This . . . is for me."

Caliph's eyes returned Alani's stare with calcified impunity. *Maybe he can see a trace of pain,* thought Alani. His injured ribs ached. But the High King's unsympathetic glare only reinforced to Alani the correctness of his choice. Caliph Howl was the right man to be High King.

"Are you sure," Caliph was saying, "that you can establish yourself quickly enough . . . to be useful in this war?"

Alani appreciated the question. Like everything else it was nononsense. It did not apologize or make excuses. Nor did it indicate that Caliph and Alani were friends.

"I have always been established in this city," said Alani. "My profession took me out of Stonehold but . . . I will not be starting from scratch."

"Then it's settled." Still, Caliph paused, seemed to hedge on asking one final question. "What are the odds," he asked, "that Mr. Vhortghast will return?"

Alani suppressed a grin. "That is something you need not trouble yourself with. I will keep an adequate amount of resources fixed in that regard." He picked up his pipe and smoked before proceeding. "I will of course need to do some cleaning." His fingers fluttered like a feather duster. "Appoint some . . . different people to positions within the organization. That sort of thing. Don't be alarmed if you see new faces around the castle or in my company. All of this, you and I," he motioned with his hands, "is based on trust."

CALIPH felt sick. Trust, specifically, was a word that chafed him.

Isca had been cut off from fresh imports for at least two weeks. Yet, even with southern commodities being conspicuously absent from shelves all across the city, Caliph held back.

He would save war plans for another night, after he had talked to Sigmund one more time and verified again that certain technical aspects were not beyond the realm of possibility.

Even so, things were moving fast. They had to move fast. Without trade, Isca would not survive the winter and winter was, according to the austromancers, barely a month away.

After Alani had finished a second pipe and the two of them had said good night, Caliph went upstairs. He pulled off his boots and tossed them under the bed. Sena did not stir. He watched her breathe for several minutes—wanting her.

"Quit staring at me," she mumbled without opening her eyes.

He wondered how many hearts lay like wreckage in her wake, wondered again if his might become one of them. Caliph cracked a window and took time to breathe. He inhaled the smell of rain as the sky grumbled.

"Mmmm—" Her purr came from behind. "I like it cold."

He turned. The candles poured gold across her skin and hair. The blue stripe looked purple in the dark.

Caliph undressed quietly and crawled into bed. Despite his desire he could not bring himself to brave the rejection he felt waiting, lurking like a quiet beast beneath the sheets.

SENA listened to him. Eyes so intent she could hear them staring at her. She waited for him to adjust his body, make some casual, seemingly coincidental touch that would serve as the starting point.

When he did nothing, she became bored and finally drifted off to sleep.

The following day, green leaves rained sporadically, petulant that they, in their supple beauty, should be ripped from their laughing parties on the limbs and tossed out like rowdy guests. They tumbled from branches, destined to be changed hideously against the ground. With irregular weather patterns along the cooling sea, the wheat fields swirled with fog.

Sena's boots stuttered through patches of blue shadow and striped sunlight. Her soles scraped over half-buried stones.

She bent down and examined one, but passed it over. With the disconcertingly early fall, she had decided to step up her timetable. She couldn't stand the duality of her relationship with Caliph any longer.

The Healean Mountains had received a dusting of white, as though some prankster with all the Duchy's powdered sugar at his disposal had orchestrated a grand hoax in the middle of the night. A sudden crispness inveigled the air.

Sena found the shift in temperature abrupt. With it, everything she had prepared for seemed to have suddenly crept up on her. The nearness to her goal, the realization of the cruelty she was about to effect brought a lump to her throat.

Caliph had already dealt with so much disloyalty. If only she could tell him what she planned to do! But the recipe was precise: *taken by theft*, it read.

Her time at Isca Castle was coming to an end.

I will go south, she thought, *before winter seals the mountains shut.*

She stopped, turned and shielded her eyes from the sun. A knee-high wall fenced in the square of untilled ground through which she had been walking. Her pack held two roundish rocks. She stooped to heft a third. She tossed it, caught it, spinning it in air, revealing its qualities.

She put it in her pack with the others and started back. As she picked her way over the weedy ground, she noticed a bent crone watching her.

Sena's lips struggled frantically. Her hand fumbled for her sickle knife. Then she realized with internalized embarrassment that it was not Giganalee that had stopped along the road. Paranoia tongued her brain.

Heart still pounding, Sena flushed under the grandmother's scrutiny. She was a caricature, old and short in a black shawl, peering and leaning on a stick of wood. Her crumpled mouth whispered syllables in Hinter to the two wide-eyed children half-hidden in her skirts. A boy and a girl stared at Sena with anesthetized alarm.

Sena stared back, warily. She pulled the strap of her pack tight against her shoulder and fingered her curls.

The old woman continued to whisper.

Sena headed for the road, departing the cemetery with a backward glance. She felt the setting sun burn orange around the contours of her face and suffuse her eyes with fire. Though unintentional, the effect seemed to startle her spectators, who trudged quickly on their way.

This was the country that hunted witches, cut off their legs and left their torsos to freeze in Ghoul Court.

Despite her immunity, or rather because of it, stories of the High King's witch had inundated the countryside. Litho-slides of her face filled the papers. People recognized her; they did not like her poking around in their cemeteries.

Sena left the fog in the valley and ascended the tree-sheltered lane that led to Nathaniel's house. By the time she reached her destination, both shoulders were raw and her back sore from the bulging rocks.

It was late. Light filled the sky like the albescent flesh of a mussel; only the land was dark and indistinct. She pushed her way through the years of wild bramble growth and tramped back to the spot she had chosen.

It was early. She had been planning on the first of Thay. But she would have to do this now because by Thay, she would be hundreds of miles away.

Sena had cut away a small section of meadow grass with her sickle knife and formed a circle in the weeds. A carefully balanced stack of round stones rose into a rough conical shape. With a final heave, the ones in her pack dropped like hammer blows, denting the ground. She placed them in the mound and stepped back to assess her work.

For a moment she rested. Finally, she began the formula.

Some of the rocks had come from Caliph's family burial ground. Others were from the woods. A few she took from the fields and the last three were from the graveyard west of Isca.

She circled the pile, walking backward, repeating the numbers and counting each repetition.

Meant to keep horrors like those at the Porch of Soth forever cordoned from physical dimensions, the numeric statement had been part of the Sisterhood's set of seasonal traditions for several hundred years. She hoped it would also keep Grū-ner Shie at bay. It was something she could do for Caliph . . . for the Duchy.

Her heart fumbled, feeling momentarily sentimental about Stonehold. Despite everything . . . she liked being here. *But I can't stay!* She banished the thought immediately and continued her numeric chant. It was almost complete when the world shook.

An explosion of panicked marsupials filled the air when the movement began. They dropped from the dreadful eves of the house like soft stones, squirming from web-thick attics and churning clumsily into the sky.

Trees swayed.

Sena, despite her nimbleness, stumbled and fell. It felt as though the ground had come alive; it tossed her into the weeds like a doll.

Then, as abruptly as it had begun, everything grew quiet. Sena's heart clenched rapidly like a nervous fist.

Her meticulously balanced pile had shaken down to a low mound. Another faint tremor rumbled deep inside the mountain.

Standing up, Sena repeated the numeric charm, no longer certain of its efficacy.

The quake had roused the last of summer's bugs. She watched them take flight, sing wildly, trying to seduce a mate. Overhead, predators circled the yard, feasting on the insects' heedless love: soft green bodies gnashed in tiny vicious maws.

Sena returned to the castle.

The streets were alive. The cobblestones and lamp-lit bistros along King's Road were packed with little crowds talking about the quake. The High King's witch went unnoticed.

Sena crossed into the Hold and over the drawbridge; she took a coach to the castle from the gate. When she arrived, she went inside and began her long climb up to bed.

Caliph's whisper arrested her. It came out of a blackened parlor that bordered the hallway, a temporary lair where he had holed-up to brood.

"Where were you?"

Sena jumped. She turned toward the tall narrow doorway that framed a curtain of negative space.

"I was at your uncle's house—thinking."

Caliph's shape materialized from the darkness as out of brackish water. Sena's imagination transformed the scene; she pictured herself hovering over him . . . his body floating in a pond. Shadows filled his eyes and collected around his limbs and neck. His robed arms reached out and pulled her slowly toward him.

It struck her both morbid and funny at the same time. She hadn't pictured him worrying about her. The realization made her feel strangely warm.

"I'm all right," she whispered.

"I thought I might have lost you," he said quietly.

It would be tonight or never, Sena thought. They went upstairs. Sena closed the bedroom door.

She slipped powder into his wine. They drank and flirted. Caliph unlaced her blouse and kissed her shoulders. She wanted him suddenly, savagely. It had been weeks now without relief. But the drug was quick. Foreplay became the only play as it slipped from delicious to slurred to clumsy and revolting. Caliph collapsed, a clouded expression on his face.

Sena sighed.

Distraught but determined, she pricked her finger and whispered the words that would deepen the rest of the mountain herb. If the narcotic did not keep him quiet, the Unknown Tongue would.

She looked at him.

Under the oil lamp he seemed like a sleeping copper figurine. Molten orange and blue-black shadows drooled across him.

Sena hesitated and touched his chest. She grew momentarily softhearted. *I love him,* she told herself. *And he loves me.* She held her sickle knife over his chest, deliberating.

With a quick jerk the blade parted his skin.

She chose the muscle of his upper arm for the task. For a moment he did not bleed. Then the dark fluid ran, an endless supply, flowing from the tissue into the silver vial she held below it. He twitched slightly, eliciting a groan.

Her thumb pressed the flesh above the cut and instantly the flow stopped. With her teeth, she tore a piece of clean linen.

Her hands moved delicately, like moth wings, fingers caring for the wound with attentive tenderness. She held the skin apart and filled it with orange powder.

Then she whispered a weak equation, using Caliph's own blood to mend him. The skin closed slightly.

She took another piece of fresh linen she had soaked in antiseptic and wrapped it several times to bind the wound, embalming him, it seemed.

With utmost care she removed the tourniquet. She stoppered the silver vial and got dressed.

Betrayal.

It caused a strange pain in her heart.

Caliph shifted. A dark wrinkle passed over his features as though from a bad dream. The monkshood would cause vivid hallucinations.

Lifting her pack quietly, Sena turned the gold handle on the door. Her skirt murmured in a rustling chill that trickled from the window. She left him to dream.

Caliph dreamt of Marco.

Vivid stripes seared the horizon like orange marmalade trapped between layers of molten tar. The color was intensely bright. Leaves rustled. Stars peeped down through a steeple snared by trees.

Caliph fought his way through saplings and emerged in a lowering black yard heavy with sinister shapes.

The creature met him in the dark.

"Hello, Caliph." He wore tattered black. "It's been a long time—"

The voice mulled stately, obsolete decorum with viperine cunning.

Caliph felt strangely unafraid. The sliver of citrus-colored light cut through Marco's faded shroud. The arms of trees remained starkly visible, showing through his body. His face and eyes startled the gloom: waxen white set with dismal inky jewels. Marco radiated displaced malice.

"It is bedtime," Marco said. He spoke as though reciting archaic poetry. "Bedtime for kings with a story for their end."

A flurry of tattered black filled the air; Marco twirled and perched on a slumped headstone. He balanced impossibly, knees pulled up under his chin, arms dangling, eyes inapprehensible beneath the brim of his hat.

"Which amuses more?" he asked. "That your nursemaid was a dead king? Or that the two of us would talk long hours—both fearing that *he* might hear? And now the irony that we talk on . . . while he slumbers underfoot?"

"Why are you here?"

"To warn you of his return," said Marco. "The teeth of his neglected ghouls clatter useless verses in the yard . . . poetry for soil . . . basking rhymes unripened by the moons."

"What poetry? I don't understand," said Caliph. In his dream he was eight years old.

"They seek validation in your ears. Our master is coming back, young Howl—and with him comes the end of kings."

Fear filled Caliph and burst through the dams of his control, cracking thick mental barriers erected from childhood as protection from the eldritch and profane.

In the dream, Caliph defiled the grave on which he stood, unhindered by the trivialities of range or barriers fashioned from zippers and cloth.

A steaming golden stream spattered across the headstone on which Marco perched.

The echo of the specter's laugh resonated through the mountain woods, behind the crickets and across the Healean Range. He dropped from his perch, stood behind the carven stone inscribed with Caliph's uncle's name.

What have I done? Caliph thought.

Uncle will be furious.

CALIPH lurched up in bed. His own sticky vapor cloying in the sheets. Cooling rapidly. He was mortified. Strange dark shapes blew around the room, shadows twisting from the open windows. He looked down at his arm with confusion.

The wound throbbed with his heartbeat.

Slowly, the realization of what had happened filled him with humiliation and loathing. Not just the bed-wetting, but the fact that he had let this happen . . . this wound. Cameron had told him about his uncle, charming a girl, using her blood to open the book . . .

He felt the aloneness. The exquisite rejection. An estranged and primal howl reverberated in the fleshy dark caverns of his chest.

Her pack was gone. His uncle's book was gone. *Sena was gone.*

It butchered his emotions like one of those senseless bulbs of meat under Thief Town.

And yet . . . he had felt it coming.

Caliph gathered up his sheets and dragged them from the bed. He turned the knobs on the tub. Stammering hot water burst from the fixture. His body rippled with gooseflesh as the bitter residue cured across his skin.

It serves me right.

Against his better judgment he had trusted her. He had wanted so badly for the two of them to beat the odds, for her to suddenly evolve and legitimize his trust.

He might as well have committed a brandy-filled chocolate into the hands of a homeless sot with the charge to guard it with his life. It was his fault, not hers.

He sprinkled soap flakes from a box into the spluttering bath. His heart pitched and frothed between damnation and forgiveness. He struggled with motive. Was the book really so important to her? Even now he wanted a reason to absolve her, grounds to purify that final, puzzling, seditious kiss.

Smooth hard fixtures turned below his hands, strangling the supply of water.

He bathed, washed his sheets and hung them from the curtain rods to dry.

He could still taste the drug inside his mouth, feel its weight roll through his head like cannonballs.

She had taken her boots beneath the chair and the bottle of oil she used to perfume her hair.

Caliph opened a panel where the servants stored the linens and pulled out a stack of fresh sheets. Her other toiletries stood nearby. He thought of David Thacker in the dungeons, pleading for a second chance. He remembered Grume's. The promises. He recalled that Zane Vhortghast had saved his life—several times.

Caliph flipped the mattress, snapped the sheet like a sail and let it float across, imagining Sena on the other side. He looked savagely at the empty space where she might have been.

"The wind blows . . ." he muttered, leaving the old Hinter proverb unfinished. His whisper fizzled with morose histrionic resolve.

THE next day was hot. Shouts and growling clangorous sounds from the steelyards in Ironside hovered in a steamy haze coming out of Temple Hill.

A new warship was nearly ready. Caliph harbored suspicions that it would prove useless in the days ahead. Yrisl still promised an aerial assault.

Caliph could see streetcars and zeppelins from a parlor on the castle's east side. Flashes of light from metal and glass flickered across the room at discrete angles, shimmering a moment, then vanishing as some wagon or whirling airship flung sunlight off its faces.

Despite the afternoon reflections, the air in the room cosseted shadows. Caliph nibbled pastries and canned fruit from a tray. He had draped himself on a plush chaise, feet up on a priceless coffee table, regarding the newly certified metholinate levels with unsettled scrutiny.

Air horns and steam whistles usually percolated through the urban effluvium beyond the window as barges and cranes fought to load and unload cargo along the wharves. But the docks today were silent, devoid of commerce.

Sigmund hadn't commented on Caliph's foul mood when the two of them had talked earlier that morning and finalized certain technical details.

The better part of Caliph's thinking had gone into one outlandish plan. Everything else had evolved into half-hearted contingencies devised to prolong the inevitable if the main plan failed—which was why Caliph had yet to tell anyone how it would come together.

Caliph sorted through a stack of paperwork he had been ignoring for some time.

In addition to the restructured metholinate reports, it contained a paper authored by the red-faced Dr. Baufent who had performed the autopsy on the ichthyoid men in West Gate.

Unfortunately, the physician had written the report as though to herself—which meant that it often became far too technical for Caliph to follow. Loquacious jumbled sentences muttered about pathogenic mucin, photophores and dense high-impact skeletal structures.

Caliph tossed it aside as he remembered her with foggy distaste. Though he was curious about the creatures' physiology, the digressive report deflated his interest.

With Vhortghast gone and all the other craziness of the past few weeks, Ghoul Court had not been raided. It was still on the agenda but the timescale had been moved back . . . intentionally . . . ruthlessly. The raid was now a critical piece of timing in Caliph's war plan.

He massaged his eyebrows where a dull ache had begun to throb. He pushed hard into the bone, rubbing in circles before daring to lift the next piece of paper—his afternoon itinerary.

> Kam 2, 561
> 10:00   Lunch & reports
> 10:40   Messieurs Stepney, Nągrüth and Bîm
> 11:40   Hazel Nantallium of Os Sacrum
> 12:00   General Yrisl . . .

The list went on. Caliph checked his watch. It was a quarter past ten. He shuffled through the remaining papers and digested what he could.

At 10:35 he strapped his chemiostatic sword around his waist, left the parlor and entered the royal study precisely on the half hour. The burgomasters of Growl Mort, Murkbell and Bilgeburg were waiting for him, chairs tugged together in a tight fraternal chevron as though huddling for warmth. They stood up the moment he entered.

Caliph shook their hands.

After obligatory pleasantries they all sat down, the burgomasters in their stiff velvet-padded chairs, Caliph at an enormous polished desk.

The burgomasters seemed paradoxically nervous and, at the same time, self-assured. Caliph supposed they had a shrewd agenda that Simon Stepney had failed to advance back in Hḷeim when he brought the ugly little factory—which had not been melted into sling bullets but been miraculously retrieved by Gadriel from whatever box into which it had been tossed and placed for the hour with expert and subtle ingenuity on the High King's desk. It sat prominently beneath a lamp, partially hidden from his guests.

Despite its presence, all three of the burgomasters looked, in a serene and well-disguised way, deeply rankled at being here. It must have been at the top of their minds that Caliph Howl had executed one of his best friends less than two weeks ago for treason. They minded their manners.

Caliph watched them. They outnumbered him. On their side were many years of experience buttressed by very high opinions of themselves. They would present their case, make their demands and force the High King to deal with their concerns. Holomorphic aberrations had not been kind to industry and time (for them) was running out.

Caliph stroked the brass nailheads on his armrest. For an eternity it seemed, he waited.

Bejamin Nạgrüth cleared his throat.

"Your majesty. The . . . fungal outbreak . . . at Vog Foundry is only the beginning of my associates' and my troubles. Business has gone slack in the face of the war. Everyone is either demonstrating or spectating or off stationed in western Tentinil."

Caliph interrupted his momentum.

"Where's Jæza?"

The last of the big industrial boroughs' burgomasters had not shown up.

Bejamin Nạgrüth looked annoyed. Simon Stepney smiled as though pained. He gesticulated faintly as if pulling cobwebs from the air. "She had—prior engagements, your majesty. Though of course this was the top priority for her, an emergency, I'm afraid . . . came up."

Bejamin Nạgrüth agreed and rummaged in an oxblood attaché.

"Yes, she did however send her regards and apologies as well as this memo expressing her unanimity."

He laid a crisp, white, notarized sheet of parchment on the desk in front of Caliph.

"Unanimity?" Caliph asked. "In what?"

Bejamin smiled and adjusted his silver spectacles. His hair was greased back in gleaming sandy bands. He forged on bravely.

"Your majesty, we haven't disclosed this quarter's profits yet, but we're vicinal to bankruptcy. If the sluggish prewar economy and holomorphic chaos doesn't get us, frankly the city's flat pollution tax will."

Caliph looked hard at the other two burgomasters.

"Pollution tax? That's what this is about? Does Ben speak for all of you?" Quick nods and muttered affirmations followed.

Caliph didn't pause. He had done his research and was ready for this.

"Ben, forgive me, but you're being terribly imprecise. Vog Foundry has survived wartime economies before. What you're really telling me here is that you can't manage your business."

Timothy Bîm let air out through his nose.

"Your majesty, with all due respect, if the four main industrial boroughs go down . . . so goes Isca."

"So this is a genuine crisis?" Caliph asked.

The burgomasters assured him that it was.

"I disagree. If it was a real crisis I don't think I'd have a piece of paper sitting on my desk. I think Jæza Tal would be here. I also disagree that Isca City is so devoid of hardworking people that twenty-two boroughs will be dragged under by the managerial incompetence of four. That's what you're suggesting. That the fate of the majority is somehow inextricably intertwined with the fate of half a dozen executives?"

Bejamin Nągrüth remained tenacious.

"Your majesty, we have a large debt both to the Independent Alliance of Wardale and the Free Mercantilism of Yorba for holomechanical resources and raw materials that were shipped to us this spring—"

"That's an inventory issue."

"Of course it's an inventory issue." Simon nearly lost control. "Our inventories were decimated by giant mushrooms, among other things!"

"What is it, Simon?" asked Caliph. "Is it the prewar economy? The pollution tax? Or the giant mushrooms? What do you want from me? You want me to bail you out?

"Gentlemen, I appreciate your industry's integral role in our economy but changing a tax law for businesses that can't keep themselves afloat is not going to help Isca survive. This is a difficult time, for all of us." He saw Simon open his mouth to speak and raised his hand. "Please . . . no more about the giant mushrooms. I know that's not your fault. I'm sure we can get you some aid for the disaster but I have no intentions of adjusting the pollution tax based on the current economy."

Caliph leaned forward, his voice unflustered, his eyes poised and cool.

"You are shrewd businessmen, gentlemen. I'm not going to rub your tummies or offer you a toddy. It is up to you to ensure your factories survive. I don't expect you'll ever again track up my office with this kind of panhandling. Is there anything else?"

The burgomasters stammered a bit and dug in their attachés but came up empty-handed.

The meeting was over and Caliph guessed he had forged several new enemies. He didn't really care. *With all the shit on my plate,* he thought, *they can eat a little too.*

UNFORTUNATELY, the worst news was just around the corner.

He endured a meeting with Hazel Nantallium, who was the bishop of Hullmallow Cathedral. She reeked of sweet incense and painted her face in a manner that indicated coquetry was not without her jurisdiction.

Over the course of sixty minutes (which was twenty beyond what Gadriel had scheduled her for) she tried to persuade Caliph to allow his name to be added officially to the church records. She offered him everything from a plaque with his name on it bolted to the pulpit, to a flirtatious glimpse of her inner thigh with the not-so-subtle hint that more explicit possibilities existed.

To be able to say that the High King was a member of the congregation would give Hullmallow Cathedral the kind of official authority it had enjoyed on and off through the past several centuries if and whenever they had been able to convert a High King.

Caliph graciously and repeatedly declined.

With a terse smile, Hazel left and Caliph hurried off, late for his meeting with the Blue General.

Yrisl brought the bad news.

"It's true," he said. "What the papers have been saying about the worm gangs. Something is seriously fucked."

Caliph sighed. "Please. I have a long day scheduled. Just say something useful that I can understand."

"A wagon full of bodies was dumped behind Teapetal Wax last night. They were carved up with traditional gang sigils. Some journalist caught it on a litho-slide. We confiscated it and took him in for questioning but . . . the wagon was marked. The men who dumped the bodies . . . they . . . were police."

Caliph sat down.

"We've questioned every one of them. They don't know where the bodies came from. All of them say they were following strict orders from high command at the Glôssok Warehouses. Does that mean anything to you?"

CALIPH sat by himself in the royal study. He had asked Yrisl for a moment alone. Intelligence had come out of Miskatoll that Saergaeth planned to issue a final ultimatum, demanding the High King relinquish his throne. He would give a deadline and then . . .

Caliph listened to the sounds of the city coming through his window. Sigmund had lied. Or someone had lied. Those canisters of solvitriol suspensate hadn't come from cats. They were human souls. Boys and girls. Gang members from the back alleys of Thief Town. Eventually he would get to the bottom of the deception. Eventually somebody, maybe even the High King himself, would have to pay. But for now, for this moment, Isca City and the entire Duchy of Stonehold was hanging by a thread.

Solvitriol power was the only thing that could save it. Solvitriol bombs. From the seedy underbelly, from violence and trash, Isca's worm gangs had become martyrs and heroes in his eyes, an integral part of Isca's defense.

He would go to Glôssok. He would curse and tear Sigmund's office to pieces if he had to in order to sort this murderous debacle out. He would sentence good old Sig to death and hang himself in chains from West Gate if he had to. But not now. Not now. The gears were in motion, his war plan already underway.

It was cruel. He agreed. It was drop-dead fucking evil and wrong. And he knew he was headed for even more lost sleep because of it. But there was nothing else to do. The last thing he could do now was stop. If it was true, if murdered street youths had been Sigmund's ingredients for bombs, by the gods of Incense Street, he had to use them to save Isca. He wouldn't allow their sacrifice to go to waste. He would use them to save the Duchy from itself.

Caliph opened the door and let the Blue General back in. "Yrisl," he said quietly, "there are some things you need to know."

CHAPTER 30

Sena stood determinedly in Nathaniel Howl's ruined estate.

She let one of the dark sweets she had confected melt in her mouth. The rest she arranged in a wooden bowl, ready to be offered prosaically as she did every year to creatures crawling out of quixotic, asomatous darkness.

She had been part of the Sisterhood too long to put away the rites. There were numbers, there were powers in the motions of the seasons. Primitive articulations in some ways transcended the grinding industrial might of the current age. She whispered to the 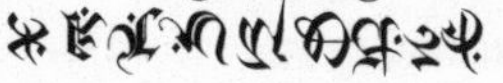 and placed the bowl in a clutch of bushes whose branches shook with a sudden gust of wind.

While buying ingredients earlier that day, she had heard about a creature in the foothills.

Farmers claimed it had snatched up dozens of chickens and other sorts of livestock. They said strange patterns showed up in the stains it left behind.

Two children—a boy and a girl—had gone missing.

Sena picked up her candle lantern and stepped back into the foyer of the Howl mansion, shutting the door Caliph had broken as best she could.

The ingredients and the kettles had taken their toll on her purse. She sat down at the kitchen table where she had cleared a little circle amid the refuse, freeing it from dust and webs. She spilled three gold gryphs and several silver beks from a clutch and let them roll around the tabletop. They were all she had, all that she could find in the bedroom before she left.

It made her laugh. A slightly crazy lost giggle that echoed off the decayed walls. She held her head in her hands and shivered. For a moment she thought about the High King's featherbed.

The nights were cooling.

She stared at the coins—more than enough to pay the sexton off.

He was a huge creature that barely spoke Trade and gouged sentences out of Hinter like a three-year-old fumbling at clay. She had met him a week ago while gathering stones.

He did not know she was the High King's witch.

Sena swept the coins back into the pouch and listened to the creatures twittering in the rubbish piles.

It must be nearly time, she thought. She checked her watch. She could hear bells ringing in the city, tolls like ghosts floating on the wind. Outside, the untrimmed bushes scrabbled at the windows, hungry for more sweets.

Sena stood up. Through one of the dirty windowpanes she had seen a lantern bobbing in the yard.

She wiped her hands on a damp rag and darted up a set of creaking stairs to one of the web-choked towers where she kept her things. With her pack over her shoulder, she ran back down to the foyer and outside where the smell of dying weeds met her.

The sexton was poking around at the edge of the estate. Sena sprinted toward him amidst the roar of leaves.

The sexton looked up.

"Moon's greetin'," he called. His voice seemed to come out of a cave. When Sena reached him, he offered her his huge gaunt hand, either to shake or to assist her in walking.

Sena dropped a silver coin in the cavernous palm and pretended to misunderstand the gesture.

"Do you think it will storm?" It was a moronic question she asked to fill up space.

He swung his head. "Mubee few drops."

Everything about him was enormous. Even his nose. Blade-like, hooked and thin. Long unkempt hair hung to his shoulders in straight uneven lengths almost too heavy for the wind. Instead of eyes, his face held tiny sunken points of obscurity.

Like a scarecrow, he towered over her, emanating an unsettling darkness from his pores.

"I been here once before," he said. "Boneyard's uver ther, ain't it?" He pointed with his spade, shouting hard above the wind.

Another sudden gust ravished the trees and a storm of plundered leaves flapped crazily into his lantern light.

Sena nodded. She led the way, picking a route through the old forest.

As they went, voices floated up from the crofts below. Faraway shouts about closing barn doors and getting livestock inside. Disembodied and broken up over the distance, they sounded like the shades of men and women mumbling near fields they once farmed.

When Sena came to the place marked with white stones the sexton stopped and lifted the spade off his shoulders. He swung it down into both hands.

"Wait," said Sena.

A huge leathery leaf slapped her in the face. She batted it away. "I need the doors opened." She pointed up the hill.

The sexton scowled but shrugged. He plodded off through the burial grounds. Sena followed.

Strandy saplings had conquered most of the cemetery. The mausoleum doors glared from a disturbingly dark recess in the hillside where crisp beveled letters had been chiseled into an arch.

Oblivious to omens, the sexton put the haft of his spade through the chains that ran between the handles and cranked down. Though the spade gave a pained crack, the well-corroded links burst apart, falling with a dull clatter to the slab.

The slab was covered with leaves and maple seeds. The sexton sorted out the chains and tossed them heavily to one side like a man who had just killed a snake.

Hunched over, Sena thought the sexton might pass as the creature the farmers were talking about.

"Hab to dig curful now," the sexton muttered to himself, "spade's craked." His lantern beamed fitfully. It cast a yellow circle across the slab and up the stone doors, making him look monstrous as he examined the damaged tool. He pulled one of the doors open but didn't bother looking inside.

"Want a tikyular one?" He picked up his lantern and walked back out among the graves.

"Any one will do." She thought her voice sounded idiotically chipper. "Make it a man. Try one that's not so old."

When she heard the chink of the spade biting into ground she walked up to the mausoleum. Fallen crab apples on the hillside permeated the air with cider. Sena poked her head inside.

The fusty silent darkness seemed palpably chancy. She crouched in the doorway to light her candle lantern. Even the flame was frightened. It fluttered down as though trying to hide in the tallow.

Once she got it going and slammed the glass, Sena saw that the vault had been constructed in crisp simplicity. An empty stone shelf for lights and flowers rested on claw-like corbels. She raised her candle box. Some roots had forced their way through the tiles overhead. They looked like pale wooden worms.

Not too windy, relatively tidy, the vault would do just fine.

She began to unpack her things, setting them out in a neat circle. An earthen bowl, a wooden pestle, several small bags of herbs, a stoppered silver vial, a skin of water, a box of charcoal, several black tapers, a pouch of powdered chalk, a bit of coiled string and the *Cisrym Ta*.

For a while she waited, straining to hear the shovel. The wind was too strong and the mausoleum door groaned, threatening to close.

An irrational fear, that the sexton might lock her in, made Sena rise. She left her things on the floor and went back outside.

The sexton's light already rested below ground. Its glow bled over the edge of a hole, illuminating pebbly sprays of flung dirt. As Sena approached, she saw him plunge the spade and violently hammer it down with the heel of his boot.

He was a Naneman and she could hear him humming and singing quietly in an old dialect of Hinter that she could not understand, a sort of chant that accompanied the rhythm of his spade.

When he noticed her, he stopped.

"There soon." His breathing came hard. "They been pushed up. Mubee frost or shifts in the grund. Ain't deep no more."

Sena could see where he had brutally hacked through roots, his long stringy arms swinging heedless of anything below. He had removed his wool shirt and his sharp shoulder blades looked dangerously close to cutting their way out every time he threw the spade. His strength and energy were horrific.

She moved away, listening to the endless cascade of leaves. She had mixed Caliph's blood with fermented creepberry juice to sweeten it and prevent it from thickening.

She leaned back against an ugly statue of a serpent and rested her hips on its brow.

At last she heard the dull thud she had been waiting for.

"Just tha hed, right?" the sexton shouted.

He had dug a hole roughly four feet square near the top of the grave, leaving the lower half of the coffin locked in the clay. The last few shovelfuls had been particularly difficult as the cracked spade finally broke.

The sexton had been forced to his knees to finish the excavation.

"Just break it open," she called.

He hauled himself out and picked up the other tool he had brought, a hooked metal bar too short to have been useful in leveraging the mausoleum chains. Returning to the hole, he set about the boards, prying them away from the face. They broke with soft mealy noises, exposing a grisly form to his lamplight.

"That all?" he asked. His tiny black eyes looked around as if making certain there were no more holes to dig.

Sena thanked him unceremoniously and gave him the extra silver she knew he wanted.

As he pulled his shirt back over his head he said, "You be all right . . . up here alone? Nuthin down there fer me but a sleepin' mule."

Sena flinched at the suggestion.

"I'll be fine."

Although he soared over her in his baggy clay-stained overalls and huge mud-clumped boots, the sexton recoiled. Maybe he found her smile unpleasant.

He bent down sheepishly to retrieve his lantern and the other half of the spade. Then he turned into the trees, following the statues out, raising a giant hand in parting.

Quickly, Sena lowered herself into the hole and with her sickle knife sliced a lock from the corpse's head. She walked back to the mausoleum with lengthened, willful strides.

On the mausoleum floor she scratched with charcoal, stepping on one end of the string and pivoting, winding the charcoal at the other end to get a perfect circle. She covered the faint line with powdered chalk, making sure the ring remained unbroken.

Swiftly now, her fingers scribbled symbols all around. Going for new charcoal when hers broke or wore down to an unavailing stub.

Her breathing grew rapid with the haste of her work. She lit the candles with a box of matches she had purchased on the street.

One blew out.

She pricked her finger and with a terse holomorphic word ignited it again.

Into a bowl went the dark contents of the silver vial along with the lock of hair and several fibrous roots and furry leaves. The pestle ground everything into a repulsive bituminous mush. She touched the stringy paste to her tongue and felt the muscles in her jaw tighten.

She set her teeth and closed her eyes and slit her arm just above the wrist. She let her part of the bizarre recipe drain into the bowl before adding a smidge of water. The paste thinned.

A few drops she dribbled into the book's grisly lock.

Sena stopped to bind her arm and double-check the directions in her journal.

Like a child dreading medicine, she raised the horrific brew. Half a teaspoonful she tried to drink but had to chew. The hairs clung in the back of her throat. She gagged, fought for control, and set the bowl on the ground.

I'm not going to puke. I'm not going to puke. She clutched her stomach. She battled to reign in the rebellion going on behind her teeth.

Finally she won. Her tongue traveled, searching for the remaining threads of hair, which (prescribed by the recipe or not) she fished out with her middle finger.

Petulant from the ordeal, she swirled the rest of the bowl's thickening contents until it broke over the lip and splashed the powdered ring.

Lastly, she deposited the *Cisrym Ta*.

Sena stood back, holding her wrist gingerly, looking at the flickering sight before her. All the ridiculous trappings of superstition . . . but she had done it as prescribed. One way or another, this was the end of a journey, the end of an affair.

Soon, her eyes would be opened to the mysteries of the world, the final blocks in raising her fortress of truth, or not.

Sena composed her thoughts and tried to breathe normally. She closed her eyes until the words that were also numbers came like familiar friends into her mind.

For half a minute, the abhorrent modulating delicacy of the Unknown Tongue filled the crypt's withered air.

When she finished, Sena's eyes opened to the stirring of wind. The silent howl of the ancient book, her constant torture for the past eight months, ceased suddenly, lulled by the words into dreadful slumber.

A clicking noise rose. All the candles save the one in her box sent long streamers of smoke from their glowing wicks.

The book shuddered, the latch popped and the heavy crimson hide thumped itself open.

A frenzy of crackling pages tried to take flight from the spine, rising in a fan of rage. For a moment, Sena imagined an old man's whisper as the pages shivered. Then a few leaves blew in from outside and Sena's head spun at a distant sound.

Was the night air thrashing the trees so fiercely? She could hear her own breathing. Maybe the sexton was playing a trick. Or had that long, high-pitched, inhuman cry been real? A gorgonian scream out in the hills, echoing off the unseen moons?

Under the estate's mercurial shadows, Sena perched like a lovely dænid reading the *Cisrym Ta*.

Its pages burst with tumid legends distended out of Soth, rendering minute archaistic details about a place called Jôrgill Deep before it had vanished from a highly theoretical, primordial world.

The stories trembled on baby-soft sheets of vellum, sounding in her head with unsettling naïveté. They spoke of happy times before Davishok and the Rain of Fire—when black pimplota flowered and dulcet laughter echoed through rampant arches and olden citadels burnished by the sea.

But every page she turned whispered of deceit. Every passing sentence conjured menaces and shadow, dusty races known now to be extinct: Gringlings, Ublisi and Syule.

As Sena read, her eyes filled with vague Yillo'tharnic undulations as great shadows moving under blue. Liquid planets refracted over primeval creatures that hauled themselves beneath the waves in massive pods whose numbers reckoned in the millions.

The *Cisrym Ta* spoke in myth better than a merchant talked money.

Melancholy verse disgorged images of darkling yellow clouds, winds that howled with voices from the stars. With the turn of a page she leapt to cantos concerning times when tendrils black as plasmic crude rose from seas that were not seas—when mountains shifted at the desert's edge.

The genealogy of nightmares lay before her. Doomed unspeakable names with magic numbers flecked each page. Nested in old thorny strokes of ink, Sena found Grū-ner Shie: the Faceless One, sleeping while Urebus crawled through his city buried in the Nocripa.

WHEN at last she lifted her eyes from the page, she felt dazed. The western sky lurked blue and lightless. One hundred eighty degrees from oncoming night, the sinking sun flared from the east and set fire to the western oaks. Their leaves made a bright patchwork of metallic orange against the horizon.

The *Cisrym Ta*'s howl had dwindled to a gentle whimper like an infant with the croup.

Since the night of the storm, Sena had taken copious notes on the book's formidable contents. She struggled to draw an outline in her head.

The first section consisted of a preface that had been stitched inside the cover seemingly as an afterthought. Roughly one hundred fifty pages long and written in Dark Tongue, it was from these preface myths that Sena had been struggling to read.

Dark Tongue was a knotty language to decipher, dead as it had been for thousands of years. Like all language it faded inside the parentheses of disuse. Suddenly faced with her lack of practice, Sena now found her mental dictionary maddeningly hard to evoke.

Tired and frustrated, she scanned ahead, gazing in wonder at page after page of Inti'Drou glyphs.

Roughly eight hundred pages of absolute power endowed the heavy tome with a thickness that paralleled her arm.

The glyphs looped on themselves distractingly, formed polysyllables Sena could never hope to pronounce. Insanely abstruse and sometimes displayed with up to five others on the same page, each glyph comprised an unsettling design amalgamated from vague primordial shapes.

The *Cisrym Ta* was organized so that an entire chapter could usually be viewed with the book lying flat open. Chapters were marked by a curious symbol that formed a break at the beginning and end of each section. There were seldom more than twelve glyphs to a chapter though Sena noticed a few instances of ten, eight and six. On some occasions, five and one glyph comprised entire chapters by themselves.

The authors of the book must not have been concerned about wasting space. In the instances where a solitary glyph embodied one complete chapter that glyph alone was given the room of two entire pages.

To stare at one glyph caused her immediate eye strain while the result of twelve in throbbing black panorama brought the sense of hemorrhage into Sena's head.

Lesser text accompanied each mark in pulsing thorny strokes, penned in the shadow of the main symbol. This lesser text, like the preface, was written in an abrogate version of Dark Tongue, as bewilderingly sophisticated as it was hopelessly obsolete.

Sena could pick out certain words but she would need other books to decipher the majority of it.

For now, she presumed more than her understanding factually allowed, that the lesser text named and described the power of the Inti'Drou glyph it accompanied and gave directions for a reader's point of attack—the place where study of the glyph ought to begin.

At the end of the lesser text sat one final symbol, the purpose of which Sena could not derive.

Sena straightened and decided to let the book fall open. Perhaps the habit of some chronic scholar would make one page in particular conspicuous above the rest.

She stood the *Cisrym Ta* perfectly vertical on its spine and pressed the covers tightly together.

Dramaturgically, she let go.

Infinitesimal moments passed.

Sena watched.

The pages seemed to breathe. They puffed with air, began to fan, forcing the covers apart. A dominant crack appeared in the solid block of vellum, like a fissure forming in a brick. The covers fell. The book toppled.

Page 379.

All around the glyph, in wide-framed margins, there were notations, cramped and written in a crisp endemic hand. The writer had penned them in Old Speech to baffle unschooled eyes.

Sena had no trouble understanding them and devoured them at once. With unreasonable shock she realized Caliph's uncle had been their author. He even signed them occasionally, like journal entries:

—Nathan H. 543 Y.o.T. Crow.

She found endless cross-references in the notes. Little trails of insight that wound back and forth like the random chewing of a worm. Nearly one-third of the pages had been marked up with Nathaniel's distinctive hand.

His years of arduous study provided Sena with an extraordinary head start. As she read, she made her own notes in the journal from her pack:

i   The inked portion of each glyph is no more important than the un-inked portion of each glyph. The Gringlings devised a system of compressing information so that each glyph is a double glyph, once in black ink and once in the empty "background ink" of the page.

ii   The eyes must be trained to read both the black ink and the "white ink" at the same time.

iii   Every curve, angle and line has meaning. Each glyph is a spatial map and the width of strokes reveal numbers and ratios upon being measured. When the glyph is stared at and the mind is drifting, the glyph will seem to move. Extra dimensional (or nonphysical numbers) are evinced when the glyph begins to read the reader and the eyes remained fixed in trance.

iv   Mortal vocals, according to the previous owner, are typically incapable of verbalizing the Inti'Drou markings.

v   Every glyph contains hundreds of objects and subjects and verbs that correlate back and forth not only within a specific glyph but in relation to the others of any given chapter. Each glyph must be studied in detail. Once that glyph is fully understood, the next may be attempted and so on until the entire chapter has been read. Then the chapter must be studied as a whole, finding the meaning in the spaces between and the correlations behind and between every glyph to every other glyph.

vi   It is obvious from Nathan's notes that he believed any single glyph subsumed a relative holomorphic gradation of power which he states is "... on scale with the creation or destruction of worlds."

Sena set her notes aside.

Now, instead of constant howling, she felt nauseous. She realized that the glyphs in the *Cisrym Ta* were so complex that singular structures of thought might take days or weeks to understand. They formed impossible pictures and indescribable movements behind her eyes. The solid surging marks, she didn't doubt, might cause blindness.

Sena looked, captured a glyph and closed her eyes to study it.

There's enough here to study three Hjolk-trull lifetimes, maybe more. She felt like a child reading for the first time, sounding it out in her head (since her vocals were of little use), trying to understand the academese of gods.

She had barely scratched the surface and already there were mysterious threads to follow, like one curious passage in the preface myths that spoke of the Last Page and that seemed to coincide with the rubbings she had taken from the Halls below Sandren.

She couldn't make anything of it:

"And the Last Page will be written before Quietus comes."

Sena felt momentarily silly as she stared at the words with profound reverence. Literal believers in even the most ensconced religions were fading.

According to the *Herald*, the congregation at Hullmallow Cathedral had dwindled; not because the organ's freakish stack of organic pipes (that twisted and splayed across the walls and ceiling like variegated trachea) had frightened them away.

Rather, the newest religion in the north was a revival of monotheism: the worship of self. There was no guarantee of purchasing friends or love or fame or happiness but hawkers sold facsimiles at a fairly going clip. As a result in the city, varietal masturbation sold far, far better than sex.

She folded her notes and closed the *Cisrym Ta*, putting the great block of vellum in her pack. She dropped from the low oak in which she had been sitting. As she paced Nathaniel's yard, fallen leaves made chewing sounds beneath her feet.

Worry consumed her.

Now she understood the trap that Nathaniel Howl had written about in the margins, the one he claimed to have chuckled ruefully over when he discovered it decades ago. And now, she guessed, it had claimed another victim who was just as inattentive to the antithetical drollery of whatever cosmic powers had created the lock.

Quite simply, there was no way to open the *Cisrym Ta*'s lock without succumbing to its curse.

It was a simple conditional, like those learned in logic philosophy at Desdae when students were faced with categorical syllogisms and the prospect of memorizing the square of opposition: if true love cannot be betrayed then betrayed love cannot be true.

Sena's hunt for the required ingredients had been a hunt for a beast that never breathed.

The trap's simplicity was also its genius.

Only a truly impassive heart would not revolt at the cost of opening the book. Only a power-hungry zealot could accept the fulsome ritual as a tolerable exchange. And only those deserving a cryptic fate would not see the blatant incongruity demanded by the recipe.

Fear tickled the heel of Sena's every waking thought.

Even the pleasant autumn evening seemed sinister and intelligent, as though the world had come alive, the ground hunkering underfoot, the air watching her. Any moment Sena expected calamity, black skies, roaring winds . . . more tremors in the mountains.

She looked toward Isca. The castle towers rose like golden needles by the sea.

Standing below the oak, she tried to decide whether to flee Stonehold before winter came or . . .

"Yella byŭrn!"

She spat the words in frustration.

Slowly the idea crept into her skull that maybe, just maybe, she had deceived herself.

Do I love him?

If I do, why now? Why now after the book is open?

She cursed again, then laughed at the mounting absurdity of her emotions.

How prosaic! She got what she wanted only when she no longer needed it.

Her humor covered the spiteful truth. She wanted to see Caliph. She wanted to tell him what she had found in the book, share her tiny discoveries thus far. She wanted to talk to him and feel his arms around her.

The guards would never let her back into the castle. Even if they did, she knew Caliph would be done with her.

She mucked around in the leaves, holding her pack in crossed arms; she had a full contingency of traveling supplies.

The wind seemed to panic her hair. Ignited by the setting sun, her unruly curls tossed this way and that against the dark western sky, a pantomime of the war going on inside her head.

With a final angry curse, Sena kicked savagely at the leaves and began walking down the hill.

CHAPTER

32

aliph's wound scabbed over.

On the fourth of Kam he sat in the high tower eating a fish and pickle salad sandwich. After sampling a side of crisped potatoes, he morosely pushed the plate away and reached down under his pant cuff to discreetly wipe his fingers on his sock.

The chef, with what he had to work with, had outdone himself but Caliph's appetite remained anemic. He had begun, for the second time, the painful effacing of her memory, the chiseling off of tokens that had snarled with surprising complexity in his brain.

At some future place or time (perhaps) the reduction of her image would obtain and something else be fashioned from the rubble left behind.

He would have dismissed his struggle as parody in anyone else. If this weren't happening to him he would have curled his lip. But she had found a hairline fracture that caused something inside him, something indefinable, to fail. *If it hadn't been her . . .*

If it had been anyone but her . . .

His mind toyed with options lodged in preposterous subrealities, masochistic cognitive abortions—games of "what if" staged in excruciating futility.

And yet he played.

Alani entered the high tower exactly on time.

Caliph could see Alani read his mood: somewhere between coal and cellar black. Caliph made it vanish with a ruffle, like a tablecloth pulled under dishes by sleight of hand. The tense angular lines relaxed, faded.

Caliph bid his spymaster sit.

He was risking everything with this meeting, trusting that unlike everyone else, Alani wouldn't let him down.

Graffiti covered the gates to the Hold. The police were terrified. The markets were dead. It was time to unveil his plan.

Yrisl had been skeptical. It relied on surreal improbabilities. Grand orchestration. Perfect timing. It relied on variables that couldn't be nailed

down. It relied on murder, deception, cruelty and chance in order to succeed. It relied on greed and arrogance and, in the end, made the handful of
murdered street youth seem like an easily forgivable sin. And yet, Yrisl
had nodded his approval. And now it was Alani's turn to hear the plan.

Initially, the old spymaster slumped slightly, legs crossed in a decep-
tively tranquil pose. But as Caliph began to talk, the old assassin scratched
his knuckles faintly and adjusted his posture in the chair. He fumbled
with his pipe, lit it nervously and laid it aside without a toke. And when
at last the High King finished, Alani sat in stunned silence, digesting
every syllable he had heard.

Finally he picked up his pipe. Without an encouraging puff, the thick
tobacco had snuffed itself. He fondled the bowl and muttered, "Do you
really think it can be done?" The old man's voice was sagely diplomatic.
It betrayed neither skepticism nor contempt. Rather, Alani's question indicated through its perfect timbre that if the High King answered yes, that
would be good enough for him.

Caliph looked hard at the spymaster.

"Everything I've told you is true. In that respect, it can be done. But
you're the man that would have to see it through.

"Risky isn't even the word. It's touch and go at best. But if we had
even a sixty-five percent success rate . . . Mother of Mizraim, if we managed even fifty percent, it would give our fleet a fighting chance.

"Logistics are what I'm counting on from you," said Caliph. "Insight.
A tether back to sanity, I guess. I've been thinking about it, bottling it up
for so long. I don't even know what it must sound like anymore, hearing
it for the first time. So . . . it's your turn. You tell me. What do you
think?"

Alani stuffed his unlit pipe back inside his vest and folded his hands
across his lap. Caliph could tell he was choosing words carefully.

"Well—since it is all true . . . and understanding the implications of
even marginal success . . . we don't have much of a choice. You have
these . . . suits ready?"

"After a fashion. Willing test subjects are, as you can imagine, difficult to find."

Alani smiled and made the southern hand sign for yes.

"It's already out that we have solvitriol power," said Caliph. "The
Pandragonian ambassador himself accused me of theft. It wouldn't be
that far-fetched for Saergaeth to believe . . ."

"We need papers," said Caliph. "All kinds of official documentation.
It has to look absolutely real."

Alani nodded and spoke with quiet businesslike decorum.

"I'll take care of the details. Just two additional items I wanted to mention.

"One is King Lewis. He may have reconsidered his position. He wants an audience."

Caliph hoisted one eyebrow but remained objective.

"That would be a welcome twist. When?"

"Lewis likes to hunt. Invite him on one . . . maybe next week?"

Caliph continued playing with his bottom lip.

"The cotters have been complaining about some creature in the hills. We could use Lewis' visit as an excuse to go after it. I'll talk to Gadriel and work something out. What else?"

"A Pplarian ship arrived this morning in Ironside . . . bearing gifts. Some very interesting weapons and, apparently, a manual on their use."

"I'll come to Ironside this evening. I need to talk with Sigmund Dulgensen."

"I had planned to bring them up to the castle—"

"No. Don't do that. I have to visit Glôssok anyway. Might as well save a bunch of soldiers having to fly them up."

Alani smiled.

"As you wish."

At first they thought it was syphilis.

White rubbery gummata or necrotic chancres metastasized from people's mouths and loins. But when it intensified and spread like pox, fear set in.

In Isca, where the sounds of coughing could easily leap between proximate windows like agile thieves, the word "plague" induced exoteric pandemonium.

Soap sold out in pharmacopolist and apothecary shops. Misinformed valetudinarians draped white linen in all the windows and doorways of their narrow homes.

Most already regarded the visitation's alleged breeding ground with fear and loathing and didn't voice objection when Ghoul Court was herded and burned.

One hundred knights and a thousand city watch converged on the unofficial borough like creatures from outlawed reality. Proboscidean masks dangled through fat tendrils of boiling air. Limp snouts swayed as they filtered breathable oxygen out of alleys swollen with plague and voluminous white clouds of disinfectant smoke.

Heavy, reinforced leather cuirasses covered the watchmen's chests. Though it created a troubling domestic image, the knights wore choratium armor. They plugged in chemiostatic goads that hummed malevolently. Rubber-coated cables supplied the power from glowing cells embedded in the armor's spines.

The *Herald* published several arguably autarchic paragraphs that labeled Ghoul Court the disease's epicenter. Caliph had composed them and given them to the press.

All necessary force will be used to protect legitimate city boroughs not only from disease but from Ghoul Court's long unchecked criminal element.

The *Herald* (and several other newspapers still cowed by the memory of Mr. Vhortghast's visits) published the High King's words without commentary on the morning of the operation.

The notion of contagion had such an effect on the populace that Caliph's outré response surprisingly rallied opinion polls at Gunnymead Square.

There were many annoyed citizens who had walked or ridden streetcars for years in order to avoid the Court. They would have supported even harsher measures while dissentients lined up against them like charged particles—pluses against minuses—some cosmic example of ineluctable binary: a natural array of checks and balances that maintained uneasy equilibrium.

A scant hour before dawn, when the onslaught trampled out of Daoud's Bend, Lampfire and Maruchine, word had leaked that troops were on their way and students from Shærzac University had shown up across the end of Seething Lane to protest.

They waited in the predawn; drinking, smoking and singing songs, linked together arm in arm across the street. They expected their demonstration to have an impact when the troops arrived.

But unlike the city watch, the knights had little patience for civil disobedience. Their objectives had been given by the High King and they did not understand the concept of failure. Because the demonstration interfered with tactical surprise they plowed through the ranks of barking students as if they had been tissue.

Startled when their lines were sundered and their antigovernment banners burst into flame, most of the activists fled. Some were struck with goads or the metal-shod bottoms of rubber shields. Many were arrested. A handful became casualties of the raid.

A sophomoric face screamed loudly that *"Violence will never win!"* His attempt to tackle one of the knights met with a gleaming bar of chromium steel. His crazed expression and vicious scrabbling with the knight's gas mask ended instantly when the goad swung out, smooth and unstoppable like a girder on chains. Its electrically charged body busted several of the student's ribs and abrogated the luxury of many presupposed civil rights.

Placards showing Caliph Howl holding a gory sword and flaunting a malefic grin were abandoned on the street.

The knights and watchmen burst through veils of whipped-cream air. Their gloves aimed billowing hoses that vomited massive canopies of smoke. Waves of men and women held rubber shields and chrome batons and wands that outpoured flame. Heavy cleated boots crashed through barricaded doors and windows. A variety of lives were crushed and mangled in their wake.

It was not a gentle raid.

The police roared into Ghoul Court with halgrin on thick chains.

Vast porcine beasts, seven feet at the shoulder, the halgrins' skeletons supported nearly a ton of mottled flesh and bone. Black and pink and hairless except for wiry strands that bristled on their humps, the halgrin mauled and shredded anything that scrambled or fell within their jaws.

Like a warthog, stipular tuberosities depended in grotesque array from jowly skulls. Their cloven hooves flinderized crates and wooden carts, pulverized bottles discarded by winos into glassy dust and thundered on the paving stones.

There were less than ten of the daemon swine, taken out of Tibium and trained from sucklings. Beyond what they could physically savage, they impacted the battle mostly through morale.

Hackles raised, the monsters' tusks splayed from mouths like overeager claws. Ropy turbid saliva draped like molasses toward the ground.

The beating Ghoul Court's occupants received was utterly severe and in many people's minds, condign.

Knights trod like heavy metal bulls through dreary tenements and filthy dens, overturning tables and beds strewn with the clutter of a hundred messy sins. Locked attics, occupied by smuggled contraband or shivering catamites, shed ugly secrets under the brutal use of rams.

Those that surrendered or welcomed the police as saviors were stabbed with bulbous hypodermics and popped with enough arcane demulcent to cure a horse. Most were summarily herded into steam-driven wagons that sputtered in the rear. If they survived the treatment and whatever sentence awaited them at West Gate, they would be released into the populace again.

Anyone found with an advanced case of the nameless malady was

ushered into quarantine wagons already packed with mounds of ulcer-
ated flesh.

The sick were driven off by men in long red trenches and insectile
masks with iridescent eyes. Though they seemed to head toward Tin Crow
and the dubious resources of Bloodsump Lane, many of the inhabitants of
Ghoul Court were lost even by the press. It was easy for them to simply
disappear.

Gleaming copper canisters that sloshed with acid burdened the backs
of enormous men who pumped liquid fire from their wands. The stones
and bricks, the very masonry seemed to burn.

Men and women in rags erupted from the drains, dislodging dozens of
thick metal lids. A grisly but euphoric effluence, like a cadence of champagne bottles. They clambered out of sewers and tunnels made for gas
lines. They danced ferociously on cobblestones that their bodies quickly
irrigated with endless rivulets of blood.

Their weapons were rude and freakish. Built of twisted nails that leapt
from boards and crudely welded pipe. The reflective pink and amber orbs
of their sunken eyes flared with intractable hatred—organic mirrors of
the gas mask eyelets that floated in the haze while subhuman bodies were
bludgeoned to the ground.

But Ghoul Court's militia was not composed of the man-things that
had besieged the opera. They were mere half-things, crawlers. They were
the shadow populace, come to defend whatever clandestine monstrosity
governed them from below.

The knights surged in and mowed them down.

Great crowds of bodies went up in sudden flame. Yellow entrails and
barely human organs splattered the streets. The stench of opened bodies
and vomit ricocheted off grisly slippery stone.

Disinfectant fog shrouded everything in gray.

Fulgurant, emerald-bellied crossbows twittered in the alleys and pol-
luted lanes.

The watch was organized and determined. They encircled their prey
with sharp-edged formations, whipped them and drove them and beat
them down.

Shackles came out, snapped over ankles and wrists. Dozens were led
away.

But the government did not have an easy time.

One unit was overwhelmed. It disappeared under leaping, peculiar
forms and arcing lead pipes lined with metal spines.

By the time two knights and a second unit came to the rescue there
was nothing left to save.

Another knight was overwhelmed, cut off from his unit and ambushed in the hollow of a barbershop.

Exultant for a few minutes, the creatures tore off his armor and dragged his body through the streets. But their celebration was brief and costly and their defeat guaranteed.

With wrath kindled by the sight of a fallen knight, the watch charged, canisters of acid spreading a strangely ebullient conflagration across bricks and flesh.

In the end, the watch won.

Men and women in uniform heaved the charred remains, took them by the wrists and ankles and swung then onto rising gruesome piles.

Caliph (as usual) had been precise.

Every stone was overturned, every building searched. Ghoul Court would be remade—from scratch.

When Caliph got the report on the sixth, he was horrified. The top page had an antiseptic whiteness with several objectives typed and centered. All were labeled: complete.

It has to work, he thought as he read the report. *My plan has to work. If it doesn't . . . if all of this is for nothing . . .* He shook his head. *I suppose I'll be paying another visit to Hazel Nantallium, taking her up on her offer.* But now that things were in motion, he wondered if all the votives in Hullmallow Cathedral could save his soul.

CHAPTER

33

aliph woke from a terrible dream that he couldn't remember. The report rested on a chair near the bed. It had settled in disarray like a white bird that had struck a windowpane.

There was little time to regret or even think about the day before.

Information had leaked that an Iscan zeppelin had crashed near Bittern Moor along the White Leech—territory now controlled by Saergaeth. It was a massive supply ship called the *Orison*.

In addition to food, medicine and military correspondence, the *Orison* had carried weapons. Gas bows, chemiostatic swords and other controlled munitions. Potentially as bad as the loss of troop locations and timetables, government sources had muttered that undisclosed highly sensitive technology had also been on board.

The papers were quick to black extras with headlines that read, ISCAN DISASTER MAY BE WATERSHED FOR MISKATOLL. And: HOW BAD IS IT? ISCAN WAR SECRETS IN SAERGAETH'S HANDS. The news was so stunning that the previous day's events in Ghoul Court were mostly overshadowed.

CREW OF FIFTY FEARED DEAD AFTER ZEPPELIN GOES DOWN!

Family members of the missing airmen were rounded up and taken to a secluded government estate in Octul Box where they awaited further developments.

By late afternoon, commanders of small arrowy spy dirigibles confirmed that despite the crash's proximity to Fallow Down, light war engines marked with burgundy emblems had already converged.

Apparently Saergaeth had no fear of the haunted wasteland of Fallow Down. Conspiracy theorists were already speculating that the two disasters were somehow linked.

Saergaeth had an array of sky sharks patrolling the region within hours. The prospect of several tons of food alone would have been sufficient to catch Saergaeth's attention. Yrisl guessed his troops were being fed from supplies seized at sea before the Iscan dreadnought and her escorts had plowed north to guard Tentinil's harbors.

Like a beached whale, the downed leviathan was to the rebellion as a carcass laid before the happy bewilderment of gulls and crabs.

Saergaeth's troops were giddy.

Spies brought Caliph the details: Saergaeth's soldiers poking gingerly through the wreckage, looking for booby traps. There were corpses strewn everywhere. Blackened and burnt or terribly marked with posthumous bruising.

But nothing sprang from the shredded compartments. No hideous automatons or holomorphic hexes triggered when grunts lifted timbers or huge sections of the punctured gasbag's drapery of skin.

The booty was tremendous.

Saergaeth's ranking officer found the schematics, the charts and battlefield maps. Caliph's spies confirmed that Saergaeth would have the locations of troops hidden in the hills east of Forgin's Keep. On top of this, there were two dozen chemiostatic swords, fifty gas-powered crossbows, five suits of choratium armor and a coffer containing a dozen trade bars in gold.

And then there was the massive reinforced tank covered with pipes and chugging engines that still hummed despite the zeppelin's violent landing. A circular door, sealed with a great wheel at its center, capped one end of the vaguely cylindrical tank.

When the troops opened it, their astonishment distilled from silence. Drooling icy vapor trickled from its frosty mouth across the tilted floor.

Inside was surreal bounty.

On great hooks, fifty enormous bulbs of unidentifiable meat depended, each several times the size of an entire cow.

A soldier stepped forward and stabbed at one with his sword but the frozen carcass was like granite. His powerful thrust wasn't even enough to set the obscene hunk of flesh swinging.

There didn't seem to be many bones. It was all meat. Enough meat, in fact, to feed a huge amount of men. Besides the protein there were bags of flour and canned goods. Pearlums and beans and salted corn.

Lastly, in a vault, were the glass tubes flanged in bolted metal, glowing peculiar hues of purple, electric-pink and blue and other colors impossible to name. They shimmered in the vault like baroque jewels.

One of the sky sharks was signaled down. It dropped tethers and an army of men strained to secure it along the river's edge.

It took four hours to load all the new cargo into the belly of a ship no longer designed to ferry supplies.

The sky shark had been outfitted like the rest of Saergaeth's fleet with turrets and ballistae and racks of aerosol bombs.

In order to fit the huge tank of meat, they had to shuttle some of the zeppelin's munitions into the already cramped war engines chugging nearby.

The two-hundred glowing canisters were left strapped in their vault. The entire closet-sized room was then winched on a crane that extended off one of the engine's scorpion-like tails and hoisted into the zeppelin's hold.

Finally, just as night was falling, the sky shark revved its engines and headed into the deadened sky.

WHEN Caliph got the news, he left Isca in the *Byun-Ghala*, escorted by several zeppelins that emerged like underwater creatures from the steel corrals of Malgôr Hangar. Dark spiny puffers floating out of candent holes, they pummeled the other side of day with their engines, left bands of soot and crossed the enormous double wall of the Hold, motoring into jellied air above the High King's Moor.

Thick amoeboid clouds clotted the night. The glitter of crofts and villages flecked an indistinct and inky landscape several thousand feet below.

Though they were stocked with epicurean delights, Caliph left the warmth of his staterooms for the chilly observation deck.

He smelled fresh vapors shredding against the propellers. Cold spongy space smacked the deck beneath the airship's turgid skin.

He had so much to think about that, for a little while, his course into darkness felt almost like escape. He soaked in the clammy wind.

With this small fleet, he had come to personally oversee the transfer of several unexpected prisoners of war. Taken in a recent skirmish west of Clefthollow and held in tiny cells, they had been confined for nearly a day aboard the same spy dirigible that had sent Caliph word of the *Orison*'s crash.

Thirty miles outside of Isca the rendezvous was about to happen in the dark, like insects coupling on the fly.

Caliph heard the engines shift; strange, auxiliary sounds reverberating through the zeppelin.

He braced himself against the rail as green lights skeletonized the dart-like shadow of some frail craft that had risen through the gloom and materialized above the deck. Like photophores on a deep-sea fish, the luminaries glistered and burned through the ether.

The spy dirigible's slender frame slid knife-like into a mooring socket on the *Precursor*, one of the *Byun-Ghala*'s more heavily armed escorts.

Caliph had insisted on being present. After all, he knew one of the prisoners.

He smiled without mirth or patience.

Just about everyone in Stonehold it seemed had become a traitor.

ALANI was blind.

Occasionally he squirmed in the tight darkness. His cramped, slippery prison had no door. His body ached.

Despite such constraints and a pair of stiff, ponderous gloves, he manipulated a slender humming device.

He twisted violently but it was no use.

He could taste his own breath against invisible glass, less than an inch ahead of his face. Like a fetus clutching its placenta he curled over a bulky bag that pressed his gut.

Swallowing fear he tried again but the slick, coriaceous walls held him fast.

He bowed his back and heaved left, thrusting with his legs. The pressure on his shoulder caused the socket buried beneath his deltoid to dislocate with a sick, internal pop.

He wrangled like something broken in the dark and managed to adjust, gain adequate leverage and proceed.

The object in his hand scraped against the wall. It still hummed and now shed a subtle light, stirring faint maroon patterns in the glass across his face.

Powered by a holomorphic tube, the instrument's calescent edge shivered with a sonic whine. It bit the wall like a scalpel working in hard rubber.

Alani clenched his teeth against the pain and pushed with his legs, trying to stretch the compartment. Nothing moved.

The instrument grew hot even through his insulated gloves.

He had to get out. He could feel the plangent reverb of the airship's engines slowing down.

He carved furiously at the wall.

A slit began to open in the thick hard blackness. He pushed with all his might. The wall began to give.

With three additional minutes of surgery and two more ferocious attempts, it finally broke. The crack stretched then tore along a fibrous grain, ripping apart like wood.

Alani fell out onto a hard metal floor covered with lumpy, bloody frost.

Above him hung a ruptured, hollow bulb of meat.

* * *

HIS metal helmet was caked with crimson ice. Rubber hoses trailed back into the carcass like umbilici. They breached the meat's upper girth where pipe had once taken the place of a trachea, poking through just below the hook where hidden stitches sealed the point of Alani's nightmarish insertion.

Chemiostatic coils warmed air in the helmet's breathing apparatus.

His thick white suit was smeared and filthy. Braided wires webbed the chest, legs, feet and hands, coursing with inward warmth. Although very little heat escaped, the cavity inside the meat had indeed begun to thaw.

Alani discarded the gloves and peeled off the heavy jacket that buttoned up his side. The bag he had been clutching unrolled across the floor, revealing an assortment of tools in sparkling green beneath the beam of a fresh chemiostatic torch.

Sena hits early snow in the mountains. She isn't ready for the cold. It takes her breath, forces her into a substandard inn at Mossloch. In the morning, she watches helplessly as the sizable flakes come down.

What am I going to do?

She is almost out of money. The pass is choked with snow. She wipes tears with the black ruffle of her sleeve, leaves the inn, trudges north. She feels worse than miserable. She feels contemptible, despicable and vile.

It has been a long time since she cried. Normally she would try to stifle it, hold it in her throat like bile but today she does not care. She walks down the mountain, beaten and blubbering.

Bilious, dissimilar voices whisper in her head. Her vision blurs. The heavy book in her pack feels like solid stone.

For several hours she doesn't have a plan.

She walks to Isca.

From West Gate, she follows Kink Street out of Gunnymead Square. The cotters have begun dragging in the grain tax and corpulent scurrying things shit and crawl and fuck contentedly between unattended sacks of barley and rye. A carriage driver takes pity on her and offers her a ride. He doesn't recognize her. He is headed home, he says, and will drop her off along the way. She accepts though she doesn't have a clue where she is going.

The driver leaves Three Cats on Sedge Way, turning north at Cripple Gate onto Isca Road. They trundle over streetcar rails into South Fell, rolling through the shadows of the Bîndash Ruins which have long been gated up but still offer weekend tours.

In Thief Town, sea-weathered towers thrust gray stoic forms above narrow ticking streets. Sena gets out and wanders aimlessly through the tepid late-afternoon air. From the mountain pass to the valley floor, she thinks the temperature difference must be at least fifty degrees.

She heads west, muddles back into South Fell where six stories of barred windows cast block-long shadows off the edifice of Teapetal Wax.

She wears her hood up for disguise, but in the ebbing light her identity is already totally diffused.

Vague human shadows inside lamp-lit shops haggle over the last transactions of the day. Clustered vertical meadows of leaded glass ripple with autumn-colored light.

Reluctant but resolved, she hurries out of South Fell into Blękton, up through fading blossomed lanes.

The smoky light of the markets dissipates before her eyes as she travels quickly through the sparsely peopled blocks near Gilnaroth and into the Hold.

The castle gates will close at dusk. A sign of urgency: above the darkened rooftops the ancient mill has locked its sails for the day.

Although factories in Bilgeburg produce great dusty piles of flour and cereal, people who imagine themselves coinsurers spend stacks of extra money in the castle mill on flavored germades, coffee beans and jam.

Sena darts through the cobbled twilight, under chimney pots spewing madder-tinted air; their pleasant-smelling smut mixes with the warm fermenting odors of dwindling summer. Autumn smells are taking over: leather and shoe polish and chemical laundries that froth through vented pipes into the cold.

Just before the sun vanishes, she arrives.

Somehow it has snuck up on her and, for a moment, her determination falters.

In the last rays, the castle stones are orange. Long blue shadows, like banners, fall between the gates. Across the drawbridge, sparkling suits of armor shuffle in the gloom.

She bites her lip, clenches her nails into her palms and takes a final breath.

She storms the gate.

At first, the soldiers do not see her coming. They are mumbling over the smell of the moat, restless with the season. They scrape around their posts.

When she is halfway across, she sees them notice. They nudge each other. There are six of them and one of her but her title must still echo in their minds. The sight of her seems to freeze them.

Like the sun's last ember trickling into dusk's ash pan, she comes out of the slanting rays.

She crosses the bridge as orange light fades from the towers in an orchestrated west to east sequence. The sentries' boots dull with cold; their ceremonial breastplates turn to tin. In her wake, the colorless ebb of day settles over the city. The sentries do not speak.

Sena levels her eyes and marches past.

She takes a carriage to the keep, dashes up the steps and into the foyer. Her feet echo down the hall, up more stairs, pulling a breeze with her that moves the tapestries.

A serving man opens a door into the passage, recognizes her and turns back, pretending to forget something. He shuts the portal with a click as the High King's witch storms past.

She takes tertiary hallways to minimize the chance of being stopped.

Reddish bands of light from the arrow loops slash her face. The steam of her breath vaporizes in the halls she leaves behind.

With anxious rapidity, she moves up even more stairs and out onto the sun-raked parapet that encloses the massive roof.

Here, the sun still shines over the eastern mountains and gleams icily off slate and lead. Her feet jump the gutters. The gargoyles seem to watch.

She opens a small door to the high tower and goes up, forever turning to the right. When she reaches the top, she throws open the door.

The highest room in the city is empty.

A surprised bird lifts out a window as Sena steps cautiously inside.

Carefully rolled maps rest on the war table along with small wooden figures of men and horses. Eleven of the wooden figures are more painstakingly carved than the others. They sit by themselves in a little group.

There is a halgrin with picked-out wooden scales, and standing by itself, the figure of a king.

She picks it up, turns it over. On the base are crude hand-carved words: For Caliph.

The wind from the sea whines harshly over the sills. Up here, she can see beyond the low mountains of the peninsula to where the sun, in scalloped pink, drowns in a cloudy film of waves.

"Miss?"

Sena jerks her head to see a young woman in black and white. She is wiping her hands on a cloth and looking both shy and concerned.

"His majesty just left, though I haven't any idea where. Would you like me to bring you something? Coffee?"

Sena shakes her head almost imperceptibly.

"We haven't seen you for days," the maid offers. "Welcome back."

ALANI helped his fellows escape their fleshy prisons: nine handpicked agents under his command. The refrigerated compartment had been fitted with a door that also opened from the inside.

His team removed the insulated suits and helmets, strapped on their gear and weapons and sprung the groaning metal door as softly as they knew how.

They gave hand signals in the blue-lit cargo hold and disappeared into the labyrinth of crates.

Quietly, the ship changed hands.

Alani's men went through the berths. They examined papers, identification cards, diaries and personal effects. They isolated their captives, told each of them that all their mates were dead.

They asked bizarre questions.

Which of the crew were loners? Which hadn't any family? Who had the fewest friends?

Some of the crew began to suspect the obvious deception. Truth remained irrelevant. They could coordinate no logical resistance. Even if they could, the bag of gear Alani clutched inside his frozen cyst contained (among other things) mostly superfluous implements of suppression.

Two would-be heroes were soothed with needles that out-flowed powerful tranquilizers. When they lulled into glassy stupors Alani's men moved them to the galley.

The period of solitary confinement came to an end.

The unmarried, the orphaned and the misanthropic were stripped of their uniforms. Naked and terrified, they were held down and injected with hypodermics full of yellow drug. Their captors didn't bother to sterilize the needles between injections.

In several minutes it would not matter.

Ten nude airmen were untied. They stumbled around the compartment in a narcotized trance while Alani's men herded them toward a shuttered hatch.

Outside, the sky blew dark and torrential.

One by one, the men were hurled into space. They fell for several thousand feet before landing with unheard thumps and clatters like bags of broken sticks among the rocks or soggy moors west of the Somber Hills.

It was messy work.

The spies did not think about it. Their mission turned Saergaeth's airmen into packages—each one nothing more than perfidious jetsam.

The remaining eight (that had not been drugged) were forced to watch. They screamed and clenched their teeth and eyes and tried to look away.

"Sorry mates," Alani whispered when all the doomed were gone. "That's the sentence for traitors to Stonehold."

His men put on the defenestrated crewmen's uniforms. They held them up, eyeballed fit like shoppers. They traded. Mixed and matched.

Eventually even Alani resembled one of Saergaeth's low rank flyboys.

One of his men had medical expertise.

He took the remaining crewmen and by means of a strange contraption forced back their upper and lower lids. Carefully he distended each man's left eyeball and inserted a bead of holomorphic glass into the underlying socket. Then he popped the eye back in place.

After an hour, all the implants had been done.

Alani's spies thoroughly explored every cranny of the ship. They gathered for the pep talk they knew was coming.

The eight remaining members of the crew were untied.

They sat nervously in wooden chairs listening to the thunder, eyeballs aching.

Alani looked ghastly in the fluttering weirdness of several lamps. At least he hoped he did. He had chosen this spot for the effect. His pocked cheeks and bristly dome would enhance his gaunt, sinister mien. He lit his pipe and puffed while resting his foot on the seat of a chair.

He could tell the crew was frightened. They paid sedulous attention to every word he spoke. They were men who ferried metholinate, not professional soldiers. Enamored with Saergaeth's leadership, they made the easy, popular choice, siding against Caliph Howl—a man whom none of them had ever seen.

"You are traitors," said Alani with slow congenial syllables. "But can still avoid a traitor's fate."

He began the propaganda he was an expert at delivering and explained that the bead in their eye was holomorphically linked to a single bead in his hand. If he crushed the one, the other eight would shatter. They were filled with toxin that would go directly to the brain.

"If any one of you should betray the High King again by compromising this mission, you will die. And you will have killed the other seven . . . your friends and crew . . . in addition to yourself."

It was a lie. The beads of glass were totally innocuous.

"When we have finished this mission, I promise you . . . we will remove the implants. You will be granted clemency, free to return to your families and your jobs after swearing allegiance to the High King.

"After this war is over we will all be Stonehavians again."

One of the men laughed even though he looked terribly afraid. "How can we possibly trust you?"

Alani didn't smile.

"Trust? I don't want your trust. As traitors to your country you are being coerced, gentlemen. Let us call it what it is."

"We're not traitors. We're patriots," said the zeppelin captain. "And you sir, are a murderous liar. The very kind we're fighting against."

Alani grinned. His teeth were yellow and crooked and he knew it. He looked the captain directly in the face for maximum effect.

"You'll get no argument from me on your second point since lies and murder are my business, sir. But I will tell you, Captain . . ." he referenced a book in his claw of a hand, "Bayans . . . that your assessment of me, while true, is inconsequential.

"Patriotism is a vagary defined by your individual hopes. Whatever you perceive national interests to be . . . however jingoistic or expropriationist. I myself am a pacifist and loyal to the crown which is no doubt where your sanctimonious diatribe springs from and why we do not see eye to eye.

"Let me be clear, Mr. Bayans, and ask you one question. When orders eventually came . . . as they surely would have . . . from Miskatoll to drop ordnance on the capital of your own country . . . would you have obeyed them?"

The captain said nothing. Perhaps some of his men were beginning to realize that the moral high ground he was clinging to was just another smear. Alani hoped as much.

"No?" asked Alani. "Either way you answer, as the commander of this airship, it's going to sound rather bad coming from those patriotic lips.

"Perhaps, Mr. Bayans, I have saved you from your sins. But I digress." Alani waved his pipe. "I see from your diary that you have a young son and daughter and a wife at home. Which brings us back to your stunning lack of choice in the matter and the truth of my grip on everything you hold dear. Do we understand one another?"

It was overkill to threaten the man's family and Alani knew it. But in the current situation he frankly didn't care.

The captain looked stricken. His men were completely cowed.

Still, one last question had to be asked. If it hadn't, Alani would have been fabulously surprised.

"How did you get on board?"

Alani ended his smoke and tapped the dottle into his palm. He had no intention of answering.

The question by itself was enough. Caliph's plan had been chillingly neat. He had tabulated casualties as a prerequisite for any plausible charade, hence the timing of Ghoul Court's violent raid.

There wasn't any crash along the White Leech. No crew of fifty airmen had gone down. But there had been bodies . . . plenty of bodies to advance that illusion.

The men of the *Orison* had met their weeping, joyful families in Octul Box at the lavish government estate. The crew had told their wives and children the only thing they knew—that their deaths had been faked to advance some strategy in war and that, for now, all of them had to stay under lock and key until the High King signed their eventual release.

Caliph too had coldly envisioned the execution of half a sky shark's crew and the psychological brutality required to ensure the loyalty of the rest. But it was only the beginning, thought Alani, only the first edge of a very complex and complicated plan.

CALIPH returned with Roric Feldman in custody and watched the *Precursor* dock over West Gate. It floated in above the heavy leaded obelisks whose panes boiled with emerald light. The beacons' gleam scintillated, created columns in the glittering rain.

After the other ships had moored, the *Byun-Ghala* pitched north across the gray-swept city. Caliph tried not to think about what Alani was doing. He tried not to think about what would happen to Roric Feldman. He supposed their paltry adolescent feud had finally ended. Caliph Howl had won. It didn't feel good.

He thought about the fresco on his bedroom ceiling, about tossing and turning during the course of oncoming sleepless nights. Isca slid by underneath him, gliding like the mottled back of a deformed nocturnal beast. He looked out from the observation deck through the rain, at the towers of his castle. There were lights, dim warm lights in his bedroom window and for a moment he dared to dream.

SENA had fretted through the evening after deciding once again not to try and escape.

She read from the *Cisrym Ta*.

Terrified of Caliph's return she shut the ancient book with restive fingers and began a series of mindless preparations.

She took a bath. She oiled her ringlets, her sex, misted her flesh with the pore-clenching chill of Tebeshian perfume. She got dressed. The clothes she picked were diabolic. She knew just which things against her skin might drive the High King mad.

She checked her glowing watch four times as the room began to blush. The rosy light faded quickly and the sumptuous shadows around the bed turned brown.

The room cooled. She called a servant to light a fire despite the groaning foment in the radiator pipes. For a while, she sat mutely, preoccupied before the mirror. She penciled in her eyes and lips while her intestines wrung themselves through a series of algetic knots.

Her reflection was resplendent. Fishnet black and satin covered up her fear. Laces on her corset and sequential cunning straps battened down her persistent bent to fly. Hair and eyes, gold and sapphire, lips of buccal ruby: she was something gleaming but restrained, dark jewels set in velveteen soot.

A beguilement, she thought, *that he will see right through.*

As the grandfather clock tolled seventeen, the storm stilled and the clouds opened on the night. She left the cluttered vanity and poised near the western windows, faced but hardly looking at the magnesium fizzle of starlight.

The room was quiet when she turned her head in the direction of the door. A figure had materialized soundlessly, shrouded in the doughy darkness that stretched like something clotting in the corner of the room.

She held her breath.

A wayward glistening twist of her perfect hair dangled, catching firelight. Sena brushed it self-consciously, presenting her lure. She calculated the forward motion of her hips, pushing her pose over the edge of art, spilling her presentation into the void of breathless concupiscence.

She moved as though blown, ignoring her heart that twitched like something in a snare.

She had already taken several steps when she realized it wasn't Caliph at the door.

A thin man in Desdae's raven-colored scholar robes seemed to hover just above the floor. He watched her with Cimmerian eyes. Narrow, pallid lips overdrew a baleful smile and hair as fine as cotton candy trembled in a cat's-paw off the sea.

The door opened behind him, swung through his semiform and erased him from the room.

Caliph stood nearly where the old man had been, slack jawed, gawking.

Despite her obvious effect on him, Sena's poise had vaporized. Whether the old man had been real remained for some·successive mental debate. Right now the moment of her opportunity was in jeopardy.

She forced her nerves to trickle back. She would not allow herself to lose this second chance—not until she had made a sterling assault.

Already she could see that Caliph's inarticulate stupor had begun to harden into skepticism. Skepticism that he hurled at her with excruciating efficiency.

It startled her—to be an outsider.

Caliph seemed newly minted, as if she was seeing him for the first time. *Palan's tail*, she thought, *he's changed! He's changed and I never even noticed.* She imagined the cruelty that must have passed like iced croissants around his table every morning. Those meetings. The endless plotting. Everyone he thought he could trust had sold him out. Even she. And now she was here, uninvited—and she couldn't blame him, she couldn't fault him in the least.

He walked past her, toward wardrobes still filled with bodices and lace.

"I'm a bitch," she whispered. It stopped him in his tracks.

He turned like a weapon on a turret: tensile, dark and cocked. Sena saw him scratch his arm.

"Not good enough."

Although his words were nasty and deliberate she realized all of a sudden that they weren't true. It was like she had climbed inside his head. She could tell that the sight of her was enough and she could hear him berating himself. *You uxorious beaten little man!* His eyes gave it away: how he loathed himself right now. His face told her that any arrows she fired would kill him on the spot.

She saw him understand that she knew. It was instantaneous. Like telepathy. And to her astonishment, he didn't attempt a charade or try to cover it up. It made her want him in a callow, unexpected way. The expression on his face was beyond her capability to exploit.

It was awkward, embarrassing and thankfully without audience. Instead of victory, Sena felt like she had melted. Her sense of vulnerability ballooned. She couldn't help it. She was ashamed of the tenderness that had jelled the air.

"You're right. You are a bitch . . ."

Tenderness noted. Appreciated. Temporarily set aside.

"I was going to leave. I didn't think you . . ." she shook her head, "would take me back."

It was a safe thing to say. Moronic and simple and clichéd. After all, Caliph's expression had made it clear that he did, that he *had already* taken her back.

Caliph said a few more sour words.

Sena fired back once or twice, explained herself with competent precision. For his part, he did an admirable job of remaining cold.

The parrying went on for two minutes at most, consisting mostly of disingenuous threats.

Finally Caliph sighed to indicate that he was done.

"You can stay here. I'll sleep downstairs."

He confiscated a pillow and left the room.

That he told her where he was going and didn't take a blanket, that he gave the bed to her, were all she needed to know for certain that she had been forgiven.

Her heart started beating again. She knew by any stretch that he had let her off easy. It bothered her.

She followed him from the room, watched him trudge down the grand stairs and plop down in front of the first floor's fireplace.

He was sulking. A sack of anger on the leather sofa. But she was trained for this. It would be like pressing a deep aposteme, forcing an eruption, getting at the core. She would squeeze his anger out. It would be surgical. Tonight it would be pårịn and . . . it would be pårịn because she loved him.

She went down. When she crawled on top of him, when she perched for him in poses that were ludicrous, he didn't look away. Her motions were smooth and daedal. Exquisite. Outlandish. It was a pantomime, a rising chaos that she stylized and turned, gripped professionally and molded into perfect form. It wasn't just a striptease or a succubus straddling a man in the huge echoing hall. It wasn't a pair of imperiled creatures grinding blindly on the edge of salvation. It wasn't that. It was Sena's adaptation. A slow-moving, living sculpture. She crafted it with subsecondal precision and gave it to Caliph as a gift.

He didn't push it away or ridicule it as another cheap pretense. She steeled herself in case he did. Instead he accepted it, embraced it and eventually wore himself out against it, collapsing into unconsciousness that lasted far beyond the dawn.

CHAPTER
35

Caliph realized that Gadriel had found them. They were draped across each other, barely covered by a blanket of black leveret. The High Seneschal had already established a perimeter around the room, using sentries to block every door and passageway that might admit a curious member of the castle staff.

Discreet bits of Sena's outfit had been swept up and whisked away.

"I've commissioned breakfast," said the seneschal. A bowl of neatly rolled washcloths steamed in his hand like an offering. Two servants erected a set of carved dressing screens, set a stack of plush towels on the table and promptly disappeared. There were slippers and soap and a basin of scalding water at the ready. "King Lewis has arrived from Vale Briar . . . on schedule. The weather is mild so I set him in the north portico."

A silver tray floated in, laden with coffee, toothbrushes and the morning's freshly toasted paper.

ALONG with the *Herald*, a copy of *The Varlet's Pike* lay ominously on the tray. Caliph picked it up, bemused by what story it could contain that would prompt the seneschal to actually purchase such a scandal sheet specifically for the High King's eye.

When Caliph read it, he was stunned not so much by the content of the article as by the speed of its being turned into print.

A source inside Isca Castle indicated that the seventh of Kam brought the return of the High King's witch. Refusing to be named, the source claimed the grand hall was the site of an alleged voluble reunion between the High King and his mistress who disappeared late last week.

When asked exactly what voluble meant, the source replied, "I wish they'd save their disgusting sybaritism for the bedroom. They ought to be restrained . . ."

A note was stuck underneath this text, penned in Gadriel's precise hand that read, *Don't worry. I've already found the source of this leak and the culprit has been terminated from our employ.—G.*

Well, thought Caliph, *I guess I haven't won over all the staff after all.*

KING Lewis was reading the same page when Caliph met him twenty minutes later on the portico. The gleaming corpulent man smiled and rose ponderously. He laid the paper aside and shook Caliph's hand.

"Freedom of the press." He grinned.

Caliph returned the smile, noticeably abridged and chilled. "Interesting preference in journalism. I'm sure *The Varlet's Pike* can offer you several good wallows at my expense. Would you like me to order you a subscription?"

"No." Lewis fanned his palms. "Already have one, thanks."

"Great. To be honest I'd hate to itemize that one on the books."

"You've gotten comfortable quickly." Lewis resumed his seat and hoisted a jelly roll.

"You think so? That's funny. Comfortable is one of the few words I would *not* have used to describe my position."

Lewis bit and chewed and spoke before he swallowed.

"I heard our meeting is being put off until tonight?"

"I've arranged a hunt today . . . for your entertainment," said Caliph. "This evening, after we return we can discuss the business that's brought you to Isca."

"How excellent!" Lewis' voice dispensed disingenuous surprise. "And the prince of Tentinil has come?"

"Yes. Prince Mortiman and several others. Like you, they've very recently arrived . . . by zeppelin."

Lewis took another bite.

"Absolutely ticky!"

THE morning sun fired the interior of the castle battlements like a kiln. Its fingers stretched down slowly to warm the men waiting in the courtyard.

They were mounted on horseback, dressed in traditional Naneman hunting clothes.

Caliph had asked Sena to come—an invitation she readily accepted.

Over the last several hours an irrational umbrage had slithered back into his heart, springing from the notion that Sena had returned to harvest her own exoneration.

He tried to chase the feeling away, but it remained. A stigma of suspicion that blurred the once crisp light in which he held her. She hadn't really stolen anything. She had asked for his forgiveness and he had given it. How could he now begrudge her?

And still . . .

His heart was full of worms. The smell of fresh crap smacked the air as Mayor Ashlen's horse deposited a steaming pile on the cobbles.

Ashlen rested comfortably in his saddle holding a long dazzling spear, huffing steam.

His son rode beside him and the barons of Bogswallow and Glanting-mire with their sons added up to an even eight. With the simultaneous arrival of Caliph and Sena, Prince Mortiman, King Lewis and his personal guard, the final tally rose to thirteen.

Chatter focused on Prince Mortiman and the war front while servants led hunting dogs from heated kennels into the chilly court. Mortiman winced at every question and Caliph thought he looked happy that the dogs were barking too loudly to continue the conversation.

"The High King has the right idea," Marsden said whimsically. He was already lit from several early brandies and his words were injudicious. "Bring a mistress and if the hunt is slow—"

"The hunt will not be slow," said Sheridan. He was the oldest son of the baron of Bogswallow and a member of some obscure cabinet. "I can smell the fetch of the kill."

You smell your flask, thought Caliph.

"Let's ride," King Ashlen shouted, raising his spear. "To hunt the minds of the peasants for this fearsome beast." The fact that they were after a monster made the outing less of a diversion in the eyes of the press. If they had been going out strictly for sport, the papers would have had a heyday.

The hunting party roared. They followed Ashlen out of the Hold, onto West Wall Road and away from the city, up into the hills.

The hounds seemed to glide before the horses.

Caliph supposed that none of them (himself included) really believed a creature haunted the foothills, but he was glad to get out, to escape for even a few hours. Horse claws provoked the marshy spice of fallen leaves and trampled turf. Clammy, fenny odors soaked the pungent air above the hills.

"Is that the old Howl estate?" Caliph heard Marsden shout. Caliph answered that it was.

The hunt meandered far above the old keep, twisting into ravines choked with bracken.

They crossed numerous gullies carved by seasonal runoff, taking occasional switchbacks to avoid rampant undergrowth. Invariably they turned uphill again.

At ten o'clock the party lunched in a clearing at the north end of Summit Wood. Afterward, they followed a beast track south. It felt unsettlingly primitive to be surrounded by horses and soughing woodland things after so much time in the city. Caliph checked his pocket watch as if to make sure the gears were still spinning.

An hour later Baron Marsden's sons, Meredith and Garrett, downed two boars. The dogs cornered them and a concentration of spears finished them off.

The hunt was about to turn home with its kill when Vaughan, Kendall's youngest son, discovered strange tracks in a nearby meadow. Everyone rode up to have a look.

The grassy patch where the tracks were located overlooked Stonehold. Far below, Isca sprawled in a halitus of gray and brown mist beside the sea.

"Come see these," Vaughan called to his brother.

Sheridan dismounted and stood with his hands braced on his knees.

"Odd," was all he had to say.

King Ashlen and his son Newl stood at the far end of the meadow. They had followed the tracks from one end to the other and were holding the dogs on leashes, allowing them to sniff and whimper.

"The thing runs with a wide limping gait." Vaughan pointed through the grass. "Mother of Mizraim! Look at that! It's like it runs on two feet and uses a hand to help push itself along!"

Prince Mortiman jumped from the stirrups and paced between the marks. "Three strides to its one," he declared.

Sheridan shrugged.

"It stands to reason not all the farmers are crazy. They've seen something up here and we've found the proof." He made a bit of a ridiculous show with his arms.

Caliph looked at the footprint closely. King Lewis crouched beside him and touched it as though skeptical.

The indentation was narrow and long and deep. The heel and the balls of the foot were hardly wider than a man's, but their length nearly doubled any boot among them. The toe impressions were also thin and long. Occasionally a tiny hole poked the ground a finger's breadth from the tip, as though a nail curved sharply down at the end of each digit.

The handprints followed the right side of the tracks nearly six feet from the footprints. They were different with every stride. Sometimes the thing had supported itself on the backs of its knuckles, sometimes on the side of the palm. One clear handprint was found in a spot of mud between patches of grass. Fingers two and a half times the length of Vaughan's and a palm that was surprisingly small, spread out under the men's eyes like the mark of a giant spider someone had mashed into the clay.

The hunting party divided and agreed that half would follow the tracks one way and half the other.

King Ashlen and his son along with Baron Marsden and his two boys went with King Lewis and his guard. Caliph, Sena, Baron Kendall, Sheridan, Vaughan and the prince took the rest of the dogs across the meadow, traveling in the same direction as the creature.

The sun had already drifted into late afternoon and the autumn day was quickly losing heat. Sena rode closer to Caliph now. She held her spear across her hips.

Despite the altitude, the underbrush remained oppressively thick. The horses had to wade through it and the ground was invisible.

They weren't following tracks anymore. But the dogs had traveled ahead. Their yelping tinkled off the mountains like broken glass.

"They're following *something*," Kendall said. He added emphasis to "something." "If the creature came this way though it's damned uncanny. Foliage is undisturbed."

Sena looked at the crushed trail behind them and then ahead at the quiet, untrod bracken.

"With strides like those, I doubt we'll catch it even horsed," Vaughan said. "We'll be lucky if the hounds don't fall down a fissure." He looked over his shoulder.

Caliph read his thoughts. *If we turn back now, it will still be dark by the time we reach Isca.*

He drew up on the reins and began to call in the dogs. They were trained from pups to ignore food even when they were starving should their master call.

It was quiet out in the mountains. Hundreds of leagues of unexplored valleys and ridges crumpled the land of the Healean Range. There must have been thousands of square miles for any kind of creature to hide.

Caliph called again.

He noticed Prince Mortiman looking at him in a kind of charmed way and felt suddenly uneasy.

Sena was looking at him too. Looking at the prince looking at Caliph. The bizarre momentary triangle made Caliph shift in his saddle as a gust of wind ruffled his hair. Mortiman cleared his throat musically and gazed off into the distance.

Caliph made one last attempt to call the dogs in.

The mountain air had turned cold. The tip of his nose was growing numb. He looked back at Sena; saw her face tense and pale. *Jealousy?* Or was she as nervous as he was?

A shuffling stirred the undergrowth.

"Ahh, here they come." Sheridan clapped his gloved hands.

But the sticks and dying leaves parted for only one hound.

Caliph jumped down, his voice a whisper. "By the trade wind!"

Blood matted the animal's coat and a great chunk of hide had been torn from the top of its head. One ear was missing altogether. It stood panting steam, whimpering softly.

"We need to go," said Sena.

Caliph tore a strip of cloth from a roll in his saddlebag. "I'll have to carry him."

Sena sounded desperate. "We need to go now!" She turned her giddy horse around and began walking it the other way. Her terror was contagious. Vaughan, a trained woodsman, sat looking anxiously into the trees. He cocked his head slightly as though listening to something no one else could hear.

Prince Mortiman held his spear, hands clenching and twisting around the haft.

"I can't just leave him," Caliph said.

His ears picked through every sound. The falling leaves, the shush-shush of wind in the bracken. Nothing strange disturbed the mountain woods but he felt a slight involuntary shiver.

Sena's voice drew his attention. He looked up, saw her eyes: wide, blue and frightened. "Caliph. We. Have. To. Go!"

She kicked her horse. Its bouquet of tails snarled. It coughed viciously and stamped its claws into the clay. Even these intimidating creatures seemed to grow nervous as evening sucked away the day.

Prince Mortiman turned his horse around and lashed its reins.

Sheridan seemed impatient. "Come on, Dad."

The baron of Bogswallow raised his eyebrows at the High King.

"If we don't want to be left, we'd best let your animal find his own way home."

Caliph abandoned his work with a sigh. He buckled his bag and hurriedly pulled himself back onto his saddle.

"This is ridiculous," he hissed.

The daylight faded as Vaughan and his father watched both ways while Caliph got his horse turned around in the thick brush.

But as the High King negotiated the terrain, he felt his well-anchored skepticism begin to crumble. Old familiar fears rose out of memory. He urged his horse into a gallop. Surreal tentacles seemed to morph and lengthen from behind.

Something snapped inside Caliph at the exact moment that the horse truly began to fly, as though the fear of rider or beast had somehow infected the other.

Clawing from the darkness of his past as much as from the mountains, a nameless horror bore down on Caliph Howl. It had eyes. Greedy, leering eyes. And teeth slick with the blood of dogs.

Caliph lashed the reins on the mad snarl of horseflesh beneath him. Branches blurred: a delirious black net above the shred of claws. He felt like he was eight again. He felt nauseous.

He couldn't tell whether he was tumbling or sliding or falling down the mountainside. A dry corn leaf, blown high above the valley like a runaway kite, wobbled through the air.

Down, down, down. The horse leapt a gully, scrambled for its footings, found balance and charged on. Down into forests of dying autumn where the bitter ale of fermenting leaves curdled air. Down where sunlight grew lost and confused. Down into nightmares he had forgotten long ago.

He had no idea where Sena and the others were. As though a mental tie had snapped on an overburdened wagon in his mind, a carefully stacked mountain of irrational fears rumbled down behind him. They burst forth in an avalanche, tumbling after his horse into the foothills.

Like a child running from the dark, there was no *why*. It was fear of the darkness. Nothing more.

Stones clattered on the steep grade. The horse roared. Its claws divorced ground. Everything grew silent for one eternal moment as the sky and trees spun past Caliph's eyes. He watched the branches pass in slow revolutions like great black swatches of funerary lace.

The muted muddy tones of autumn twirled past him. Rough bark. Ragged leaves. Sticks and stones. The black markings of ghostwoods, like a million sinister eyes, stared at him from pallid faces.

They watched him fall.

He should have died in the mountain woods of the Healean Range. He should have cracked his legs or neck in half or crushed his skull on numberless boulders.

Instead he landed in a deep patch of decomposing leaves that had accumulated in a wash where two hills met.

Like a dart thrown at a board he landed miraculously, standing up, planted to his shins in spongy compost. Behind him, his horse lay silent as though exhausted by the long run.

The rational part of Caliph's head yammered at him to stop, but instinct drove him on. He forgot the freakish rarity of his landing, relinquished one of his boots to the suction of the bog and fled on foot.

Away!

He galloped with an uneven gait. His unshod foot tore against fallen branches and stones. He cursed. He could feel the darkness behind him, a creature that mimicked his limp, pushing itself over the ground. He could hear it clawing through the leaves, hunting him between the blackened trunks.

Without looking back he sprinted up one of the wooded hills and began down the other side. From behind, he heard the heavy sound of pursuit change to an echo of his own feet shredding leaves.

The thing moved fast—faster than he could run.

Tears from sprinting in the cold blurred Caliph's sight. But up ahead, something gleamed. Something the light picked out at odd angles. Pink flat shapes standing in crooked rows amid the saplings.

Caliph coughed up, nearly choked on a sour laugh.

His bare foot felt like it was on fire. Icy tasteless air burnt his lungs. Limping, cackling at the irony, he stumbled into the Howl burial grounds.

His voice escaped, broken and dissonant from his parched throat. It snagged in the trees. He whirled, nearly blind, jerked the safety ring counter-clockwise, and drew his chemiostatic sword with a crackle of green.

A flurry of dark cloth filled his vision. Something flew through the air. It had launched itself just before he turned around. A black-and-gold shape struck him heavily in the chest, sending him sprawling amid the graves.

His sword, jolted from his grasp, did mindless cartwheels on the spot, sent its bolt of electricity harmlessly into the ground.

The creature pinned him with expert efficiency. Everything went black.

"Caliph? Caliph? It's okay."

A cloak's heavy folds parted revealing a yellow sky, shadowy branches and a disheveled but gorgeous halo of golden hair.

Sena's lips gasped, forming airy words just above his face. Her body pressed him into the carpet of leaves.

Even though Caliph's horror had already given way to dazed surrender, his mind, for some unaccountable reason, had snagged on the memory of their struggle in the library.

His hand fumbled reflexively for his sword but it was stuck in the ground several yards away.

"I think you're bleeding," she wheezed.

She was real. Caliph's hideous exhaustion-strangled laugh echoed through the trees. He closed his eyes and began to cough.

"Thirsty—"

"Me too. The water is a hundred yards back with my horse."

She rolled off and lay on her back like him, staring up at the tangle of limbs. For a minute they both gulped oxygen.

"I don't know where the others are." She swallowed. "I think Sheridan fell. I saw you go down the slope and followed you. Your horse is dead."

Caliph winced and tried to sit up.

"Don't—" She forced herself to all fours, pulling a leaf from her hair. "You stepped on a branch and ran part of it into your foot. Hold still."

Her fist took hold of a fat twig protruding from the tender skin between his toes and yanked it out with a swift straight jerk. "It's a mess down here," she said.

Caliph bit back on the pain that exploded in his foot.

"Thanks." He sounded ridiculously apologetic.

She examined the wound for fragments.

Caliph swore under his breath. It felt like she was digging with a shovel.

"What did you say happened to Sheridan?" he asked, trying to stay still.

"I don't know. Maybe he got eaten and that's why we're still alive." She scrunched her nose in distaste and put her mouth to the wound. She sucked hard and spit.

"I'll go to the horse. I think brandy and linen is all we have to work with." Crouched at his feet in the twilight like a beautiful ghoul, lips red with his pain, she made efforts to reassure him. "I'll hurry."

She stood and started walking, quick as her tired legs would move. She wished she could see what might be lurking in the woods. Her eyes ached from studying the *Cisrym Ta*.

She blinked several times, rubbed her eyes with her palms. A brilliant migraine was exploding at the back of her head. She could see Inti'Drou glyphs when she closed her lids, like someone had stapled the pages to their undersides. Then it dawned on her that there might be a way . . . a way to see them more clearly and still ease the pain.

I'll carve my eyes.

She marched through the dying wood, thinking of the procedure, still aware of the leaves falling around her, aware that they glowed with velvety redness in the sinking sun, scarlet bodies twinkling like dozens of eyes between the trees. They were there, beyond the geometry of the wood, haunting her steps. The Yillo'tharnah. They squatted. They followed from angles that could not be protracted with instruments made by men.

She could feel them watch her as she topped the low hill and found her horse. They stared while she inspected the creature's right front leg. It was bleeding and didn't look good.

Patiently she led the animal back to Caliph. She bandaged and cleaned his wound, continually glancing behind her at the invisibles she felt breathing across her neck.

She rinsed her mouth with brandy and gave Caliph some to drink. "It's probably not a good idea to walk on it, especially since we don't have a boot." She took back the flask and had another hit.

"Are you going to carry me?" he joked. Sena didn't laugh as he struggled to his feet.

"You can ride my horse," she said distractedly. "I think it's starting to founder." It was a baseless guess. She knew virtually nothing about horses.

Sena sniffed. The cold was making her nose run.

"Caliph? Are we going to go . . . or are you going to stand there and stare at me all night?"

But Caliph didn't answer. An alarmed expression, blazoned in red light, was crawling over his face. He was talking. But not to her.

"It was just like this," he whispered. "A cemetery in the woods . . . and I was standing . . . over there."

He looked around.

"It was right here." He limped in a circle. "I think."

"What was?" Sena asked. She had never seen him like this.

He didn't answer. He hobbled farther into the yard, tracking toward the pile of dirt the sexton had left behind. Sena's heart quickened.

"Caliph, it's getting dark. I'm worried."

But his black eyes were fixed on the marker that leaned above the half-exhumed grave. The sky grew darker by the moment. When Caliph reached it, he sat down heavily on the mound. Sena looked down with him.

Several feet below, the ripped-apart boards of an ill-made coffin made it look like the corpse had forced its own way out. They lay splintered, thrown carelessly aside. The gray shriveled form mocked her with empty eyes partly covered by leaves.

Caliph was sick. Neither of them had eaten much when the party stopped for lunch and his stomach turned up thin, clear bile in substitution of a good vomit.

Sena suddenly understood his reaction. Her eyes grew wide, a pall coming over her face.

The night she opened the *Cisrym Ta* she had not paid any attention, but the sexton had excavated precisely according to her words, one that's not so old . . .

NATHANIEL HOWL, DIED 545 Y.O.T. WREN.
THE HOLOMORPH ON THE HILL.
MAY THE BENEVOLENCE OF ADUMMIM
KEEP HIM IN CLAY FOREVER.

He lay exposed to the air like one of his own freakish experiments.

"He's come back," Caliph gurgled. A viscous line strung between his lower lip and the mound where he crouched, looking away.

"Caliph." She bent down beside him. "It's only grave robbers. He's not alive." Weird glyphs from the *Cisrym Ta*, however, made her doubt her own words. She had read the necromancer's notes, seen the secrets in the margins, found the truth behind Cameron's stories.

"I dreamt it. Can't you smell it?"

"Smell what?"

"Piss!" For the first time since she had known him, Caliph's face looked truly pale. His skin was clammy against her fingers. He babbled without sense.

"I did it. I shouldn't have, he was just . . . gods! Why can't he just be dead?"

"He's dead. He's dead." She rocked him in her arms, suddenly frightened. "He's dead."

The words ran together in a macabre lullaby. Darkness settled in around them. Only faint light ebbed through the black thatch of trees.

"We have to go, Caliph."

She felt an approaching presence. In her mind's eye she imagined something stop to sniff the dead horse on the other side of the hill. It tilted its small head to listen.

Caliph wiped his mouth on his sleeve. Cold light had filled his eyes.

"Caliph! Where are you going?"

He had begun crawling quickly, angrily through the leaves, heading for where he had dropped his sword. She tried to stop him but he threw her off. The blade gleamed.

Sena leaned against a marker and watched in rapt fascination, enspelled by his bizarre behavior.

A weird windy cough came from the direction of the dead horse. Something was actually there. It lurched slowly uphill from the body of the animal and supported its weight on one deformed hand. It rested, moved uphill then rested again, something that should not have had corporeal form.

When it stopped, it listened against the wind. Sena could almost hear it pause, eavesdropping above the soft clatter of leaves.

Her fingers gripped the headstone and pulled herself up. Naobi's eroding face fell apart behind the trees. It didn't seem possible that night could come so fast.

Caliph was slogging back, oblivious, ignoring his foot, walking toward the grave with sword in hand. He looked monstrous. His black hazy shape hunched over the hole and lunged downward stroke after stroke, stabbing at the corpse. He made horrible noises like a crying animal.

Powerful electric currents flashed in the pit, made the corpse lurch and jolt.

Somewhere, near the crest of the hill, whatever was listening must have both seen and heard. Sena's horse bolted. It gave a startled high-pitched snarl and left.

No sooner had the animal vanished than a terrible sound echoed off the mountains. It ricocheted through the trees and sank into Sena's blood like teeth.

Caliph's body seized in midthrust. He stopped his insane demonstration over the grave and looked around.

Sena stumbled.

She stared blindly toward the origin of the inhuman echo but it was too dark to see.

"Caliph." Her throat had constricted and his name came out as an exsiccated whisper.

Strangely, the scream seemed to drain Caliph's fever. He stopped, clicked into motion, cogs running smoothly, measuring, guessing. His voice was quiet and rational again. "Sena, run for the house."

She continued to stumble for a long moment then she turned and almost bumped into him.

What is the use in running? she thought.

"Run for the house," he said again.

And then she obeyed. She could hear Caliph close behind her. His feet made shuffling noises in the leaves, painful limping sounds. She wondered if he would fall.

Sena broke from the trees into the overgrown lawn before the house. She could feel the creature coming now. It ran clumsily but with unreal speed. Long spindly limbs flung it with horrific strength over the ground. It tore silently through the graveyard, bearing down through the trees, hardly disturbing the forest through which it sped.

It could see her. It could see them. Its teeth were bared. By daylight it might flee from men and dogs, but when the sun set, it grew bold.

CALIPH ran headlong after Sena, his pain swallowed up in the urgency of flight.

He could see her body moving like it had been made only to run. She leapt the front steps in a single bound and vanished into the house.

He almost did the same but the gears clicked out a different course and pushed him into the overgrown bushes instead. Though still afraid, it was a cool fear.

Quickly, efficiently he felt the ground, searching for the thing he knew was there. There was a clink and he pulled a cracked little bowl from the weeds. It was the little bowl he had nearly crushed when Sena and he had ridden up earlier that fall. The same terrible little bowl his uncle had used.

Caliph drew his depleted sword across his palm, letting the metal bite into his flesh. He clenched his fist over the little bowl just like his uncle had shown him so many years ago.

Now Caliph's life ran into it instead.

"Holomorphy needs blood," Nathaniel used to say. "Holomorphy is blood. Blood is numbers." A thin old man seemed to stand on the mansion steps with Caliph, a ghost mumbling in his ear. It reminded him. Prompted him at every step.

"If I am gone and you need to be safe in the house, this is what you must do."

The bony fingers of the necromancer rested on Caliph's head, stroking the boy's hair.

"You must not be afraid."

Caliph could almost see the silver knife Nathaniel used to cut his hand. One cut deep enough to count as three. The words were coming to him with the same speed as the creature.

"Caliph, come inside!"

Sena's terrified voice hardly registered behind him. Distantly he heard her moving the broken door. His blood ran into the bowl. He spoke the math.

Whether or not he wanted to be a holomorph, the syllables of the Unknown Tongue had been his nursery rhymes. He slopped his life on the front step and drew in it: the curious three-stroke mark with the toe of his boot.

Then he set the bowl down, a blank expression on his face.

Across the meadow something parted the trees and swung its huge gaunt frame into the grass. Caliph stepped backward into the house; he helped Sena shut the door.

Inside, they could do little but hold the panel in place and wait. Listening. Their labored breathing and the wind pushing through the chinks made it impossible to hear.

Pressed together, they leaned against the thick wood portal and doubted the clawing noises on the walls were only bushes.

The door, hanging from its one hinge, could not even keep the wind out. It took all four hands to keep it in place.

In the blackness, they stared at each other.

A guttural, bestial snort puffed softly through the crack. Whatever it was, it was only inches away.

It scraped on the steps—talons or claws. Slobbery heavy breathing drew the air backward.

A hissing like the release of steam from a kettle made Sena's breath catch audibly in her throat. Then there was a whimper and the sound of claws dragging off the steps.

"Upstairs," Caliph gasped.

Sena nodded. She knew exactly where he meant. Caliph shoved several bricks against the bottom of the door then raced up the tower steps and pushed their way through the trapdoor into the onetime bedchamber of Nathaniel Howl.

The walls of the tower still held their strange geometry. They had been carved with sigils and glyphs that plaited and interlaced, surging generally upward like rushing voices frozen in stone.

A bedroll lay along the far wall. Aside from it, and the carvings in the ceiling, the room looked empty and remarkably clean.

"So this is where you stayed?" Caliph surmised, limping to one of the windows and trying to peer down at the dark yard. "After you disappeared?"

Sena sniffed and blew her nose in a handkerchief for an answer. She had a hundred lies in her head, but none of them would have worked. Anyway, she was too out of breath to lie. Instead she latched the trapdoor and walked over to the bedroll where she sat down and drew her knees up to her chin.

Caliph was fiddling with the window.

"I have to give you credit," he said. "I don't think I could have stood sleeping up here even one night." He got the window open and the room became colder.

"What are you doing?"

For a reply he swung his leg over the sill. The tower had been built of stone and square holes set at intervals down the outside wall formed an invisible ladder that descended to the roof.

Caliph's bandaged foot tapped gently until he found one of them. As impractical as it seemed, Nathaniel's bedroom escape route finally found a purpose.

"Don't worry," Caliph said. "Whatever is down there won't be making it inside."

Sena stood up, her curiosity forcing her to follow.

"What did you do? I've never heard a formula like that."

"Something my beneficent uncle taught me."

Sena swung her legs out the window and sat on the sill looking down at him.

"How old were you?" she asked.

"Probably seven."

His hands and feet worked the stones in a backward rhythm until he reached the roof. He waited until Sena found her footings. Once she had gotten halfway down he set off between the gables, sidestepping toward the edge of the roof to have a look at what might be prowling in the yard. He could see the lights of Isca from here.

Sena reached the roof and went to stand beside him.

"You seem to be getting around all right."

Caliph smiled faintly.

She decided not to follow him.

"The shingles look rotten. Be careful." Then her face went white.

Both of them stopped.

The creature was right below the eave. Its bestial breathing snorted from the bushes. Caliph got down on his knees and put his head out over the edge. The sight made him draw back quickly.

"It's enormously tall," he said. "Small head. Could almost reach the second-story windows."

It had been gibbering quietly to itself. But it must have seen Caliph because suddenly a scream burst loose from its great rib cage and shivered the air.

The sound, so close beneath their feet, made Sena convulse. She scooted backward toward the peak.

"It might actually be able to do it with those arms," Caliph whispered. He scrambled after her, heading back to the tower.

Agitated by its unreachable prey, it now sounded like the thing was running in circles around the house, cackling and crashing through the brambles, dragging its long talons over the walls.

When they had hauled themselves back inside, Sena went directly to the bedroll and sat down. Caliph shut the window and came over beside her.

"It's amazing that something like that actually lives out in the mountains."

The creature brought back blobby memories of his uncle muttering incoherently. The old man would stand at the window in his scholar robe, white haired, mumbling into his fingertips as he scanned the mountain woods for shapes that moved between the limbs. Caliph had already begun formulating plans to hunt it down and kill it.

"It's unreal."

"It's very real," Sena whispered. "It's one of them."

Though she said more than she wanted to, her currently jumbled sense of reality made it mercifully incoherent.

All she could remember was that same scream echoing in the mausoleum as she had unlocked the *Cisrym Ta*. All her fearless rationality seemed to fall away in chunks. Her whole person felt like it was disintegrating along with her mind. Oblivion buckled the doors of reality, seeping out into a once logical world.

"What do you mean?" Caliph asked.

"I opened your uncle's book," she said quietly. "I lied and they know it."

"They? Who's they?" It was Caliph's turn to watch Sena come apart the way she had watched him in the graveyard.

"The Yillo'tharnah," she barely whispered.

"The what?"

She felt certain the creature had come for her, drawn by the book.

Outside, the monster let loose a horrid chilling shriek followed by a cackle that freshened her reserves of fear.

"See," Sena licked her lips and continued to whisper, "that's why I needed you . . . to open the book. Only I didn't love you in time."

Her smile looked crazy. It crossed the borders of sanity. Took on a reckless look—one that didn't care anymore, one that laughed at virtually everything.

Her expression frightened Caliph more than the creature clawing at the walls.

She stood up suddenly, smiling, her intentions all too clear. She headed for the stairs.

"Sena, sit down." He grappled her to the floor.

"Yeah. Fuck me," she whispered. Her hands fumbled with his belt. "It's what I do best."

Her breath smelled like brandy but Caliph knew she wasn't drunk. Her mouth went wild.

Caliph pinned her to the floor for her own protection. He refused to move. She changed personality again, screamed at him, kicked and fought, but he locked himself over her like a cage. She imagined him one of the crumbling stone guardians in Sandren.

In the end she stopped cursing and grew still.

"I hate you," she whispered. "I hate your damned logical mind."

An hour later she slept.

Caliph did not.

An inhuman gibbering noise came from the window and he saw her turn fitfully in her sleep.

Far away in Isca, Caliph heard an alarm horn sound. Its blare floated into the foothills and the creature outside grew quiet. More horns took up the note and carried it far above the blackness.

The High King had turned up missing.

ena woke quietly.

Her lids flicked open to see Caliph staring at her. He sat across the comfortless room with his arms resting on his knees. A band of light from the window marked his face like a welt.

"Didn't you sleep?" she asked.

"It stopped making noise a few hours before dawn."

Sena sat up. "I'm cold. Come warm me up."

Caliph sighed. His eyes made a circuit of the floor. He walked over to her.

"Feel how cold I am?"

Caliph nodded.

"How did you stay so warm?" She burrowed against him. A queer disavowal of the night before.

"We should get back," Caliph said. He pushed her gently away, repulsed by her variance.

The whole way back to the city, Sena cracked brittle jokes while Caliph watched people flee Isca on tractors and steam cars piled with possessions. When Caliph didn't respond she accused him of being grumpy.

He looked through her as though she were a curl of smoke from the farmsteads along the road. He saw behind her smile where men with enormous axes were herding furry pigs to slaughter.

A moment later a patrol of soldiers put an end to his self-absorbed metaphor and whisked the two of them back to Isca Castle.

AFTER their return, Sena lost track of Caliph.

As often happened, he disappeared abruptly into the unremitting political cauldron that cooked the insides of Isca Castle.

But today's level of activity was extreme even by wartime standards. More odd, it didn't seem to have anything to do with the previous night.

Sena watched as men in suits ushered Caliph toward the epicenter of an administrative stew. For a moment they patted his back, asked briefly if all was right and then got down to the business of thrusting dossiers and charts into his vacant hands while yelping highlights above the chatter.

Sena could tell something had happened during their time in the hills. Maybe it was something to do with Saergaeth. She would find out eventually. In the meantime she was simply too tired to care.

Caliph hurried off, surrounded by advisors and bodyguards and a constant, migrainous din.

Sena took the stairs, ascending the city's quintessential cupola, climbing wedges into the sky. She headed like a moth, despite her exhaustion, for the drab garret with the occult beacon no one else could see.

When she reached the room she stared out over the bleak mansions and hollow-eyed factories. The city was like one of the glyphs. So intricate, so vast in meaning. It seemed impossible to understand. She turned and looked at the book: red, fouled and indifferent.

She opened it. The cover folded back unhindered, mundanely submissive to her demands.

Her skin prickled like a weather prophet feeling electricity or something tighter than air. She gathered items: antiseptic, clean cloths, a bowl of water. Megan had given her the shylock two years ago as a contingency. In case she ever decided to carve her eyes. Sena found it at the bottom of her pack, tried it on, felt it move slightly like a leech adjusting its grip. It covered only her eyes.

She took it off and set it aside.

She opened a little wooden case. Inside was an instrument with chrome loops, opposable tunsia blades and an adjustable arm with a mirror the size of a coin. Sena looked into the tiny mirror where the dark scalpels hovered over her reflection.

Yella byūrn! What am I doing? Her stomach turned. She put the instrument down and looked at the *Cisrym Tạ.*

Black voluted glyphs spread profligate like curled legs, amphibious and strange. They wrapped thorny triple-jointed arms around her mind; clutched, jerked, teased and baited her.

Centric figures, bolide detonations in ink, swept out across the page in comet patterns. Stellar holocausts. Cosmic orgies. Transient metempsychosis: like sheet lightning, stuttering through ten thousand bodies in an instant, through clouds and rich celestial humors.

Sena's eyes raced, struggled to stay ahead of the darkness that devoured the tail of every symbol she understood. The inked pictures played tricks.

Dead things walked.

Suns burnt out amid cataclysmic trauma. Cold alien oceans sparkled and slithered with a million breeding things. Harsh light stabbed out of primeval mist, out of cells that were neither plant nor animal nor anything in between.

The *Cisrym Ta* might have been the sacral vade mecum for creatures capable of profound modulation. But there was too much of it. Too much in it.

Sena's pulpy head couldn't help abbreviating the abstruse concepts, shortening perfect structures into imperfection, substituting across the prevaricated line that separated beauty from horror.

Her brain, her body, in the context of the *Cisrym Ta*, was a fibrous cyst: temporal, momentary, riddled with lethal flaws. Already, on reflex, she had pulled a comforting shroud over the blinding concepts, coddling herself from a toxic rarefaction of truth.

She pushed the book away.

I can't avoid it. In moments I've lost centuries.

Words in Dark Tongue made sounds inside her skull. They searched for sustenance and found nothing.

I will fix my eyes, she thought. *I will master this thing.*

She picked the scalpel back up, made sure her bowl and rags were ready. Carefully, carefully, she began to cut into her eye.

She felt the blades touch her cornea, slide into it at an angle. The clear coat flopped up, granting access to the lens. Her movements were subtle, careful. She whispered as she went, using tiny bleeding capillaries to work the Unknown Tongue. She crafted facets with the double knife, cut inscriptions that would have made a miniaturist gape. There were numbers. There were shapes. Angles and circles and tiny triangles engraved on multiple layers of cornea. She cut her eye into thin sheets of film, put diagrams on various strata, sandwiched them together, compressed them.

She dabbed at her tears. An endless gush of fluid poured across her face. Finally she was done.

Now . . . the other eye.

After several more hours, throbbing in pain, she slipped the mask over her head. It was dark but the Inti'Drou glyphs still floundered in her brain. She concentrated on something simple, something capable of restoring her identity. She thought of Caliph and the way Prince Mortiman had looked at him.

SENA woke up blind. She could feel the mask working on the swelling. Like a smell-feast, the shylock was actually a more docile cousin of the scarlet horror. It was brown, silent and sleepy. It could be cut and sewn like a sheet of leather in order to fashion gloves or boots. This one had been hibernating in her pack for two years. She felt its gentle suction on her swollen eyes.

She fumbled for the bed. Caliph's side was still made, pillow undisturbed beneath the quilt. "Caliph?"

She was seeing things, bits of light that could not be light. The shylock kept her in darkness. *Am I hallucinating?*

She got up. She could tell where the fireplace was. She could see it, snagged against the wall like a tuft of cotton in a thicket. It moved. It was ephemeral. Its shadows seemed to breathe. The room swayed as if underwater. Sena stumbled and fell. She felt blood trickle down her cheek.

"Godsfire!" Her head hurt. Her bladder was going to explode. "Caliph?" Bluish impressions tracked across her cerebellum from the right. She turned as if toward a light, smacked her forehead on the bed. "Yella byūrn! Fuck!" She reached out, touched the wooden pillar, groped past it, trying to make sense of what she interpreted as sight. She tried to shut her eyes then cursed at her stupidity. She couldn't close her mind against the impressions even with the shylock clinging to her face. "Mother of Mizraim I have to pee!"

The shylock left its presence in her blood and forced her kidneys to work overtime. She wondered how long she had been asleep. *I can't make it!* She thought of the agonizing walk to the toilet.

Pastel colors rinsed her brain. She could see the bank of windows in Caliph's bedroom. She reached out, walked toward them, uncertain they were real.

One of the panes swung in and folded against the wall admitting a chilly mass of air, fresh with rural smells.

She undid her belt.

The ledge beyond the room was wide and deep and draped in cool blue. Diamonds of gold sparkled on the tower's skin as the sunlight crept east, dragging over rough stones, catching every chink and mortar line. The colors were bizarre. Too saturated. Too bright.

Below the castle wall, architecture snarled and stirred as part of some remote world seen through veils of dream. Her pants unsnapped on either leg and crumpled to the floor in leather folds. Thin metallic sounds and indistinct voices curled out of the Hold. Her mind bucked again at the realization that she was not seeing anything. *What if I fall?*

She climbed out onto the ledge, clothed only from the waist up and the knees down. She set her boots several feet apart and leaned back on her palms. Like one of the grotesques on Hullmallow Cathedral, she perched at the brink of disaster.

The cool air felt delicious; it mouthed her vulva and sent a tingle through her. She relaxed and allowed herself to foul the sky. Her boots grated. She moved backward on her palms, withdrawing into the room. She resnapped her pants, found the basin, washed and sat down.

She was dizzy. She thought about taking the shylock off but reconsidered. Although she wanted to try her new eyes on the *Cisrym Ta*, she would have to wait. Other sisters had warned to keep the shylock on for several days. She laid back across the bed, dreaming that the ceiling moved with impossible colors.

I can't sleep.

She got up and left the room.

General Yrisl passed her in the hall. He looked at her, assumed she couldn't see him and raised an eyebrow in what must have been a hint of scorn. He was in a hurry, still buttoning his shirt. Sena's brain saw everything: his torso, muscular but slightly flabby at the same time, white with the telltale sag of middle age. She dreamt past his shirt, through the fibers, caught a glimpse of something dark and twisted at the center of his belly. A twirl of ink. A shadow, small and indistinct, nested behind a thick patch of hair.

Only then did she recognize his faded resemblance to the tall gaunt forms of Mr. Naylor and his friends. His glassy eyes contained a redoubling significance, suddenly odious.

"General?"

He turned, surprised. "Yes, ma'am?"

"Nothing. I just wondered if it was you."

"Yes, ma'am. I have to hurry. The *Byun-Ghala* is leaving."

"Where is it going?"

"I'm sorry." He sounded sincere. "I'm afraid it's classified."

She let him go, terrified of the sudden symbology associated with him. *But was it real? Was it true?* She dreamed where he was going and picked a route that would let her watch him unobserved.

She avoided the main corridors, not wanting to be seen. Some crazy girl walking with a blindfold. She felt ridiculous.

She skirted through rooms and hallways, picking her way toward parts of the castle that did not see regular use. Finally she came to an oriel that overlooked the zeppelin deck. From here she could sense Caliph's luxurious airship ballooning over the huge expanse of concrete and old stone, casting pincushion shadows from its outspread spines.

Yrisl was marching across the field of masonry toward a body of knights whose huge ornate carapaces glittered with colors like emeralds and rust.

At the center of the knights she sensed Caliph leaning against a stack of chiseled gun-stones.

As the Blue General approached, Caliph seemed to levitate slowly like oil smoke in the frosty air. The knights shuffled. Some conversation took place. Then the whole party headed for the docking tower.

Sena still couldn't make sense of it. Had she imagined the mark on Yrisl? It confused her enormously. He had been less than six feet from the *Cisrym Tạ* on many occasions. It had rested in the high tower in plain sight. If he was from the Cabal, why had he not seized the book?

Her thoughts went back to the night it had disappeared from the desk in Caliph's bedroom only to reappear in the same place.

She sensed the party of knights had come out onto the tower roof, into thin sunlight. They were followed by Caliph and Yrisl. They boarded the *Byun-Ghala* while men in dark leather made adjustments to several new-looking weapons that jutted from the airship's belly.

Silvery gadgets with smooth, organic-looking segments, hoses and ornate gears hung from refitted turrets. Sena recognized the craftsmanship from other sources she had seen around the city as being (possibly) of Pplarian design.

Almost as soon as the bridge lifted away, the zeppelin's engines gave a slurred whine. Heavy fan blades poured air across the fins, dislodging the ship like an enormous bumblebee from some gruesome flower. It hovered, clumsy at first, moving in imperceptible increments, inches at a time.

It turned. It raised. Its turrets spun. Spines bristled. Guns shone. The blue pennant of the High King uncoiled, a silken lioncel, a serpent of cloth unwinding in the zeppelin's wake. Then the airship found itself between the castle's piled spears of stone. It no longer moved in inches or feet but sprang, bloated with sluggish violence, a bullfrog leaping out between towers, hauling its girth west.

Sena felt it go. A strange sensation of abandonment distilled within her. He hadn't even said good-bye. The image of him lounging against the cannonballs seemed frozen in her mind.

She made her way from the oriel to their bedroom, took a bath, brushed her teeth, drank a cup of coffee Gadriel had left by the door and brushed her teeth again.

She read the *Iscan Herald* with the shylock on, the only copy in the castle. She sensed her lukewarm bathwater funnel down the drain. It ebbed from the tub's enameled roses like rain. *I must be seeing,* she thought. *What else can this be if it isn't sight?*

But the bathtub seemed to breathe, the pages of the paper modulated in her hand. She felt the water in the pipes slipping down the drain. She followed it for a while.

There must be something wrong with the furnace. The pipes were cold. She used the *Herald* to start a fire. She left the room, fetched the *Cisrym Ta*, brought it back to bed. She got out her notebook and scribbled a page of notes: all with the shylock on.

Am able to see better than I thought. Will attempt to decipher part of a glyph with the shylock still on.

Yillo'tharnah seem to be following the book. I don't know how, but a corporeal manifestation nearly killed us at Nathan's mansion: a ꝏꝏꝏꝏꝏꝏ ꝏ![25] *Why? Are there Linshin'thn too? Are there limits to Their hierarchy?*

I assumed the One I bound at the Porch of Soth was alone.

---

[25] U.T. Approximate pronunciation: Cal'cr'Nok.

Am having nightmares. Shapeless things. I see insuperable slithering masses in the dark. I feel giddy all the time. Something is happening.

This glyph. This jellyfish glyph. I have no other name for it. It terrifies me for reasons I cannot describe. Ref: page 847 of C.T.

Cataclysm. Creation. Things I can't explain. Can't explain. Yella byūrn! It's like I've become a child again, without vocabulary to describe a thing!

One thing is certain. Nathan Howl was brilliant. I think his house is a transdimensional fortress. Something I can use. Not now. Not even in a month from now. But soon. Soon.

Find it funny how They (the Yịllo'tharnah) are trying to get in. I'm trying to get out and They're trying to get in. Each of us pressing against our respective side of the membrane. A case of greener grass? Or just a singular truism common to both our species: the need to explore, to conquer new territory. To learn, expand and grow. The need to create and destroy. The evolution of the inner beast. Becoming more of whatever it is we are. Creator, killer, philanthropist . . .

Just another natural increment in our progression. In the development of gods. They are gods. Not the deaf blind disconnected gods of Incense Street. They are waking gods. Undying. Planning gods. Proximate and looming.

SENA tucked the notebook between a pillow and her thigh. She picked up the *Cịsrym Tạ* and opened it to her mark. Just ahead was another passage about the Last Page.

She swore.

The Last Page of what?

She flipped to the back of the book. It ended like most books, abruptly. There was nothing special about the final page except one small thing.

Nathaniel Howl had written in his precise scholarly hand: *Ha! Clever Pun. And so like tattoos they now seem to me!*

Always another mystery.

Cameron had told her Nathaniel had gone crazy. Maybe it didn't mean anything at all.

She studied through lunch into late afternoon.

THE pages were smooth and cool. Like dead things, the old necromancer's hand had marked them up. She was starting there, with pencil and ink, with wide margins filled with notes and references.

"The jellyfish glyph."

Sena looked up, startled. An old man's voice had whispered the words. They scraped along the curves inside her ear, tracing from the outer edges in, sounding like the weird dry brush of a fingertip moving. A sensual exploration, analytic and at once perverse. There was no one in the room.

The words had been so clear. She had never verbalized them and had written the approximation of them in her notebook for the first time earlier today.

Could someone have been watching while she wrote?

Deeply disturbed, she set her studies aside and slipped out of bed. She checked the door first. It was shut tight. Feeling childish, she felt around under the bed. She wanted to remove the shylock, to see with her real eyes that she was alone. She opened the wardrobes, batted around jackets and shirts and dresses until she felt positive no one could be inside. She even checked the windows and the ledges for intruders. All she found was birdlime and chilly air.

I'm not going crazy, she told herself.

This is holomorphy.

Perhaps the Eighth House had composed an argument against her. Perhaps Giganalee could send glamours from leagues away . . .

Sena waited for the voice to come again but it did not.

For roughly one week Sena was alone in Isca Castle. Caliph did not return and Gadriel either truly did not know where he had gone or masterfully hid his knowledge.

Her eyes were black and purple, tinged with green. Badly bruised, she still slept with the shylock at night.

No one seemed capable of telling her where Caliph had gone. The weather turned cold. Though the castle boilers had been fixed, she had the servants keep a fire roaring in the bedroom and a thermal crank besides.

The servants snickered. They told her this was not cold. Cold had not even come to Stonehold yet. There was frost, yes. There was snow in the mountains. But the crops still stood in the fields, defying the shift in season. The corn stood out to dry, right down to the wire according to promises in the almanac. Every year the Duchy held its breath and hoped the austromancers were correct.

Sena shivered under blankets and quilts. The maids, the butlers, even Gadriel seemed to have abandoned her. She started drinking to keep warm.

She started drinking to bullwhip the coarse black ink strokes twisting through her brain. She could feel them cutting into the meat inside her skull. She started drinking to dull the pain.

In the dark, she whispered to her bottles. Behind the black glass, lutescent liquid hung in suspended animation. Inked labels with recent dates denoted when each of the delicate sherries had been sentenced to life below the cork. She regarded the bottles as tombs. Prisons that kept out light.

She drank for the sake of the sherry. She drank to free them. In the twinkling blackness, she drank while watching a bottle she had flung from the neck, burst against the hearth. It shattered with a triumphant explosion of tiny shards and pale juice. Each splinter of glass, each droplet, they glistened midair, turning slowly, exultant. She drank in celebration.

She knelt down as if at a grave and patted the wet floor like she might have patted the place Nis' ashes were buried. When she lifted her hand, a ringlet of razor-edged glass dangled from her thumb. It hung there like a piece of strange jewelry, like a parasite. She took a drink and pulled it out, watched her blood ooze from the slit. It seemed too dark, nearly black against her cold white flesh. *Like ink*, she thought. *As I move, so moves the quill of the gods.* She smeared her thumb in fantastic random patterns over the floor. "They will not hold me," she said, laughing. "They will not lay me in some catacomb to ferment." She dragged her gushing thumb in ever more erratic circles. "They will not use me!" she shrieked. "As a tool—"

Two of the servants found her and dragged her from the glass-strewn room.

They bandaged her hand. They swept, mopped and swept again. They got out a clean charmeuse robe with lace that plunged past her waist. They tied it around her and put her in bed. Then they took away her bottles and left her in the dark.

The darkness thickened into layers of wax. Layers of murk and loneliness and irritating fear. She felt herself suffocating: an insect below a dripping candle. The servants slept. Solitary guards rasped and scraped through the empty hallway beyond her door.

Sena pulled her knees up under the covers. The lacy robe barely covered her ass. She held herself for warmth while the castle's silence tore into her. This, she decided, was a deeply haunted place.

I'm not mad. I'm not mad.

She found herself watching the tapestries, hung in silent folds, animated by the coals in the fireplace. The coals cast nimble black demons off every piece of furniture. She stared for so long that when it finally came she couldn't tell if it was just another illusion.

In a small terrible hour, like a plume of soot, an ancient scholar's robe rose on the draft and dragged across the floor. Dreadfully thin and hunched it sat in the tall carven chair near the door and whispered of the immutable past.

I'm not mad. But she did not sleep.

In the morning, bleary and wasted, she capitulated with the specter's demand and opened up the grimoire. Her life had became its pages.

SEVERAL days later, she noticed the *Herald*. It was her only link to events beyond the castle.

The newspaper told her King Lewis had been arrested the same day Caliph had left and that he was being detained in Isca Castle, a captive guest in one of the towers.

A peculiar insult, the article validated her recent feelings of debarment. She thrust the article at Gadriel and demanded an explanation. The seneschal glanced at her eyes as he did every morning and quickly looked away. He demurred pathetically, presented her with a choice of northern coffees.

His disavowal put her in a rage.

She threw the *Herald* down in front of him and screamed. But the High Seneschal was a formidable adversary. In response to her tantrum, he offered her cream.

Recognizing the iron wall for what it was, Sena ordered him from the room.

THAT night, she strapped her utility belt around her waist, tugged on her soft black boots and slipped her kyru in its sheath. King Lewis would be well guarded. She closed her eyes and the colors returned, guiding her. She knew the way.

Time became something she could gloss before it happened. She could see castle guards before they turned the corner, saw their numbers like halos in the air. Probabilities. Angles. Algorithms of the next.

Her vision didn't compute in three dimensions anymore. It was ghosted with time, future happenings all around her. Sometimes they blurred where probabilities split, made whole corridors hazy with risk. But if she waited, silent and safe, things changed, pathways opened, unpredictability passed away and she could move again. Pale cones of perception spread out from people's eyes, both current and future. All she had to do was walk or stand outside their line of sight.

She left the High King's bedroom through a window. Since her outburst, Gadriel had placed sentries just outside the door . . . in case she felt ill again, he said, or needed assistance.

Sena smiled at his pathetic attempt to cage her and stretched for the cornice above the window, touched it and left the bedroom empty in her wake. She moved quickly, like an arachnid, fingers sticky with holomorphy. She was blindfolded but she could see. She sensed Lewis in the towers above, behind a locked and brightly guarded door. He sat by himself, play-ing with a stack of ivory plaques, fortune-telling devices once trusted by the general public, now sold in Three Cats only to amuse.

Sena saw the guards as well. Her new eyes made everything easy. She re-entered the castle through an open window twenty stories up into the night. It was a lightless side room and she paused to listen to the men out-side the door.

Her eyes were well, but she still wore the shylock. She had discovered a new use. With a single word she could pinch it, goad it with a cantrip and the thing would tighten to her face, appendages that normally hung like decorative leather straps writhed. She felt it take a deeper bite. Blood oozed below the mask, ran in perfect painted lines along her cheek.

She spoke, robbed the creature of its meal, forced it to draw more sus-tenance as she burnt her own holojoules in prosecution of the air. Logic twisted. The Unknown Tongue sentenced six castle guards to coma.

Sena opened the door and stepped over their sleeping bodies. The shy-lock squirmed. It took only what it needed then stopped. She bent to re-cover a heavy ring of keys.

Beyond King Lewis' door she could tell the coals were dying, dribbling purple light across the floor.

She pulled the bolt back with a loose clank and the thick portal opened slowly, heavy timbers floating on oil.

Lewis looked up to see her standing in the door frame.

He scowled, obviously trying to make sense of it. She imagined the extraordinary image: a blond woman, seemingly blind, the fallen guards, the little trails of red oozing from her mask.

Encircling her was an oversized belt that holstered her sickle and other tools. In her right hand was a potion, a decanter she had just pulled out. It was made of glass and filled with something red.

She saw Lewis toy with the idea of taking her hostage but the gory potion and her mask seemed to distract him.

"I wouldn't," she said. "I'm the High King's witch."

"So I've read in the papers. Midnight snack?" He gestured to the de-canter.

"Something like that. Holomorphic provisions."

"Ah." Lewis lifted his eyebrows and then gestured to the bed. "I'm afraid I'm short on furniture, but please . . . sit."

Sena placed herself on the edge of the mattress, one knee draped over the other, perched like something weightless. She dangled the decanter between her fingers.

"It's dark in here."

Lewis chuckled. "Try taking that..." he noticed the blood tears again, "... mask off."

Sena came to the point.

"I want to know why you're here."

Lewis smiled. "You're not here officially are you?"

"I'm not asking," said Sena.

Lewis glanced out at the incapacitated guards. "No. I suppose you're not. Pretty as a seashell though. Maybe my friends contracted you through Skellum to clean me up?"

"What friends?"

Lewis only chuckled. He seemed prepared for this, ready for some assassin to end his journey through the courts. Sena realized that he wouldn't talk, that she was wasting time. She liked him. She liked his false resignation, his sense of humor, the calculations she could feel him making underneath it all. And yet, she let the decanter slip from her hand. Delicate facets shattered on impact, a sloppy crunch that burst against the floor like a bloodsucking arachnid made of glass.

Already, her survey of the *Cisrym Tạ* had augmented her skills. She recycled Caliph's mind-reading formula from the library in Desdae and pared it down, added to it and pared it down again.

King Lewis' mind went blank and Sena rummaged in it, semimethodically, as if searching a head of lettuce for bugs. She found all kinds of things. She knew why Lewis' chest hurt.

It had started after a squad of Iscan military personnel had escorted him forcefully back to Isca Castle. Alani's men had discovered his alliance with the Pandragonians.

Lewis himself had helped smuggle the solvitriol blueprints out of the country.

But he hadn't confessed or denied. He had simply stood, chest hurting, wishing that he hadn't been caught.

Lewis knew the Pandragonians and so Sena knew them too. She saw them clearly in his head. Bjorūn Amphungtạl and Msgr. Pratt.

She knew how they had stopped on their way to Isca Castle on the second of Kam, pausing at Kennan Keep to meet with Roric Feldman. They had moored. They had disgorged great piles of weapons and supplies onto Saergaeth's new flight deck. They had signed contracts and promised to help remove Caliph from the throne in exchange for favorable trade agreements once Saergaeth took the throne.

And that was Lewis' secret: that Pandragor and Yorba and several other countries were watching Stonehold's civil war with vulture eyes. That other countries had become intimately involved in Stonehold's civil war and were counting on Caliph Howl to lose.

The ambassadors that had flown to Isca Castle had only ever been a ruse. Deals had already been cut with the Shrądnæ Sisterhood, with Saergaeth, with Peter Lark.

David's set of blueprints had already been sent south.

And now Pandragor would be sending zeppelins, actual troops to bolster Saergaeth's mighty fleet.

For the first time, Sena understood with sudden numbing fear, the precarious position of Caliph's reign. The impossibility of any chance that he would succeed. She swore in a whisper. *Saergaeth was going to win!*

Sena withdrew from Lewis' brain, lobotomized the memory of her, locked the door and crept spiderlike back to her bedroom. The guards would wake, confused to find the shattered vial, and that would be her only trace.

Sena did not sleep that night. She pondered instead how she might use the *Cisrym Tą* to help save her king.

CHAPTER
38

When Ghoul Court is cleaned, it is like doing a thorough brush across the front of the city's teeth, the visible gunk comes off. But the more conniving criminal element sinks further out of sight. Sena sees them with her new eyes, waiting in Isca's deepest cavities and cracks. She dreams of them at night, moaning creatures in the sewers, far below the opera house, bellowing a nameless emotion.

She can no longer talk about what she sees. Her eyes are healing, the corneal layers gelling into a single lens, a single filter that delivers transcendent messages to her mind. She cannot talk about what she sees because there are no words to describe. Only old words. Words that call things as they used to be, not as they are now. Once she saw a chair, a gas lamp, a wine bottle. Now she realizes that what she saw was really only what she thought.

Adumbrations.

She used to see sketches of meaning, instantaneous renders of objects flickering through her mind. She could categorize them quickly, use them as signposts, directional cues. But now she understands that it wouldn't have mattered how many adjectives she attached to the wine bottle, or how closely she might have studied it with her old eyes. Even if she had measured it, weighed it, calculated its yaw pitch and roll, its potential kinetic energy, its tensile strength . . .

A textbook full of wine bottle statistics would have still been an approximation. A pile of different disconnected thoughts.

Now she sees. She sees the whole bottle. She sees its layers unified, interpreted and as it is. She sees it emotionally, potentially, with sunlight streaming through, casting colors and shadows. She sees it in every possible light. Every angle, temperature and locale. She sees it physically, every molecule, every particle in its composition. She sees it chronologically before it is a bottle, being made into a bottle, as a bottle now. She sees it broken, shattered, molten, every kind of death. She sees it spiritually, *diagramed in ether, its eternal planning in a thought. She sees it lovely, as a sentimental gift, a talisman, embodying the memory of a celebration, an anniversary, a first drink, a last drink, a love, the method of seduction, a habit, something forgotten or ignored, a bauble, an implement of cruelty and limitless torture. She can still call it a bottle. She remembers the old word. But the word is empty and cannot pass any of the bottle's meaning as she sees it now, nothing of the true thing.*

And it is not just the bottle that she sees this way. It is everything in the world.

She sees all objects not as symbols but as they are, whole, unified, with nothing lost in translation between her consciousness and her eyes. She sees the thing, all things. Directly. And this, she understands suddenly, is also the power of the Cisrym Ta.

Inverted.

She has realized. The problem with other books is their length and imprecision. So many sentences, ideas, chapters . . . all tied together perhaps, but fragmented . . . hidden, buried in the pages. The concepts must be explained, diagramed, with paragraphs, examples, forcing the words to do their job, to communicate clearly all the steps of cooking veal, or building a centrifuge, or getting along with one's lover. And in the end, there are bits that stick, like a red flower in the grass, the main idea or several key ingredients. The mind sorts through the pile left behind, the chunks it can remember.

But not in the Cisrym Ta.

In the Cisrym Ta, the Inti'Drou glyphs are so much more than blueprints for systems, for worlds. They are not just symbols on a page. Inti'Drou glyphs are nothing less than the objects they describe. Not pictograms. The math of the thing is there, trapped, twisted into īrlian ink. The math is alive. Compressed. Like in a spring. Undo the latch, release the mechanism, and the glyph unfolds, into planets, into creatures, into stars and subdimensions. The glyphs are more than real. They are reality.

And the glyphs are whole, on one page, captured in a glance. No chapters to sort through. No metaphors or diagrams or grammar used at all. The initial confusion she faced between hundreds of subjects and objects has gelled, cleared. With her new eyes she sees the raw ethereal information contained in particles of light. In ink. All of it together. Together. Precise.

Words in Hinter, words in Trade, haunt her through the night. Torture her with their constraints. She dreams of definitions that do not fit.

But there are some words, strange, cooling words, like moon sweat, that dapple her pia mater during sleep, running molten cold through her sulci, soaking deep into her brain. They sound smooth . . .

Sslîa. Ooil-Üauth. Ķhloht.

They are giving her direction. They are telling her what to do. And despite her desire to help Caliph she finds herself instead looking out across the world, perhaps because the facets of her eyes derive from cuts meant for hunting. But she has modified the angles, used the Cisrym Ṭa to adjust the purpose of her eyes. It is safe to say that no one in the Sisterhood has eyes like Sienæ Iilool.

In the autumn chill, she sits at night, facing south, staring through her bedroom wall. She looks from her vanity through Blękton, South Fell and Maruchine, through phantasmagoric drainpipes in the substructure of Ghoul Court.

She sees the slaughter of the muck spies, the venting of blood into cavernous byways. The Lua'grǫc are cleaning up. The flawless are moving. The huge maggot bodies she associates with the attack on her cottage are abandoning Isca's drains.

Yrisl will be the only muck left, protected by the castle and his loyalty to Caliph Howl.

The Lua'grǫc are not angry with him though they would kill him if they could. Yrisl does not answer the dispatches they have sent him.

But the Lua'grǫc are removed from human emotion. They would kill him out of utility rather than rage.

The city watch now recognizes the Lua'grǫc half-breed spies. The mucks are of no further use. So they are eaten, bones and all, rich nutrients ingested, the blubber and talons of the cannibals fortified preparatory to the journey ahead.

Only the flawless survive.

But they are not a vengeful race. For them, carnage is holomorphy, tactics and something close to joy or delight. They have no rituals for their dead, no tombs or graveyards. The dead are eaten without thought as a matter of course.

Sena watches through the wall, and begins to understand them as the flawless grow fat and sink from Ghoul Court into deep reservoirs and cold abyssal bourns that gush or leak south below the world crust. She begins to understand them as ancient organisms that follow routes like salmon where the water has not seen sun for many thousand years.

The Lua'grǫc abandon Old Duny's brumal backwash, migrating south into less frostbitten waters. Sena sees them course through tunnels across the convoluted miles. Under the continent's blind-making shadow, their journey will take several months to complete. But Sena has read about them, knows that eventually they will find their way by touch or sense of smell or some more primitive perception no human ecologist has ever cat-alogued or named.

In the end, the legendary Seas of Yǫloch will welcome them home; they will pour their bodies in, mingling with slurry spilt from culverts older than the Duchy of Stonehold. They will drizzle out of sewer sys-tems designed by the slaver race before the advent of the hexapala's eight thousandth year. And for a while they will be at home in olden structures built up in the deep, waiting for word to come from Ŭlung where the last of the true Lua'grǫc, the last of the true flawless dwell.

So this is what it's like, *she thinks.* This is what it means to be Sslîą . . .

SENA *orders a servant to buy two crows in Octul Box and bring them to the high tower garret. It is time she did something. Stonehold is the only place she has to lay her head and she knows acutely, since rifling Lewis' brain, that Caliph is not winning.*

The black wisp of soot that haunts her, tells her what to do. But first, like all good holomorphs, she decides . . . she insists on running a proof.

Sena locks the door. The servant has come and gone. A large cage hanging from the rafters contains a pair of rooks. They blink angrily and grouse for space. They will save her badly bruised eyes; she has left the shylock in her room.

As she moves, the birds' agitation increases. A sporadic drizzle of sable feathers touches the floor. She does not attempt to soothe them.

She stands before a blackboard and makes the calculations, scrib-bling out the numbers she will translate into words. As the chalk moves she begins to whisper, the sky outside begins to turn. Her eyes notice it as if from miles away, vast gouts of chocolate stratosphere and sapphirine vapor rotating like toilet water centered on Isca's tallest spire.

She sees the streets, the pavement nymphs and worm gang members and gadabouts from Winter Fen to Ironside who stop to marvel at the snail shell of cloud. But when little fingers of lightning begin to play the city's cables like discordant strings, when the lines that carry short sup-plies of power begin to lap the wind and a fine gray sleet begins to fall, she sees the rubbernecking end. People run for cover.

Sena opens the Cįsrym Tạ. Her vocal cords are incapable of pronounc-ing any of the Inti'Drou glyphs. She must dilute them, take parts of them and transpose them with the Unknown Tongue. Something she can use. Even so, its primacy is extant.

She speaks ạ word and both rooks die in an explosion that splashes the floor. Her tongue moves, knocking out words made of numbers made of blood. They are brighter and darker than the Unknown Tongue. They are smoother. They are pure. She cannot reduce them further any more than she can use a stick to draw a sunset in the dirt.

Her incantation pours several different algorithms into one; then puts her argument in place.

It is a proof so she follows all the rules, doesn't cut corners, makes everything painfully clear.

The test she has chosen is the equivalent of tipping a dart with an unknown chemical and hurling it at a creature in a cage. After it is done, she will wait and watch, morbidly, because she doesn't know exactly what the Cisrym Ta's concoction will do.

Her conscience troubles her minutely in a purely scientific way. She has to know. So she aims her missile at a seemingly overeager volunteer, a target she has been saving all her venom up for years.

Sena speaks and her lips launch the invisible and ancient bolt, hurling it beyond the Greencap Mountains, across the Valley of Eloth, into the Country of Mirayhr. Her aim is perfectly precise, pointed at a parody of family that has so often made her choke. With long-anticipated retribution, with angst grown bitter as a root, she spits her dart at Megan.

ALANI knew everything.

He knew how carefully Caliph had planned this war. He knew how the bodies from Ghoul Court had been dressed in zeppelin uniforms and laid at the site of the *Orison*'s crash. He knew how the timing had been so critical, perfectly synchronized with the departure of Bjorūrn Amphungtạl's airship from Isca. King Lewis could be arrested and imprisoned but Mr. Amphungtạl was a diplomat: far beyond the reach of Stonehold's criminal system. He was untouchable.

Alani imagined Amphungtạl's smile as he bid Caliph good-bye the evening before his flight left. How he must have relished the fact that the blueprints had been recovered, that Caliph Howl was doomed and that he, Bjorūrn Amphungtạl, was escaping via airship just before calamity struck! But such was not the case.

In clear dawn, Mr. Amphungtạl's zeppelin was brought down under a hail of gunfire. Its gasbags were rent. Its luxurious cabin was riddled with holes. It crashed near Clefthollow in broad daylight to the amazed eyes of townsfolk and soldiers stationed below. There were no survivors.

The news rocked the Duchy and spread south: that a Pandragonian ambassador had been fired on, murdered as the papers said, killed ruthlessly

and illegally by a Stonehavian airship. But the airship that killed Mr. Amphungtal was not part of the High King's fleet. It was a sky shark flying
the colors of Saergaeth Brindlestrøm.

Alani smiled.

Caliph had made it impossible for Pandragor to publicly support Saergaeth in Stonehold's civil war. He could do nothing about the munitions
and supplies that the Pandragonians had already delivered, but there would
be no southern zeppelins in Saergaeth's fleet. The war was back to being
fair. As fair as it would ever be.

Alani and his men had landed behind enemy lines after shooting down
the southern ship and moved swiftly to the next stage of Caliph's multi-
phase plan.

But despite Alani's pride in a mission well done, when he reached
Miskatoll, his hope faded. Like reading ahead in a novel, he knew what
was going to happen. He could skip all the intervening chapters of pointless violence and exposition and know with the solid assurance that his
many years of experience provided, that nothing Caliph Howl could do
would change the inevitable.

Alani omitted this grim personal assessment in his note to the High
King and wrote simply that he had discovered the date and time of Saer-
gaeth's main attack. He sent this (and only this) information back to the
High King.

CALIPH received the note within two hours, pulling it from the exhausted hawk's leg. Alani had cranked the tiny golden screws on the
chemiostatic governor in its brain to maximize speed.

Day after tomorrow, read the note, *second of Thay. Saergaeth will be
coming.*

Caliph's eyes wrestled with the crumpled hazy darkness of the western mountains at the limit of his sight. He took tablets from a red-coated
physician on the *Byun-Ghala* who assured him they would moderate the
pain. He chewed them like candy but his discomfort never flagged. His
stomach gurgled with acid.

He was headed home.

After visiting his generals, ferrying the prince to Tentinil, completing a
long schedule of meetings, Caliph was finally headed home. He had made
every decision he could make.

He shredded the note from Alani in his palm and let it fall like the
first snowflakes from the *Byun-Ghala*'s outer deck.

The zeppelin powered south, clearing a geothermic swamp and gliding
over a jumbled pile of hills gone bald with autumn brown.

In the fast-moving zeppelin, the landscape never stayed the same. The drumlins that had just replaced the swamp receded in minutes like diseased gums, exposing the blackened incisors of Murkbell and Growl Mort, basking in their own slaver by the sea. The industrial districts offered drooling abscesses that outpoured spew as yellow as infected pus. Caliph could see the grime-encrusted seawall, the arches of the great arcade. Like a sleeping dark but restless thing, Isca seemed to slither into view. But Caliph didn't wonder if it was worth saving.

The *Byun-Ghala* motored in quickly and moored on the deck at Isca Castle. He instructed Yrisl to deploy all remaining engines on the city's western flank. Not the trundling lightweights . . . but the juggernauts. The big heavies.

As the airship docked, Yrisl jumped the gap, not waiting for the plank, and ran without pretense to obey.

Caliph *did* wait for the plank. He was exhausted and wanted only one thing: two hours. Two hours of sleep.

He headed to his room.

When he entered he found Sena looking wild.

She was draped in the tub, hair pulled up, covered with bubbles, cradling a bottle.

"You're late," she slurred.

"Really?" He pulled off his gloves and boots. "By whose clock?" He had already noticed her eyes.

"Mine." Her voice was repugnantly wanton. "Come fuck me." The bottle slipped, disgorged its blush into the bath.

The radiator was boiling and the bedroom felt like a roasting pit. Caliph pulled off his coat. He twisted a knob that isolated the room from the rest of the boiler's circulatory system.

Her eyes!

Caliph walked toward the tub, speechless.

They were dazzling and awful. Ringed with bruises and glowing in shadow: molten blue. The closer he got the more he saw, little flashes, tiny engravings that caught the light. They were exquisite, without a pupil. Pure blue. The iris had grown shut. Caliph was horrified. Her eyes looked like jewels.

Sena stumbled from the tub. She nearly fell but Caliph caught her by the arm. Her towel hung from a nearby chair. He jerked it free and draped it over her shoulders.

She bit her lip as if in concentration and made it to the bed.

Her body smelled of perfume, soap and wine, glossy with the creamy lace of bubbles gathered on her skin. Her form unrolled, escaped the towel's rubric. Caliph gazed at the gleaming provocative compilation of her parts. He felt disjunct, as if part of him was still standing on the *Byun-Ghala* staring at war charts. But her topography mapped a place far removed from anything that reeked of war. A rolling golden landscape. Left shoulder dipping sleekly into waist. The supple hollow where her skin grew taut across the pelvic arch.

Caliph ran his fingers over her. She stretched at his attention, slid her legs along each other with the soft whisper of skin.

Maybe in the morning she wouldn't remember him kissing her like he was starving for her mouth. Maybe in the morning they would talk and sort things out. She wouldn't be drunk. She would explain her eyes. He would apologize for leaving her without good-bye. Maybe she would forgive him and he would forgive her and she would tell him, finally, that their love wasn't something base; that they weren't just a pair of junkies whipped by what they craved or a set of people using one another for comfort or power or anything else.

Caliph trembled and held her like something on the verge of being lost, like something irreplaceable that he couldn't save or hold onto tightly enough. Afterward he cried.

Sena woke up alone. Meetings and war formed her primary suspects. She didn't bother getting out of bed.

Last night remained a blur. She smiled, pulled a heavy shadow toward her and opened the *Cisrym Tạ*. The day passed quietly with the knowledge that she had sent an ancient ball of blackened numbers like a meteor into Skellum Hall. If Megan couldn't or wouldn't do it, she knew the Eighth House would soon dispatch a qloin. Retribution was inevitable.

During the past few days, Sena had killed things, used a vast amount of holojoules to drape the castle in a veil. Her eyes could not penetrate the Eighth House and she hoped the inverse was also true. She kept the shylock close at hand.

In the evening, a servant brought her dinner and a bottle of ridiculously expensive sherry. She hardly touched the meat. She took the bottle to the window and stood looking at the distant west. Since she had been in Lewis' head, tenuous loyalties had begun to blossom in her chest, something she had never felt before, a weak and unfounded brand of nationalism. It seemed ridiculous. Her allegiance had always been to no one but herself.

She flicked her kyru out, cut the foil below the lip and popped the cork. The smell of Stonehold wafted from the bottle's throat. She wiped the top and poured a taste of her new country, her new home.

Her eyes clawed through the mountains—past the war, but parliament, all of Skellum, remained dark. She could sense the chaos, sense the Sisterhood changing hands. She guessed her proof had been a raging success. Now all that remained was to find a way to use what she had learned to help Caliph win this war!

Sena swallowed two ounces and poured herself another glass. *Stonehold will be my home,* she thought.

A shadow in the room whispered to her, urging her to lug the *Cisrym Tạ* from its perch, open it and begin to read.

* * *

THAT night, winter fell like an anvil. From Kjnardag's glittering slopes a cold snap stabbed south and crackled in the Iscan Bay. Snow descended. A parasitic host bedaubed the north with grotesque white.

Cold inveigled every cranny of the city. Steeples, bathrooms and bedrooms of the poor became its nests. Buckets of frozen night soil were tossed from door stoops of tenements devoid of plumbing. They bobbed, half cones of solid filthy ice, thudding dully along fouled concrete tunnels. The watch dumped chemicals in the sewer to keep them mostly liquid.

Caliph looked out from his study windowsill that had draped impossibly during the night. All across the skyline surreal sculptures drooled, white as frosting, defying gravity in a bake shop of the mad.

As predicted, when Isca's stench had been dulled by snow, when things seemed almost sanctified and suddenly still, all-out war erupted on the western plains.

Word reached Caliph for the second time, a correction from Alani confirming that airships were lifting out of hangars in the border keeps far away: one day early. Irony of ironies, he attended one last meeting. Then, by hawk and word of mouth, he disseminated to his generals the signal that would finally put his plan in motion.

He felt numb.

Vaguely, he became aware of transitions taking place in the streets below the castle.

People couldn't flee. Instead, they braced themselves and hunkered down, cracking un-laughed-at jokes in order to distance themselves from outright hysteria. He could see Octul Box from the parapet, where grocers' shelves sold bare by half past six and storefronts closed as owners hurried home.

People changed. Priorities about-faced. There were no demonstrations at Shærzac University, no more antiwar sentiment in the major press. Zeppelins. A countless host of zeppelins was coming and everybody knew it. Chemical bombs would fall on the capital of Stonehold, on Hullmallow Cathedral, on Cripple Gate, and Dimult Hall. Terror and destruction would mar the ancient statues at Shærzac University and kill the helpless in the slums of Gorbür Dayn.

Of course there were factions that still insisted a peaceful transfer of power could be achieved through several rather optimistic channels. They published rushed articles in flyers and held rallies in tiny bistros with an attendance of half a dozen souls. But their rhetoric had become the lunatic fringe and it drowned quickly in the tumult of a rising indignant mass. People were incensed by Saergaeth's attack.

How dare he? How dare he attack Isca! The capital of Stonehold?

While the citizenry of Isca voiced their outrage, the military turned abstract anger into tangible force.

Caliph left Isca by zeppelin at seven fifty-six on the morning of the advance. He and a crew of twenty airmen headed west.

Boys in black flight uniforms tumbled across the decks, winding up the nickel-plated Pplarian guns. They adjusted slides, bolts, and loosened various clamps with ratchets, pulled safety pins that prevented rotation and fine-tuned a variety of other obscure settings on the clawlike turrets.

Caliph had sent word to Klơ, thanking him.

Klơ had sent eight strange cannon that Caliph divided judiciously among Isca's fleet of forty. One he had harnessed to the *Byun-Ghala*. The rest he placed on his fastest ships.

Their long slender barrels gleamed with alien elegance, vaguely phallic. Glittering hoses coupled compression units to six-inch bores that conducted a unique shell down the weapon's length.

Ammunition was limited.

Twenty shots per gun. The shells, like strange silvery seeds nested in racks to the loader's right flank. Pointed at both ends and screwed together at their meridian, the shells were designed to break in halves after launch. Once the twentieth shot was fired, the cannon would be reduced to decoration, worthless until more of the special ordnance arrived.

Unfortunately, brigs from Mortūrrm had sunk a Pplarian frigate carrying just such a load. A second shipment was not likely to arrive until the war with Saergaeth had become a matter of historical debate.

Caliph gazed at the twenty alien bullets with a sinking feeling. He wasn't counting on one hundred sixty Pplarian shells winning this war.

The *Byun-Ghala* slid west, following the Trịll Hills that separated the mud pots to the north from the village of Bụrt. A thousand feet below and receding fast, brown lanes chugged with gray shapes. Steam engines, horses and carriages. Small platoons of local men stood in formation in the village square.

Caliph aimed one of the railing-mounted spyglasses and discovered they were armed with swords, pitchforks and probably a handful of chemical grenades. They were local militia lacking uniforms or armor. Some of their fellows loped along trails presumably hidden at ground level, darting under leafless trees that hardly camouflaged them from the sky.

They were getting ready.

But Bụrt cowered in the folded hills eight miles west of Isca. And if Saergaeth made it to Bụrt, Caliph knew nothing else would stop him.

In the cold air over Glụmwood, Caliph squinted, checked charts and finally made out at nearly twenty-five miles just exactly what he was up against. Tiny flecks of red had begun to resolve against the hazy western chalkboard of the sky. Saergaeth's zeppelin fleet numbered one hundred thirty-four according to the latest intelligence.

As the intervening miles shortened, the young soldiers on the deck looked solemnly west. Saergaeth's cloud of measles swelled to the size of ruby-bellied reed flies, then cherries and, finally, they looked like great crimson balloons filled with blood.

Saergaeth had dyed his entire fleet red.

The crew began to take turns looking through the spyglass. They smoked nervously and peered into the lens.

One of the men cursed and grinned. He read the numbers painted on the taut skins and started calling them out. Caliph was looking too. He could see the enemy airmen walk across somehow hostile decks, smoke and look east through similar spyglasses. Caliph felt awed by the resolve. All around him, his men were ready to die and Saergaeth's aeronauts were strange mirrors or doppelgangers.

The landscape below drifted in pastel grays, surreal and quiet except for five choratium horrors plowing through the snow. The Iscan heavies were heading west, ordered to provide ground support for the High King's tiny fleet.

The *Byun-Ghala* had caught up with the rest of the airships. It slid between a pair of leviathans, a spiny minnow between goliath pike. Airmen on the other ships flashed signal lights in salute as the High King's tiny dirigible sped past.

A condensation trail arced suddenly into the sky, launched from one of the Iscan heavies. Like a crayfish darting in clear water, it left an organic muddy-looking trail. The projectile reached its zenith over a cavalry of light Iscan engines and plummeted past them into Saergaeth's ranks of heavy foot. It detonated remote catastrophe. Orange smoke surged like a sudden mushroom. An exclamation point above imperceptible carnage that served to mark the beginning.

Saergaeth's array was highly visible now. Floating from the Greencap Mountains with a kind of fatuous malignancy. Perhaps Miskatoll had built more. By Caliph's estimate, nearly two hundred zeppelins darkened the sky, many nearly half a mile long.

They bristled with weapons and spines.

Faint concussions echoed across the plains as the first artillery burst from flight decks and engines on the ground. Legions of infantry and horse marched in eccentric, primitive formations between the lumbering machines. They made easy targets against the white fields.

From launch decks and skyhooks, one-man gliders slipped into the air. They leapt from massive leviathans like a swarm of papery bees. Powered by a single cell and one propeller that its pilot engaged only occasionally to gain speed, the agile gliders dominated the sky around their hives.

They wheeled and banked in helical twists, swooped and darted, serving up high-velocity dismemberment with trundle guns. A frenzy of saw-toothed blades crisscrossed the sky and unfurled bloody, seemingly random paths.

The Iscan zeppelins scattered as Saergaeth's massive fleet pounded east.

Caliph's legs felt numb as he watched. It was a dreadful, graceful and utterly ferocious aerial ballet. Steel balls hissed past the observation deck, fired from a host of giant tubes.

Caught in the sights of an oncoming sky shark, the *Byun-Ghala* pitched suddenly, evasive maneuvers executed without warning from the pilot.

Bottles of single malt slid from a buffet in one of the staterooms and shattered on the floor. One man, not hooked to his tether, fell, slid across the deck and slipped through the railing.

Caliph looked to where he had vanished with a horrified expression.

There wasn't time to scream.

Caliph turned away mechanically. He helped his men reload the Pplarian gun. He checked his tether, tugged it several times just to be sure and donned a pair of leather-clad earmuffs that would help muffle the sound.

The gunner made hand signals, scrutinized his sights and then pulled an enormous floor lever. Pumps began repressurizing the tanks even as the cannon fired.

The gas that propelled the bullet produced enough recoil to rock the entire airship hard to port. A faint purple glow traced the shell's wake as if some kind of plating on the bullet was burning off from friction with the barrel or the air.

Caliph coughed on a dozen odious chemicals.

A rolling boom filled the sky as the Pplarian shell went supersonic seemingly after the fact. Caliph watched the purple trail until the bullet found its mark. As designed, it broke in two releasing its unique orgonomic power. Charged ions and orgone manipulated through holomorphy filled the air.

A sudden electrical impulse found its way over one hundred fifty footsteps toward the fields below. It traveled at thirty-eight miles per second.

From the ground a streamer rose to meet it.

Purple lightning stuttered. One hundred sixty thousand amperes channeled into the zeppelin Caliph's men had fired on. The airship's chemio-static batteries exploded with an impressive green pyrotechnic display.

Billowing black smoke, the stricken ship folded like wax paper, metal ribs tearing through its crimson skin, and plunged, irrevocable calamity waiting below.

Still, another sky shark was coming.

Caliph braced himself as the *Byun-Ghala* continued its precipitous dive. He imagined the pilot pulling certain knobs, telescoping long metal shafts from his control panel. Caliph felt the airship bank as tightly as it could to port. Overhead, a flock of white balloons lifted from compartments along the *Byun-Ghala*'s dorsum. They floated swiftly up into the face of the oncoming sky shark, each one encumbered with a miniature chemical grenade.

The sky shark wrenched its engines but the wall of white balloons enveloped it. They bounced along its skin. Popped as tiny detonator spines collided with the body of the ship. Several airmen in gliders were similarly overwhelmed. Acid-based fires engulfed them and sent them on a mile-long funerary procession toward the ground.

It was spare joy. Caliph's men reloaded the Pplarian gun and waited stonily for another target to enter medium range.

All around, bizarre colors and fires arced and streaked and burned. Radioactive orange and red and green. Hot purples and blues and saffron yellows. Spreading oily smoke and sporadic showers of blood added horrific authenticity to an otherwise shockingly beautiful display.

The blue lions of the High King were on the run, harried and dogged by Saergaeth's scarlet ships.

Then, disaster.

One of the Iscan leviathans exploded. Two thousand seven hundred feet of airframe twisted, melted and mushroomed: black and searing. Orange butterfly tints melted inside a mephitic and enormous cloud. Some chemical shell capable of reacting with the denatured gas in the airbags had produced unthinkable results, uncasing holocaust.

The inferno ballooned in every direction, engulfing scores of gliders on both sides of the conflict. They dropped like singed moths around a popping gas lamp.

Caliph felt the blast from several hundred yards away. A swell of scorching air rolled over him, hit him squarely in the face. His eyeballs dried instantly. Sticky and hot. It hurt to blink. He gagged and clutched the railing.

When he looked down he saw more calamity, Iscan engines unraveling to enormous canisters of gas. Puffs of noxious toxins gloated over the hills and meandered with prevailing winds, killing everything they brushed.

Airship cannons powered by enormous compression hoses fired stone and metal balls inscribed with Naneman battle runes. War engines a mile below suffered devastating trauma.

Occasionally, gun-stones would shatter or bounce off thick choratium plates but more often than not, the high velocity of the missile would turn an engine's boiler inside out or render tracks snarled piles of useless grinding scrap.

Paralyzed and broken or pierced with ragged puncture wounds that rent from top to bottom, the smaller engines were abandoned by their crews. Canisters of deadly fumes burst nearby and sealed the crewmen's fate.

With miserable fascination Caliph watched the impotent retaliation of his lights. They fired shells of hardened clay packed with incendiary pellets, shot from powerful ballistae. They traveled interminable arcs and sometimes splashed through rigid zeppelin skins, adding to a paltry tally of influential blows. Unlike Saergaeth, the High King did not have shells capable of reacting with what everyone had thought to be inert zeppelin gas.

Even one or two direct hits often failed to bring Saergaeth's airships down.

The relentless front swept east.

Since the *Orison*'s "crash" Caliph's only communication with Alani or his spies had been the two hasty notes.

He couldn't tell if something had gone wrong, if his elaborate plan would meet with even marginal success, but he decided he couldn't wait any longer. Saergaeth was tearing him apart. From the back of the *Byun-Ghala* a battery of metal tubes had been bolted to flashing on the deck. Caliph gave a signal and one of the airmen flipped a switch. Current from the airship's giant cells coursed down a length of wire to where the strange artillery piece pointed astern at seventeen degrees.

Half a dozen chemical rockets thumped from the tubes and hissed into the air. Nondescript streamers of smoke mixing with the more breathtaking violence that choked the sky. The rockets traveled only a hundred yards before bursting into glittering multicolored flares.

Fireworks.

They were the signal.

Isca's heavy engines crawled out of Glumwood like unreal castles cobbled from choratium and steel. Each of their eight cleated tracks were ten feet tall, thirty feet across and twice again as long. One track: a single belt of bladed metal churned through elaborate sequences of toothy wheels. One tread could individually crush a two-story house of mortared stone.

Eight such belts comprised the clangorous foundations of the heavy engines whose stacks spewed a soup of brimstone and inky grit.

They defied and boggled the mind. Moveable fortresses, tactical strongholds that could be positioned as defiles or inching juggernauts, the foes of which had but one realistic maneuver: a slow relentless rout.

But against the comparative agility of zeppelins, the cumbersome heavies could only wait, hoping an airship would blunder within range— something not likely to happen even if a zeppelin captain showed gross incompetence and total disregard for all things sane. The crew would mutiny long before coming within a mile of such a monster's reach.

But when the gold and blue fireworks discharged behind the *Byun-Ghala* the Iscan heavies stopped launching conventional missiles of steel and stone.

They filled their guns with tunsia-reinforced holomorphic glass.

Cannonballs filled with souls.

Brobdingnagian compression units sent a volley of solvitriol bombs into the air. They were rudimentary. Untested. Caliph saw the heavies fire but lost track of their supersonic ammunition.

His stomach twisted three directions at once. His bowels needed sudden emptying. Everything depended on this moment.

Had Alani really done his job?

Caliph sweat profusely.

For unbearable moments nothing seemed to happen. He scanned the sky for any trace of success. His eyes moved from one dirigible to the next. Keenly attentive despite agonizing discomfort.

The Iscan heavies gave another volley, compression cannons rolling like thunder across the hills.

No visible effect.

So that's it? Nothing?

"Fuck thunder!" It was not a curse of rage. Fear filled Caliph from the boots up. Isca was doomed. The worm gang youths had truly died in vain!

His flesh went clammy. He felt himself surrender to prickles, uncontrollable convulsions and finally retching fits. His head would decorate the walls at West Gate: a distinctly irritating but not entirely inconvenient method of escape.

But he wasn't being honest. After all, he did care. Not for himself. He still had to pay for the worm gang murders. Sigmund had lied, but the High King had authorized the project. No. Caliph didn't have much hope for himself, but he did wish the unaffected best for Isca.

He didn't really care that he was about to become a piece of history except that many hundreds of loyal men and women were dying on his behalf.

He chuckled at what he guessed would be tomorrow's headline:

Saergaeth Puts End to War!

And then:

High King Saergaeth Brindlestrom restores order to the Duchy of Stonehold after months of conflict and scandal. Caliph Howl, whose family name had suffered a history of alleged political impropriety and corruption was arrested sometime this morning and taken into custody on charges of treason and witchcraft.

Caliph's execution would take place in Nevergreen along with the other traitors. Caliph felt torturously ashamed of that.

People are going to die because they followed me.

Who am I? Some misanthrope out of Greymoor? Incapable of planning any kind of war or strategy that works!

Caliph was gagging.

Three of the airmen unlatched his tether and dragged him into the stateroom. Warm lights fluttered on the walls. The piano stood silent. Outside, detonations filled the air with a pungent biting stench.

Caliph unzipped his flight jacket, tossed his earmuffs and goggles aside and stumbled into a cramped closet outfitted with plumbing and a tastefully decorated stool.

He jerked his leather pants down between his ankles and dropped onto the seat, colon exploding with pent-up anxiety. His guts tightened, struggling to wring out every drop of stress.

Klaxons sounded.

Caliph laid his head in his lap, exhausted. He focused on purging himself of any residual disquiet.

Again the horns. Urgent. Sequacious. Unremitting.

Detonated wood paneling and a sudden spray of splinters suffused the air. Winter wind howled through the tiny bathroom.

A ragged opening just above Caliph's head yawned brightly, somehow comical and grotesque.

A gun-stone must have torn through the *Byun-Ghala*'s hull leaving a trail of like-sized holes. The opposite wall was similarly destroyed. Beyond it, the floor. Strake smashed. Planks flinderized. Wind screaming underneath.

Caliph swabbed himself, agony devitalized by fresh crisis. He buckled his belt and crawled out of his ruined water closet.

The hole in the stateroom floor showed a jagged picture of war-torn landscape several thousand feet below.

Caliph gritted his teeth, donned his gear and marched back out to the observation deck. He reattached his tether and got to work on the Pplarian gun.

No, he told himself.

You conceited prickish ass! They aren't fighting for you. They're fighting for Stonehold . . . for themselves . . . for the place they want to live. And you, as the High King, owe it to them not to give up before it's through.

Every firing shook the cannon's inner mechanisms so that after three such volleys certain bolts had to be readjusted.

Off the starboard side, one of Saergaeth's airships listed oddly. As Caliph worked he noticed its decks devoid of movement. The flaps in the tail were banked hard. The bloated bloodred thing was going in vast protracted circles.

The Iscan heavies fired again.

Caliph saw the shot this time by virtue of the obscene chance that the propelled tunsia sphere actually impacted one of Saergaeth's gliders. Caliph's attention was drawn to the missile's arc just after impact.

The glider had turned to fragments of wood, metal, leather and gore and the faint orb that had destroyed it had left a visible wake of fumes from the glider's cell. It had also slowed tremendously. Caliph could tell it was about to begin its return trip, plummeting through clouds to lodge deeply in the frozen fields.

But something astonishing happened instead.

It did not fall.

Its velocity increased. It changed direction. It swooped like a gumball on a string. Swung in a smooth arc, impacted an Iscan airship, tore relentlessly through and accelerated toward an invisible gravitational pull. It hit another of Saergaeth's gliders, disintegrating the aeronaut and his lighter-than-air craft into a spray of tiny bits.

Caliph could follow it with his eye because its track was faintly visible. Not a trail behind, but its path ahead. And it was growing clearer every fraction of every second. Like the negative image the Pplarian lightning left on his brain when he closed his eyes, a dark line, a blackish foreshadower materialized, showing where the ball would go.

Then Caliph lost track of it amid the chaos and the noise.

What could it mean?

At least some mechanic of his plan must have succeeded. Alani must have installed the devices on a portion, no matter how small, of Saergaeth's fleet.

Hope returned as the heavies fired again. Roaring lions. Angry personifications of some overused political symbolism.

"Tell the captain to board that ship!" shouted Caliph.

He pointed to the derelict zeppelin cutting mindless circles in the sky.

"Yes, sir!"

The Pplarian gun concussed the air and another gout of lightning split the sky.

FIFTEEN minutes later, they were docked above the *Mademoiselle*. The coupling was tricky. A set of additional controls existed in a kind of inverted crow's nest below the *Byun-Ghala*'s observation deck. The copilot had climbed down via an exposed spiral staircase.

He used the secondary controls to put the upside-down steeple into a coupling dead center on the other zeppelin's crown.

They stacked on top of each other, floating like fat cacti in air.

It was extremely difficult not only because of the ongoing battle but because the captain had to fly the *Byun-Ghala* at exactly the same speed and direction as the other ship. If he did not, the coupling might snap.

Caliph and several other airmen descended the stairs, gripping the freezing iron tightly against the wind. They made it to the dorsum of the other airship by way of metal rungs.

Above, the *Byun-Ghala* billowed, obstructing much of the sky. Below, the great airbag of Saergaeth's ship stretched pincushion-like. A floating red island covered with petulant limbless trees.

Near the coupling, a hatch opened into the hull. Caliph spun the handle and pulled up. Narrow dark steps descended through a slender cavity between the gasbags. They slithered down several flights.

Finally they emerged on the ship's bridge.

The pilot of the enemy craft was slumped at the helm, an arm hanging through the wheel like a crowbar. His dead weight had jammed the flaps, caused the propellers to beat against fins laid perpetually to the right.

The airmen drew swords and spread out.

Caliph checked the pilot for wounds.

Nothing.

There was minor trauma to the ship, easily visible. A cannonball had entered on the port side, strafed through every intervening structure and cut through heavy reinforced stanchions as if they had been bundled straw. The missile's velocity must have been unreal at the time of impact.

Its remains were found after several minutes, lodged deep inside the zeppelin's belly. Wholly melded with another object. A twisted mass of tunsia and shattered glass. Both objects had been driven up the middle of a support wall, wedged between duralumin beams, stopped at last in their catastrophic path.

"Everyone's dead, your majesty."

The analysis came back after a three-minute survey of the ship.

"No signs of struggle. It's like they all just fell over."

"It's not right," said another man. "Creepy as a night on Knife and Heath."

But Caliph's fear had dissolved. He ushered his men back toward the *Byun-Ghala*. When they reached the top of the *Mademoiselle*'s hull he took a moment to gaze in panorama at the battle that compassed them on every side.

Many of Saergaeth's airships were now doing strange things. Going in circles like the *Mademoiselle*. Others were ascending or descending without apparent reason. One made a spectacle of dragging through Glumwood's upper fingers, ravaged by the forest's claws.

Caliph suppressed a cheer.

Back on the *Byun-Ghala* he heard another salvo assault the sky. The Iscan heavies were firing again.

As the sun went down, Alani watched the war from the ground.

He felt the wind; it walked restlessly up and down the cheerless hills. His men had installed nearly fifty cells.

Split souls. Half-damned creatures.

They were separate from the real solvitriol cells Saergaeth had found on the *Orison*. Half-souls couldn't power engines. At least not conventionally. Their only force lay in the path of attraction.

Alani's men had carried tiny cells, barely the size of chicken eggs. They had used tunsia bolts, securing them to the frames of as many zeppelins and engines as they could. They chose places where even if the bolts gave way or the material of the frame twisted and tore under the strain of mutual attraction, the damage would be catastrophic.

When the Iscan heavies started firing, the other half of each of Sigmund's bisected human souls overcame whatever plasma diversion had temporarily negated their collective pull. Both halves sought each other out.

The bullets homed in, finding the one and only target they had been made unerringly to strike.

Unheard collisions rocked the ether, ripped bodies and souls apart while every inanimate thing remained unfazed. But it was intrinsically unpredictable.

The Iscan heavies were firing blind, not knowing which zeppelins housed which targets or what paths their bullets would take. Some struck ships already engaged with Iscan ships. The result was indiscriminate slaughter.

Just outside the radius of ethereal disturbance, Alani had heard other aeronauts complain of queasiness and acute unrest. Alani himself had felt the diminishing ripples, disturbing something he had never felt before, threatening to dislodge him from his fleshy shell.

That was when Alani had taken a glider to the ground. Most of his men were dead. Despite his best efforts, extortion could only last until his psychological hostages lost hope, decided it no longer mattered whether any of them lived or died. Their beliefs were at stake. And one or two had talked, risking themselves and their fellow crewmen to the surgically implanted beads behind their eyes. The jig was up.

Six of Alani's men had been discovered and killed.

Alani had fled. His men had been able to install only fifty units.

Fifty! Less than thirty percent of what they were supposed to have done.

Alani cursed and smoked his pipe from his hidden vantage south of Clefthollow. That meant that if every missile fired from Caliph's heavy engines found its mark, Saergaeth's zeppelin fleet would still be double that of the High King's.

Somewhere in the skies, the spymaster of Isca knew that Caliph Howl was already dead.

MORE snow brought the zeppelin battle to an eerie standstill during the night. The flakes were thick and the ships stopped for fear of colliding with other vessels.

But early in the morning, from the west, the snow was replaced by defeat: falling silently out of the clouds. Caliph couldn't help but notice it from his dizzying position on the starboard deck. He watched mutely as the massive red bellies shredded tendrils of vapor. It had to be a dream. A nightmare. The rail became his only connection to reality. No ship. No deck. No crewmen running. Just a shaft of cold, pushed hard into both hands, solid and immovable. He gripped it tightly as the *Byun-Ghala* tilted in the sky.

The directionless sense of perspective afforded by vertigo made the vast crimson skins bursting out of the clouds look like a pod of red leviathans breaching in an ocean of white. Except that it was upside down. All of it. The clouds above the battle had created a false ceiling over the entire war. Now they ruptured, spilling a second armada, scores of dark red fruit popping into existence, falling on the remnants of Caliph's ragged fleet.

How could Saergaeth have hidden them? Holomorphy? Caliph watched the red ships' bays open and vomit a host of chemical bombs. The storm of canisters passed through the aerial battlefield and plummeted toward the ground. The bombardment brought even the Iscan heavies, trundling through the snow, to a creaking stop that Caliph felt physically against his heart.

So cold, at the very center of his chest, it was like the weight of all those zeppelins had come crushing down on him. He couldn't breathe. Saergaeth had outwitted him after all. Stonehold's old hero had pulled together a battle plan that a boy from Desdae hadn't been able to overcome. It had been ruthless. It had depended on superior numbers. And just when Caliph thought he had seen the full force of Miskatol brought to bear, Saergaeth had pulled back the curtain and said, Look: I have more.

Someone was talking to him. But all he could hear was the faint explosions in the fields below.

"Your majesty! Your majesty!"

Caliph turned his head slowly. One of the deckhands was shouting at him, tears gushing from his eyes. Why was he crying? Men were yelling incoherently. The *Byun-Ghala* tilted again, sharply, engines revving. The captain was turning her away from the battle.

"Where are we going?" asked Caliph. He felt so out of breath. "We can't run . . ."

The deckhand was close, right in his face. Why was he so close? He was younger than Caliph, tears streaming down his cheeks, "It's going to be all right . . ."

"I think I need to sit down," Caliph whispered. But he could not move. He tried again.

Strange.

He looked toward his feet and suddenly saw that the deck had been blown apart right in front of him, metal bent into crazy branch-like fingers. Wood had been blasted away.

Part of the railing, or maybe a support beam, was projecting through the center of his chest. He felt embarrassed, as if he had made a terrible mistake. He wanted to apologize to the deckhand for not realizing what had happened.

"Oh," said Caliph. "Oh . . ." The clouds swept by, beautiful and gloomy; the wind was cold.

"We're going to get you home." The deckhand was bawling. "Hold on . . . hold on!"

CHAPTER
40

The tailors presented Sena with a dozen options. She settled on a pale suede jacket, trimmed with white fur. It fit her torso like a glove, buttoning up the front with wooden toggles, cosseting her neck in a stiff fur-lined collar similar to those worn by monks in the western hills. Gorgeous wine and rose-colored embroidery flourished up and down the suede. She put it on, checked herself in the mirror and went down to deal with the commotion in the great hall.

Even though it was practically the middle of the night, the royal huntsman had come, accompanied by the taxidermist and a group of other men.

They had brought the creature down.

The patio doors were opened to admit the massive head. Gadriel had balked at first but Sena was back in power (Caliph had left specific instructions) and she ordered him around with satisfaction in exchange for his treatment of her the week before. She had them haul the specimen in and hang it in the great hall.

It was a terrifying thing. The head was small only in comparison to her memory of that night, being roughly the size and shape of a giant pumpkin.

"Incredible specimen, my lady. An aberration perhaps never to be catalogued again." The taxidermist held a repugnant kind of reverence for the thing.

Sena looked at it closely. It was no less odious under the castle's metholinate lights.

From a distance, it might have passed as a hideous human head infected with gigantism. But closer up its brow curved too sharply back in a drastic ovoid dome stippled with dark occasional hair. The ears were tall, multipointed and labyrinthine beyond the folds of subterrestrial echolocators. Once soft and sallow, the flesh was now hard and speckled like the eggs of feral birds.

Its nose was snubbed despite the bestial protrusion of its snout. The lips were broad, thin and indescribably cruel.

"Took a dozen chemiostatic spears to bring it down," said the huntsman.

Sena felt herself grow cold as she looked at the eyes, placed by the taxidermist beneath drowsy alien lids. Their smooth black surface glistened. Midnight waters without whites. A nictating membrane slipped up at an angle, forming a milky sheath that clung laconically across the glass's bathyal deeps.

In the reproduction, Sena could only imagine the cosmic blackness of the originals. The replicas had been flecked by the taxidermist's hand with ever deepening layers of tiny golden motes that glittered in the great hall's light like twin galaxies.

"The body is being sliced into cross sections and inserted into panes at Grouselich Hospital. It will be pickled. No doubt to be a key attraction at the Ketch Museum." The taxidermist spoke as if everything were bright.

Sena paged through the report that said ten men had lost their lives during the hunt, victims of the creature's teeth and claws.

She examined the jaws, protruding hinges that exposed multiple rows of fangs. She shivered before the trophy's insensible gaze and defiantly extended her finger. Something compelled her to touch it. She needed to know, on a visceral level, that it was real.

But feeling its death did little to reassure her. On the contrary, it made what she had read in the *Cisrym Tạ* all the more frightening because something was happening.

For several nights, since she had hurled her formula at Skellum, she had felt *Them* . . . primordial bodies stirring, churning through lurid ghastly throes.

Horrors far richer and more rarefied than the ꝏꙨꭤꞬꝇ, whose head was being hung in Caliph's hall, crooned strangely through the ether. Sena could feel them in the castle, inchoate forms, reverberating, trembling: monstrous catacombs of flesh.

Flesh was an approximation.

"They are my gods," Sena whispered. She could not see them, even with her eyes.

"Excuse me?" said the huntsman.

Sena ignored his incredulous expression and left the grand hall without excusing herself. She wandered out into the icy halls, feeling dizzy, not knowing where she was going. A whisper pulled her down a passageway she had never used before, drawing her into a deserted tourelle. From its windows she could see occasional flickers of purple light through the glass, stammering from the Pplarian guns. Seven miles out, war was raging and she knew that Caliph was losing. *I need to help him* . . .

But the thought was blurry, strangely inconsequential, like the memory of something she had meant to do but then changed her mind. Sena whispered in the dark. "Soon . . ." She heard scratching voices in her head, like the needle on a phonograph with no recorded sound.

"Soon, soon."

Her skull churned. A bottle full of newts. The whisper that had pulled her here was familiar now. Old and damp and chilly. Disjunctly, it induced the smell-memory of decomposing leaves. "Soon . . ." Around her, the forgotten baggage of a dozen High Kings seemed to brood. Fur cloaks, carved coffers and ugly diplomatic gifts nested like lonesome birds in the loft, dreaming darkness and betrayal.

Sena looked out through the dirty panes at the snow-covered land. Tentacles of light filled the sky, oozing between the mountain peaks.

She watched the veils slowly ebb and ruffle. The tentacles were breaking up as dawn approached. They refracted and moved over the north.

She stepped closer to the window, felt the filthy panes rattle in the wind. She rested her palms against the glass and mused that maybe, just maybe, she was going mad.

An anomalous noise from overhead jolted her back to reality.

An old man's whisper licked her ear canal. "Go up."

There was a wooden staircase that pulled down. Above it, a trapdoor glowered in the ceiling. Sena scowled and pulled the rope. The staircase lowered with a creak. This particular turret did not connect with the rest of the battlements. It hung alone in a forlorn crevice of the castle's northwest face like an unnoticed tick in a vertical fold of hardened skin.

There were no conventional means to reach its rooftop except the rusted door.

Sena took hold of the bolt with both hands.

Perhaps it's something flapping in the wind.

The sound came again. Precise. Betraying intent. The bolt popped back suddenly, scraping her knuckles on burred iron. She swore. Hesitantly, she put the back of her shoulder against the door.

Ice crackled. A cold dark wind whistled in as she managed a half-inch crack. She pushed with every muscle in her body, relaxed and took another step, working her way expertly up the rickety stairs, maximizing her leverage.

Finally the heavy hinges gave a painful snap and the trapdoor swung all the way open, smashing back against the roof, a thick sheet of ice shattering in every direction.

A square of cloudy sky grumbled overhead. Despite the crushing cold, she wasted no time pulling herself up.

The turret's architecture formed a small octagon, obscure and shadowed by the castle's walls. From its solitary rooftop she gazed down on Stonehold wrapped in snow from a perspective that obscured the city.

To the north there was something black, as if a giant had thrown a fistful of mud at the castle wall. It clung, oblique, opaque, hiding in the gloom of the castle's own acre-wide shadow. The air around it trembled as though thick fumes like fuel vapor, heavier than air, drooled out of it and down across the frozen moat. That, or parts of its shape were slavering back out of physical space, into the ether.

"Why are *You* here?" she whispered.

The massive thing did not move. It wavered. It writhed almost and seemed to slurp at the sky even though it made no sound. It did not move from its position on the wall. A point of light, exquisitely bright, shivered in its central void, surrounded by other lights, all of them the color of welding sparks. Its exact shape was impossible to tell, even for Sena's eyes, because it seemed to have an invalid structure. The more she looked, the more it occurred to her that it was somehow imploded, a re-entrant polygon, though softened and organic, a mushy concavity or hole rather than any shape at all. Light bent around it. It exuded cold.

One of Them. One of the Thæ'gn. Maybe it was the one she had bound to protect her at the Porch of Soth, responsible for utterly discreating the flawless Lua'groc that had attacked her in her home. Maybe it was from the Halls under Sandren. One of the Hidden. A black lump of mucus, a cancer of space. Gleaming.

The lights inside it fizzled in and out of sight except for the great one at its center. Like a cell, that bright gleaming nucleolus surrounded by cosmic black cytoplasm, shimmering lysosomes . . .

She was making up metaphors primarily because she had the feeling that, even with her new eyes, she wasn't seeing it correctly, as if the gigantic thing refused to translate properly through any kind of sight.

There was no communication from it. Nothing she could sense, except for the logical assumption that it had been drawn here by the book . . . just like its lesser cousin whose head hung in the great hall. Sena envisioned more of them, attracted by the *Cisrym Ta*, cementing themselves like barnacles to Isca Castle, great abysmal vacuums of them. Deep plastered colonies of empty holes, drawing together like negative cells, building a gulf of tissue, a void, a parody of oyster flesh around a pearl, growing over the irritation of the book.

Maybe.

In truth she had no idea why it was here or what the book meant to it.

The incomprehensible smell of the thing washed over her. So sweet.

Like rose flesh. Like a flower she had never smelled before. It was cloying. Overpowering.

Maybe her proof, her bolt aimed at Megan, had drawn it. After all, it was the first time she had taken numbers from the *Cisrym Ta* and turned them into holomorphic force. Again, it was just a guess. Her legs felt weak. Her body modulated, softening as if subject to wavelengths emanating from its core. She had the unpleasant memory of Megan's hex at Deep Cloister and felt like she might wobble apart, muscles waggling free of her bones.

Is this an attack? Or am I simply too close? Like trying to swallow a strandy web of phlegm at the back of her throat, Sena had to concentrate on simple systems. She couldn't walk; it felt like she was standing in pudding. Her thoughts slowed.

Maybe the head of the Cal'cr'Nok, hanging in the great hall, had drawn it. *But would something so powerful and different from its physical cousin hold a grudge? Would it even care about murder?*

Sena didn't know. She had no answers as she stood, trapped, feeling its cold, unseen secretions envelop her like gelatin.

There was a potion in her belt. *Hemofurtum,* she thought dully and reached for it with exaggerated sluggishness. She had kept it close in anticipation of the formula that would help Caliph win. She had been planning to perform it . . . right now . . . or earlier. She couldn't remember. Why hadn't she done it earlier? Instead of wandering aimlessly through the castle halls?

She didn't know.

She pried the potion's cap off like a clumsy drunk and watched the crimson fluid purl upward in the air. *That shouldn't be happening,* she thought dreamily.

A shadow, like a brushstroke, had appeared beside her. It hung just above the left side of the battlement in her peripheral sight, smoky and gaunt and curled. Black, with a vague wisp of white hair and within it, a hint of cimmerian eyes, burning through the cold, staring across the empty gulf between the tourelle and the thing that boiled on the wall.

"Nathan?" she asked. But the specter only watched. Sena felt like laughing, everything was so bizarre. She opened her mouth to speak, trying to gather holojoules from the weightless potion. Panic. She couldn't breathe. The heavy invisible slime poured into her mouth. Into her nose and throat. She couldn't speak. She struggled. She thought she heard an old man humming far away.

Sena twisted as her feet came loose from the stone. She flailed. Floating. Fighting for her life. She couldn't hold her breath any longer, she began to choke. As the jellied air poured in, deep inside her throat, she felt something bite.

On the side of the castle, the godling-stain bubbled, a black honeycomb of flesh pouring from its hole, plasmoid, tentacular, hideously fast, a complex mollusk unfolding.

The black pseudopodia foamed toward her, silent as thrown ink, glistening with deep cribriform patterns. There was a burst of prurient pink, an outward thrust of bright color trimming those impossible lobes. The pseudopodia didn't move in concert. They were not like the anemones from Desdae's biology labs or any other creature with a cognizant grasp. The outpouring flesh, if it was flesh, moved like an abruption . . . like something that had exploded from a wound. Mentally, Sena screamed.

The blood potion floated in front of her like the glowing tube at Grouselich Hospital, the disgorged red contents hovered, roiled, and remained suspended. Her eyes glazed, her throat relaxed, the slime-thick air poured into her lungs. Something bit deeper, like serrated teeth, slicing into the soft tissue of her pharynx, biting, slicing, she could taste her own blood.

Those ebbing holojoules . . . waiting for her voice. She thought of Megan's transumption hex, of the Devourer: Grū-ner Shie.

In the distance, the sound of thunder or zeppelin guns tortured the sky. Sena's body convulsed from lack of oxygen . . . the black flesh was all around her. And she was floating, stuttering. Catapult. Zoetrope. *Where was Caliph?* The Thæ'gn's sweet mucus filled her sinuses with incomprehensible alien dreaming, scent-shadows of her own death. The curl of smoke that was shaped like an old man did nothing.

Snow fell. *Odd.* It seemed unaffected by the thick air. Her vision was blurring. Then suddenly, she was assaulted from every direction, both internally as well as all across her skin. Her jacket tore away in parallel strips. Her clothing disintegrated. She could suddenly breathe but the pain was exquisite. Black tendrils sliced gill-like slits into her skin. Those arms that looked so slippery, surprisingly powerful . . . and rough. Like coarse sandpaper grit. They snagged and tore at reality. She could see them shredding the fiber of space with every subtle movement that they made, reality turning to mist, threadbare wisps that dispersed slightly, revealing glimpses of someplace else . . . someplace hidden . . . hovering just behind. Space closed as the arms moved, re-weaving, healing, but vaguely warped . . . vaguely scarred.

She was breathing through her skin . . . or maybe she had stopped breathing altogether. Her body had been filleted, every part of her exposed, like a child's snowflake cut from paper. She hung in tatters in the air, bones and organs twisting. A gory paper doll.

Black filaments of something like mist condensed, forming webs below her dangling guts. They braided, wound up, tugged gently at her tattered flesh. She felt the manipulation, not from without, but from within, at a cellular level, a molecular level.

Her smallest parts, the fibers of her tissue, the atoms themselves were grinding against each other, turning, realigning, tuning themselves to some new atomic pole. They snapped suddenly, locking together, fundamentally changed, perfectly attuned to this new orientation.

And Sena was back together, packed tight and sutured shut and the great black mass trimmed with vaginal pink was collapsing, withdrawing, once again becoming a void, an empty hole on the castle wall.

Sena dropped, no longer floating. The potion of blood now spun, falling as it should have done minutes ago. She had been struggling so hard to scream that now the sound ripped from her throat, filled with numbers.

"Not that one," the curl of smoke whispered. It had not moved from its position during the entire ordeal, while the godling-stain had chined and sliced and then reinvented her anew. "Use the beacon." It was a command not spoken in Hinter or Trade. Sena had no clear sense of individual words, only the collective meaning.

Without thinking or questioning, she obeyed. Words gushed from her mouth, a torrent of repellent sounds. Was she imagining it, or could she actually hear a ghostly stopwatch drumming through its tiny gears.

Faster!

The old thin voice sequenced like a horologe, just outside the hurricane of her concentration.

Her flesh prickled.

Faster!

Sena let the Inti'Drou glyphs sink their blackened compound forms into her eyes. She could see them even shut, behind her eyelids, played like picture lanterns across her brain. She was preparing to inject portions of their compressed multidimensional data into her argument.

Sena nearly choked on the glottal sounds that tumbled up her throat. Lightning rived the towers of Isca Castle. Snow fell. Thunder boomed as if the compression crack of the Pplarian guns had finally reached the parapets half an hour late.

She gathered the holojoules from the whirling blood before it splattered across the floor.

To focus Megan's transumption hex, she called out, sending up a beacon from the tourelle, screaming at Grū-ner Shie to *see* her. Forgotten were her plans of helping Caliph. She was obeying the whisper in her head.

The beacon went up, a meaningless pillar of math that bent every dimension, useless except in pinpointing her location to the thing that had been roused for the sole purpose of devouring Stonehold.

"You will save the Duchy," the trace of smoke assured her, sibilant and dry like a leaf-rattle in the wind.

Glassy shapes spread suddenly from the direction of the zeppelin war. Delitescent palpi puffed the sky from the other side of nothing, fungal forms swelling. The stratosphere burst like fluted glass gone wild. Sena saw jelly slipping through crystal pearls, glistening worms the color of empty air.

Colors played across her face. *So beautiful! Incandescent pink. Flaming, cerulean blue.*

There was no doubt that the thing that had eaten Fallow Down had found her! This time it was not a random abrogation of luck. It was cognizant as it groped its legion parts in the direction of her voice.

But then, while the heavens went berserk, something happened that she had not expected. The snow hovered, retreated, fell backward, the dawn eclipsed by unseen mass. Some continental shadow spread like an infection below the maggoty celebration in the sky.

No thunder.

No sound.

Just freezing silence across miles of air.

And then the distant zeppelins buckled like red gelatinous creatures caught in riptide. Not just Saergaeth's airships, but the High King's as well. She saw them fold in on themselves and vanish from the sky. The armies on the ground, every building west of the Hold, was unmade. Even the clouds, the great storm front moving west, evaporated like a clot of steam.

Sena felt the plurality of their deaths as an impact in her chest. So many people at once! But the madness in the sky was not done yet. Its glassy writhing mass surged toward her. It homed in on her position atop the battlements, spreading east. Sena steeled herself. She felt the temperature drop suddenly and then: the godling-stain exploded a second time, thrusting from its hole like something hidden in a shell. Its untamed limbs skewered the clouds, then curled, as if gripping prey before pulling back into the void.

Sena looked down to find herself lying on the roof amid shattered chunks of ice. Her naked flesh had gone mausoleum gray.

here was nothing anymore. Nothing on the wall. Nothing covering her skin. The curl of smoke, the whisperer, had dissolved if
it had ever been there at all.

Sena looked down at herself, albescent with an oyster-colored glow.
Whorls of blue flickered under her fingernails, luminescing. Her body had
been extraordinized under an obscene stylus. She looked at the patterns
and laughed out loud. "I see! I see!"

ZEPPELINS hit the city from the east. They drifted in over Monk Worm,
dropped chemical bombs in Daoud's Bend. They were from Vale Briar, ignorant of the fact that Saergaeth and his entire armada had disappeared.

The city fumed and hissed. Two war engines, left to protect Isca,
erupted in sudden fire. Gargoyles exploded as gun-stones passed between
tower and sky. The glowing ornate face in Maruchine's clock tower imploded. Coped gables were blown away. Crockets fell in a heavy rain of
carven stone. They broke like ice against the street. Rent pipes spewed
steam in ugly patterns on avenues suddenly alive with running people.

Sena heard the Klaxons from her prone position on the other side of
Isca Castle. But time had fractured. *Is this the past? Is this the present?*
The western skies were dark. The Pplarian guns had ceased to fire. She
couldn't see a trace of battle in the clouds.

She rolled her head to the left.

On the turret roof a sprinkling of hollow metallic granules rolled sor-
rowfully in the wind, inches from her cheek. A bitter fume wafted from
them.

There were stones missing. Great blocks displaced like knocked-out
teeth.

Something had coddled her in that brilliant terrible light. Something
had stroked her like a tongue, beautiful and languorous and left her in
this state of dread.

Sena tried to move but could only fumble. Her vision was skewed in

new indefinite ways. She could see magnetic bands across the sky. The
city's architecture looked slippery and unreal.

Her head throbbed.

In the west, nothing stirred. She looked between the battlements, past
a star, through a distant galaxy and into someplace lightless and deep.

The explosion tore her eyes back, up, or down . . . completely disoriented. An orange blossom. A pinwheel. A zeppelin on fire. She watched
the *Byun-Ghala* tip into Isca Castle. Metal screamed against stone.

Sena spun. Her limbs were weak like molten candy. Her eyes refused
to blink. She was looking at the accident. The airship crunching like an
accordion against the castle cliffs. She was looking at the sun.

TIME stutterd.

Snow or ash dwindled beyond the windows.

People stirred. Men in red coats. Cycles of light and dark. Sena's eyelids fluttered open just in time to catch a dark shadow flicking over the
room as a sheet of melting snow fell past the glass. She heard whispers.

"The High King is dead."

The story came to her in pieces. His airship had left the battle, racing
back to Isca in an effort save his life. The details were still foggy. A hawk
had brought a note stating that Caliph had needed transfusions and surgery. Stat. The *Byun-Ghala* had escaped granulation, only to be hit by Saergaeth's smaller front coming from the east. That offensive had stopped
quickly when it was realized that Saergaeth himself had been vaporized
with the rest of his fleet. But it was too late. By the time they surrendered, the *Byun-Ghala* had already been hit, crippled, crushed against the
castle.

Sena sat up in Caliph's bed. A doctor in a red coat looked at her from
across the room with a terrified expression. She saw the *Herald* on a
nearby stand, read the headlines in the largest, boldest typeface available
to the press. Three words covered the entire page.

HIGH KING SLAIN! And below it: BURT VANISHED LIKE FALLOW DOWN!
Perhaps people will start calling the town "Burnt" even though it doesn't
rhyme, like they call Fallow Down, "Fallen Down," like Stonehavians
have always used humor to deal with crippling loss.

What? How could she think about that! How could she be distracted
from the headlines proclaiming Caliph's death? There was a low ringing
like tinnitus: musicians in the grand hall, she realized, playing subtle
fugues. Why was the doctor staring at her so strangely?

Sena looked through the walls of the bedroom to where the High King's
body lay surrounded by several thousand candles that melted the grand

hall into a dignified but ritualistic-looking cave. Around him, tapestries hung like chthonic draperies and flowstone.

Gadriel entered the bedroom. His eyes were red and frightened, devoid of their usual brightness. He nodded to her, almost shaking, and placed several embossed envelopes on a tortoiseshell table before stepping backward, shrinking, almost creeping away.

"Condolences are pouring in," he whispered.

Am I . . . gods, what's happening?

"Gadriel?"

His answer to her question was tense and fearful. "You are the queen. The Council, what is left of it, called a meeting . . . last night. With the exception of General Yrisl, all of our ranking officers are . . ." He stopped.

Obviously there were too many details to explain. Too much horror behind the reason. "You are queen of Stonehold, my . . . lady. According to the vote."

Impossible! They would never . . .

Gadriel and the physician left the room, not waiting for her reply.

SENA got up. A whisper etched the air inside her left ear. Nothing intelligible. The gas lamps had been put out until shipments of metholinate could be resumed. There were candles all around. She took a bath, got dressed and sat down in front of her vanity. She stared into her eyes where the black islands of her pupils had been buried under a brilliant flood and then, slowly, took notice of her skin. There were markings, shimmering and pale, nearly invisible. Distinctly, from far away, she could hear an old man's voice . . . humming.

"Ha! Clever Pun. And so like tattoos they now seem to me!" His voice sounded whimsical.

She echoed it. Whispered it to herself. "The Last Page."

The memory was hard to grasp, sleek and slithery, the instant that the sky had gone wild, but pieces of what had happened were falling into place. The gill-like slits . . . her body opening like a flower . . .

These tattoos must be the scars! But they're so . . . beautiful!

Head to toe, they covered her. Fully healed into elegant designs. *What had the Thæ'gn been trying to do? Strike that! What did it do . . . to me?*

Something was wrong.

She had just realized that she wasn't breathing. She was sitting at the mirror, thinking . . . not breathing. Frightened, she drew air in through her nose. She could feel it pull down into her throat, cool, crisp, she could feel it filling her lungs, a pleasant chilly expansion. Relieved, she noticed that she could smell. She could smell so acutely that it reminded her of when she had been a child. The faint dampness of the wood at the windowsill. The pleasant waft of her perfume bottles and lipstick tubes. And then she realized that she wasn't breathing again.

She inhaled. Exhaled. Inhaled. Exhaled. Everything worked. She stopped. Seconds passed. No panic. She flipped open her watch. A minute passed. Nothing. Five minutes passed without a breath. She didn't need to breathe.

She remembered the terrified expression on the doctor's face, the way Gadriel had seemed frightened of her. *What's happened to me?*

She checked her pulse.

Nothing.

She felt under her chin, cupped her hand under her left breast. Nothing. She felt herself. She was warm, except for the tattoos. Fear rising, she took a hat pin from her vanity and stabbed her finger.

It didn't bleed. It didn't even hurt.

She rubbed her fingers together. They weren't numb. She could feel the brush of one against the other. She found her kyru and sliced into her palm.

For a moment, the flesh parted, but she had the distinct impression that it had done so only because she had desired it to happen. There wasn't any blood. Shocked, she sliced again, deeper. The skin parted without pain, showing perfect pink muscle tissue all the way to the bone. The skin fell back together without so much as a mark. Not a trace. Perfectly whole.

And she wasn't breathing.

She examined her tattoo-scars in the mirror, the way they carved her up with screaming lovely poems. She recognized the designs from the *Cisrym Ta*. Inti'Drou glyphs. The Thæ'gn had written on her.

Slowly it began sinking in that the entity hadn't actually attacked her. Even when her intestines had been dangling in the wind and her skin had been flayed open like a tattered kite, it had never attacked her. It had done something on its own, outside her small sphere of logic, like a lab technician re-engineering some small speck of life in order to study it. And then, *They* had used her.

It felt mysterious and sinister but mostly it felt invasive. *What did They do to me?*

But, in the same self-exploratory moment, Sena felt like she could already answer that question.

Caliph's ships had held the brunt of Saergaeth's armies at bay, gathering them, holding them in one place where Grū-ner Shie's mindless gluttony could stop dead the entirety of the war. In that respect, Caliph's plan had been a success. Precisely timed, the Abomination from outside reality had transmogrified her, even her vocal cords, giving her the ability to pronounce the glyphs.

The beacon had gone up, called forth the Devourer. By destroying Saergaeth's army, by destroying everything, it had put an end to the threat of Sena's removal from Stonehold. Or rather, it had ensured that the *Cisrym Ta* would stay where it was, safely ensconced at Isca Castle, and that it would remain in Sena's possession, with time purchased for her to continue studying its contents.

Once the threat had been eliminated, the Thæ'gn that had written on her skin had removed Grū-ner Shie from the equation, before it could reach the object of its hunger, before it could devour the newest owner of the *Cisrym Ta*.

"Ha! Clever Pun. And so like tattoos . . ."

The old man's voice again. A splintered trace, an echo of sound.

She whirled around but there was no one in the room.

"The Last Page."

Why me? thought Sena. She felt like some rare virus in a dish that They had been waiting for to reach critical mass. Waiting for some simple, predictable chemical reaction that They could then exploit.

She felt like a paramecium that had eaten a specific type of agent, as if the *Cisrym Ta* had been a lure. Once she had ingested the contents of the book, the next step in the process had been administered with clinical care, like gene therapy, something that would bring her to the next phase of her development.

The questions she couldn't answer were: *why?* and: *what now?* What would They expect from her now?

She used her new eyes and looked out, far away, and saw the planet as a single cell, hovering in space, ready for insertion of a foreign bud. *Am I that bud?*

The word games began. *Last Page. Page of what? The* Cisrym Ta*?* She scowled. *Or could page mean usher?*

She thought of gardeners turning what was living into compost, preparing for the next season. She thought of the coiled, tightly packed realities waiting in the *Cisrym Ta* . . . tightly coiled, packed . . . like the blueprints of life.

Not a paramecium. I am an oöcyte, ripened by the book, fertilized in a test tube by the Thæ'gn. I am a zygote.

I am not breathing!

SENA felt her body move when she stood up in front of the mirror. She felt perfectly healthy. Perfectly rested. She had never felt like this before, like she could run for miles, jump over mountains. It was impossible for her to be sad. She sat back down and outlined her eyes and lashes, stroked color into her lips. She changed into her best black dress, which clung to her body like something starved for warmth.

She left the bedroom and went down to the grand hall, one step at a time, watching the marble steps come up at her, hearing the noise increase as she approached the room where Caliph's corpse lay in state. "I have no time for this," she whispered to herself.

There was a great crowd of people; a line of lesser gentry passed through an exterior candlelit hall. The music was soft but piercing and everywhere the smell of food.

Curious, she stopped, plucked a glass of wine from a serving tray and lifted it to her lips. She drank, felt the wine go down. She realized she was neither hungry nor thirsty but the wine tasted excellent at the back of her throat. The smell. The tingle. She enjoyed it.

There were people watching her now, scrutinizing her, wondering why she wasn't mourning. She glared back at them with her scintillating eyes. She glided between them, heading for the bier.

Caliph's body had already been embalmed. He looked gray and glossy under the candles. She saw through him. All his organs had been removed, turning him into an empty puppet wrapped in expensive silk.

He was dressed loosely in a white robe, like a priest, shining in the light like fresh soap. Sena lifted his sleeve and found the place on his arm where, a month ago, her unswerving desire had wounded him. It pained her. That scar had accumulated so much meaning. It seemed the symbol of their relationship.

Gadriel was pushing through the crowd. But she didn't care whether he was coming toward her or running away. She whispered abruptly, stopping on a spirant sound. Gadriel stopped. Everything stopped.

But there wasn't any blood in her veins. She paused only momentarily. Another word blossomed on her lips, this one powerful enough to reach through skin, below tissue, to find holjoules at their source. Sena spoke and suddenly, all the pets in the room detonated. Dignitaries had brought them, fluffy creatures with pedigrees they carried in their arms. Mayor Ashlen's hounds died where he had leashed them. Cats and dænids and other more exotic things, like the rooks in the garret, all of them disploded with a gory popping sound.

The guests screamed as the wake plunged into a sacrificial bath. Many sobbed and puked. Many more of them ran . . . not because a dozen loyal animals had died but because, on the grand hall bier, Caliph Howl was sitting up.

Metholinate supplies are restored. Masons work to fix damage to the castle and other buildings especially in Barrow Hill, Temple Hill and Daoud's Bend. The brief warm spell doesn't last. The rest of the repairs will have to wait for spring.

All the major papers have ruled Caliph's death an elaborate charade. They say that records of his trauma and time of death could have easily been forged. Several dignitaries from the wake go so far as to tell the press point-blank about the sham.

"We weren't fooled."

"It was a disgusting prank and the acting was poor. The murder of animals, family pets, was a revolting over-the-top theatric for which the government will have to pay. A public apology is in order."

They fill the opinion section of the Iscan Herald.

And then, of course, there are others who believe.

Caliph feels lost for a while. He reads the documents, sees the canister that supposedly contains his stomach. He talks with the physicians and the embalmer but all of them seem frightened and quickly go away.

He remembers the jolt when the gun-stone must have hit the deck, remembers the metal sticking from the middle of his chest. He had remained conscious as his men turned the airship home, running from the battle, engines pounding to get the High King home. He had been conscious even when they were struck again over the city . . . so close . . . only a hundred yards from the mooring deck. And he had felt his stomach pitch as the Byun-Ghala had finally lost power, drifting into the walls of Isca Castle with graceful, violent repercussions.

The memory of the impact comes to him in third person, at a speed that feels dreamily slow. Engines ripping through gas cells, officers flying over lightweight rigid frameworks. His agonizing stomach pain finally . . . finally goes away.

Days pass and the papers spin one journalistic counterpoint after another. Mostly, however, they focus on the thousands and thousands of dead.

* * *

SENA stayed out of public sight.

Caliph watched her spend hours on end poring over the *Cisrym Ta*. She had sent a huge order to the book buyer, calling for a veritable library to be brought back to Isca Castle. Caliph was forced to send several zeppelins to haul the enormous collection in.

Surprisingly, he didn't have trouble believing that he had died. There were distinct memories of the time after the zeppelin crash that he didn't talk about. Who would believe him anyway? Except Sena?

Gadriel had tendered his resignation. So had the royal physicians. Almost all the servants that had worked closest to the High King and his queen had left, seeking employment elsewhere. Only Yrisl and Alani stayed.

Sometimes Caliph felt like he was functioning in a dream, thinking back to those hours where he was certainly someplace else. Someplace far away from Isca. During those moments, he found himself touching his chest where the duralumin beam had been and thinking about Cameron Howl and his uncle's book.

The worm gang murders had been nearly forgotten. The journalist who took the litho-slide had become a casualty of the attack and his story turned to hearsay, brushed aside amid new turmoil surrounding the postwar and the tragedy at Burt.

The litho-slide, now property of the Iscan government, tormented Caliph for a while. He pondered the possibility of turning himself in. Sigmund had told him it was Zane Vhortghast who had replaced all the caged-up cats with human beings. It was a story that carried the ring of truth. Certainly Sigmund must have capitulated but Caliph didn't want to think about that. He didn't want to think about anything pertaining to the war. Instead, he shut down Glôssok and moved Sigmund Dulgensen to another project.

Caliph couldn't feel the guilt anymore.

I died for Stonehold.

ON a morning just a few days after his wake, Caliph met Sena in the library for breakfast. The meeting had jumped out at him from his itinerary for the day. The thought of her scheduling it with the new seneschal made him smile faintly as he entered the huge chilly room.

Sena looked up and smiled at him from across the hazy blue space. She didn't move. She wasn't breathing. His own breath was frosty in the air. Caliph walked toward her, studying her in that gray square of light below the window. Where shadows clung along her neck and beneath her arm, he could see the pale designs, the platinum tattoos that painted her with specular. So fluid and cunning. They glittered every time she moved. She had told him everything, about how they were the same kind of glyphs as those found in his uncle's book.

The closer he got, the wider her smile became until finally, he reached out and touched her. She let him feel the lines as he always did. They were nothing like the raised ridges of scar tissue, tactually they were no different from her skin . . . except that they were cold. When he crossed a line he felt it tingle under his fingertips. Fleshy warmth veined with soft icy designs.

He could rest against her. The warmth of her body compensated. The designs were delicate and thin.

"You scheduled breakfast?" He asked it with obvious amusement.

"Yeah. I scheduled breakfast." She got up from her stool and led him by the hand through the shelves to a great fireplace. There was a chaise and coffee table and a perfect breakfast spread out beside the flames.

"It's cold in here," said Caliph.

"I know."

"Fire's for my benefit?"

"Our benefit."

Caliph sat down. Sena let her slippers drop and crawled up beside him on the chaise. She plucked a berry from the tray and put it in his mouth.

"I want something," she said while he was chewing.

"More books?"

She shushed him. "It's hard to explain what I want . . . the macroscopic . . . the microscopic. All those physicists trying to manipulate objects from the outside looking in. They can't help it because their eyes are like stone. They can't help the grains slipping through their fingers. Can you imagine? Creating from inside? An inflow of matter, without wind, attaching itself, precisely, without flaw, without smoke or machinery? Attaching itself to your thought, your intention, to the soul of what you're trying to create?"

"What?" Caliph looked at her quizzically.

"It's the evolution of engineering . . . perfect atomic alignment that transcends matter as we know it. Perfect alignment. Absolute attraction."

"I don't understand."

"Caliph." Her tougue peeked out between her lips as she wrestled with the words. "I want to have a baby."

Caliph picked up a pastry and looked into her jeweled eyes, her perfectly sculpted face so convincingly inlaid with chromium. She sounded crazy. She hadn't been herself since his funeral. He didn't know if it was possible. He had listened to her chest many times in the past few days after they had made love and heard the silence, the absence of her heart-beat. She could always wear him out and her breathing never changed. She breathed for him, intentionally, to comfort him, to keep it as close to normal as it could be. But she didn't grow tired. She never had to catch her breath.

The only sounds she made were for his benefit.

Caliph felt disjoint. He didn't know whether she was really alive. Or whether she was really Sena. She seemed to be Sena. She had all of Sena's memories. She had brought him back, given him life, if he was to believe everything that had happened in the last few days.

He looked at her; swallowed his berry. "A baby," he said. "Are you sure we can . . . ?"

"I don't know." Sena's smile faded. She looked down into his lap. Her hands tugged softly at his belt.

He ached for her suddenly.

Then the pastry in his fingers slipped and dropped, scattering flakes and icing across the floor. Not pleasure but fear.

Something dark, like a shadow or a wisp of smoke moved out of her. It brushed along the bookcase and curled toward the wall. It drifted quickly over the marble floor. Its movement was deliberate, its shape slightly stooped and very thin. Like an old man leaving a building, the shape paused for an instant. The impression of a clawlike appendage gestured faintly, as though waving. Waving at him. Caliph blinked and the horrible apparition with its familiar posture and gait disappeared.

"Sena?"

She lifted her beautiful face to him.

"What?" She smiled and stretched up to kiss him, tasting of fruit. He recoiled. She didn't seem to notice. It was a familiar kiss, reassuring and strong. It held nothing back. Caliph felt his resistance slide away.

"I love you, Caliph. You and I belong to the stars . . ."

PRONUNCIATIONS

Ạ   *A* in *father*. Mirạyhr.

Å   *O* in *home*. Dåelôc.

Â   *I* in *high*. Barâdaith.

Æ   *EY* in *whey*. Sienæ.

Ẹ   *UE* in *hue*. Mrẹsh.

Ê   *E* in *bend*. Nêlẹa.

Ị   *I* in *ill*. Nịs.

Î   *E* in *eel*. Înẹ.

Ḵ   Approximated with a glottal sound between *k* and *h*. Ḵhloht.

Ọ   A slightly softened vowel articulated between the *o* sounds of *over* and *on*. Sọth.

Ô   *O* in *oat*. Dåelôc.

Ü   Approximated by a punch to the stomach. A guttural *u* similar to that in *fun*. Ooil-Üauth.

Ǖ   *OO* in *tool*. Brǖak.

Ụ   *OW* in *now*. Nụmạth.

Ŭ   A diphthong combining the *e* of *hem* and the *oo* of *tool*: eh-oo. Ŭlung.

Y   In words unique to Adummim, *y* is almost always pronounced as the *e* in *eel*. Mirạyhr.